To celebrate the

Three Nights in New York

Poolbeg Press ana
Award-winning American Holidays
OFFER **YOU** AND A FRIEND THREE
FUN-FILLED NIGHTS IN **NEW YORK!**

Book online at www.americanholidays.com

This amazing prize consists of return flights from Dublin or Shannon to JFK with Delta Air Lines, and three nights accommodation in the well located Holiday Inn in the heart of Manhattan.
You can also enjoy a New York City Showbiz Insiders Tour and go behind the scenes of the entertainment industry!

To win this fantastic prize all you have to do is answer this question:

What is New York also know as?
A. The Big Pear B. The Big Apple C. The Big Kiwi

Answer: _____

Name: _____

Contact number: _____

Address: _____

Email: _____

Send this page in an envelope to: *Three Nights in New York* competition,
Poolbeg Press, 123 Grange Hill, Baldoyle, Dublin 13.

ALSO BY MICHELLE JACKSON

Two Days in Biarritz

PUBLISHED BY POOLBEG

Three Nights in New York

Michelle Jackson (signature)

MICHELLE
JACKSON

POOLBEG

Published 2009
by Poolbeg Press Ltd
123 Grange Hill, Baldoyle
Dublin 13, Ireland
E-mail: poolbeg@poolbeg.com
www.poolbeg.com

13 5 7 9 10 8 6 4 2

A catalogue record for this book is available from the British Library.

ISBN 978-1-84223 -404-4

Typeset by Type Design in Bembo 10.5/14.5

Printed by
Litografia Rosés, S.A., Spain

www.poolbeg.com

NOTE ON THE AUTHOR

Michelle Jackson is the author of the bestselling novel *Two Days in Biarritz*. She enjoys travel and gets immense pleasure from the research that she has to do for her books. She lives in Howth, Co Dublin, with her husband and two children.

If you would like Michelle to visit your book club or talk to community groups etc, see her website www.michellejackson.ie

ACKNOWLEDGEMENTS

I thought it was going to be easier to write these acknowledgements as this is my second novel but that doesn't seem to be the case! As always I would first like to thank my publisher Paula Campbell and all of my colleagues and friends at Poolbeg, especially Niamh, Sarah and David – I don't know how you put up with me!

To Gaye Shortland – editor extraordinaire. You whip through the jumbled-up words that I put together and call a manuscript and make them a wonderful read for everyone to enjoy.

Thanks to my dear friends and readers – especially my mainstays Clodagh Hoey and Suzanne Bolger.

To Sarah Gallagher, thank you for bringing me to New York and introducing me to your fabulous brother Daragh McDonagh. Daragh, you make a tremendous tour guide – amongst your many other talents. Thanks to Niamh Hopkins of www.howthwebdesign.ie for doing such a great job on my website.

Many thanks to Detective Sergeant Gary Kelly for all his help with matters of the law.

Thanks to John, Deirdre and Jack Teeling for your support and generosity with Tyrconnell Whiskey.

To Juliet Bressan and Conor Kostick – thank you for bringing me to Annaghmakerrig and the Tyrone Guthrie

Centre. To all the wonderful people I met at the centre – and friends I made who helped me through the manic few days I spent there in July editing this book.

Thanks to my father Jim for the wonderful gift of storytelling that he has passed on to me and my mother Pauline whose creativity knows no bounds.

Finally, thank you to my husband Brian and wonderful children Mark and Nicole – without you I wouldn't be free to be me.

AUTHOR'S NOTE

The High Line is unique to New York. Standing thirty feet in the air it runs through Chelsea, the Meatpacking District and Hell's Kitchen. It is a one-and-a-half-mile-long park in the sky. It was once part of the industrial fabric of Manhattan's Westside as trains carrying meat and baking supplies ran along its tracks. Completed in 1934, it was designed to take the freight trains off Tenth Avenue, but use for it declined in the 1960s as more and more companies started to use trucks. The last train ran before Thanksgiving in 1980, carrying a cargo of frozen turkeys. It was left unused for decades. As a layer of soil built up on the gravel, the wind and birds scattered grasses and seeds over the tracks and a wonderful wild park was created. In 1999 a group of residents met to discuss the proposed demolition of the High Line and they formed a group called Friends of the High Line. Through persistence and hard work they convinced the city government in 2002 to renew the area and create a public park for the residents and visitors. An international design competition was proposed in 2004 and work on the winning design commenced in 2006. At the time of going to press the first stage of development of the High Line is in progress.

For the purpose of this novel, the characters Alex and Rachel find a corner of the High Line that is secluded and not under construction – just yet!

To find out more about the High Line visit www.thehighline.org.

NYC & Company is the official marketing, tourism, and partnership organisation for the City of New York. For information on the hottest restaurants, latest NYC trends and "must do's in New York" go to www.nycgo.com.

To anyone who's ever been to New York and loved it!

PROLOGUE

February in New York

Eve Porter wished that she had stayed in New York. Her transition to the London branch of the Just for Coffee exclusive dating agency had been good for promotion, but London didn't have the same buzz. However, just now that same "buzz" was creating a problem. Standing on a snowy Seventh Avenue, surrounded by a cacophony of blaring car horns and gridlocked traffic, she wondered how she was going to make her appointment with Lucille on time. She could always catch the subway. Most New Yorkers didn't think twice before using it – even the mayor was reported to take it to work – besides, she did get the Tube on the odd occasion now that she lived in London.

She held her breath as she descended the steps for the subway and avoided eye contact with the masses on their way to work. She pulled back the sleeve of her coat to see the face of her Rolex. John had given it to her for Christmas and even though she'd removed every trace of his existence from her flat in Chiswick she continued to wear the diamond-studded watch.

One of its benefits was the dual-time system. Although it was now five years since she had left New York, she still liked to know what time it was in the Big Apple – and it was convenient when conversing with Lucille across the Atlantic.

She gave her arm a shake and the sleeve fell back over the watch as she teetered at the edge of the platform. She was anxious to be first on the carriage – near the door so she could make a rapid escape.

The tiles on the wall at the other side of the track were shiny – whiter than they should have been with the bombardment of trains passing by every few minutes. She thought she heard the train get nearer but it was only her stomach rumbling. Eating in the mornings was a chore and a cup of black coffee was usually all she could manage to keep down. She was sorry now she hadn't forced herself to eat a piece of toast at least or a few spoonfuls of muesli – anything to keep this unpleasant sinking feeling at bay. As a child she was regarded as anaemic and her doctor had warned not to fast for too long between meals. But Eve was now a professional woman and well able to make her own mind up about if and when she should eat. Another rumble from her stomach and she felt a light and airy pressure rise from the top of her spine and rush around her skull. Hypnotised by the tiles in front of her eyes and a gentle breeze brushing past her face, she began to sway.

Conor pulled the collar of his leather jacket up over his ears. The February wind was sharp and he'd known that morning they were in for a cold one as the snowflakes fell on the window of his Greenwich Village apartment. The subway was on the corner of Prince Street and as the snow fell harder he quickened his pace and plunged underground. He had to be midtown in half an hour to check on a venue for his next day's work. He had arranged to meet a friend of his who had told him about a cavernous restaurant that would be a perfect backdrop for the indie band he had to photograph – they hadn't a big budget but their manager was hot and liked to tip Conor off when he had a talented new act to market.

Conor had given up wearing a watch since a shoot with The Pixies two years before. He knew the constraints of time affected the quality of his work – and that was such a big job he really needed to get absorbed in the present and forget about how little time he had. He had taken his watch off and experienced the longest and most productive hour of his professional life.

So far doing without a timepiece had worked very well during the creative process but obviously not when it came to being punctual.

As he approached his platform he thought he heard a rumble in the distance but it was only the after-effect of a train in the next tunnel going in the opposite direction. The station was busy today – bodies everywhere. He could improve his chances of getting on by moving down the line a bit so he would be ready to jump off when he reached midtown.

Head and shoulders above most of the commuters on a busy Friday morning, he stopped short of a little old lady. She could only be from one place in the world with that lilac hair – Brooklyn. She lifted her head up and stared at the tall Irishman. It was the mixture of crystal-blue eyes and jet-black hair that made him stand out – even in New York.

He knew that she was looking at him but didn't mind. He was very lucky. Living in the most exciting city in the world with one of the best jobs, he got to go to all of the best parties and hang out with famous people. He had it all as far as his family in Ireland were concerned and this was one of those mornings where he had to agree with them.

Conor glanced over at the other side of the track. Above the heads of the other commuters he could see shiny white tiles on the wall opposite.

Then his head swung left as out of the corner of his eye he glimpsed a woman flopping off the edge of the platform. His heart gave a great leap. Was she a jumper or had she fallen?

The old lady with the lilac hair screamed, "My God, somebody help her!"

All around people were looking down onto the track – staring at the woman who was now lying face down on the steel girders.

Conor pushed through the crowd. He felt a rush of adrenaline through his body as the sound of the train in the distance started to rumble from the dark tunnel. It was too late to stop the train. Something had to be done – and fast.

At the edge of the platform two dudes laden with gold chains – boys in the hood – looked on, shaking their heads.

"She's a goner, man!" one of them said to Conor.

A force from deep inside swept over Conor like a wave. He didn't think he had the time to do what he was about to do but he didn't have a choice. He was in autopilot mode as his feet hit the steel girders. The vibrations from the approaching train rumbled down the track. Shockwaves shot through his legs as he felt it getting closer and closer. He could feel them running through the woman's body as he gathered her into his arms. She was out cold. He heaved her onto the edge of the platform, head first – it took every ounce of his energy to lift her legs. It was the elderly lady and a public transport worker who pulled her to safety.

A shrill whistle blew down the tunnel and the lights from the front of the train were approaching quickly. He tried to get a grip on the side of the platform but his palms were sweaty and he rolled off and back onto the track.

"Here, man, give me your hand!"

One of the dudes reached down and grabbed Conor's wrist. The other guy joined his friend and they heaved Conor up and onto the platform with less than a second to spare before the train swept by.

A commotion gathered around the still unconscious woman. Conor stood up and brushed his hands clean on his jeans. All he could think of was whether the woman was all right. The little lady with lilac hair held the woman's head in her lap and stroked it gently. The majority of those around boarded the train. The dudes gave him the thumbs-up from behind the doors of the carriage as it pulled away. He hadn't had a chance to thank them for saving his life.

"You're gonna be all right," Lilac Hair whispered to the woman.

Conor moved closer as the old lady brushed the strands of auburn hair from the face of the woman who was now starting to show signs of coming around. She was definitely a looker, the kind of intelligent businesswoman that he would be slow to approach in a bar – but would like to. He didn't have problems meeting women but it was usually the enigmatic and more serious type of woman that really caught his interest – so different to the models and singers that he usually dated. Her hair was pulled back in a roll and her expensive-looking full-length coat had come open to reveal a smart suit underneath. Conor wondered for an instant why she had taken the subway at all – she was more the type of woman who would be taking a courtesy car to work.

Suddenly her eyelids lifted and exposed a pair of dazed green eyes, as her head rocked from side to side. She seemed vaguely familiar but after living in the great ethnic melting pot that makes up New York for twelve years he felt most people on the planet looked familiar.

The sound of the next train rolling to a standstill disturbed his thoughts. He was going to be late.

A subway guardsman pushed his way past Conor and leaned over the woman as she pulled herself up onto her elbows.

"I have to go now," Conor said to Lilac Hair. "Will you make sure she's all right?"

"You go on. I'll see she gets home."

As the doors of the train opened, Conor reluctantly boarded it. Another subway worker was running over to the woman with the auburn hair and he knew that his part in the saga had been played. The memory of her green eyes stayed with him as the train followed the line uptown.

Eve pushed the guardsman away as he tried to help her to her feet. She grabbed her left arm as a dart of pain shot up it.

"You gotta be careful, honey," the old lady with lilac hair said kindly. "You've had a bad fall – you were nearly killed!"

Eve looked down at the old lady, clad in woolly hat and matching thick cable-knit sweater with a basket in the crook of her arm, and winced. This was definitely the last time she was ever getting the subway – what was she thinking of?

"Where's my bag!" she demanded.

The old lady looked around and picked the cream leather Gucci bag off the ground.

"Here you go, honey. I don't know what happened to your hat."

Eve grabbed the bag and with her other hand brushed back the stray auburn tresses indignantly.

"Thank you!" she said to the old lady – without meaning a word of it.

The attempts of the subway workers to calm her down were in vain. Eve wasn't sure exactly what had happened but remembered staring at the tiles on the other side of the track, feeling faint, and then one instant later falling forward. Not only

6

her left arm but her whole body ached and felt like it was covered in bruises. Lucky it was winter and she had been protected by her voluminous coat and padded gloves. The palms of the gloves were torn – she must have broken the fall with her hands. Gridlock or no gridlock she would stick to a cab in future – and for now a quick shower in the Soho Grand was called for to wash the unfortunate episode out of her life.

"Ma'am, you need to see a doctor," the subway worker said gently. "You fell on the track – you need to get checked out."

The track! Eve put her right hand up to her head and smelt oil on her glove. She had fallen onto the track!

"You're in shock, honey!" the old lady said with a shake of her head.

"How did I get back up?" Eve asked as the realisation of what had happened to her finally took a grip.

"That handsome young man risked his own life and jumped down after you!" said the lilac-haired woman. "He was only just back on the platform when that train pulled in!"

Eve steadied herself. Did a complete stranger risk his own life to save hers? She felt uncomfortable in the presence of these people – she had to get as far away from this nightmare situation as quickly as possible. Her six-figure salary meant that she never needed to take public transport again and after this fiasco she had no intention of doing so. The entire experience was surreal.

But she was curious about this strange man who had rescued her from death. She didn't generally believe that knights in shining armour existed – especially as she was in the matchmaking business.

A pain shot through her left arm and she looked at the sleeve of her coat. She pulled it back to study her watch as a trickle of blood dribbled along her wrist and onto the back of her hand. It was only then that she noticed the huge rip in her coat.

ONE

Three months later

May

"I can't believe we're really here!" Rachel exclaimed as she slipped off her four-inch heels.

She watched her companion Nicky nervously strip as she herself had done a few seconds earlier. She was down to her shirt and jeans, and her watch was resting in the blue container.

The man in the crisp white shirt and dark tie nodded at her waistline and grunted.

"Your belt as well, madam."

Rachel leaned over and whispered in her friend's ear. "Knickers and bra also, please, madam!"

The security guard grabbed the pan filled with metal objects and shoes from Rachel and glared at them with furrowed brows. She smiled at him and gave a flick of her long blonde curls as she breezed silently through the security gate.

Nothing could dampen her mood – she hadn't been at Dublin Airport with Nicky for sixteen years. On that occasion they were students coming back from a long summer working in

London to pay for their college expenses. They were both in completely different situations now and the break was well earned.

"Would your brother like us to bring anything over?" Nicky asked.

Rachel clicked the roof of her mouth with her tongue – remembering stories of fellow students begging for Tayto crisps and Lyons tea from across the Atlantic Ocean. There was little nowadays that couldn't be got in either country. Except . . .!

"Damn, I forgot to get a couple of Swiss Rolls!" she groaned. "Hang on – we'll get a few Crunchies – that will do him!" The preparations required before leaving her three children with their father for the next four days had left her little time to think about a gift for her brother Conor.

Nicky beckoned as the doors of the bar in Boarding Area B opened. "Come on – let's have a little tipple before we board!"

"But it's ten o'clock in the morning!" Rachel exclaimed.

"Exactly, and when do we ever get a chance to drink a nice crisp Sauvignon Blanc at this hour?"

Rachel nodded in agreement – there was no way that she could admit to Nicky that she often had an early morning tipple after taking the kids to school and before facing her day in suburbia. But that was part of Rachel's secret world and there was absolutely nobody that she could confide in about the insecurities attached to being a stay-at-home mum.

"What would you be doing if you weren't here?" she asked.

Nicky smiled. Normally she would be sitting at the desk of Virtue Publishing Ltd, studying the finishing touches of this week's magazine.

Leaving the final editing to her PA made Nicky nervous as she knew that the young girl was chomping at the bit to slip into the assistant editorial position. But it couldn't be helped. The last time she took a break was five years ago and even now the thought of leaving her son Daniel with his friend's family was heart-wrenching. But she had dedicated many years of her life to keeping him and his needs fulfilled and the time had come to do something for herself. Besides, her fourteen-year-old son would rather spend time with his friend's family. There was a lot more on offer there – a father figure for a start. Daniel needed more men in his life and Nicky realised that painfully – even more so now that he was hitting puberty. Her own father had died when she was only fifteen so Daniel had never known him. At times Nicky was riddled with guilt and fears about the way she was bringing him up but she could only do her best as a single mum and her wages as assistant editor for a women's magazine left them both with little choice about it.

"I'm glad I'm not sitting behind my desk – that's for sure!" Nicky lifted her glass and clinked it off the side of Rachel's. "Cheers – here's to a great four days in New York!"

"Don't forget the three nights!" Rachel said buoyantly. Secretly she was worried sick. The thought of Derek at home on his own with the children sent shivers up her spine. How were they going to manage? But everyone agreed that she deserved this break badly – everyone except Derek of course. And then there was the other worry . . .

Nicky recognised the glassy expression on Rachel's face and shook her head.

"Don't go all funny on me now – you know you want to go – you jumped at the idea of visiting New York when I told you about the cheap flights!"

Rachel smiled nervously. Yes, she would miss the kids but that wasn't the real reason why she was feeling apprehensive. Her mobile phone could ring at any moment and, although she wanted it to, she didn't relish having to explain the conversation to Nicky if it did happen.

Rachel knew her friend would be furious if she knew what she had done but the feud between Nicky and Eve had gone on for long enough and a reunion was well overdue. It was great having Nicky back in her life for the last five years and this was a golden opportunity to bring the three of them together – wasn't it?

The registrar in Trinity College Dublin had been surprisingly helpful when she rang earlier in the week and the list of alumni far more comprehensive than she'd expected. The registrar said there was talk of a fifteen-year reunion of the English faculty as they had failed to organise one at ten years – this was more than likely due to the fact that they were the last of a student brain drain that had steadily dribbled out of Ireland after graduation during the later decades of the twentieth century.

The Just for Coffee company was easy to find on Google and she sent the emailed message for Eve's attention, unsure if she had changed her surname. It was as light-hearted as she could make it – surely she would answer? The rift between Eve and Nicky should be all water under the bridge by now.

As she took a sip of her ice-cold wine she felt a shot of relief. "I'm fine," she said with a smile – hoping that Eve would ring but not yet. "We deserve this!"

Nicky lifted her glass and took another sip from the frosty rim. Something inside told her she shouldn't entirely believe her friend. But, if anyone had a right to be nervous, she herself had! After all, her son was staying with a friend – not even family. She envied Rachel's stable marriage with her husband for the last thirteen years – while she herself had staggered from one disastrous relationship to the next.

Nicky sat up straight in her chair and blinked. She craved a cigarette – especially with a cold glass of wine in her hands. How was she going to get through the long flight to JFK? Then she remembered her nicotine patch – she had to put it on.

"Let's go through Immigration soon!" Rachel said.

Nicky nodded. The sooner she was on the big green airbus the better.

"I just need to go to the little girl's room for a minute," she said. How she wished that Rachel smoked too – maybe then she would understand how difficult this smoke-free flight was going to be. No cigarettes and all kinds of nightmare scenarios to conjure up about Daniel. There was only one thing to do when she boarded the big green airbus and that was drink some more.

Eve breezed through the doors of 1680 Broadway, swinging her super-light briefcase in her right hand. It felt great to be back in New York. Her last visit had been disastrous but she made sure this time that she came to the Just for Coffee offices in a cab.

"Morning, Arthur," she said to the doorman who permanently sat at the desk of the Howards Building.

Arthur nodded his head respectfully at the tall red-haired lady in the sharp grey designer suit. She didn't usually come to the offices more than twice a year but he knew who she was. Something must be up for her to visit again so soon.

"Mawnin', Miz Pawtah," he replied with his slow southern drawl. "How you been?"

"Fine, thank you."

Eve couldn't comprehend how someone could spend most of their waking hours sitting at a desk watching the world go by through glass doors. Especially a world as exciting and invigorating as New York. She imagined this poor man skulking onto the subway back to Queens in the evening, having done nothing all day but watch and wait for those who had a real life to pass him by.

Eve made her way to the lift and put her perfectly manicured fingernail on the button embossed with the number twenty-three. From that level Lucille Baron's office had a spectacular view of mid town that was a testimony to the success of the Just for Coffee franchise. In eight short years Lucille had built the business from scratch to one of the world's leading dating agencies.

It wasn't a typical dating agency where man meets woman and goes for dinner or to a show. The clients on the Just for Coffee database were all high-flying business people who were much too busy to waste a whole evening getting to know someone and far too sophisticated and intellectual to delve into the world of speed dating. Just for Coffee suited a lot of business people who could fit in an hour over lunch or in the afternoons during their heavy schedule. The hard work was put in by Lucille and her staff to ensure that the matches were made between equally successful and well-heeled individuals. They had even been involved in getting certain celebrities together but were such a professional organisation that no trace of the events would ever be leaked to the press.

Eve walked up to Lucille's secretary and the young girl sat upright in her seat. Eve had this effect on the junior members of the company – she carried an air of superiority and aloofness that made them uncomfortable.

"Hello, Ms Porter, how are you?" The secretary smiled as she searched her desk for a sheet of paper. She passed it to Eve. "This came in yesterday and I thought I should give it to you in person as you would be in the office today. I wasn't sure if it was a genuine email or spam."

Eve nodded at her and started to read the sheet of paper as she strolled over to the door of Lucille's office. The message was sent by rachelsloan@eircom.net. Subject: Reunion.

It was a shock for Eve. Rachel was a genuine type of girl – but why on earth would she contact her? She wondered where

Rachel learned that she worked for Just for Coffee – she mustn't know that she had moved or she would have sent the email to the London office. She read the opening lines, which informed her that Rachel would be in New York for the weekend and included her mobile phone number in case Eve wanted to meet up. A torrent of old memories started to flood her mind and drag her into the last century. But she had an important new client to meet on this trip and really didn't have the time. She didn't know whether she would respond or not.

The door swung open when she was only a few centimetres away from it. The woman at the other side was in her early forties and perfectly groomed with poker-straight blonde hair – she beamed at her colleague with a dazzling white set of teeth.

Eve leaned forward and kissed Lucille – first on her right cheek and then on her left.

"Eve, baby, it's so good to see you!"

Lucille's blue eyes sparkled like diamonds. She had a captivating effect on everyone she spoke to but Eve wasn't taken in by all the gloss and panache of her business colleague.

"Wonderful to see you too, Lucille," she said, returning the welcome with a wide smile.

She folded the email and slipped it into her handbag as she took a seat at Lucille's desk. The stunning view of the top of the Chrysler building and the rest of Manhattan shifted her focus and steadied her nerves.

"Things must be very good if you're calling me back to New York so quickly!"

"Darling, things are fantastic. The London office is thriving in your capable hands but this particular client that I want you to meet today needs special attention and I could only trust you to look after him properly."

Lucille sat down and took out a brown file from a concealed

drawer in her desk. The folder bulged with paperwork and made Eve curious about its contents.

"I've booked him into the Soho Grand so you can keep an eye on him and he does most of his business downtown so that suits. When I tell you his details you will understand why I needed you to see his file in person. I understand your reservations in dealing with Irish clients but you're the best person to handle this guy – he is real important."

Eve was intrigued but didn't want to show it by reacting too strongly.

Lucille opened the file with the reverence of a preacher about to make a sermon. She lifted the first page and cleared her throat.

"I'm really excited about this," she said. "It's rare that we get one of the most powerful men in Ireland as a client – even though he is officially retired he will never stop working."

Eve didn't often see Lucille so excited. "Is he extremely wealthy?" she asked.

"Absolutely, and he is so well connected he could open all sorts of doors for Just for Coffee! He isn't officially divorced but has been separated for years. His ex-wife has a new partner and he has two daughters – both grown up and successful in their own right."

Eve usually kept abreast of Irish news from *The Irish Times* on the internet. This man sounded familiar. "Is he looking for a permanent partner or discreet sex with someone who isn't likely to spill the beans?"

"Not sure but he's much too powerful to want his dealings with us spread all over the tabloids. He held the stopwatch for the Celtic Tiger in his hands for years."

"Go on then – tell me who he is – I know you're dying to."

Lucille grinned. She didn't often get a reaction like this from Eve. "Our new client is . . ."

A loud knock sounded on the door and Lucille's secretary appeared.

"Excuse me for interrupting, Ms Baron, but your client is here."

Eve sat up straight in her seat. Who could be coming all the way from Ireland, looking to Just for Coffee to find a partner?

"Hi, Conor, we're here!" Rachel giggled down the phone excitedly. She longed to see her brother so much. It had been three years since he had last visited Ireland and she had only ever been to New York with Derek who hated the city.

"Hey, sis! It's about time! Where are you?"

Rachel craned her neck and looked out of the window. "In the back of a yellow cab driving through Brooklyn. Will we go straight to the hotel?"

"That would be best – I'll make my way there now. How was your flight?"

"Great – no problems. Nicky drank Aer Lingus out of baby bottles of champagne and slept for the guts of three hours so it all went well!"

Nicky mock-glared over at her friend but couldn't stop a big grin from creeping out.

"You should be here in about twenty minutes," Conor calculated. "I can't wait to see ya."

"Me too – can't believe I'm here at last – see you then!" Rachel flipped the cover of her phone shut. "Look over there – that's what I told you about."

Nicky turned to where Rachel was pointing through the front windscreen and stared at the New York skyline unfolding before her eyes. Thousands of cars resembling dinkies sped back and forth over the bridge. In the distance thousands more were flying by on the overpass. The massive skyscrapers were pulsating with life and down below in the Hudson River, ferries and water taxis went about their business.

"Wow!" she exclaimed.

Rachel looked on as Nicky's eyes sparkled at the myriad architectural jewels before her.

"Nothing prepares you for your first sighting of the Brooklyn Bridge, does it?"

Nicky's mouth opened wide as the cab turned onto the massive suspension bridge.

"It's beautiful," Nicky gasped. "Look, there's the Empire State – and, oh my god, it's the Chrysler Building!"

Rachel smiled. She knew exactly how her friend was feeling. The first time Derek had brought her to New York she felt the very same. It was the eve of their first wedding anniversary and was meant to be the trip of a lifetime. The Celtic Tiger hadn't started to purr and the prospect of doing Christmas Shopping in the Big Apple was reserved for those with special concession flights or the rich and famous. The air at JFK was icy and sharp – unlike today. Christmas was everywhere in the city even though it was only the end of November. It should have been a wonderful trip but Rachel was in the first phase of pregnancy with her eldest child and suffering from morning-sickness for ten hours a day. She couldn't even go ice-skating at the Rockefeller Center – it looked so magical with the massive Christmas tree and trumpeting angels providing the perfect backdrop – such a symbol of Christmas in New York! Derek blamed her for ruining the holiday – even though it was his decision to start a family so early in their marriage.

"This is fantastic," Nicky said, looking over at her friend, unaware of the feelings of inadequacy and low self-esteem that Rachel's memories had reawoken.

The yellow cab brought them to Washington Square a few

minutes later and up to the door of their hotel. Standing at the railings with his leather jacket swung casually over his left shoulder was a tall handsome man in his early thirties.

"Is that Conor?" Nicky asked, pointing out the window.

Rachel craned her neck to see. "Yeah!"

"Wow, I don't remember him looking like that – I mean, he was always kind of cute but now he's gorgeous!"

Rachel grinned and searched distractedly in her purse to pay for the cab ride.

"It's okay, I've got a fifty-dollar bill," Nicky said, reaching across and handing it to the taxi-driver.

"Thanks, Nicky, I'll get it on the way back." Rachel opened the door of the cab hurriedly. She put her four-inch-heeled boots onto the pavement and rushed up to throw her arms around her brother.

"So good to see you, sis!" he said, giving her a tight squeeze.

"It's good to be here," she replied, gently pulling away from his embrace. "You remember Nicky, don't you?"

Conor stretched out his long arm and pulled Nicky closer for a peck on the cheek.

"Of course I do – even though I was an unbearable school kid while you guys were all graduating from college."

Nicky blushed – the few years' age difference was nothing now that they were all in their thirties and she berated herself for the short-sightedness that had made her ignore her friend's younger brother.

"Let me help you with those cases," he said, leaning forward to take Nicky's.

"No, really – they're very –"

Conor lifted the first one that Nicky had left at her side and swung it up in the air. "Wow, I wasn't expecting it to be so light!"

Nicky smiled and raised her shoulders timidly. "I'm hoping to fill it for the return!"

Conor grinned. "Of course. You girls are going to hear more Irish accents than American on Fifth Avenue. This town is thronged with shoppers from across the Atlantic."

He lifted Rachel's case with his other hand and shook it — it rang hollow also.

Rachel led the way up the granite steps of the small but respectable boutique hotel. Icons from the 1930s covered the tiled walls of the foyer and there was a distinct art deco feel to the place.

"Jesus Christ!" Nicky exclaimed, causing the attractive receptionist to lift his head. "It's Denzel Washington!"

Rachel giggled. "I hope you're not going to make a show of me all over New York!"

Nicky had to stop herself from swooning on the spot — it was just as well that Rachel had made the reservation and was checking them in.

"Do you guys want to drop your suitcases upstairs and then maybe we could go to a little café a couple of blocks away?" Conor asked. "I usually meet Alex for a coffee mid-afternoon."

"Who's Alex?" Rachel asked.

"He's a guy that I hang out with. We met at an exhibition through mutual friends and he's kinda cool — with no bullshit!"

Rachel nodded her head — she knew what he meant. He was prone to criticising the glamorous New York set in his sporadic emails.

"We'll be a couple of minutes. Do you want to come up?"

Conor looked at Nicky and then back to Rachel. "I'll let you girls do your thing and I'll wait outside. It's turned into a nice day!"

"Okay," Rachel smiled.

Conor moved out to the pavement and sat down on the steps

that led up to the hotel entrance. It was a discreet boutique hotel that he had carefully chosen to cater for his sister's and her friend's needs. Rachel had warned him that Nicky hadn't much cash to throw around. That suited Conor because he liked to have his sister near him instead of in one of the many dull and generic uptown hotels where she usually stayed when she came to visit with Derek in tow. Lately, however, she hadn't been over much and he could sense that it was Derek's decision to cut back on time spent in the Big Apple. That was why he was surprised and delighted to get the email from Rachel telling of her impending trip. He would do everything he possibly could to make it a memorable experience for her.

He scanned through his phone looking for missed calls or text messages. Business had been brisk after Christmas but there was a lull now with the onslaught of summer – hopefully things would improve and he always got the odd call to photograph some of the open-air gigs. Only one missed call from Mandy and he wasn't tempted to call back and see what she wanted. A text from Alex made him smile:

Waiting for you in Tart's . . . A

"Were we quick?" a voice whispered behind his ear.

Conor turned around and smiled when he saw his sister and her friend.

"Follow me, ladies. I'm going to bring you to a real New York café!"

Nicky marvelled at the colourful shop fronts and familiar yellow traffic lights that she associated with the New York she saw on TV and in movies.

"It's so relaxed and pretty – I expected New York to be frantic!" Nicky remarked as a yellow cab stopped politely before they stepped onto a zebra crossing.

"That's because we're downtown. Live here a little while and you'll never want to go uptown."

"Oh!" Nicky replied meekly. She didn't understand what he meant but, apart from the tip of the Empire State in the distance, the buildings didn't seem that tall and life was pretty laid-back all around.

Conor beckoned the girls across a tree-lined street and over to a pretty little café with the most delicious-looking muffins and pastries filling its windows. The pale green awnings with *Once Upon A Tart* scripted across them protected those who sat out in front from the mid-afternoon sun. Sitting at a small round wooden table with a cup of coffee in front of him was Conor's friend. He was doodling on a white paper napkin and as Conor approached he looked up and smiled.

"Hey, man!" Conor said flippantly.

Alex looked at Rachel and then at Nicky – then back at Rachel again. He surveyed her blonde curls and blue eyes as a wide smile beamed across his lips.

"When Conor said he had a sister I thought 'if she's anything like him she'll have a wooden leg and a hump on her back'! But I can see that the looks in the family all went one way!"

Conor smirked at his wisecracking friend. He was used to his sense of humour and he was a good foil for his own laid-back manner.

"Rach, Nicky – it's with great misfortune I introduce Dr Alex Thoreau."

"You're a doctor?" Nicky asked in amazement. Wearing a thin leather necklace, small silver sleepers in his earlobes and a scruffy red tee-shirt, he certainly didn't look anything like her GP – not to mention his spiky white-blond hair.

"Yes, but don't let this shabby exterior fool you. Sure, if you were to have a heart attack on the spot I could do nothing to help you." He smiled as he spoke and shook his head gravely. "However, if you had a canvas and a bucket of paint I could throw something together to save your wall!"

"Doctor of Fine Art – just the guy you need in a crisis," Conor smirked. "Of course he got it in one of those American art colleges so it's pretty worthless."

Alex protested with a wave of his arms. "What about Pollock and Warhol – you guys would still be painting chocolate boxes in Europe if it wasn't for us Yanks!"

Nicky was just about to butt in and say that Picasso was European but she didn't want to seem like a total nerd already – even if she did think this artist guy was a bit of a jerk.

"Sorry, girls, he doesn't usually get like this until after his fourth whiskey of the day," Conor said with a smile. "What will it be – something savoury or sweet?"

Rachel and Nicky looked at each other and then back at Conor.

"I guess we should have a look inside," Nicky said.

"Get me a cappuccino, sis, and a cinnamon muffin!"

Rachel rolled her eyes as her brother sat down next to Alex. "Who's on holiday here?" she grinned.

The smell of cranberries and spices wafted from the kitchen to the rear of the café. Chickens and rabbits moulded from chocolate and candy mixtures decorated the shelves. At the counter an assortment of savoury delights – including frittata and pizza were on display next to the multitude of different muffins and home-baked cookies.

"I don't think I've ever smelt such gorgeous food!" Nicky exclaimed. "It's a good place to have the munchies after all that champagne I drank on the way over! Totally divine!"

"And the food isn't the only thing that's divine around here." The words had rolled off Rachel's tongue before she even realised that she was saying them.

Nicky looked over at her friend with an exaggerated mixture of shock and incredulity.

"Is this my married friend eyeing up the opposite sex while her good husband is at home minding the kids? I take it you are referring to that scruffy white-haired jerk?"

Rachel felt embarrassed despite Nicky's jokey tone. And secretly she felt annoyed. Married she definitely was but Derek was no saint. He had always been difficult to live with at the best of times and recently he had become downright dismissive of her. His standards of perfection were so high that Rachel was made to feel a failure over most of the things that she did during the day.

"I didn't mean it like that," she said lightly – trying to conceal the attraction she had felt on meeting Alex. "Just he seems like a nice guy – funny!" She didn't want to dig a bigger hole for herself than she could feel herself slipping into. "I'm glad my brother's got a somewhat normal friend."

"Honey, if you think that guy Alex is normal you need to get out more. Apart from that blueberry muffin that I am going to devour in about thirty seconds, Conor's the only dish around here!" She turned to the waitress and ordered food and drinks for everyone.

Rachel paid the cashier and carried the tray out to her brother and his friend. It irritated her that Nicky had spoken so forcefully about Alex – she had hardly met him after all – and she was cross with herself for letting her.

"Sorry, girls – I should have told you," Alex said as Rachel put the tray down on the table. "I gotta shoot – not like my friend Conor here shoots – I gotta get a ten-foot by five canvas finished by six o'clock."

"Will you join us tonight?" Conor asked. "I thought I'd bring the girls to Kelly and Ping later for something to eat."

Alex lifted his sweater off the chair and casually threw it over his shoulders. "Sounds good – one of my favourite places to eat," he said with a nod of his spiky peroxide-blond hair. "That is, providing the ladies could bear spending the night with a real American."

"You're hardly a real American, Alex – your mother was from Rome," Conor quipped.

"But I grew up in Massachusetts! Later, dude! Nice meeting you ladies," Alex said with a little bow and then he was gone.

"He's a great guy," Conor said as he watched him go. Then he turned back to the girls. "What do you two want to do after this?"

"Can we do some shopping?" Nicky asked eagerly.

"Look at her!" Rachel laughed. "She's chomping at the bit. Let's take her downtown to Fifth Avenue."

Eve liked to shop around SoHo and it was one of the reasons why she chose to stay in the Soho Grand. If it was good enough for U2 then it was just about good enough for Eve Porter.

She made her way to the Armani shop first to get a few make-up essentials and she was running low on her favourite Armani Code perfume. Then she made a quick detour to get some La Perla lingerie. This trip had been organised in such a hurry she hadn't made any arrangements to meet up with her old New York friends for tonight. She looked down at her Blackberry and remembered the email that Rachel had sent. She was between two minds whether she should answer her and decided to check out her New York friends first. She typed up two emails: one to Ingrid who used to work for Just for Coffee – Eve was probably the only person in the company that she would still socialise with – and another to Tom who was a married man she liked to call for casual sex whenever she came

24

to town. She appreciated the merits of her sex-only relationship with Tom now that she was single again. It was ironic that she worked in the matchmaking business while the need for a constant companion and partner simply didn't exist for her personally.

As she browsed through the lace-trimmed bras sized 34C she heard a bleep from her Blackberry and knew instantly who the message was from.

Hey gorgeous. Are you staying in the Soho Grand? How about 5 o c? T

She replied and then, smiling, slipped her phone back into her bag. He was so reliable. She checked her watch – two and a half hours was plenty of time to get some more shopping in – she might even have a bath before he arrived. Hell no! She'd have the bath when he got there.

As a rose-coloured two-piece set made entirely of lace was next on the rail she felt that serendipity had handed it to her. Tom loved pink! She made her way over to the cashier and joined the short queue.

Tom was always on time. He was so reliable there was no way Eve could stand him as a permanent fixture in her life. He was, like most men that she had dated and the one that she eventually married with such disastrous consequences, a solid dependable individual. She wondered if he was like that with his wife. Probably not if he could be there for her after one email. He always appeared fascinated by her and had told her he was attracted by the aloof way she carried herself. She enjoyed the way most men buzzed around her like bees when in her company – it made her feel like a honey pot.

She sprayed a little of her new perfume on her neck and loosened the belt of her luxurious black bathrobe. There was no need to beat around the bush with Tom – they would enjoy an hour of making love and perhaps order some food up to the room – then she could decide what to do for the rest of the night. She didn't relish the prospect of sharing the evening with her old college friend but part of her was curious. She still had unfinished business to thrash out with Rachel and New York was probably as good a place to do it as anywhere.

The North Loft Suite of the Soho Grand was Eve's favourite place to stay in New York now that she was a visitor. She was far enough away from all of the tourist hotels uptown and lucky that Lucille allowed her to charge the expensive room to the company. She strolled over to the large glass doors that looked out on the towering landmark of Manhattan. Later in the evening the Empire State would be illuminated like a glittering prize in the midst of the other skyscrapers and she could sit and watch it for hours. The cubist furniture and modern lines of the suite made this the perfect setting to enjoy the Manhattan skyline. She opened the door and stepped out onto the patio which was furnished with deckchair-striped couches and chairs. Maybe she should treat herself and Tom to a bottle of Bollinger – she deserved it.

Suddenly an impatient knock sounded on the door of her suite. She slowly walked over to open it – there was no need to appear overenthusiastic. She turned the handle and it was slowly but forcefully pushed from the other side. She could smell his Boss aftershave before she saw his face. Then his dark hazel eyes appeared around the door and they fixed on hers. Eve didn't want to talk – there was absolutely nothing she had to say to him. Instead she pursed her lips and drew him close enough to kiss. He smelt of work and the splattering of aftershave that he used to try and conceal the odours of the day. She didn't care – she loved his scent.

They shuffled, using tiny steps, inside the hotel suite – Eve walking backwards while Tom slammed the door with his left hand.

"Eve, baby. It was great to get your mail. I'm so glad to see you!"

Compliments didn't impress Eve. She had most of the people in her life departmentalised and her relationship with Tom was based purely on sex and she didn't want to waste the short time that they had together whispering niceties in his ear. She slipped the robe off her shoulders, revealing her nakedness. Her body was in such good shape that most women in their twenties would be envious of it.

"Wow, you are amazing . . . I've missed you!" Tom panted as he brushed his lips along her collarbone and rounded the curve of her shoulder. He was moving slowly down to her breasts when he suddenly stopped and studied her left arm. "Eve, honey, what happened to you?"

Eve glanced down at the scar along her upper arm and rolled her eyes. "I had a fall in the subway last time I was here – it's nothing – just a silly little scar." She moved her hand over to snap the buttons open on Tom's shirt.

"What happened? Why didn't you call me?"

"I didn't have enough time to see you – it was a quickie visit for our AGM."

Tom seemed hurt. "I can't believe you were in New York and didn't call me!"

Eve was getting impatient. "I said I was busy. Anyway if I wanted to be examined I'd have called a doctor."

Tom took a step backwards. "Hey, honey, I'm just concerned – I haven't seen you in months and now it's like you don't even want to talk!"

Eve snapped. "If I'd wanted to talk to you I would have phoned!"

Tom flinched at her sharp retort. It had been a crazy week in the world of fund-management and he didn't need grief from a woman that he only saw a couple of times a year – even if she did drive him crazy with desire.

Eve rolled her eyes and picked up her bathrobe – slipping it on over her shoulders as she flopped down on the square grey couch.

She looked up at the dishevelled Tom as he fixed the buttons on his shirt.

"So, how's the wife?"

"Jeez, Eve, is there any need for that?"

Eve pulled punches harder than most of the guys he'd had to deal with on Broad Street in the past few days and it looked like she was in fighting form tonight.

"I'm merely asking a polite question as you came here for a chat – I thought you were here for sex!"

Tom sat down on the luxurious couch opposite Eve. His legs spread wide, he rested his palms on his thighs and shook his head. "I like you, Eve, I'm glad to see you – it's been a while."

Eve dragged her French-polished fingernails through her hair and sighed. "Yeah, well, it's been a crazy day for me – I've had emails from long-lost friends and a new client who I can already tell is going to be trouble . . ."

Tom shrugged.

"Yeah, well," she continued, "I just want to forget about it and chill out this evening . . . and I thought that you would help me."

Eve smiled for the first time since Tom entered the suite. She would give him one more chance to turn this evening around and give her what she wanted.

He cleared his throat – holding a clenched fist up to his lips. "Eve . . ."

"Yes?"

Nothing could have prepared her for his revelation.

"Eve, Monica is pregnant."

Eve felt an inexplicable dart in her chest. She didn't give a damn about Tom's wife and she certainly didn't envy her but the fact that Tom had come to tell her the news brought a mixture of emotions up from the pit of her stomach.

"So, you're going to be a father – how lovely for you."

Tom wasn't sure if it was sarcasm or genuine regard in her tone. "I didn't want to tell you over the phone 'cause I haven't seen you for ages."

"I already told you – I didn't have the chance to call you the last time I was over," she replied sharply.

Tom rubbed his hands through his short hair. It was shades paler than it had been when Eve had first met him as more grey had crept through the black strands with time.

"I know I'm not a priority in your life, Eve, but I always regarded you as someone special in mine. But things have changed for me now . . . I can't see you when we are expecting a baby."

Eve threw her head back and laughed. "Why did you come here then?"

Tom drew a sharp breath. "I wanted to see you one last time."

"You can be so mushy. Give yourself a break, Tom. I'm really not bothered." She stood up and walked towards the door. "Actually, I'm meeting people later and I'd like to take a bath, so why don't you go home to Monica?"

Tom stood up and nodded. He knew in his heart that Eve had never really cared for him but he needed to show her the respect that he felt their relationship deserved – illicit as it was.

"Goodbye, Eve."

He leaned forward to give her a parting kiss on the cheek but she turned her head away.

"Goodbye, Tom," she replied and, as he disappeared out the door, she shut it sharply and stood for half a minute with her back leaning heavily against it.

She couldn't stay here on her own tonight. Her mind was made up – she would ring Rachel and see where she was staying. If she was in New York shopping, chances were that she would be in the Fitzpatrick like the rest of Dublin that thronged Fifth Avenue from one end of the year to the other.

She rummaged around her handbag until she found the piece of paper that Lucille's secretary had given her earlier. It was dog-eared but the mobile number was all that needed to be legible. She tapped the digits into the smooth chrome hotel phone and waited – unsure what she was going to say to her old friend. Fifteen years was a long time and all that she was certain of was that a lot had happened in both their lives.

TWO

Rachel was applying a coat of Virtuôse Divinehold mascara to her eyelashes as her phone rang. She looked at the caller ID and flinched when it showed an unknown American number. She knew that it was the phone call that she had hoped for all day.

"Hello!" she said cautiously.

"Rachel – it's Eve."

Rachel gulped. "Eve, hi! Thanks for getting in touch."

"Where are you? Have you arrived?"

Rachel checked that the door of the en suite was firmly shut. "Yes, I'm here and thought it would be nice to hook up after all these years – are you free at all over the next couple of days?" The sound of dripping water from the shower meant that Nicky wouldn't be able to hear their conversation and made her anxious to say all that needed to be said before her friend emerged from the en suite.

"Actually, Rachel, I don't live in New York any more!"

"Really? So where are you now?"

"Well, I'm staying in the Soho Grand – I just happen to be here in New York on business for a few days."

Rachel's heart started to beat faster. "That's an amazing coincidence – where do you live the rest of the time?"

"London – for the last five years." Eve relaxed as she started to fall into the memories of friendship with Rachel. "I married a Brit who dragged me back across the Atlantic."

"Wow – so you're married – any kids?"

"No – well, I'm newly separated actually – no kids – you know me, Rachel – they were never a priority."

So much information all at once – Rachel was ecstatic to be conversing with her old friend and found it difficult to stop the momentum now that she was talking to Eve at last. "That was a long time ago, Eve. People do change!"

Eve didn't need reminding of that but there were some people from her past that she felt would never change. "So, do you still see anyone from college?"

Rachel bit her lip – now was as good a time as any to tell her about Nicky. "Funny you should ask – I've actually seen a good bit of Nicky for the last few years."

Silence came from the other end of the line.

"So," Rachel continued hastily – maybe now wasn't the time to tell her that Nicky was with her – "are you free tonight – would you be interested in meeting up?"

"Have you got D-d-david with you?"

"It's Derek actually but, no, he's not with me. I'm visiting my brother and staying in the Washington Square Hotel."

Eve considered the location – it wasn't that far away from where she was staying. "What are your plans for tonight?"

This sounded promising, thought Rachel. "Actually we're going to Kelly and Ping. Do you know it?"

"On Greene Street. It's a dive but the food's okay. Tell you what – I might call over later at some stage."

"Great – that would be really great!" Rachel gushed but she felt disappointed – somehow Eve wasn't responding in exactly the right way to the prospect of meeting up.

"Okay then – have to go. Take care, Rachel."

"Thanks for getting back to me at such short notice," Rachel said apologetically.

She felt like a total fake when she turned off her phone. Why did most of her relationships leave her feeling inadequate or foolish? She lifted her hairbrush and ran it through her blonde curls – it was holding up well considering the journey across the Atlantic only a few hours earlier.

Seconds later Nicky emerged from the en suite.

"Everything okay at home?" she asked as she dried herself off briskly.

Rachel nodded her head frantically. "Absolutely great, yes, fantastic!" Honestly, she had dug a hole for herself now and had no idea how she was going to get out of it.

"I'm going to give Daniel a quick call," said Nicky. "What time is it at home?"

"Nearly twelve o'clock."

"Damn!" Nicky sighed and took a comb to her brown hair. It was shoulder length and looked longer and darker when it was wet. "I really wanted to talk to him before he went to bed."

"Maybe he's still up?"

"I don't want to disturb Karen and her family – she's so good to put him up for the weekend."

Rachel nodded in agreement. "You can ring him in the morning," she said with a weak smile. She wondered how her friend would feel in the morning after meeting Eve for the first time in a decade and a half!

33

Eve went into the luxurious en suite and put her head into her hands. It had been an awful day and did she really want to finish it off with a reunion with Rachel Moore – now Rachel Sloan – who quite possibly had morphed into a yummy mummy with tales of how wonderful Ireland now was?

She lifted her head and looked at the tiny lines that were starting to appear around her eyes. They weren't there a couple of years ago. It's just as well she had her Armani designer foundation make-up to hide the flaws. Her lenses felt tired and dry in her eyes and she flicked them out carefully before putting on her glasses. Back in the college days she'd have let them turn to sandpaper before she would have removed them but not any more. She had the confidence now to wear her glasses with panache and know that she was quite literally head and shoulders above most women her age.

The black DKNY suit was perfect for tonight with a pair of four-inch heel Jimmy Choos. If she was going to meet up with her past she wanted to look her best.

The walls of Kelly and Ping were lined with row upon row of tiny blue and white medicine bottles and china plates. Floral centrepieces on the small and rickety wooden tables resembled tropical twigs rather than flowers. Rachel had never been in such a dark restaurant in her life. In the background she could just about make out the silhouettes of two small Chinese men in white chef's uniforms in the midst of billowing white smoke – but the aroma of richly spiced and delicious food was palpable.

"I love this place!" Conor exclaimed as a tiny Asian woman scurried over to the threesome standing at the entrance door. "Hi! I booked a table under Moore."

The waitress beckoned them to follow her.

"It certainly is atmospheric!" Rachel said.

"If you could see your way around!" Nicky agreed.

Conor seemed to know exactly where he was going and took a seat at a table to the right of the corridor-like room.

"This okay for you girls?"

"Um . . . it's for four . . ." Rachel said anxiously.

Nicky raised an eyebrow. "And there are only four of us dining!"

Rachel shrugged. She turned to the waitress who stood waiting nonchalantly. "This is fine!" She really needed to warn Nicky.

"I'm surprised Alex isn't here yet," Conor said as he looked all around. "He's always eating – always hungry."

Rachel sat down at the rickety wooden table, feeling a bit uncomfortable. She had spent less time than usual getting ready in the small but hygienically clean en suite of the Washington Square Hotel. She normally kept her appearance pristine – Derek wouldn't allow her to present herself in any other way – but for now she would have liked to appear casually trendy with her younger brother and his stylish friend. But as all she had bought so far was a pair of cream trousers in Banana Republic and a white cotton Calvin Klein shirt, she was left with very little choice of what to wear except the now-smelly clothes that she had travelled in earlier. She felt prissy and too old for the company that she'd be keeping for the evening. She would have to buy some trendier gear tomorrow.

Today she had been occupied getting items from the list Derek had made. She wouldn't be able to go home without them and felt relieved that she had found the shirts and jeans that he had requested with such ease. Hopefully he would be pleased with them because she knew that it would be bad news for her if he wasn't.

Nicky had been luckier with her purchases and gone all out

in one of the trendy but exquisite boutiques on Broome Street. She also bought a top in Prada that easily cost a week's wages but was definitely worth it. As the afternoon's shopping was drifting into the evening Rachel had a job pulling the paper-bag laden Nicky out of Old Navy as she bought enough jeans and T-shirts for a family of four sons rather than one.

Conor must have read her thoughts.

"I can't believe the amount of gear you guys picked up today," he said as he took the card menus from the waitress and distributed them to the two girls. "Nicky, I see you're as mad about shopping as my sister."

Nicky sat upright on her seat and rested her elbows on the table – holding her menu tightly. "There's so much to do in this city. Just one shop after the other – and the Prada shop was just . . . well, I thought I was in heaven."

Conor grinned. "You probably were."

Suddenly he jumped and looked around after receiving a swift slap on the back.

"Hey, man! Sorry I'm late," Alex said as he took the last seat at the table for four. He turned his gaze directly to Rachel. "Nice to see you again, girls." He turned to Nicky. "How was your first day in New York?"

"Good!" she nodded. "Do you mind if I slip outside for a minute?"

"Not at all," Alex declared. "It's charming to have a smoker in our midst – do your friends ever make you feel like a dinosaur?"

Nicky stood up sharply and grabbed her handbag. "Actually most people smoke in my business. Excuse me!"

Nicky manoeuvred her way successfully out to the street but couldn't find a comfortable piece of façade to lean against as she lit up a Marlboro Light and took a slow leisurely drag. She was finally in New York – no sign of Carrie or Miranda yet but she figured she still had a lot of the city to explore before she could feel that she had really been to the Big Apple. She would never have got here had she not bumped into Rachel that day on Grafton Street five years ago.

They had gone for coffee in Bewleys a couple of times after that first meeting. Both found it amazing that they lived only six miles apart yet hadn't seen each other in the previous ten years. Rachel had been busy giving birth and going through the motions of the other stay-at-home-mums in Portmarnock – keeping her home nice and doing the after-school runs from one activity to the next.

So far it had been good renewing the friendship but, even though Rachel's house was thronged with children and women calling in for cups of coffee, Nicky felt that there was something lonely about her friend. On more than one occasion she had opened up and told Nicky what a relief it was to be friends with someone who understood the real her. However, Nicky had no other real evidence of this loneliness.

Nicky, on the other hand, was on her way to work at eight o'clock every morning. When her mother was alive she used to take Daniel to school and go through all of the other routines that Nicky wished she herself was able to do for her son. Living with her mother had seriously stunted her chances of forming a romantic relationship in the early days when Daniel was small but life would have been intolerable if she'd had to pay crèches and minders to look after her son. When her mother died four years ago Nicky only then realised how hard it was as a single mum living in Dublin. But Daniel was coming to an age where his friends and after-school activities were becoming more and more important in his life and for the last couple of years he was consuming nearly all of her resources. That was why she came up with the suggestion of visiting New York with Rachel. It really was time that she started to look after herself – because before she realised it Daniel would be gone!

"I don't seem to be making a good impression on your friend," Alex said to Rachel when he was sure that Nicky was well out of earshot.

"Don't mind her – she's tetchy at the moment – I think she's missing her son."

Alex nodded although he had no idea of the emotions experienced by a parent separated from their offspring. "Are you missing your kids?"

Rachel leaned forward and said confidentially, "Actually I haven't thought about them since I landed! But I was very anxious before getting here and even had last minute jitters before getting on the plane!"

It was true. She had been wondering about Eve for a good deal of the day and wallowing in the enjoyment of spending some time in New York without Derek leaning over her shoulder and watching her moves every step of the way. It felt like she was visiting a different city this time around and she knew already that this was going to be her best visit to New York.

"Good for you!" Alex exclaimed and called the waitress over. "Tiger beer, man?" he asked Conor who nodded.

"Me too," Rachel blurted. She hadn't drunk beer since her college days but it seemed like a new and exciting change on finding herself in unfamiliar laid-back surroundings.

Alex looked even better in the dark atmosphere of Kelly and Ping. He was wearing a black crew-neck tee-shirt and a faded denim jacket hung on the back of his chair. The thin leather necklace still rested around his neck and he had spiked up his peroxide-blond hair even higher than earlier.

Rachel found it difficult not to stare into his dark brown eyes. His lips were full and perfectly symmetrical and when he wasn't talking he had a constant smile firmly fixed across them. His conversation was directed at Rachel, which was awkward as she didn't want her brother to think that his older and married sister was in danger of turning into an irresponsible flirt.

The Tiger beer arrived – without glasses. Rachel took a swig from the top of the bottle and felt alive as the fizzy golden-coloured liquid trickled down her throat. Derek would freak if he saw her taking a drink like that in public and she got a thrill for an instant as she thought about it. Now was as good a time as any to warn Nicky about the possibility that they might have another guest at dinner – she felt braver after a swig of beer.

"Excuse me for a moment, guys!" Rachel squeezed past Conor as she left the table.

"You haven't started smoking again, have you?" he asked.

Rachel shook her head. "I just need to warn Nicky – I called an old college friend today and told her that we would be here tonight and she said she might join us."

"Bring it on! Irish girls are great!" Alex said with a wicked wink.

Rachel scurried out of the restaurant – tripping up en route in the darkened foyer.

Nicky was taking a last satisfying drag from her cigarette as Rachel came out to the brightness of the streetlights.

"What do you think of this place?" Rachel asked nervously.

Nicky smiled. "It's not exactly *Sex and the City*, is it?"

Rachel nodded in agreement. "But Conor swears the food is great." She took a deep apprehensive breath. "Nicky, I've a bit of a confession to make . . ."

Nicky frowned and eyed Rachel apprehensively. "Go on!"

"Well, before we left Dublin I made a couple of calls to see if I could get Eve's address in New York and I got an email address for her and I . . . well, I contacted her . . . and . . . and she's living in London now but she's here on business . . . and she said she might come here tonight."

Nicky suddenly flung her cigarette butt on to the pavement and stamped it out firmly.

She tilted her head – not quite believing her ears. "You are joking, aren't you?"

Rachel didn't answer but shook her head timidly.

"Why in the name of God did you do such a thing, Rach?"

Rachel had completely underestimated Nicky's reaction. She'd genuinely thought that she was doing the right thing. This was bad. And also, in hindsight, Eve hadn't been exactly thrilled to hear from her – how would she feel if she did actually turn up to Kelly and Ping tonight and saw Nicky there too?

"I thought it might be a good time for you guys to make up – look how great it's been between us for the last five years."

"But Eve doesn't hold a grudge against you – not like she does with me!"

"I think it would be good for us all to move on."

"Rachel, some of us *have* moved on!" And Nicky strode back into the restaurant, still shaking her head in disbelief.

Nicky wasn't able to hide her feelings of upset when they returned to the table. She slapped her handbag down on the ground and rolled her eyes as she sat down opposite Rachel. She was glad she wasn't opposite Alex as that meant she wouldn't have to make constant eye contact with him for the evening – meeting Eve was going to be painful enough to endure.

"I felt like a leper out there!" she exclaimed, hoping the guys would put her bad humour down to that. "Does anyone smoke in New York?"

40

"Just about every model and artist – apart from Alex," Conor said with a grin.

Nicky wished she could drop the habit. But another part of her worried what size she would be if she didn't smoke.

"This menu looks interesting," she said, tilting her head and trying not to appear as agitated as she was feeling at the prospect of meeting Eve Porter again. "What's everybody having?"

Alex found these women amazingly cute with their lilting Irish accents – especially Conor's sister. He leaned forward over the cup filled with chopsticks and the paper napkin dispenser until his eyes were fixed on Rachel's again.

"I recommend the Yam Ped Krob duck for starters and the Pad Thai here is the best you'll get in Manhattan."

"Don't mind him – the salt and pepper shrimps and Dak Bulgogi are the way to go!" Conor interrupted, feeling more than a little possessive of his sister. He saw Alex in action most weekends and knew how effortlessly he cut to the chase with one waif-like beauty after another. He didn't feel comfortable watching his sister in the role of one of his friend's prey. He cared deeply for her and, even though she was older, he always felt that she was the more naïve of them, hence his instinct to protect her from his philandering friend.

Alex sat back on his wooden chair following the subtle but effective glare from Conor that said these women were not to be trifled with.

The brief tension was dissipated by the waitress who was suddenly getting busy as more and more people filled the room. She efficiently took their orders and scuttled away to the steamy kitchen at the back of the restaurant.

"What are your plans for the weekend?" Alex asked.

"I was hoping to get to the top of the Empire State to be honest," Rachel said wistfully. "I've never been."

"I brought you up the Twin Towers the first time you came over!" Conor blurted.

Nicky watched the dynamics of the other three. She wondered if Rachel had any idea of how envious she was of her. Not only had she a reliable husband at home waiting for her but here, thousands of miles across the Atlantic, she had a hunky brother and his friend fussing over her. When she'd bumped into Rachel initially she'd wondered if they could ever be friends again. She carried a lot of hurt from the time when Rachel abandoned her. Those were the hard days – pregnant and single in a Dublin that didn't even have the basic human right of divorce in its constitution. But Rachel was easy to forgive and in hindsight it was more than likely pressure from Derek than Rachel's own decision to stay away from Nicky. It wasn't as if Rachel sided with Eve after their friendship broke up – she just sat on the fence and if Nicky were in her situation she couldn't say that she wouldn't have done the same.

"Penny for them?" Conor asked Nicky, taking a swig from his Tiger beer.

"Sorry – I shouldn't be daydreaming in the city that never sleeps!" Nicky sat upright. "Did Rachel mention that we may have an old friend joining us?"

"Yeah, just a few minutes ago. Who is she again?"

"A girl called Eve – from college."

It was difficult to read his expression in the dim light but Nicky felt sure that he was unaware of the story and the tensions that related to the coming meeting with Eve.

Conor shook his head. "I didn't get to meet all of Rachel's pals when she was in college. Don't forget I was an undesirable schoolboy, and anyway Rachel was never home in those days!"

Nicky nodded. That much was definitely true. They all hung around in Eve's rooms in Trinity. Often the tiny cramped lodgings slept five or six students who had missed the last bus home. They were good days, ducking and dodging the dormitory porters. But that was a long time ago and they were all very different people now and she couldn't help but feel that somehow Rachel had ruined not only their first night in New York but quite possibly the whole weekend.

She decided to warn him. "We have a history, Eve and I. When we finished up in college I had a relationship with her boyfriend while she came over here to find work."

Conor pulled his top lip down, covering it with his bottom lip. "Happens, I guess!" he said with a shrug.

Nicky nodded. "Yeah but I fell pregnant and Eve found out and didn't want anything more to do with me – I can't say I blame her!"

"What about the father?"

"He did a runner out of Ireland as quick as he could!"

Conor picked up his bottle of Tiger beer and took a mouthful. "Nice guy!" he said dryly. "Sounds like you did her a favour!"

Nicky wasn't able to quantify how she felt about James Holden any more. But she did carry a certain amount of guilt towards her friend.

Meanwhile Alex and Rachel were engrossed in each other.

"So what do you do in Ireland?" Alex asked, his left cheek resting on the palm of his left hand, his elbow propped on the table. His eyes were firmly fixed on her face.

Rachel could feel a pink flush rush over her cheeks. "Nothing much – I'm a stay-at-home mum!"

"Hey, don't I wish I had one of those when I was a kid! Don't knock the great service you're doing."

Rachel blushed even harder.

"My mom worked in Real Estate and she was never around,"

he went on. "It was my job to cook the vegetables when I got home from school – my sister made the fire and cooked the meat."

Rachel reached out and gave him a friendly poke in the arm. "It didn't do you any harm by the look of it!"

"Maybe not – but it didn't help my relationship with my mother. We never really got to know each other and she died of a heart attack when she was only fifty-three."

"That's awful – how old were you at the time?"

"Twenty-seven and just finished my doctorate. We never had quality time together and now we never will."

Rachel took a drink from the now lukewarm bottle of beer and smiled timidly. "That's awful!"

"Sorry – I didn't mean to get all morose – you're on your vacation." He beckoned to the waitress as she was passing. "Some more cold Tiger beers, please!" he called.

The waitress was balancing three plates full of various starters precariously on one arm.

"You wan fooh furst?" she asked Conor.

"Yes, of course, if it's ready," he nodded.

The presentation was superb and Rachel and Nicky gazed at the food hungrily.

"Wow, good choice!" Nicky said, taking a pair of chopsticks from the small jar in the middle of the table.

They finished two more rounds of Tiger beer before the main courses were put down in front of them. Alex was completely honed in on Rachel and she loved the attention so much she got a start when a tall figure loomed ominously over the table.

Rachel looked up first and then Nicky who quickly put her head back down into her food. She was grateful for the first time all night for their dark surroundings.

"Hi, Rachel," Eve said and nodded at the two men. With her

eyes firmly fixed on Rachel she seemed oblivious of the fourth member of the group.

Rachel jumped to her feet and embraced her old friend who was head and shoulders above her. She planted a kiss on the side of Eve's cheek but she only reciprocated with an air-kiss.

Conor stood up and held out his hand. "Hi, I'm Conor – Rachel's brother." Eve looked vaguely familiar to him in the dim light – he must have met her previously after all though he couldn't remember doing so.

"Hi," she said curtly and responded with a limp handshake.

Conor had intended to fetch a chair for her but, with manners like that, she didn't deserve one. He sat back down.

Instead a waitress came over with a chair.

"You wanna join?" she asked.

Eve nodded and the waitress put the chair near the corner of the table next to Conor.

With a flick of her long thick auburn hair Eve sat down. She then glanced at the fourth person at the table, who still had her face bent over her plate, and in an instant recognised who it was.

"Nicky!" she exclaimed loudly. "What are you . . ." Shock took over and her mouth dropped open.

Nicky looked up and gave a half-smile. "Hi, Eve." What else could she say?

"You guys came over together?" Eve asked, looking first at Rachel and then at Nicky.

Rachel nodded.

Alex and Conor swiftly realised that they were embroiled in a drama in which they had no part to play.

"Why don't you check out the menu," Alex said, handing it to Eve in an attempt to deflate the tension.

"I've eaten, thanks," Eve lied and held up the palm of her hand. This was a big mistake and she shouldn't have come.

"Have a beer?" Alex tried again – even he could feel the tension.

"I don't drink beer," she replied curtly.

"Sake, wine?" Conor suggested.

Rachel took her cue to intervene. "It's brilliant to see you, Eve – you look fabulous. When did you start to wear glasses again?"

"About ten years ago," Eve replied dryly. Looking around the table, she wondered if she would have been better off in the loft staring at the Empire State for the evening.

"Tell us what's been happening," Rachel said in overtly bubbly tones. "Fifteen years is a long time."

Eve took a deep breath and sighed – the spotlight was definitely on her. There was no way out of the situation for the moment so the best thing to do was to play along. This was not the sort of place she frequented and these were no longer the sort of people that she normally associated with.

"I lived here for eleven years – probably shouldn't have left New York at all really. It's the only city in the world that has anything you could possibly want condensed into the one reasonably small space."

"It's great, isn't it?" Alex said. This Irishwoman wasn't like the others. He felt almost afraid of her. She wasn't dressed like the others either – her expensive designer suit made her look years older than Rachel – or maybe it was her black-rimmed spectacles.

Eve looked Alex up and down and dismissively turned her attention back to Rachel.

"So how is D-d-d – your husband?"

"Derek . . . he's great," Rachel said. "We have three kids."

"Yes, I had heard – I met one of the girls from college on a flight a couple of years ago who bumped into you – can't for the life of me remember her name now!"

Nicky stayed silent – she hated telling people from her past that she still wasn't married – especially as most people knew that she had a son.

"What ages are they?" Eve asked.

"Sarah is twelve, Ben is eleven and Holly is six."

Eve turned to Nicky. "Your boy must be almost grown up now!"

Nicky nodded in reply and their eyes met for an uncomfortable moment.

"Daniel is nearly fifteen," she said.

"Eve, do you want to sit nearer the girls?" Alex said suddenly, standing up. He could sense that his and Conor's presence was becoming more inappropriate as the conversation became more personal.

Eve stood up and Alex took her seat next to Conor so that the men could talk together while the women continued to fill in the missing years of their lives apart.

"I'm sorry to hear you're separated!" Rachel said sympathetically now that Eve was sitting nearer.

"I suppose I am technically – we are living apart but neither of us is in any hurry to get a divorce."

She looked at Nicky and added, "Never marry an Englishman."

Why does she presume I'm not married? Nicky thought angrily but gave a wry smile and nodded. Eve had more reason to be annoyed with her than she had with Eve. It was fifteen years since she had slept with Eve's boyfriend and the shame still hung over her. God only knew how much she had paid the price for that one night but she wouldn't change it for the world – even if she could.

"What are you doing now?" Eve was asking her.

"I've been working for Virtue magazines for ten years," Nicky said and hated herself for sounding so timid.

"Are you still living with your mum?"

Nicky knew that Eve couldn't wait to get the dig in any way that she could. "No, actually – Mum died four years ago."

"I'm sorry to hear that," Eve said, lowering her eyes. "So, when do you guys go back?"

"Monday night," Rachel replied.

"Three nights in New York," Eve observed.

"And four days!" Rachel added.

"You'll be shopping for most of it, I presume."

Nicky and Rachel nodded their heads in unison.

"Are you working tomorrow?" Rachel asked.

Eve nodded. "Actually, I may have to work this evening – I received a call from one of our new clients before coming here and I agreed to meet him later."

"I Googled Just for Coffee when I sent you the email. Who uses your agency?" Rachel asked out of genuine interest.

Eve threw her head back and ran her fingers briefly through her hair. "Lots of people – most are highly paid professionals but we do get the odd celeb."

"Anyone we'd know?" Rachel pried.

"I have an Irish client at the moment and you would definitely have heard about him in the papers and on TV. But we have a confidentiality clause that means I can't tell his name."

"It sounds very exciting," Rachel smiled.

Eve shrugged. "I suppose it can be interesting – it's quite mathematical really when you balance it all up."

"What about love?" Nicky asked – staring intently at Eve and waiting for a calculated retort.

"If you want to get your hair to look better you go and see a qualified stylist so why should getting a partner be any different? Our clients are too busy to find their own and we can do a much more thorough job of vetting potential partners." Eve rolled her eyes. "And as for love – it has to be the most grossly overrated emotion in the world. Anyway, most of the time when people talk about love they are really talking about lust. Our clients have too much to lose by picking the wrong mate up – at least this way they are both financially secure and money won't be an issue or problem in their relationship."

Nicky took a sip of her beer as Eve's phone bleeped. Eve was obviously doing well while she herself still waded through the small-time magazine industry in Dublin. She couldn't help but admire the woman who used to be such a good friend. Her stylish clothes and ultra-confidence signalled that she had made it in the business world. Eve always pushed herself forward and Nicky had no one but herself to blame for the position that she was in. Maybe she should think about joining a dating agency when she got back to Dublin – after all, she hadn't done a very good job finding suitable dates for herself.

Eve nodded and hummed as the person on the other end of the line spoke.

"Okay, I'll meet him in half an hour – see you tomorrow."

She snapped her mobile phone shut and turned her attention back to the two girls who used to be her friends.

"That was Lucille – I have to go and meet this guy – but maybe I have time for one glass of wine." She sighed. "It's much the same as baby-sitting at this stage – some of our clients haven't got a clue."

Conor was laughing, deep in conversation with Alex.

"Conor!" Rachel called. "Could you get a glass of wine for Eve?"

He turned and smiled at his sister. "Why don't I get a bottle? Red or white?"

Eve coughed. "I only drink red – but they probably don't have anything drinkable in a place like this."

"Hey, what's your problem? This is a place where people

who live in this city like to go," he said, a bit more forthrightly than he had intended.

"I lived in this city for eleven years and never came here – even when I had no money!" Eve snapped.

"Maybe you should go uptown to the Astoria or somewhere you might feel more comfortable then!" Conor said, lifting his Tiger beer and taking a generous swig.

"There are plenty of cool places to go," Eve retorted. "Why come to this dive?"

"There's no need to be so rude." Conor looked over at Rachel and then back to Eve as he scratched his head. "You know, I'm not surprised your boyfriend went off with Nicky!"

Rachel went puce and frowned at her brother, then dropped her gaze. Out of the corner of her eye she saw Eve pick up her handbag and stand up abruptly.

"I didn't realise my private life was public knowledge," Eve said, glaring at Rachel and then at Nicky. "I have to go."

"I'm sorry, Eve," Nicky blurted. "I told him that I was the one who was in the wrong. I didn't say anything derogatory about you."

"We were only trying to help him to place you!" Rachel pleaded. "I really want us all to be friends again."

But Eve wasn't giving in and was utterly embarrassed by the situation.

Alex looked on inquisitively.

Nicky shook her head. She was beginning to see the merits in Rachel's actions. There were plenty of unfinished business between the two of them and she didn't want Eve to leave.

"Don't go, Eve," Nicky begged. "Not like this!"

"I have to meet this man back at my hotel – Rachel has my phone number!" she said. "We might get a chance for coffee before you go back."

Nicky stood up too. "Let me come with you. Just as far as the hotel."

Eve shook her head. "I'm meeting a client and it wouldn't be appropriate."

Nicky grabbed her coat and walked around the table. She leant down and whispered in Rachel's ear. "You guys will be here for a while? I'll get a cab back – what's the name of this place?"

"Kelly and Ping – Greene Street!" Rachel said wide-eyed – still shocked at the exchange between Eve and Conor – it was so unlike her brother to lash out like that.

"I can phone you if I get lost," Nicky called as she hurried out after Eve.

"Really, Conor," Rachel berated him, "was there any need for that?"

Conor rolled his eyes and took a swig of his Tiger beer. "Some people are so far stuck up their own asses they need to be told how it is sometimes."

"She was my friend – I invited her here – you should have just said nothing."

"I tell it like it is, Rachel – that's what comes from living here. She should know that if she lived here for as long as she says she did."

Alex clapped his hands down hard on the table. "Hey, guys – stop it – you're family. Besides, we haven't had our dinner yet."

"I'm not hungry any more," Conor said taking another drink from his bottle of beer.

As if on cue, the waitress came over with three plates balanced precariously on her arms.

She placed the food down in front of them.

"Where you fren?"

Rachel looked up at her. "She had to go."

"Don't worry – I'll eat hers," Alex said. "I'm starving."

THREE

Eve and Nicky sat silently in the back of the yellow taxi.

"I shouldn't have gone there tonight – it's been the freakiest day ever!" Eve exclaimed.

"Well, everything happens for a reason, I guess." Nicky couldn't believe that she was sitting in the back of a taxi in New York City with Eve. It was totally surreal and she felt like she was twenty-one again. "And I'm glad that Rachel emailed you. We still have stuff we need to talk about."

Eve shook her head. "The past is the past and really it doesn't matter any more. I've been through one separation and maybe you spared me from another. But that brother of Rachel's is an absolute pig. I never would have thought he was related to Rachel Moore."

"Rachel Sloan," Nicky corrected.

"Yes," Eve said with a sigh. "I don't blame you for telling her brother but I don't like getting the past thrown up in my face like that. I mean, nobody has it perfect and to be honest

I'd be worried about Rachel."

"What do you mean?" Nicky asked defensively. "She looks great, she has a steady man and three gorgeous kids. She's probably doing the best out of the three of us."

"She hasn't found herself," Eve stated. "She may have a husband and three kids but she doesn't seem to have moved on since we were in college."

Nicky wondered if Eve was slightly jealous of Rachel – for one thing, she was undoubtedly the most naturally pretty of the three. "Have you?"

Eve smiled. "When you leave home young and come and live in a city like this you must learn to eat or get eaten." She turned her attention to the traffic rushing by the window beside her as if needing to be distracted from something else that was bothering her. "Then life's lessons get thrown at you along the way," she added.

Nicky could tell that Eve was hiding something but it was too early in the rekindling of their friendship to pry. "You know, Dublin's frantic to live in now!" she said, nodding her head. "It's all about what you have and what you want next!"

"From what I've heard – it's probably worse than here! But when I left Dublin it was still a sleepy little city on the edge of Europe."

Nicky tilted her head and smiled. "Would you ever think of coming back?"

Eve laughed and shook her head. "I'm from Galway – Dublin was never my home – and there's no place for me there now. Most of my relatives are dead or not living in Ireland any more."

The taxi slowed down as it pulled up in front of a large brick building with clear modern lines and large windows.

"This your hotel?" Nicky asked, her head craned upwards at the postmodernist exterior.

Eve nodded. Her mood and tone had mellowed considerably during the car journey.

"Tell you what – why don't you come in for a nightcap? The concierge will get you a cab back to the restaurant."

Nicky smiled. She wouldn't mind a look at how the other half lived and she was enjoying Eve's company – something she thought she would never be in, let alone enjoy, ever again.

"Why not?" she shrugged. "But what about your client?"

"To be honest, I couldn't give a damn about him." She thought for a moment. "I'll tell him you're an employee of the agency."

Nicky felt like she was walking into a different world as she passed through the large glass doors of the Soho Grand – one filled with glamour and wealth such as she only ever got to write about between the pages of the glossy magazine that she edited.

The floor of the large and modern foyer was covered with stone and marble and the grand staircase was constructed from glass bottles and iron, unlike anything Nicky had ever seen. This was the sort of place a supermodel or rock band would definitely hang out – so different to the images she had seen in movies of hotels like the Ritz Carlton. This was definitely a twenty-first century hotel.

"The best bar is upstairs," Eve said leading her toward the remarkable stairway.

The steps were minimalist in style and made of glass, making Nicky feel anxious as she ascended. She looked around in amazement. There wasn't a hotel like this in Dublin. The occasional tables had tropical flower arrangements effortlessly decorating them and reaching high up to the vast ceilings. Another feast was waiting for her eyes as she entered the opulent lounge. It was luxurious and ultra-trendy in furnishings and design.

"What will you have?"

"A glass of beer – do they have Carlsberg?" Nicky asked.

Eve rolled her eyes as they approached the long and beautifully proportioned bar counter.

"Two Cosmos," she said with a nod.

The waiter didn't reply. Instead he promptly took out the cocktail shaker and set to work.

"This guy I'm meeting seems to be always late," Eve said, glancing at her watch. "I was looking at his file earlier – I think we're going to have problems finding anyone in Dublin who would suit him."

"What's he like?"

Eve gestured to one of the large and luxurious sofas. Together the two sat down and then Eve turned to Nicky with a grin.

"I'll give you a clue. He is tall and smart-looking. He has been separated for years – with two grown-up daughters. He is extremely powerful in most circles in Dublin and Ireland and had a long-time public affair with a woman who he never committed to. He has been on his own for some time now and is looking for company. He is officially retired but over here on business – as far as I can make out he's still working!"

Nicky's mouth dropped. Eve had described in detail the last taoiseach – the equivalent of the Irish prime minister.

"You're joking!" Nicky exclaimed.

Eve shook her head. "He's coming this way now."

Nicky sat upright and scanned the room. Only one person was approaching apart from the waitress with their Cosmos. His steps quickened as he noticed Eve. He was tall and wide-set, wearing a smart grey suit . . . and a taoiseach he most definitely wasn't. Nicky's mouth was no longer open but she couldn't hold back a giggle that was trying to escape from her lips. It struck her as comical that she had been expecting to see Ireland's ex-taoiseach! She held her hand up to her mouth in an effort to conceal her reaction.

"Stephen!" Eve exclaimed as she stood up to greet her client. "Good to see you again."

Stephen held out his hand and looked down at the other woman who was very obviously trying to compose herself from a fit of giggling.

"Stephen Delaney, this is Nicky Blake – you will have to excuse her – she works in the London office with me and this is her first time in New York," Eve leaned forward to whisper in Stephen's ear. "She's a bit excited – you know how it is!"

Stephen smiled and looked down at Nicky. "Hi, there."

Nicky beamed back up at him. He looked like a kindly Pierce Brosnan – dark hair peppered with grey and a definite twinkle in his eye. But Nicky was never the sort to be attracted to an older man so the twinkle wouldn't do him any good with her!

"Very sorry. Delighted to meet you. I hope *Out for Coffee* will be of great service to you," Nicky said, trying to act in what she thought was a professional manner.

"Really?" he said with a grin as he surveyed her blue eyes and dark hair. Her Celtic looks were typical in Ireland but unusual and attractive in the New York setting. "I thought it was Just for Coffee that I was employing!"

He liked the natural and childlike way this girl behaved – different from the people he usually met.

"I've got to have a cigarette – excuse me!" Nicky exclaimed, grabbing her handbag. How could she have jumbled the name when she was trying to make an impression? And how could she have thought that the taoiseach would possibly employ a dating agency? But Eve did have her going for a few minutes.

Eve looked to see her client's reaction and hoped that he wouldn't pass remarks about Nicky to Lucille.

"I may make my ex-wife laugh but I don't usually have that effect on women who are meeting me for the first time!"

"She's new and I'm trying to train her in – sorry!"

Stephen shrugged and sat down opposite Eve as a waitress hurried over.

"Can I get you anything, sir?" she asked.

"I'll have an Irish whiskey with a small jug of water and a packet of Marlboro."

The waitress hurried off.

"How long are you in town?" Eve asked – she knew that she would have to see him again if he was staying for longer than the weekend and show him the full range of possible dates that she had on file.

"I'm going back Monday evening. I have to hang around for a meeting on Monday morning on Wall Street."

Eve nodded. This could be a very boring weekend if she didn't take care.

When the waitress returned Stephen picked the box of cigarettes from the tray and nodded at Eve.

"Back soon!" he said and left her.

A shiver ran up Eve's back – she hadn't bargained on him being a smoker – she hadn't been through his file with a fine-tooth comb yet. This would make it even more difficult to find him a partner.

Stephen made it to the front of the hotel as Nicky was finishing her cigarette.

"Pity," Stephen said enigmatically as he walked up to her.

"What is?" asked Nicky, startled.

"I was hoping for some company with my cigarette."

Nicky smiled. "I know what you mean! Non-smokers drive me insane. They are so bloody condescending when we sneak out for a quick drag. Do they make you feel guilty?"

Stephen carefully lit the tip of his cigarette and slowly blew out a cloud of white smoke. He nodded. "Especially if you're having dinner and you're the only one that smokes. I mean, I even put down in my file that I didn't smoke in case it put people off."

Nicky nodded. "In the old days it was great – if you were in a place and you saw a guy smoking you knew exactly where you stood. Now it can get you into all sorts of trouble. I followed this guy outside once for a smoke, as I thought, and it turned out that he was going to his car. When he got back and saw me with my Marlboros you'd think I'd just contracted some sort of contagious disease."

"I know what you mean," Stephen said, blowing a smoke ring into the air.

"I have to say, Stephen – I'm really surprised that you're using our agency – I mean, your face is always on the news and in the paper. Why do you need us?"

"I thought you lived in London with Eve?" Stephen asked with his brow furrowed. "I'm surprised that you recognise me!"

Nicky had to think quickly. "I'm new – you're not exactly anonymous in Ireland and I'm only in London a couple of weeks."

"And they send you over to New York so soon? Nice company!"

Nicky knew that her story would become more and more transparent the longer she spoke to Stephen on her own.

"I'd better get back to Eve – big boss and all that!" she said, stubbing out her butt in the metal ashtray at the side of the large rotating doors.

Stephen followed suit and joined her in one of the revolving doorways.

"I think your company is a brilliant idea – a personal friend of mine found his bride-to-be with Just for Coffee."

Nicky tried to act like she was privy to company protocol but she felt lost and quickened her pace, leading the way back to Eve.

"Back so soon?" Eve said with a smile, holding her almost empty cocktail glass up to her lips. "Your smoking will seriously cut the base we have to work with, Stephen, but I've been looking at your preferences and I'm confident we'll find plenty of prospective dates for you."

Stephen clapped his hands together and sat down on the sofa opposite Eve. "Great news – now let's get another drink in. It isn't often I get two such pretty women for company when I'm on my own in a hotel like this."

Nicky smiled. Her first night in New York wasn't turning out anything like she had expected it to.

Rachel looked at her watch as the waitress cleared away the dishes.

"I think she's trying to drop a hint!" Alex said with a grin as the tables emptied.

"I hope Nicky is okay and hasn't been eaten by your other friend!" Conor said to Rachel.

She frowned but inside was feeling anxious. "Maybe I'll give her a call – I don't want her to get lost!"

She rang Nicky's number but didn't get a tone to indicate if she was engaged or just out of coverage.

"No reply! What should I do?" she asked Conor and Alex earnestly.

"You could try and go to the Soho Grand and find her," Conor suggested.

Alex looked over at Rachel – this was his chance to pounce!

"Or you could leave a message on her voicemail or text," he said, "and let me take you up the Empire State Building?"

Rachel looked at her watch again. Ten o'clock – it was three in the morning at home and she still felt wide-eyed.

"Well?" Alex pushed a little harder this time.

"I don't think I should leave her," Rachel sighed. "I mean, it wouldn't be fair."

Conor was about to interrupt as a hand tapped his shoulder.

"Hey," he said, turning quickly in surprise.

A girl who was easily six foot in her Manolo Blahniks stood waif-like, holding a strand of fine straight blonde hair. Her skirt was so short it made her legs look like two very long, albeit sexy, walking sticks.

"I didn't expect to see you tonight, Mandy," said Conor, not sounding too pleased. "I told you that I was meeting my sister."

The girl stared vacantly at Rachel and then looked at Conor again and shrugged. "I thought what the heck – that party in Pravda was dumb and I knew you'd be here."

"Pravda?" Rachel asked.

"It's a people-spotting bar – full of musicians, photographers and . . ." he didn't need to state it – it was obvious that it was also full of models and Mandy was definitely one of them. "Why don't you sit down?" he added unenthusiastically. "This is my sister Rachel."

Mandy plonked herself down on the chair that Nicky had occupied earlier. "Hi-i-i!" she hummed, fiddling with her hair again.

The new visitor to the restaurant made Rachel wonder exactly what sort of life her brother led in this city. She definitely would only be getting to see what he wanted her to see – that was for sure.

"I think I'll try ringing Nicky again to see if she is okay," she said, taking her phone in hand.

Nicky jumped as her phone rang out of her handbag and she rushed to get it before it made any more noise in the swanky bar of the Soho Grand. Already she had told Stephen some of her best jokes, while he contributed his best yarns, and she felt that she was doing the Just for Coffee brand a great service — even if Eve was trying painfully to smile while cringing at the obvious lack of professionalism on Nicky's part as a company employee.

"Rach — hi. I'll be back soon," Nicky said, trying to hide the giddiness she felt after a long flight, lots of airline champagne, shopping and now two Cosmos in rapid succession on an almost empty stomach.

"Are you having a good time?" Rachel asked.

Nicky nodded her head frantically as if Rachel could see her. "Yeah! It's great here."

Eve felt a desire to make Nicky disappear. For one she didn't want to sit and listen to Stephen and his stories for much longer and Nicky was acting like a complete idiot.

"Alex wants to take us up the Empire State Building," Rachel continued. "He says it's open until two a.m. but we would need to move now — sometimes they close the doors early if it's really busy."

Nicky looked over at Eve and Stephen. "I'll get a cab now — why don't I meet you outside the Empire State in a few minutes?"

"Okay. I don't know how long it will take you to get there but the traffic can't be that bad this time of night."

Nicky smiled at the other two, who had been silent while she was on the phone. "I'm going up the Empire State Building!" she said excitedly.

Eve looked at her watch. This meeting was futile to say the least. "I'm beat. Do you mind if I go?" she asked Stephen.

"Not at all – don't let me hold you up," he said apologetically. "It was good of you to meet me tonight."

Nicky stood up and picked up her handbag.

"I'll see you later then," she said to Eve, almost forgetting that she was meant to be a Just for Coffee employee. Then she added hastily, "If that's okay?"

"Sure, just don't stay out too late – we are meeting Lucille in the morning."

Thinking up lies on the spur of the moment came naturally to Eve.

Nicky shook Stephen's hand. The fact that he was a good deal older than her made her think he would make a terrific big brother/father figure. It was probably why she was able to be so relaxed in his company.

"It was very nice meeting you, Nicky. I hope we meet again before I go back."

Nicky nodded, still shaking his hand warmly. "Yes, absolutely. Great to have someone to smoke with. Bye, Eve, and thanks."

Nicky clip-clopped across the marble floor and gave a little wave before she moved out of view.

"She's good fun!" Stephen said when he was left on his own with Eve.

"We try to employ the best," she said, taking a final sip of her Cosmo.

"I'll probably see you in the morning for breakfast?" Stephen asked hopefully. He was enjoying the company as he usually was very much alone when he came to New York on business.

"I don't normally eat early in the morning but I might slip out to the Village for breakfast – old habit. The food is great in New York."

Stephen nodded. He would slip outside for another cigarette before going to bed.

"Goodnight, Eve."

"Goodnight, Stephen," she said, smiling.

He walked away, leaving Eve alone on the large couch, contemplating her day. It had certainly been crazy from start to finish.

Nicky was putting her cigarette out as Stephen reached the doors of the hotel.

"This is a bit like *Groundhog Day!*" he said as he came face to face with her again.

"Oh, hi." She was a bit dismayed – she didn't want her cover to be blown with this man for Eve's sake.

"I thought you would be gone?"

"I was just having a quickie before the cab ride."

"I envy you," Stephen said. "I've never been up the Empire State in all the times I've visited this city."

Nicky giggled. "Well, I've never been here before today – it's cool, isn't it?"

Stephen couldn't help smiling at the open frankness that this girl expressed so naturally – so different to the hard-edged women he came across in business and the silly glamour girls who made it so blatantly obvious that their only aim was to become a trophy wife.

A yellow cab pulled up as Nicky waved it down.

She grinned at Stephen as she got in.

"Have a good night, Nicky!"

"Hopefully I'll see you tomorrow." She gave a little wave through the window as the cab pulled away and she breathed a sigh of relief. Part of her felt as though she should have asked him along but her cover would definitely be blown if he was to meet Rachel and the guys.

The taxi drove up Broadway on a straight run to Fifth Avenue and her destination which was clearly visible in the New York skyline. The cab driver turned up the music playing on a Hispanic radio station – shouting through his phone back to the cab control-centre in Spanish. Nicky felt a rush of excitement run through her at the prospect of climbing to the top of the tallest building in Manhattan. Today had been amazing and it wasn't over yet.

The biggest surprise of all was meeting Eve Porter. She did think of her on the odd occasion – especially in March – on her birthday. Nicky never forgot birthdays that happened around holidays or prominent dates. Eve was born on St Patrick's Day and the three friends had spent many long national holidays of celebration in the Pavilion Bar in Trinity College. They would start off after the parade in O'Neills of Suffolk Street and then search out some music in Bruxelles or some such place, but they always ended up in Eve's rooms in Trinity. Nicky had envied the fact she was living on her own. Now, however, she felt glad for the time that she had spent with her mother. How different things might have been though if she had untied her mother's apron strings back then just like Eve had done. Maybe she would be the one with the high-flying career. Then she thought of Daniel and smiled. No, she was very lucky the way things had turned out. She always had her son.

The taxi stopped outside the vast and towering façade of the Empire State Building. It was almost prison-like with tall thin windows that ran up to the fifth floor – above them the vast majestic tower that made the Empire State the tallest building in Manhattan ran up to almost touch the sky. She craned her neck, looking for Rachel, and spotted Alex's spiky blond-white hair first. Then she saw Rachel. But where was Conor?

"Thanks, how much?" she asked the driver.

He held up his fingers to indicate eight dollars.

Nicky realised that really meant ten including the tip. She paid him, stepped out of the cab and crossed the street – dodging the free flow of cars and taxis that flooded the thoroughfare.

Alex spotted Nicky first and waved.

"Where's Conor?" Nicky asked Rachel when she reached them.

"We left him in the restaurant – it looked like he was having a spot of woman trouble."

"Mandy is trouble," Alex said, nodding his head in agreement. "She lives on coke and is dependent with most things – especially men. Conor was crazy to get mixed up with her. I think she was more out of it than usual tonight."

Rachel stared at Alex and gave a small smile. She hoped her brother had the good sense to keep away from drugs. She was desperately naïve when it came to such matters and visiting New York like this only highlighted what a small parochial existence she had etched out for herself and her family. It was such a contrast to be going for a night-time vigil on the top of the tallest building in New York!

"So, lets go!" Rachel said excitedly as Alex held out his arm to point the way into the massive and imposing lobby of the Empire State Building.

"Funny – it's like visiting the electricity supply board back home with ESB written everywhere," Nicky said, craning her neck and scanning every bit of the lobby in case she missed a thing.

"Security first," Alex said, leading the two girls through the barrier.

None of them bleeped and the girls followed Alex over to three long lines that ended at the ticket desk.

"This place is enormous!" Nicky exclaimed.

"Great art deco lines though," Alex added.

Nicky nodded — not quite sure what he meant but not wanting to sound foolish by asking.

"We are lucky tonight — it isn't usually this quiet," Alex observed.

"I'd hate to be here on a busy night," Rachel said, looking at the hundreds of people rushing from security to queue to lift.

"This is my treat," Alex said, putting a fifty-dollar bill through the slit at the ticket-desk window. "Three adults, please."

"That's really nice of you!" Nicky and Rachel said together.

Alex hurried them along past images of the Seven Wonders of the World that decorated the corridors.

"This place was called the Eighth Wonder of the World when it was finished in the 1930s."

"Wow!" the two girls said in unison.

They joined a short line under a fluttering star-spangled banner hanging above the entrance to the lifts. A massive illustration of the building filled the entire wall at the end of the corridor and captured all of the lines that pointed heavenward like a great gothic cathedral.

"Sixteen maximum, please," the porter called as the lift next to Alex opened and they shuffled on silently.

Rachel was very much aware that Alex's eyes were firmly fixed on her as the elevator doors shut and they began to move, starting their ascent to the eighty-sixth floor observatory.

"I can't believe we are really here where *Sleepless in Seattle* and *An Affair to Remember* were made," Nicky squealed excitedly.

"How did you get on with Eve?" Rachel whispered as the power in the lift cables started to push them at a rapid speed up through the floors of the building.

"Oh, she was grand! She had calmed down by the time we got the taxi. We met her client and he's a nice man."

"You make him sound about seventy!"

Nicky chuckled. "No, he's mid-to-late forties I'd say and interesting. Eve has a great job – the Soho Grand is fabulous and I had my first proper New York Cosmo – well, two of them actually."

"No wonder you're so giddy!" Rachel said and smiled over at Alex who still had his eyes fixed on her.

He pointed up at the numbers above the doors – they were now at floor eighty.

"This thing is quick!" Nicky exclaimed as the lift came to an abrupt and sudden stop.

"Observatory," the porter said in the New York drone that the girls were becoming accustomed to.

"Nothing prepares you for this . . ." Alex said as they walked out into the night.

"Amazing!" gasped Nicky as she got her first glimpse of the view with the illuminated George Washington Bridge in the distance. "It's like the stars are sparkling down on the ground and we are watching them from above."

Rachel was breathing in the experience but was also beginning to feel very aware of the unspoken attraction that was building between her and Alex. She really liked him too. She loved the little knowledgeable remarks he made about art, history and design. He was a really interesting yet unpretentious guy.

When they were out on the deck a cold breeze blew around them.

"I know what you mean about stars on the ground," Rachel said. "It's so much nicer to see the city by night. The roads look like diamond bracelets."

"That black band around Manhattan is the Hudson," Alex said, leaning in very close to Rachel until his chin was resting upon the crown of her head.

It felt good there and she could catch his warm masculine smell wafting in the air.

"Over there on a very clear day you can see the next state!" he said.

He didn't move and Rachel didn't want him to.

"Hey, has anyone got change for one of these telescope things?" Nicky asked, still not noticing the chemistry unfolding between her married friend and the Doctor of Fine Art.

Rachel searched through her bag frantically. She was all fingers and thumbs. She put a handful of change into Nicky's palm and hoped that she would leave her for a few sweet moments of indulgence with a man who she would probably never see again but would be able to fantasise about on the days when she got home and living with Derek became as painful as it always was.

Mandy slapped Conor across the face.

"Oh, sweetie," she then sobbed, putting her hand up to the red mark that she had made on his left cheek.

Conor withdrew his face from her touch. This girl was out of control and he had to get her out of his life.

"That's the reason why we need to stop seeing each other," he said, shaking his head. "I don't want to live the way you do, Mandy – going from one party to the next – watching who is going where and when."

Mandy put her hands up to her face to cover the smudged mascara tracks around her eyes. The effects of her last line of cocaine were well gone and she was as low as she could feel.

"Please come up to my apartment," she begged, running her thin fingers along the buttons of his shirt and letting them rest on the buckle of his belt. "You can't leave me like this."

Conor looked with pity at the woman that he once thought he was in love with. Rachel's arrival couldn't have come at a better time. If he was going to get serious with a woman she would have to have the same values and ideals as his own and seeing his sister confirmed that. Only two months ago he had contemplated moving in with Mandy and he was so glad that he had escaped with his heart intact. He had no idea how bad her habit was back then but she almost overdosed at the last party they were at together.

"I have to go, Mandy. My sister is in town and I don't get to see her often. I told you I wasn't around this weekend."

Mandy threw her arms around his neck and started to sob louder. "I don't want to be alone – you've got to take me upstairs!"

Conor knew that if he stepped inside her apartment he was in danger of losing control and slipping into her bed. He had to be cruel to be kind. Firmly, he took hold of her wrists and put them down at her sides.

"I have to go."

He took a few backward steps and then turned around. A taxi fortuitously was passing by and he hailed it. With a bit of luck he would catch up with the others and be able to join them on the top of the Empire State.

"Hey, man, the view is stunning!" Alex said into his cellphone, with his eyes firmly fixed on Rachel who was precariously edging forward to peek over the side at the long drop down.

"I was hoping you guys were still queuing," Conor said. "Are you on the top?"

"Yup. We're on the eighty-sixth floor," he replied, staring at Rachel and speaking loud enough for her to hear every word.

"Will I meet you outside when you're finished?"

"That's a good call," Alex nodded. "I'd say we'll be down in about fifteen minutes."

"Okay," Conor said, flipping his cellphone shut.

Conor sat back comfortably on the black leather seat of the cab. He was glad that he had made a decision about Mandy – he could have let it drag on and on but he knew in his heart that it was never really going anywhere.

His mind started to wander and he wondered for a moment what happened to the woman he had saved at the station a few months before. A part of him was curious to find out who she was. She was a little older than him and dressed like a business executive – that much he remembered. Maybe she was a jumper and he had saved a life that didn't want to be saved – he hadn't thought of that as a possibility at the time. Her hair was wrapped up the way his mother used to wear it, in a roll, but some stray wild tendrils had come loose. He closed his eyes and pictured her perfect skin and her sharp green eyes – she looked kind of similar to Rachel's obnoxious mate – the one with the black-rimmed glasses.

"Empire State Building!" the cab driver called as he pulled up.

Conor paid him and waited at the bottom of the steps for the others to get there. The hustle and bustle of life in the city rushed by.

"Conor!" a shrill voice called excitedly. "We're over here!"

He looked around over the heads of the people who were filtering down the steps of the ESB.

"Amazing, Conor!" Nicky said, almost jumping up and down. "It was unbelievable up there!"

Conor grinned. "Glad you enjoyed it. What do you want to do now?"

Rachel yawned. "I think I need to get to my bed – the jet lag is starting to catch up with me."

Alex nodded. "You've got loads to see tomorrow. Hey, would you like to go see the Met?"

"Is that where the baseball players play?" Nicky asked.

"I'm talking about *The Met* – the Metropolitan Museum of Art," Alex smiled. "You gotta go."

"I'd love to," Rachel said, coming to life at the suggestion.

Nicky's expression turned to disappointment. "I thought we were going to Century 21 – you promised, Rach!"

Rachel turned to Alex. "Sorry, I did. We have to get runners for the kids. Nicky has brought a cardboard cut-out of her son's foot to get the perfect fit."

Alex shrugged. "No problem. I can take you after lunch if you like – a free guided tour?"

Rachel looked over at Nicky.

"As long as I get to Century 21, I'll be happy!" Nicky exclaimed.

Rachel grinned and nodded to Alex. "Sounds great." She hadn't banked on him hanging around for the weekend – but she wasn't complaining!

Conor frowned, surely it was up to him rather than his friend to make arrangements for the girls. He didn't like Alex butting in on quality time he wanted to spend with his sister.

"I can meet you guys back at your hotel and take you to a great place I know for breakfast. You can shop and then we can have lunch in the Village," Conor said, taking control. "Then if you really want we can go to the Met!"

Rachel smiled at her brother. "Sounds like a plan."

Nicky flopped onto the bed wearing her T-shirt and underwear – she didn't have the energy to put on her pyjamas. She closed her eyes and felt waves of tiredness sweep down through her body.

"Here," Rachel said, pushing a minute white pill into Nicky's palm.

Nicky lifted her head and looked down at her hand. "What's that?"

Rachel grinned. "Take it – Conor insists."

"I'm not doing drugs!"

"Don't be silly – it's a sleeping tablet – he got them at the drugstore around the corner."

Nicky put the tablet on the bedside locker and lay back down on the bed. "Is he nuts? I'm absolutely exhausted – there's no way I need a sleeping pill."

"Trust me, if you don't take that you'll be awake at four in the morning and you won't be able to get back to sleep."

Nicky looked over at the locker and back at Rachel. "Are you sure?"

Rachel nodded. "It's the only way to counteract jet lag."

Nicky examined the tiny pill suspiciously before putting it in her mouth. Rachel wasn't normally so bossy so she must have good reason to make her take this. Rachel handed her a small bottle of water and she washed the tablet down.

It was only a matter of seconds before she was sound asleep. Rachel just managed to put a blanket from the cupboard over her before she too fell fast asleep on the other bed.

FOUR

Suddenly Nicky's phone rang out – louder than usual. The sun shone brightly through the narrow window, telling that it was now morning, as she searched frantically in her handbag to answer it. It kept slipping through her fingers but she persevered and finally took a firm hold. She pressed the green button and put it up to her ear.

"Hello?"

Daniel was crying at the other end of the line. "Mum, you've got to come home!"

Nicky panicked – she hadn't heard her son cry since he was seven and that was because he had broken his leg.

"Calm down, honey." She tried to conceal the alarm in her own voice. "What's the matter?"

"Please come home! This man wants to take me away to live with him – he says he's my father!"

Nicky shook with horror. She should never have come to New York.

"What about Matthew's parents – where are they? Are you in their house? They're meant to be looking after you!"

Daniel started to sob harder. "They've gone to work – I'm on my own here."

Nicky looked at her watch. "You should be at school – it's one o'clock."

"Mum, it's Saturday. Please come home – he's banging on the door. P-l-e-a-s-e!" his voice cried down the phone – leaving Nicky more powerless than she had ever felt in her life.

"Lock the doors – I'll ring the police – you ring the police . . ."

Rachel sat up in the bed and gave a loud groan. She looked at her watch and smiled. Conor had been right yet again. She went over to the window and drew back the curtains to let in the beaming New York sunshine.

Nicky jerked in the bed – still asleep – as the light crept around the room.

"Ring the police!" she called out.

Rachel leaned across the bed and gave her friend a gentle shake.

"Nicky, good morning – there's no need for the police just yet!"

Nicky opened her eyes and stared at Rachel like a rabbit looking down the barrel of a shotgun.

"It's only me," Rachel smiled. "You look like you've seen a ghost!"

Nicky jumped up in the bed and put her head into her hands. "Thank God!" she exclaimed. "I had a terrible nightmare."

Rachel undressed and pulled a towel around her midriff.

"What happened?"

"Daniel was ringing me – there was a man trying to take him away – it was his father!"

"I don't think there's much chance of that, do you? More

chance of finding James in New York than Dublin!" Rachel said lightly. "Well, at least the tablets worked – it's nearly nine and I feel as fresh as a daisy."

Nicky picked up her phone from her bedside locker and checked it – no calls or messages. But the dream had seemed so real. Maybe it was her mind playing tricks after seeing Eve again after all this time. She'd had deep emotions hidden away for so long that maybe the only possible way they could manifest themselves was in a dream.

"I'll shower first," Rachel said, banging the bathroom door behind her.

Nicky looked at her phone – she longed to speak to her son but it was Saturday and he would be playing football and then golf with his friends like he usually did. But the dream had woken her to the reality that someday he could be faced with his father. As the years rolled by she had begun to think that the likelihood of such an event was minimal. But up until yesterday the prospect of sharing a drink with Eve Porter had seemed just as unlikely.

Nicky hit the button on her phone that showed Daniel's name and waited. There was no reply and she wasn't surprised – it was nearly two o'clock in Dublin. As the voicemail came on Nicky spoke briefly.

"Daniel love, it's Mum, I hope everything is okay and you're enjoying yourself – I'll call later."

She stepped out of bed and rooted through the lists and papers that she had neatly sorted in her suitcase. The cardboard cut-out of her son's foot made her smile. She would put the past behind and enjoy the day – her first full day in New York. She had to be positive and do what she came to do – shop!!!

Conor was waiting at the steps of the Washington Square Hotel as the girls made their descent to him.

"Morning – sleep well?" he asked, giving his sister a kiss on the cheek.

"Fantastic," Rachel smiled. "Poor Nicky had a nightmare but she didn't wake until nearly nine!"

Conor looked down at his watch. "Come on – I'll take you guys to a nice little French place on Houston for breakfast. Where do you guys want to go first today?"

"Well, I want to shop –" Nicky said and stopped.

Conor smiled. "You don't want to make it too obvious that you're Irish. The streets are thronged with hungry Irish shoppers with mad stares – mouths open. It's like the end of the world is nigh and they have to shop to survive!"

"Is it really that bad?" Rachel giggled.

"Not so bad this time of year but November and December are grim. You won't hear an American accent the length and breadth of Fifth Avenue."

Nicky gave him a friendly nudge. "Go on, you're teasing!"

Conor shrugged. "Wait and see for yourselves."

"What's that?" Nicky asked, pointing over to a fenced area that was buzzing with activity.

Conor nodded his head. "That's the Washington Square dog run."

"The what?" Nicky stared and could only guess that this was where the apartment-bound K9s got brought for their daily exercise. "That's crazy – look, some of the animals are wearing coats and it must be in the high teens!"

Conor grinned. He had become accustomed to the Americans pampering their pets. "There aren't that many kids in Manhattan and lots of people are single so they treat their pets like kids."

"I can see that," Nicky gaped.

Conor strode off.

"Where are we going to now?" Nicky panted as she kept pace.

"La Guardia Place, then Houston – the architecture is pretty cool around here – you're in NYU heartland."

Nicky rooted inside her handbag as she tagged along behind the others. "I've just realised that I haven't taken a photo yet."

Conor grabbed the tiny digital camera from Nicky's hand and turned it on. "The thing about this place is there are photo opportunities everywhere you look."

Immediately he held the camera up to catch the morning sun reflecting off the fire escapes that covered the façade of one of the buildings nearby. He snapped once – then twice – checked it back a couple of times and then handed the camera to Nicky.

"Wow!" she exclaimed. First looking at the building and then looking at the picture Conor had taken. "That's fantastic. I never would have noticed the colours and shapes just walking by."

"Maybe you're too busy looking in the shop windows – don't miss out on New York while you're here!"

Nicky blushed. The guy was a genius. He was even more gorgeous than she had first thought because he was obviously talented as well. "You'll have to tell me about your work when you get a chance."

Conor shrugged. "Sure."

Rachel's brother was gorgeous and now that she was away from her normal daily routines and caring for her son she realised more than ever that she needed a man!

"I thought you didn't eat breakfast in hotels!" a voice whispered over Eve's shoulder as she spread a thin layer of *Lite and Low* butter on her golden toast.

"Stephen!" she exclaimed, remembering her position and smiling as sincerely as she possibly could at nine fifteen in the morning. "I didn't sleep very well and I have to be uptown soon . . ."

"Is Nicky not with you?"

Eve wasn't usually caught off her guard. "S-s-she got up earlier," she stammered. "Had to go to the office."

Stephen nodded. "I have to do some work myself – meeting a developer on Broad Street. Hopefully we can meet up later for a drink?"

"Sure," Eve smiled. "I'll be in touch at some stage. Have a good day."

She picked up her linen napkin and wiped any traces of toast from her lips. Then grabbing her handbag she threw an overly sweet smile at Stephen and walked out of the dining-room.

Stephen grinned to himself. There was something strange about the girls in that agency but then it would take a strange sort of person to work in matchmaking. He felt brave employing them, now that he was three thousand miles across the Atlantic Ocean, but wondered how he was going to feel about it when he returned home. It was under great duress that he'd allowed his business partner, Frank, to contact Just for Coffee on his behalf. Frank had been hit more than once by lecherous females, gold-digging for a husband, and swore by the skills of the women in the agency. It was only six months since he had married an up-and-coming barrister who was so well set up in her own practise that it was she who recommended that they draw up a prenuptial agreement. Stephen remembered the look of total bliss in Frank's eyes as he relayed the story of how he proposed, certain that he had found his true love.

Stephen didn't like the clinical way that Frank assessed his fiancée's virtues. He liked to think that there was still some romance in the world. Of course he enjoyed looking at and sharing the company of good-looking women but most of the women who hung around the Shelbourne Hotel and concentrated on presenting themselves as the most beautiful and well-groomed women in Irish society left him feeling cold. He needed more from a relationship. He wanted a woman with a good heart – he wanted a woman that would make him laugh.

He thought about the excitement on Nicky's face as she told him that she was going up the Empire State Building and smiled. He wanted to experience joy again. Making millions over the last twenty years had been fun but he couldn't honestly say that he got any real joy from doing so – that was why it seemed like a good idea to cut back on work – but that left him bored. He needed to find fulfilment in his personal life or there wouldn't be much point in going on. He looked down at his watch. He would have loved a small whiskey. He had taken to drinking a couple with his lunch and his biological clock was telling him that it was nearly time for his first of the day. For the last five or six years he relished his tipple during and at the end of the day. If he wasn't careful he'd be falling into the abyss of becoming a lone drinker.

"So where to next?" Conor asked Nicky.

"Well, I was kind of hoping that you would tell me," Nicky said, wide-eyed. "I mean, I haven't a clue where I am."

Conor pushed aside the empty plates that had been filled earlier with delicious pancakes and mixed berries. He took her guidebook and opened it at the map of lower Manhattan.

"See, we are here and it's only a few blocks down to that place Century 21 if you want to go there – it's right beside Ground Zero."

"Wow!" Nicky gasped.

Conor wasn't sure if the "wow" was for the department store or the most poignant landmark in the city.

"I think that's where we're going," Rachel said with a smile. "Any word from Alex yet?"

Conor shrugged. "He doesn't usually get up until midday."

Rachel was disappointed but could tell by the tone of Conor's voice that he wasn't going to give any more information.

"I have to hand it to the New Yorkers – they do a great breakfast," Nicky said, tidying away the plates into a jumbled-up pile.

"Right, are we ready?" Conor asked as he stood up.

The three caught a cab on Houston that brought them down Broadway to the site of the World Trade Center. Protestors marked the site with huge banners and slogans, chanting.

"What are they protesting about?" Rachel asked her brother.

"They think 9/11 was an inside job," Conor said casually.

Rachel's mouth dropped. "Do you?"

"Possibly," he said with a shrug as the taxi pulled up at the kerb.

Nicky was almost shaking as she got out of the cab. "I can't believe I'm really here!"

Rachel arched her neck up to whisper in her brother's ear. "I think she's talking about Century 21."

"Do you want to go over to the station and look at the boards around the site?" Conor asked. "It's a detailed account of the events of 9/11."

Nicky scrunched her face up, which to Conor could only mean a negative.

"Hey, look at that little church – isn't it gorgeous!" said Rachel. "I didn't notice that when you brought me here before." She made her way over to the railings to get a closer look at the group of young people who were dressed in black with white-lace skullcaps and involved in some kind of ceremony.

"It's worth taking a peek – honestly," Conor said with raised eyebrows.

Nicky sighed. "Okay, I suppose we can spare a few minutes."

Conor led the way as his mobile phone rang out. He looked at his watch and it read ten thirty in the morning but the name showing on his phone was definitely Alex.

"Hey, man – what has you up so early?"

Rachel looked at her brother and could tell that it was Alex by his expression.

"I don't know what the girls want to do for lunch – we're at Ground Zero." Conor rolled his eyes and gave pointed expressions in his sister's direction as Alex spoke on the other end of the line. "I don't know how long we're going to be. If you want to get a table at Gitanes that would be good – make it for seven o'clock – okay, man."

Rachel was aching to find out what the conversation at the other end had been. Did Alex want to join them for the day? She wouldn't have minded. Did he still want to bring her to the Met? Art galleries were such romantic settings and the thought of visiting with Alex made her tremble with excitement.

"Okay, let's get a bit of history," Conor said, mounting the steps through the graveyard that led to the church entrance.

The church interior was simple and Protestant but the vibes were something the girls were not prepared for. Large boards surrounding the rectangular church walls were covered with images of the hours and days after the Twin Towers were destroyed in the terrorist attack in 2001. Photographs of men – most in NY Police and Fire Department uniforms showing tremendous courage were dotted along the walls between the sad images of death and despair. Most were heartbreaking – all were touching. Rachel could feel a lump in her throat as she surveyed the images of these heroes dropping from sheer exhaustion as they plodded to and from the doomed buildings on that sombre day.

Items on display included pans and medicines and an array of emergency foods used in the makeshift hospital and living accommodation that the church was used for. The three observed silently like the rest of the congregation and sightseers.

But Rachel couldn't stop her mind from wandering. She was distracted – a certain person from the previous night was responsible for invading her thoughts.

"I wonder what Alex wanted?" Rachel whispered in Nicky's ear.

Nicky frowned. "Shame on you thinking about a man and you walking around this shrine to such a horrific disaster!"

Rachel was taken aback for a moment. "I just …" then she noticed the cheesy grin develop on Nicky's face.

"Listen – this place is amazing and all but I'm a little distracted myself," Nicky said with a smile. "I'm really desperate to get to Century 21 – do you think Conor would mind if we made a move?"

Rachel knew her brother only too well and he, like all the men in her life, hated shopping. She couldn't even get her son to go to the local shopping centre to size up for his school uniform. As for Derek, he didn't like her shopping and always inspected her receipts afterwards. If the other women in Portmarnock knew how tight her well-heeled husband was they would be truly shocked. This time in New York was really precious and she wanted to make the most of it – but there was more to it than shopping and last night Alex had made her feel alive in a way that she had forgotten she was capable of feeling.

"Conor, this place is great but Nicky needs to shop," she said finally.

The prospect of traipsing the grim and tasteless floors of

Century 21 was unappealing to Conor at the best of times and not exactly the sort of place that Conor wanted to spend time with his sister.

"Can I take you guys to see Wall Street or anything else? I mean, you've got all day tomorrow or Monday to shop!"

Rachel was torn – Nicky really wanted to shop and she could tell that she didn't want to be left on her own. She could only do what she did best on a day-to-day basis as she ran her home – compromise. She touched the side of Conor's sleeve gently.

"Why don't we go to Century 21 for an hour and a half and then meet you afterwards – is there anywhere near here that we could meet for lunch?"

Conor scrunched up his cheeks. "Okay, I could check out some spots for work next week – what about if I meet you at Balthazar for lunch – do you remember that place from your last visit? A cab will take about ten minutes to get there."

Rachel thought for a moment – it was back up Broadway, the way they had come. "I think so – is that where they had the golden statue pillars and the red awning?"

Conor nodded his head. "That's the place. Half twelve okay?"

"Should be," Rachel said, following Nicky out onto Church Street and the big doors that led to the bargain department store, Century 21.

Conor watched as the two women disappeared. It was an unusually warm day for May but the sky looked strangely ominous – a powder blue with misty haze – and Conor thought for the first time that day about Mandy and hoped she was doing okay. It was strange that she hadn't rung him by now but he felt amazingly relieved and liberated by her absence. Maybe she realised, just as he had a few weeks before, that their relationship was futile and it would never go anywhere.

Just then his mobile phone rang out. He didn't recognise the number on the display panel. Holding it up to his ear he said, "Hello."

"Conor, it's Tonya – Mandy has OD'd. She's in St Vincent's Hospital." Her voice was shrill and hysterical. "Are you there?"

Conor held his left hand up to cover his ear from the surging traffic that hurried along Church Street. "Yes, I'm here – it's just noisy. Is she okay?"

He could imagine Tonya with her long black shiny hair – Mandy's crazy yet not so dizzy friend. She was even more beautiful than Mandy and had been on all of the major glossy magazine covers at some stage over her short career.

"Of course she's not okay – she's unconscious – what did you say to her last night? She was frantic when I got in – she must have taken the drugs when she went to bed."

Conor didn't like Tonya's accusatory tone. "It's none of your business, Tonya, and you and I both know what Mandy is like. She takes too many drugs for her own good."

Tonya clicked the roof of her mouth with her tongue. She couldn't figure out what Mandy saw in the Irishman. He was too boring and poor to feature in her circle of friends – she couldn't care less if he was on first-name terms with David Bowie or Bob Dylan – they were dinosaurs or freaks as far as she was concerned.

"Look, just get in here and see her – she's on the fourth floor."

Tonya was gone and Conor was left looking at his phone. When was he ever going to be free from that crazy woman? Now she was attempting to sabotage his weekend with his sister. He turned his phone off so none of her other model friends could call and wondered what he should do. His head told him to stay away but his gut instinct was to try and help Mandy and he felt left with no option but to go to the hospital – it was only a short walk from where he was anyway.

Alex was pleased and surprised to get the call from Conor. The prospect of lunch with Rachel and Nicky in Balthazar sounded very appetising.

"I thought you were having special brother and sister time?" Alex wondered what could possibly have kept the two apart.

"Oh, Nicky wanted to shop and I couldn't face it. Now I can't get through to her on her cellphone to say I might be late – she's probably buried under a mound of Ralph Lauren shirts in Century 21."

"Leave it with me – she'll be safe," Alex grinned to himself. "Have you booked a table? You know what that place is like."

Conor was now certain that Alex fancied his sister. Still, it was better that she was with a man he knew than some stranger who would be only too delighted to chat her up. "Josef always fixes me up – tell him I'll be coming for lunch too."

Alex moved over to the huge mirror that covered the back wall of his studio and checked himself out. "Listen, take care and don't get caught up with Mandy – she's bad news."

"Don't I know it!" Conor huffed under his breath. "Later, and thanks."

Alex took a few strands of spiky hair and pulled them up higher. A bit of gel, his Billabong tee shirt that he loved so much and he'd be ready to meet the cutest dame in Manhattan as far as he was concerned.

"Are you sure you'll be okay on your own?" Rachel asked.

Nicky looked up from the mountain of Quiksilver tee shirts that she was almost hidden behind. Daniel was going to be the best designer-clad teenager in Dublin if she continued at this rate.

"I haven't even got near the shoes and you've seen the amount of trainers they have – I think I'll have to buy a suitcase at this rate."

Rachel shook her head. "Relax, Nicky. There are tons of other shops in Manhattan. You might regret it if you buy too much here."

Nicky resembled a squirrel surrounded by a mountain of nuts who was just too greedy to let any of them go. Confusion was etched across her forehead and she let out a sigh.

"I think I need a cigarette break – you wouldn't mind these bags while I go out for a quick one?"

Rachel was beginning to wonder if her friend was losing it totally. "We can come back here later," she said. "You need to eat something."

Nicky wasn't convinced. "No, I have to keep going. I'm on a roll."

"You're in Manhattan – there are more shops here per square metre than anywhere in the world!"

Nicky looked at the shirts and then back at Rachel. "Go ahead without me," she said, swinging the cardboard cut-out of her son's foot in the air. "It's a tough choice to make – lunch with your hunky brother or leave this place. If I break the back on it I won't have to shop as much tomorrow or Monday."

Rachel reached into her handbag and tore the corner off a piece of paper. She scribbled some details on it and put it into Nicky's sweaty palm. "Balthazar on Spring Street. We'll be there until three at least – will that give you enough time?"

Nicky nodded. "You haven't got some water, have you?"

Rachel reached into her bag again and produced a bottle of Poland Spring. "Three o'clock and no later – okay?"

Nicky opened it and took a deep refreshing gulp. This was all she needed to continue her marathon shopping expedition.

Rachel wondered how safe it was to leave her in such a state but she also wanted to see Conor. She had plenty of time with Nicky throughout the year and it was rare and wonderful to see her brother without Derek watching her every move.

He hadn't always been that bad. Sure, when they were married initially he was possessive and did blame her for things that she had no control over, but lately she had become a prisoner in her own body. She often felt afraid to breathe too loudly at night or he would snap at her for disturbing his sleep. If she were really truthful he changed the day she got pregnant. She had never developed her own talents or skills or used the degree that she had earned from Trinity. From that day she had become totally dependent on him – she had no career to fall back on. Her sole status was that of Derek Sloan's wife and his children's mother. Nobody really knew her as anything else. The other women in Portmarnock that she had contact with on a daily basis all loved her because she was the one they could ask to do anything and she would always oblige. She wouldn't be doing anything very much anyway that didn't involve the running of her family and home.

Hailing a cab on Broadway felt wonderful. The simple act of doing something for herself alone was so alien that she blushed inwardly.

"Balthazar," she said through the driver's window as the cab pulled up.

She sat in and watched with awe as the hustle and bustle of the city passed her by. The ride was so enjoyable she didn't want it to stop but as the red awning came into view she recognised the restaurant that her brother had brought her to on every occasion that she had visited before.

"Eight dollars," the driver said.

Rachel handed him ten dollars and exited the car. She loved

this restaurant. As the art-nouveau furnishings came into view she felt a rush of pleasure inside. Standing at the desk inside the door was a short man – made taller by his mop of curly black hair. He looked like he had stepped out of the nineteen-thirties with his pinstriped suit and cufflinks clinking against his chunky gold signature bracelet. His teeth were so white next to his dark skin that Rachel wondered if they could possibly be his own.

"I'm meeting my brother – Conor Moore."

Josef threw his head back and smiled widely as he clapped his hands in delight.

"Ah, my favourite client! I have a table for him when he arrives."

Rachel's face dropped. "Is he not here?"

"Conor will be late but he phoned – the rest of your party is waiting at the table," he said in an accent that could only be described as Arabic.

"Oh!" Rachel blurted.

"You come this way," Josef said, holding Rachel's arm a little more firmly than she would have liked. "Conor such a good man – he get me Bob Dylan autograph."

Rachel could see by the dreamy expression in his eyes that he was a big fan. She followed him to a square table in the corner by the window that looked out onto the thronged Spring Street. Sitting facing her was Alex, looking even more delicious in daylight than she had remembered from the night before.

He got to his feet as she approached and held out his arms – expectant of a hug. Rachel planted a kiss on his cheek and he responded with another on hers.

"Rachel, I'm afraid you have to put up with me," Alex said cheekily. "Conor will be here as soon as he can."

Rachel didn't mind one little bit. In fact it was a fantasy of hers to be alone in a foreign city with a handsome guy in a plush restaurant. One of the many she used to help her through the lonely nights when Derek ignored her.

"Where is he?" she asked as she sat down.

"He got a call from Mandy's friend – apparently Mandy tried to OD last night."

Rachel's mouth gaped open. "Oh my god! Is she all right?"

"I don't know the details but she's still alive – Conor has gone to see her – I told him he was crazy having anything to do with a chick who was so out of it all of the time."

"I hope she's okay."

Alex was less sympathetic. "I hope she leaves your brother alone. He's a good guy. You know, whenever we go out he has lots of women drooling over him and he hasn't a clue most of the time. It makes them go even crazier for him!"

Rachel took a menu from the little French waitress who was dressed as if she had stepped out of the turn of the twentieth century instead of the twenty-first.

"I almost forgot about your friend – where's Nicky?"

"I'm afraid she's totally lost it. I had to leave her in Century 21 where she is about to buy a suitcase to carry all of the stuff she's bought."

Alex looked on sombrely. "She has it bad, which is a good thing – it's a bigger treat for me to get you on my own!"

Rachel hid a coy smile behind the large menu card. Compliments – especially from a handsome single man – were something she was definitely not used to.

"Looks like you made it on time – the weather is changing," said Alex.

Droplets of rain fell on the large windowpanes as people outside on the street darted for cover.

"It's good to be inside," said Rachel. "I hope it doesn't last – it's really hot today and I'm enjoying the nice weather."

"It's certainly got hotter since you arrived," Alex said cheesily and then was sorry – he didn't want to frighten off this attractive woman who was after all very married.

Rachel slapped his arm playfully. As her hand brushed over his skin she felt how soft it was. "Really, Alex, I bet you're like this with all of the women you know. Artists are notoriously wicked when it comes to the opposite sex!"

Josef appeared again with two glasses of champagne.

"Sssh!" he said holding his finger up to his pursed lips. "On the house for the romantic couple!"

Rachel could feel her cheeks turning red. "This is embarrassing."

"Enjoy the adventure, Rachel. It's just you and me – no one need ever know – even Josef can see the chemistry between us."

His eyes were fixed firmly on Rachel's which left her feeling unnerved. She couldn't deny that there was a chemistry between them but she didn't feel like she had the wherewithal or guts to do anything about it.

Nicky rolled her newly purchased Ralph Lauren suitcase behind her as she edged her way out into the daylight. The shop assistant had given her funny looks as she piled her other purchases into the new suitcase. She had managed to get most of the things that she wanted for Daniel as well as a few more items for next year. She was feeling buoyant until the large drops of rain started to seep into her blow-dried hair. It had been so expertly done the night before – so much for it lasting the weekend. A terrible thought hit her as she looked up and down the street. She didn't recognise it and had no idea which direction was uptown or downtown or which side of the street she should get a cab. The rain didn't look like it was going to stop anytime soon and it was already gone two forty-five. If she didn't hurry Rachel would be livid and she couldn't say that she would blame her. She took shelter in the doorway and sent her a quick text to say that she was delayed and would be in Balthazar as soon as possible. The rain was pelting down when she returned to the kerb and she waved frantically for a taxi to stop. They all seemed to be full as the rest of New York took refuge from the deluge. She was in a Catch 22 situation – if she went back into the store she would never get a cab. If she stood at the sidewalk for much longer she could get pneumonia. Still, a little voice inside told her to persevere and she waved her arms at every cab that passed by.

Suddenly a large black limousine pulled up and the back door opened. Nicky jerked back swiftly as water splashed up from the tyres. Visions of being kidnapped and sold into white slavery came into her head until a familiar face peeped out from behind the door.

"Are you going to stand there catching your death or will you take a lift?" His Irish accent was distinctive.

Nicky gasped as a big smile came to her face. She never thought she would be so pleased to see Stephen from the night before.

The driver hopped out, took Nicky's case and put it in the boot to the sound of horns blaring from the cars behind.

"Don't mind them," Stephen said kindly as Nicky plonked down beside him, water dripping from her clothes onto the back seat of the limo. "Looks like I came at the right time."

If ever there was knight-in-shining-armour moment this was it – it was as close as she had ever come to one in her life – it was just a pity that it was an older man and, she just remembered, a client of the company that she was supposed to be working for!

"You're a lifesaver!" Nicky panted.

"I'd offer you a cigarette but I can't smoke in this hired car," Stephen groaned.

"Hey, the lift is more than enough," Nicky said, running her fingers through her drenched tresses. "Thanks a million."

"I only wish I had a towel – that's some downpour. But I bet the sun will be shining in half an hour."

Nicky looked down at her shirt which was almost transparent and sticking to her skin.

"I'm not exactly dressed for the rain!" she admitted.

Stephen longed to say that he thought she looked great but didn't want to say anything inappropriate.

"I hope you're not going back to London early?" he asked inquisitively.

Nicky frowned. "What do you mean?"

"You've got your luggage with you, I see."

Nicky threw her head back and laughed. "God no, I was just doing a bit of shopping."

"So you were shopping for a suitcase?"

Nicky laughed even louder. "Not exactly. I bought a bit more than I thought I would and needed the case to get the stuff back to the hotel."

It was Stephen's turn to laugh out loud. "I have to say I like your style, Nicky. And everything is for yourself, I presume?"

Nicky didn't know the right answer – she didn't want to tell him about her son but she didn't want him to think that she would be so self-indulgent either.

"Most of it's for my boyfriend actually," she lied.

This seemed to throw Stephen to Nicky's surprise. There was a pause, then "You're in a steady relationship?" he pried.

Nicky was caught in a web of lies and she didn't know how to stop. It was as if each lie she had told since meeting Stephen had caused her to tell another. He was a nice man and she didn't feel comfortable telling so many fibs.

"No, well, yes, actually. We met at work – well, my last job."

Her expression was confused and dizzy and Stephen could smell a rat in her story. He was enjoying the look of sheer panic on her face as he asked her the next question.

"So you didn't have to work today?"

Nicky felt trapped. Which was the right answer? "No."

Stephen's brow furrowed.

"I mean yes," she blurted. It would be much easier to tell the truth but she didn't want to make Eve out to be a liar – especially as the reunion had gone so well the night before.

"I was working earlier but, when I got in, there was nothing for me to do so they told me to take the rest of the day off."

Stephen gave a small smile that left Nicky wondering if she had got away with the tall tale or not. It was definitely time to change the topic of conversation as it was getting too personal. She peered out of the window past the towering architectural marvels of the old courthouse, city hall and the Woolworth building.

"I feel like I'm in a film set," she said with a big grin etched across her face – she recognised the buildings from the *Spiderman* movie.

"Are you usually this excited when you are away?"

Nicky thought for a moment – for some reason she became a looper in Stephen's company and she wanted to get this one answer right. "Definitely."

"I wish I saw things the way you did," he said in a voice that Nicky thought sounded sad.

Suddenly his phone rang and he delved into his suit pocket.

"Eve!" he exclaimed. "You guys do a great service – I have one of your employees with me right now!"

If the car had stopped Nicky would gladly have leapt out and run for it, leaving her Century 21 purchases in the boot.

Stephen was smiling as Eve spoke and Nicky could only assume that she wasn't furious at the other end of the line.

"I was hoping that she might stay with me for a drink after she changes out of her wet clothes. I have to hand it to you girls – you really are there whenever a client needs you."

He started to nod and the smile left his lips for a moment. "Okay, but then you have to promise to meet me for a drink at the very least – Nicky is going to join us too – won't you, Nicky?"

She was speechless. The car was pulling up to the Soho Grand and she was meant to be in Balthazar. As Stephen finished his conversation with Eve she had to think of another fib and quick. The car was parked and the driver had already taken her suitcase out of the boot.

Stephen politely thanked the driver and then did the most natural gentlemanlike thing in the world and started to pull Nicky's suitcase through the doors of the foyer.

Still dripping, she trudged along after him as he approached the lift.

"What floor?" he asked.

Just one more lie and hopefully she could run.

"Ten, please." She hoped he wouldn't ask her the room number.

"Ah, pity I'm up in the loft!"

The rapid lift jerked to a stop on the tenth floor.

"Why don't I help you take your bag to your room?" Stephen offered.

"Not at all!" Nicky said a little too abruptly. "Thanks, you've been really good."

Stephen held the doors open.

Nicky walked out, hoping that she would go in some sort of convincing direction.

"Maybe I'll see you later?" he said. "Your boss said that she'd meet me. I hope you'll be there."

Nicky just wanted to be out of Stephen's sight now. "Sure!" She would have said anything just to get away. "Thanks for the lift."

As the doors of the lift slid closed and she watched him disappear, her watch read ten past three and inside she had a mini-panic. She rang Rachel but when she got no answer she sent her a text telling her to wait and then made a beeline for the lift to get back down to the ground floor as quickly as possible.

"What was your favourite part of the meal?" Alex inquired with his right brow raised.

"I think the goat's cheese tartlet was probably the best I've ever tasted," Rachel replied after some thought.

"Yes, pretty yum," he said as he scooped a final spoon of crème anglaise from his almost empty plate. "This lemon tart was pretty special too."

Rachel watched as he carefully licked the edges of the spoon with his long tongue.

He placed the spoon down on the plate and slapped his palms down on the table.

"What are we going to do now?" he said with a wicked smile. "It seems your brother and friend have deserted us for the afternoon."

Rachel shrugged. She looked at her watch and then out at the street. Only a couple of puddles remained around the kerb to show any sign that it had been raining. "There's hardly any trace of that downpour," she said.

Alex laughed. "You Irish certainly love to talk about the weather. It's something I've got used to, hanging out with Conor."

Rachel glanced at him, then looked down. "I'm a bit worried about him, to be honest. I mean, going out with girls like Mandy – girls who take drugs – I thought he might want to settle down at some stage and maybe even come back to Dublin." For a moment she berated herself for sounding like her mother but then thought of Sarah at home who was now a teenager. She would hate to see her own beautiful daughter wasting her life away taking drugs.

"Mandy hounded Conor for months – she's crazy about him and he was for her for a little while – until he saw sense."

Rachel wondered if Alex was interested in the same sort of girls but from his tone he didn't seem to enjoy the company of models. She didn't need to ask him as he continued to explain.

"I avoid places where women like that go. Conor sometimes has to go to bars for work and meet music promoters or PR people and there are always models hanging about. He's a good-looking guy but he's got substance. I wouldn't worry about him."

Rachel smiled at Alex. She never imagined that she could have such a wonderful lunch with a gorgeous guy in New York City – it was all too dreamlike. Her Flake moment was disturbed by her phone ringing with a message from Nicky.

Wait for me. There in ten N x

"Who is it?" Alex asked.

"Just Nicky, she'll be here soon."

"That's a shame. I was enjoying having you all to myself!" Alex grinned.

As Rachel had put her phone back into her handbag it rang out again – with a call this time.

"Hello?" Rachel said.

The voice on the other end of the line sounded anxious and terse.

"Rachel – what is Nicky doing with Stephen?"

Rachel had to pinch herself first and then she figured out who it was.

"Eve, hi! I'm waiting for her in Balthazar – she's in Century 21."

Eve huffed loudly. "Well, I've just spoken to the client we met last night and she was sharing a ride with him."

Rachel shook her head. "I'm sorry, I haven't a clue what you're talking about – she was shopping for Ireland the last I saw of her."

"I just don't want to mess up with this client – I really shouldn't have let her stay on last night. Anyway, how are you getting on?"

Rachel blushed and hoped that her cheeks weren't as red as they felt. "I'm at Balthazar actually – but, listen, I want to say sorry about last night."

"Forget it – I was just a bit sensitive. Had a bit of a scene earlier and I guess I overreacted."

"Well, I'm really sorry. Listen, what are your plans for later?"

Eve didn't want to appear to be at a loose end but for the first time she felt like she didn't belong in New York. The visit from Tom the night before had left some sort of emotional bruise inside and she didn't know how to turn herself around.

"I'll probably do a bit of shopping uptown," she said.

"Hey, can we go with you? Nicky is dying to go uptown – she keeps saying that she doesn't feel like she's in New York – it's not enough *Sex and the City* for her downtown."

Eve laughed. She knew what Rachel meant. "I'll call around to Balthazar in a few minutes – we can go on from there if you like."

"Thanks, Eve – that would be great."

Rachel had only snapped her phone shut when a damp Nicky with a wheelie suitcase appeared. Alex got up and grabbed a chair from a nearby table.

"You look like you could do with this," he said. "It's a jungle out there!"

Nicky sat down heavily onto the chair and looked longingly at Rachel's wine-glass.

"That's just what I need – my nerves are shot – you've no idea what I've been through."

Alex poured a glass from the bottle of white wine that they were slowly enjoying.

"We're all ears," Alex said, handing the glass to Nicky.

Looking around and then down at the table with two empty dessert plates it dawned on Nicky that something or someone was missing. "Where's Conor?"

"I haven't seen my sister in three years," Conor explained to Tonya. "Mandy and I broke up before and I was only making it clear to her last night that we were over for good. I know you blame me but it isn't my fault."

Tonya chewed harder on her gum. "I have to go to work and I think someone should stay with her."

Conor shook his head vehemently. "It's up to her family to do that."

"They live in New Hampshire – you're only a few blocks away."

Conor felt like he was talking to a brick wall. "I'm really sorry but I've got to go – I'll call and see her tomorrow."

Tonya blew a large bubble that made a loud pop as she burst it. She threw her bag over her shoulder and turned her back on Conor as she walked down the hospital corridor. Conor watched her walk away with relief and returned to Mandy's bedside. She looked even skinnier than usual wearing the thin hospital gown.

A nurse walked over to Conor and gave him a kind smile.

"She's stable, you know – there's not much you can do. We managed to contact her parents and they should be here in about an hour. Why don't you go home? We'll take good care of her."

So there had been no need for that drama from Tonya after all, but then he had come to expect that from Mandy's model friends. It really was time that he thought through his dating habits. He took a last look at Mandy who was well and truly intravenously wired. It was such a waste. Her beautiful face and hair weren't visible any more under the veil of the coma. Instead she was shrouded in a kind of tortured sleep and, even though he knew that it wasn't his fault, he felt partly responsible.

Eve launched herself over to the tight little group that sat by the window. She wanted to give Nicky a right telling-off but she had to find out how she had ended up in Stephen's car in the first place.

Alex looked twice as the tall woman with the stunning green eyes approached. She looked very different to the woman with spectacles from the night before.

"Your friend's here, Rachel," he nodded.

"Eve!" Rachel said and jumped up to give her a kiss on the cheek.

"I didn't realise you had company — your brother's not around, is he?" Eve scouted the room but there was no sign of the guy she considered the rude Irishman.

"He had a bit of an emergency to attend to," Rachel informed her.

Eve took a seat between the two girls and turned to face Nicky.

She cut to the chase. "So, how did you end up in Stephen's car this afternoon?"

"It was pure coincidence — I was leaving Century 21 and he was coming down the street — he spotted me in the pouring rain and pulled over to give me a lift — that's all!" Nicky assured her.

"Jesus, Nicky, you have no idea how vulnerable our Just for

Coffee business is. We promise discretion and complete confidence with our clients – it's what our reputation is built upon and Stephen knows a lot of very important and influential people."

Nicky felt like a teenager getting lectured. "I don't know why he's gone to your agency at all if he's as important as you make out!" she declared. "I mean he's a nice guy and all but with all of that money surely he can get himself a wag somewhere."

Eve rolled her eyes. "You just don't get it – do you?"

"Girls!" Rachel called them to order – she had always had the role of peacemaker between the others' scuffles. "Are you going to eat or what are we going to do?"

Eve and Nicky called a truce without blinking an eyelid and for the first time in fifteen years Rachel realised that they had all fallen back on the roles that they'd played in the old days. They might just as well have been in the Buttery café in Trinity College instead of a swanky New York restaurant. She smiled silently with pride that she had brought the three of them back together. For the first time all weekend she felt that she had done the right thing by organising the reunion and she felt good inside just to be Rachel.

FIVE

There was a time when Nicky saw Rachel as a role model. She was the centre of attention whenever the three girls were together. Those were the days when Nicky was two stone heavier, Eve's hair was more red than auburn and Rachel's hair was more golden than blonde. Nicky was dating Gordon from Cork and everyone called him Gin. He was the only guy that Nicky really felt she'd ever had a proper relationship with. He was studying microbiology and he joined the girls in the Pavilion Bar for lunch most days. He was good fun and even Eve had time for him. But he flitted off to London the year before Nicky graduated. They tried to continue the relationship by long distance but it didn't work. That was the last serious relationship that she had until a few nights after graduation. Though she could hardly call her relationship with James serious — it was more of a fling — a fling that lasted a week — most of it in bed. He was a talented student of music and had the knack of twisting any girl that he wanted around his finger. Lots of his faculty were shocked when he started wooing the hard-edged debating student Eve Porter. They were even more stunned the day he walked into the Pav with his arm around the frumpy but pleasant Nicky. She thought that it was true love at first but she didn't have to wait long to find out what James was truly like. She missed her period two weeks later and James made a snap decision to take a year out and try his luck as a DJ in Ibiza. He fobbed her off with an offer of £200 for an abortion but when she wouldn't hear of it he shrugged and told her that it was her problem.

Nicky cried for a month – in between morning-sickness and odd looks from her mother.

It was definitely the lowest point in her life. Then, to make matters worse, James was the one to break the news to Eve that he had made her best friend pregnant. He was almost proud of the fact and seemed to enjoy rubbing Eve's nose in it too. He was jealous that she had got a green card to work in the States. New York was where he wanted to be. He could have tried his luck as an illegal alien but after the episode with Nicky he took the quickest option to get out of the country and that was the last either Nicky or Eve had heard of him.

For a while after Daniel was born, Nicky used to dream that James would appear at the door some day and say that he had made a terrible mistake. He would say how he longed to see his son and make it up to Nicky for leaving her on her own. But as the birthdays passed and Daniel turned from a toddler into a boy, Nicky's longing turned to dread. She didn't want her son to have anything to do with his father and she secretly harboured this fear day in day out as she went about her business. It had turned from fear into a recurring dream and one that had returned now that she was so far away from Daniel.

"What's your plan for the afternoon, girls?" Alex asked.

"I'm off to Abercrombie and Fitch to get some bits – who's coming?" Nicky said as she got ready to stand up.

"I would have thought that you were done with shopping by the look of that case behind you," Alex said.

Eve rolled her eyes and took a deep breath as she turned to Nicky. "If you like I'll show you a bit of uptown while we're there – I don't suppose you've even been brought to Time Square?"

Nicky's eyes lit up. "Oh Eve, thanks so much – I'd love to!"

Alex grinned. "Sure – you gotta see Time Square but there are lots of other great things to do in the city – I think the Staten Island Ferry is the best ride in town – and it's free!"

Rachel lifted her ears at the mention of the ferry ride. "I've always longed to go on that since I saw *Working Girl*."

Alex looked straight at Rachel. "Let me guess – your husband wouldn't let you go on that either?"

Rachel didn't know how to reply. She didn't want to seem like a moan and yet her life and choices did seem to stop and start in accordance with Derek's.

"Okay," said Alex, "you can twist my arm – I love the ferry and if you don't want to go to Abercrombie and Fitch I'll take you on it – we can visit the Bull off Wall Street on the way!"

Rachel looked around at Eve and Nicky but they were busy discussing their attack on upper Broadway and Fifth Avenue.

"I've seen the Bull actually but if you don't mind I'd love to go on the ferry." Rachel smiled at Alex but her smile turned to a look of concern when she thought of Conor. "What time is it now?"

Alex looked at his watch. "It's after four – but don't worry, he'll be back soon. We're having dinner in Gitanes tonight – you're gonna love it."

That's a given, Rachel thought, but tried not to show it.

"Are you ready, Rach?" Nicky asked, now standing up with her suitcase at the ready.

Eve stood up too and looked down at Rachel who was showing no sign of moving.

"Would you mind if I took the ferry with Alex?" said Rachel. "I could meet up with you at Schwarz in a couple of hours?"

"You wouldn't see me dead in a kids' shop, Rach," Eve replied, "but we'll get as far up Broadway and Fifth as the next couple of hours will allow."

"You will come with us to Gitanes tonight, won't you, Eve?" Rachel begged.

Eve shrugged. "I don't think that's a good idea – I mean, what if your brother's there?"

Rachel certainly hoped that he would be but couldn't honestly promise that he would behave in a more gentlemanly fashion.

"Don't mind him, Eve! He'll probably still be caught up with whatever – or whoever!"

Eve didn't look convinced but she was beginning to enjoy this brush with her past – and there was nothing more interesting to occupy her until her flight back on Monday evening.

"We'll text you to let you know how we're getting on," she said, taking a look around for Nicky and her suitcase. "Where's she gone?"

Rachel smiled. "I'd say she's popped out for a quick fag before the next phase of shopping starts."

Alex smiled to himself as Eve left them and made her way to the door. He was getting to be with Rachel for a while longer and was curious to know if he could peel away the layers of insecurity that shrouded her pretty face.

Conor looked left and right on Spring Street as the red awnings of Balthazar came into view. He was anxious and aware that he had already missed precious hours with his sister. He pushed his way past a horde who were queuing for tables until he spotted Josef.

"Hey, my man," he said, patting the curly-headed maître d'hôtel on the back. "Where have you got my sister?"

Josef looked terrified as he checked the table in the corner and looked back at Conor.

"She went with your friend – was I meant to keep her here?"

Conor dragged his hair back from his forehead and sighed. He hadn't thought that she'd have gone on without him. He suspected that Alex was behind her departure and he wasn't sure how much he trusted his friend any more. He was a great comrade to philosophise on life, death and politics but his track record with women left a lot to be desired.

"I don't suppose they said where they were going?"

Josef shook his head. "Sorry, Conor, I don't know!"

"No worries, thanks for looking after her, Josef." Conor turned on his heel with his mobile in hand.

"Where's the cash register?" Nicky asked, a lime-green T-shirt in one hand and a navy crew-neck in the other.

"Sorry, I can't hear you!" Eve shouted back.

It was so dark that Nicky felt it difficult to believe that it was still daylight outside. The heavy rhythm from the massive speakers dotted around the shop reverberated through her chest.

"This place is more like a nightclub than a shop!" Nicky shouted – even louder than her friend.

Eve nodded in response. Although she enjoyed purchasing the trendiest fashion and accessories while she was in New York, Abercrombie and Fitch was one shop she could comfortably walk past.

"Ask that girl over there if she can help!" Eve roared and

pointed at a wafer-thin girl wearing hipster shorts and a tight T-shirt.

A mahogany-trimmed glass counter stood between her and the masses that swarmed and heaved forward along the narrow aisles. She chewed gum and stared vacantly into the distance as if she were no more than a living mannequin.

"*Excuse me!*" Nicky hollered. "Can I pay for these here?"

The girl barely blinked and, without looking directly at Nicky, said nonchalantly with a southern drawl, "This is the denim bar."

Still none the wiser Nicky looked over at Eve who was now stuck in the crowd but waving frantically towards the back of the room. Hidden in a corner was a guy who looked like he had stepped out of the latest Abercrombie and Fitch catalogue. He was taking credit cards from the person standing at the top of a massive queue that stretched the length of the shop. He was aided by another waif-like assistant who was slowly putting each person's purchase into a paper bag.

Eve and Nicky emerged into the brilliant sunlight, tarnished and exhausted from the ordeal, but as Nicky looked down at her paper bag she found it easy to convince herself that it had been worth it!

"So, where to now?" she asked the frazzled Eve who was looking up and down Fifth Avenue for a yellow taxi.

"I have to get back to the hotel," she snapped. "That place brings out the worst in people. Anyway we haven't got enough hands to carry the stuff we've bought."

Nicky looked longingly down at her purchases and back at her friend. "You can't leave me on Fifth Avenue on my own!"

"It's just a long straight road with loads of shops – you'll be fine!"

Actually, Nicky was beginning to tire of shopping, and

dragging the suitcase behind her wasn't exactly making the expedition easy. "I suppose I could always go back to the hotel and leave my stuff there."

A yellow cab pulled over and Eve had the door open before it had stopped fully.

"Washington Square," she said to the cabby who jumped out and put Nicky's case and bags into the boot.

Eve ushered Nicky onto the back seat and breathed a sigh of relief as the cab set off down Fifth Avenue.

"I need a massage or something to chill out," Eve said.

What a great idea, Nicky thought. She really had to get into the correct vein of thought and look after herself properly. A massage was something she had only ever had once when she was sent to write a review of a spa in County Wicklow. It was newly opened and looking for as many reviews from women's magazines as possible. Nicky thought that she had died and gone to heaven – even though it only lasted 24 hours. She wrote a rave column about it but never got the opportunity to go back.

Eve lifted her mobile and rang the spa at the Soho Grand.

"Will you join me?" she asked Nicky.

Nicky nodded enthusiastically as Eve began to discuss the appointments with the girl on the other end of the line.

Alex gently placed his left hand on the small of Rachel's back. Nobody but her husband ever touched her there and she felt a tingle of excitement race up her spine at the brief contact. He was protecting her from the large crowd that was now gathering at the exit gate with the number one painted above it.

A voice with a Bronx accent boomed over the intercom. *"Passengers taking the four thirty ferry to Staten Island should proceed immediately to Gate Two."*

The mass of bodies propelled themselves towards the other

exit and Alex grabbed Rachel protectively in the excitement of the moment.

"It's best just to go with the flow!" he said with a wicked smile.

Rachel let herself be carried along with the crowd to the doorway that was now opening and led to a short jetty. A large orange ferry was waiting at the end of it.

"If you look to the left out that window you'll see the Statue of Liberty," he said, pointing to his right-hand side.

Rachel couldn't see over the throngs of heads bobbing up and down as they approached the gangway. She was surrounded by a great mass of people in their tracksuits and work clothes, from the great melting pot of ethnicity that makes the city so unique. She wondered what it would be like to be one of those people who made this journey twice, and sometimes four times, a day.

As they boarded the big orange craft Alex let go his hold of her waist and ushered her to a row of seats. From the window beside them they had a perfect view of Ellis Island and the Statue of Liberty. Sitting opposite, their travelling companions were a young couple whose combined ages couldn't have been much more than Rachel's own. A buggy carrying a small and wrinkly infant was parked up beside them, reminding Rachel of her own children so many miles away on the other side of the Atlantic Ocean. She hoped they were okay. She thought of Derek briefly and winced – more importantly she hoped they were safe.

Rachel reached for her handbag and a tissue to block the pungent smell of the diesel fumes.

"Do you fancy going outside?" Alex asked, aware of her discomfort. "The fumes aren't so bad out there."

Rachel nodded. Damn, she thought. She didn't want him to think that she was some kind of precious lightweight – barely able to take a public ferry without becoming nauseous. Alex led the way out to the back of the ferry which was empty to his amazement and delight.

The fresh sea breeze filled her nostrils and Rachel breathed in deeply. It was such a relief to breathe clean air that she let it out with a loud sigh. She leaned forward against a rail as Alex put a protective arm around her again.

She sensed him so near to her that she was afraid to turn her head in case it came too close to his. Standing on the rear deck of the Staten Island ferry she didn't feel like she was Rachel Sloan any more. She didn't feel like Derek Sloan's wife. She didn't even feel like a stay-at-home mum of three gorgeous children. She wasn't sure who she was but she did know that if she let Alex get any closer she was in danger of jeopardising everything that she held dear.

"Wow!" she exclaimed as the Manhattan skyline unfolded before her eyes. "It's so beautiful – even without the Towers."

"When I'm here in the city I paint nature and everything that I miss about the countryside. And when I'm in Massachusetts I paint New York!" He moved aside, resting both of his elbows on the rails of the deck.

"Will you go back there someday?"

"Maybe! New York is for single people. Sure, it's great for art and parties but there is something missing for me," he said reflectively. "Sometimes I need to get out of here and go home to the ruggedness of the countryside – especially in the fall when the colours and light are something special. I need that to survive."

Rachel's eyes were fixed firmly on Alex's as he spoke and she felt a deeper intimacy develop between them as each second passed.

"There aren't that many people I'd say this to. I don't know what it is about you, Rachel, but you seem to touch a side of me that I only reveal when I'm painting – and even then I'm only revealing it to myself."

Rachel gave a half-smile. She waited as he moved closer until the warmth of his breath whispered past her cheek and their lips were only centimetres apart.

Suddenly her phone bleeped.

"It's only a text – leave it," Alex said with his eyes fixed firmly on hers.

Rachel wanted to ignore it. His deep brown eyes were drawing her into him and she longed to find out where they would take her. Her mind raced off on a tangent, thinking that Derek could sense where she was and how she was feeling. She berated herself for thinking of him now at this moment when she was on the verge of letting herself go. This was her chance to escape from the confines of Derek's clutches, even if it was only for a little while. She moved her thoughts to Alex and the warmth of his breath and focused for a moment on his moist full lips. So what if he was to kiss her right now? No one would ever know.

It was as if Alex was reading her mind perfectly as he slowly moved his head forward and closed his eyes. Rachel opened her lips slightly as she felt his touch hers ever so gently. Then their tongues searched to find each other. He was the gentlest kisser. She shivered as he took her face in his hands. It was a gesture of warmth and desire and so new for Rachel that it felt like a dream. Only in her heady days of first romance could she remember being kissed like this before. The breeze from the Hudson swirled around them tenderly, caressing her as she moved into a trance. Tingles shot through her body as he placed each delicious caress of his lips onto hers.

Five or more minutes passed before her phone bleeped again. She was the first to move her head away – albeit slowly.

"I'd better get that," she whispered, delving into her handbag.

Alex remained silent as she pressed the digits on her phone and read the message.

"Conor is looking for us," she said without lifting her eyes.

"I'm glad he hasn't found us!"

"Me too!" Rachel said, looking up to meet Alex's gaze. "I'd better try ringing – he could be worried."

"If he knew what we were just doing he definitely would be!" Alex said with eyebrows raised.

Rachel held the handset up to her ear and waited for several seconds. "He's engaged," she sighed, flipping her phone shut. "What do you want to do?"

Alex said nothing but the expression in his eyes told a multitude.

Rachel blushed. "Maybe I'll leave a voicemail that he can meet us at your place?"

Alex nodded knowingly. "Now that's a good idea."

Stephen rolled over on his back as the masseuse began manipulating his triceps. His head was full of figures and plans from the meeting earlier and he needed to relax before he met the syndicate on Monday. So far this was turning out to be an interesting trip. The land he was proposing to develop was getting cheaper as each day passed, thanks to the weakening dollar. The Just for Coffee people were turning out to be good fun – and he hadn't even been fixed up with a date yet!

He smiled as he formed a picture of Nicky and her suitcase standing in the rain outside the department store. She was a total cookie and so unlike the women that he usually met. She didn't seem interested in the slightest by his income or status and she treated him with the same sort of amusement as his own daughter did.

The gentle strumming of oriental chimes filled the air and he fell into a half-sleep of blissful relaxation until the masseuse stopped.

"Take a rest until you're ready, sir, I'll be outside," the masseuse said, taking Stephen's plush black bathrobe and putting it on a stool beside him.

Stephen opened his eyes and reached out for the robe. He was happy that he had everything he wanted – except for a drink!

Outside the treatment room Nicky giggled in anticipation of the forthcoming pampering.

"I'll see you back in the loft if you're finished before me," Eve said as she disappeared inside.

Nicky lay back on the luxurious couch and sipped on a glass of mineral water. An array of glossy magazines was piled high beside her and she couldn't resist the temptation to have a peek – it was a bit like a busman's holiday to indulge, she thought, as she started to flick through the first *Vogue* that came to hand.

"Nicky!" a deep voice called.

Nicky jumped when she heard her name and wondered who could possibly know her in a New York spa.

His silhouette was becoming hauntingly familiar and she was beginning to wonder if she could go anywhere in the city without meeting him.

"Stephen!" she replied. "I didn't recognise you without your clothes!"

He smiled at her. "I'm glad I recognised you without yours!" he said as he studied her fixing the black robe around her bare neckline. "Is Eve around?"

"She's in there." Nicky pointed towards the treatment room beside her.

"I think I'm in the wrong business – you girls seem to have a great set-up."

Nicky nodded in agreement. If only you knew, she thought.

"Where are you off to tonight?" he asked.

Nicky wasn't sure but she felt by the tone in his voice that he was asking for an invitation. Weird, she thought – why doesn't a man as well known and wealthy as Stephen have loads of people to dine with?

"Not sure yet – probably going to some place called Gitanes, I think."

Stephen shook his head. "Never heard of it."

"It's probably grotty," she said, making excuses. "I don't think it's your sort of place."

Stephen picked up on her vibration instantly. Such a shame she saw him as an older man and not boyfriend material. "I'm not invited then?" He didn't care how it sounded – he was a speculator and risk-taker and he only had two more nights left in New York. He wanted to spend some of that time with Nicky.

A petite blonde peeked out from the treatment room and smiled at Nicky.

"Madam, are you ready for your treatment?" she asked.

Nicky was never so pleased to be called for an appointment. "Eh, yes, thanks," she said hurriedly as she nodded at Stephen. "Better go – I'll see you again, I'm sure!"

He didn't reply but his smile assured her that he would.

She felt like an adolescent as she lay down and let the beautician cover her face with a pungent aromatherapy cream. That man was everywhere she turned in New York. It was getting freaky. She closed her eyes and thought of Daniel but flashes of Stephen continued to interrupt her thoughts. There was something very comfortable and reassuring about him but he didn't seem to realise that the world she inhabited was so completely different to his. To him the Soho Grand was just a hotel. To her it was sheer luxury, the likes of which she would probably never be able to afford to stay in.

As the facial progressed and the soothing aromas caressed her nose she found herself thinking of Stephen again but this time in a very different way.

Conor sipped on his lonely cappuccino and stared vacantly at the phone. He tried to think where Alex could have taken his sister but this was New York and there were countless sightseeing and pleasurable places to visit. She should have got his text by now but there was no reply.

Then the screen on his cellphone lit up and he grabbed it in anticipation of hearing his sister's voice.

"Hi!"

But the voice at the other end was definitely male.

"Conor Moore?"

"Eh, yeah!" he said, surprised.

"I'm Jim – I was given your name by my producer Nat Lincoln."

Good old Nat, Conor thought. He had him to thank for so much work and he had a knack of signing on hot new acts more frequently than any other producer in New York.

"Right! I've done a lot of work for Nat over the years. Have you got a band?"

"I've got my own musicians but I'm solo."

Unusual for Nat to take on a solo artist, Conor thought – he preferred bands – this guy must be good.

"So what can I do for you?" Conor cut to the chase.

"I'm looking for some good shots. I need to get some promotional material around the city – I'm doing a number of gigs and I also need them for my website."

Conor was slack next week and this call couldn't have come

at a better time. "What's your sound? Have you any ideas of where you'd like me to take the shots?"

"I was thinking of using the city as a backdrop. I'm Irish – Nat told me that you were too."

Conor wondered where this guy's Irish accent had gone – unless he wasn't actually born in Ireland but was second or third generation and still called himself Irish.

"Really? I'm from Dublin – where are you from?"

"Wicklow, but I've been living here for five years."

Conor was still baffled as to how someone could have a strong Manhattan accent in such a short time.

"Right – so when do you want to do this?"

"Soon as you can, man. I need these pictures quick."

Suits me, Conor thought to himself. He had a job on Thursday and Friday but he could always do with extra cash.

"It's really short notice but you're lucky that I have a make-up artist who is always on call and if she can't make it she usually gives me one of her crew. We could go over to Brooklyn and use the bridge as a backdrop if you want to do an outside shoot – or we could use a stage if you want to work inside."

"I don't really mind."

"Why don't I have a word with Nat and see what he thinks?"

"That would be cool – I really appreciate this!"

Conor remembered Rachel and considered what he was about to commit to – it was unfortunate that she would be here and he had to work but Nat was an important customer and he had to keep him happy. He might even get this gig finished by lunch-time if he got some good shots quickly.

"Okay, Jim – I'll sort something out and see you on Monday."

Jim felt a great sense of relief as he put the phone down. So it was finally happening. God knows he had waited long enough to get to this stage. Nat couldn't have come along at a better time. A few months longer and he might have had to go back to Europe – he always made a good living in the sunny resorts along the Mediterranean. Now his perseverance was paying off and he was finally going to be a recording artist with his own record deal.

Alex walked along beside Rachel as they emerged from the subway on the edge of Chelsea.

"Is your apartment near here?" Rachel asked. Her eyes scanned the imposing decorative facades as they passed.

"Around the block – I have a loft – it's a brownstone."

"Oh!" Rachel couldn't imagine living in an apartment anywhere – especially not here in downtown Manhattan. Her own home was the epitome of Dublin suburban living. It had recently been renovated to the highest specifications. The whole family had moved out for four months while builders ripped out the insides – then landscapers came and renovated every inch of the exterior. All the neighbours and friends that she had made locally loved her new home and she was happy with it too, but the changes that were needed in her family were larger than could be fixed up with bricks and mortar. Already Ben was showing signs of animosity towards her that she found difficult to handle. His father was such an authoritarian that he only had to say anything once and Ben would submit but then he seemed to take his angst out on Rachel instead.

Her neighbour Veronica assured her that it was only a phase with boys and that he would grow out of it but Rachel knew that she couldn't expect Ben to understand or learn how to speak to her when he saw his own father give so much abuse each night when he came home from work. It had become a pattern and one that Rachel had come to expect now. Derek seldom came home in good form – especially since the Irish Stock market had been through such a pounding. She tried to convince herself that it was the pressure that he was under in the world of high finance that made him this way but deep down she knew that this was the way he always had been and he had used his manipulative powers of persuasion to control her since the day they had met.

On the odd occasion when Derek did come home in good form she didn't know how to handle the situation and usually said something that wound him up until he was in bad form before too long. She couldn't put a finger exactly on how long things had been like this but she did know that she didn't have any confidence around Derek – unless they were having guests and even then lately he had been known to slag her off for some inadequacy or other. That's why it felt so special to be alone with Alex. He was interested in her and she was enjoying the attention.

Alex stopped outside a brownstone building, four stories high. He pointed up to the top floor.

"That's my pad," he said, reaching with his other hand into the pocket of his jeans for the key.

Rachel wasn't sure but she thought she saw his hand shake slightly as he turned the key in the lock. She couldn't imagine why he would be nervous but deep inside she could feel butterflies dancing in her own stomach as he guided her gently up the stairs.

Rachel led the way, unsure where exactly she was going. Adultery was a path she hadn't taken before and although they both knew where they were aiming to go neither felt certain that they would definitely get there.

As they came to the last set of stairs a pair of sneakers came into view. Alex recognised them instantly but Rachel wasn't sure who they belonged to until she reached the top.

"I thought you guys might come back here!" Conor exclaimed as he got up to his feet.

Rachel smiled at her brother but felt a surge of disappointment inside. She would never know now what might have happened if Alex and she had been left in the apartment on their own.

"Hey, man! We were on the Staten Island Ferry!" Alex informed him brightly in an attempt to hide his disappointment.

"Where's Nicky?" Conor asked.

"She's gone shopping with Eve," Rachel said hurriedly.

"Is that one not gone back to wherever she came from?"

Rachel frowned. "She's not that bad, Conor. Can you give her a break just for me? I'm only here for a couple of days."

Alex pushed open the door of his apartment. "Drink, anyone?"

Conor shrugged. "I'll have an iced tea, man."

Alex made his way over to the open-plan kitchenette to the right of where they stood.

"Would you like one, Rachel?"

She nodded and turned to Conor. "How's your friend?"

"She was unconscious when I left the hospital but I'm just after getting a call to say that she has come through."

"I am glad," Rachel smiled. "I think I'll give Nicky and Eve a call – what's the name of the place we're going later?"

"Gitanes."

Nicky felt like she had stepped into the pages of a Jack Kerouac novel when she arrived in Gitanes. A guy in his twenties with blond curls and a stripy beatnik-inspired jumper slouched contemplatively with his back to the wall. Propped beside him sat his friend who looked like an art-student, with shoulder-length hair and a wispy goatie on his chin. They were accompanied by a Brigitte Bardot lookalike with long blonde tresses and a vacant expression etched upon her pretty face.

"Are we in the right place?" Nicky asked. "This is more left bank than left of the Atlantic!"

Eve pointed at the poster on the wall. It looked as if it was a print from the seventies and represented the sovereign state of Morocco.

"I hope you like spicy!" she said. "I think we have Moroccan fare to look forward to!"

The waitress — who could have been a client by the way she sauntered casually over to the women — handed them a menu and gestured at a table for two by the window.

"Actually, we're meeting people — at least two others, maybe three," Nicky informed her and then turned to Eve. "I wonder what name it's booked under?"

The waitress shrugged. "You can take that table over there — you wanna glass of wine?"

Nicky smiled. "Two glasses of red, please."

Eve nodded and the two sat down on the sixties-inspired plastic chairs.

"Another gem of high-society living from Rachel's brother," Eve said, running her finger along the edge of the table to inspect for dust.

"I think it's kinda cute — I mean you wouldn't find anywhere like it in Dublin," Nicky said in defence of his choice.

"There are plenty of places like this in London," Eve said, taking the glass of wine from the waitress, "but you wouldn't find me in them!"

"I can see why Conor annoyed you so much last night but don't you think he's a fine thing?"

Eve looked with pity at Nicky. "Did you not learn anything from your encounter with James Holden?"

Nicky took a large swallow from her glass of wine and drew a deep breath. She had no answer to Eve's sharp retort.

But Eve wasn't finished with what she had to say. "I've made it my business to keep away from arty types – whether they're musicians or photographers or painters. You know where you stand with businessmen usually."

"I wouldn't pick on a guy because he's arty – they can be really sexy," Nicky sighed. "Besides I don't seem to have the time for any men except Daniel for the last few years."

Eve shook her head slowly. "You've got to do something about that before it's too late."

Nicky stared vacantly into her glass of wine. Of course Eve was right and now that Daniel was independent of her for most things except food and money she knew that she had to think about her own future.

"Look, if you want I could see if there's anyone on our books that might suit you and you wouldn't need to pay Just for Coffee," Eve suggested.

Nicky lifted her head and smiled at the suggestion. "Maybe you're right and a blind date is the kickstart I need to get back into the relationship game!"

Eve tapped the end of her nose with her index finger. "It's not just a blind date – don't forget we do our research properly so you will only be set up with someone who is completely compatible."

Nicky got excited at the prospect. "Thanks a million, Eve. I don't know what to say!"

Eve shrugged. "No problem. At least one of the three of us can be happy."

"Rachel is happily married," Nicky said in her absent friend's defence.

"If she's so happy why was she rushing off to the Staten Island ferry with that spiky-haired freak this afternoon?"

Nicky frowned. "That's not exactly fair – he's her brother's friend and what can you do on the Staten Island ferry with hundreds of people all around?"

Eve said nothing but raised her eyebrows to suggest she had a pretty good idea of things that could be done.

Nicky's eyebrows arched as she fixed her gaze on the group of three entering the restaurant.

"Hi, girls!" Rachel said in visibly buoyant mood. "How did you get on?"

"Not as well as you by the looks of things," Eve said provokingly as she sipped on her glass of wine.

Rachel blushed and hurriedly beckoned the waitress over. "Can we have the menu, please?"

Conor had been busy texting and had missed the brief exchange between Eve and Rachel – much to the latter's relief.

"Rach, I meant to say it earlier," he said, slipping his phone into the inside pocket of his jacket, "but I have to do a job on Monday morning – I'm really sorry that I won't be around again." Sitting down, he glanced across the table and for an instant wondered who was sitting next to Nicky – she looked completely different to the woman of the night before but he couldn't understand why.

"She's not wearing her glasses," murmured Rachel, interpreting Conor's puzzled gaze.

Conor realised that was it. She was wearing a crossover floral top that softened her look completely and she also had the most dazzling pair of green eyes he had ever seen. They looked so familiar! Yet he had no memory of having met her in Ireland. Surely he would have remembered those eyes if he had? Well, not if she had been wearing her glasses apparently.

"Rach," he muttered back, "I'm beginning to think I must have met her in Ireland in your student days – she looks so familiar!"

121

"No, you never did. I'm quite sure of that."

Rachel had arranged the seats in a diplomatic order so that Eve was at the top of the table and Conor at the far corner. Eve was engrossed in conversation with Nicky but Conor found himself drawn to look closer at her penetrating eyes. It bugged him that they seemed so familiar.

Then Rachel's phone rang out. She picked it up and shook when she recognised the number – it was home. She wondered how Derek was coping and if he was angry with her for something she left undone before setting off for New York. She hurriedly got up and moved away from the table.

Alex watched her avidly as she spoke subserviently to the person on the other end of the line.

Rachel felt his eyes upon her and she gradually moved over to the door and went out into the street so that the others could no longer hear her conversation. She turned her back on those inside and leaned against the large windowpane.

Inside, Alex turned to Conor and murmured, "What's her husband like?"

"Who – Derek?"

"Is that his name? He sounds like a dork!"

"Actually, he is a bit of a dork all right. I can't stand the hold he has over her. She never did anything for herself outside the home unfortunately so he's in total control."

Alex nodded and watched as, from the other side of the glass, Rachel sighed and nodded in a way that he could hardly stand to watch.

"I'm sorry that I didn't leave the baby-sitter's number on the list," Rachel was saying apologetically to Derek. "I have it in my phone and I'll text it to you when I hang up."

"You really don't make things easy for me, Rachel," Derek

berated. "I mean if anyone needs a break at the moment it's me – just when you think the stocks can't go down any further they crash again – it's getting ridiculous."

"I'm sorry!" Rachel had got into the habit of apologising mid-sentence as she spoke to Derek – it made it easier to fill in the gaps. At least from three thousand miles across the Atlantic she didn't have to worry about him lashing out with his fists. "Are the kids all right?"

"Of course they are," he snapped. "There's no minding them now."

Rachel knew that Sarah had done all of the cooking so far because she had texted earlier to say that everything was fine and that she was feeding everyone.

"Anyway, I have to go into work now for a couple of hours and try and clean up the latest mess before the next onslaught on Monday."

"Of course," Rachel replied. Even though she realised that he was trying to make her feel bad, it didn't work. She had such a boost of confidence from her day spent with Alex that she felt invincible. The best thing to do was get off the phone as quickly as possible and return to the dream world she was inhabiting for a few short days – it would give her strength to go on once she got home.

SIX

"That was a fantastic meal," Eve said, taking the paper napkin and wiping her lips.

"So you approve of this dingy joint then?" Conor said from the other end of the table in an effort to break the deadlock between them.

"I have to admit that was better than any Moroccan cuisine I've ever had and I spent two weeks in Marrakech interviewing the country's minister for finance."

"Was he using Just for Coffee?" Rachel asked in disbelief.

"He was looking for a partner for his daughter – we don't have many Muslims on our books but we are one hundred per cent up on last year."

Conor looked dubiously over at Eve. He wasn't convinced that she was the super-efficient businesswoman that she appeared to be. He was determined to find a flaw in something she said tonight and this was just the kind of thing he was looking for.

"I thought they were into arranged marriages anyway, so

why would they use you?" he called down the table.

"Exactly," Eve said with a nod. "We arranged a perfect match with a very affluent Arab from Dubai. I know that we did an excellent job because he sent me a gold bracelet as thanks!"

"It's amazing, this whole thing," said Nicky. "I can't wait until you fix me up!"

"You're kidding, aren't you?" said Conor. "Why would you put yourself through something like that?"

"It works for some people," Rachel interrupted, keen to keep the peace as best she could. "Where are we going to after this?"

"What about Raoul's?" Conor suggested.

"Hey, Conor, we can show them the best place to play chess in New York!" said Alex.

Minutes later the five were walking down Thompson Street as shop after shop displayed the most fabulous array of chess sets that Rachel and Nicky had ever seen.

"Look at that *Shrek* set – I have to get that for Ben," Rachel sighed.

"Does he know how to play chess?" Nicky asked.

"No," Rachel sighed yet again.

"Do you?" Nicky asked.

"Maybe I'll leave it!" Rachel said hurriedly, not wanting Alex to think she was dumb.

On the side of the street, two tables illuminated by small lamps set the scene for the battles that were in progress there.

"It's amazing to think these are ordinary people playing on the street!" Nicky remarked.

"Look over there," Alex said, pointing.

Rachel and Nicky gasped as they saw a long line of tables occupied by pairs of players deep in battle filling the other side of the street.

"Only in New York!" Conor said proudly.

As they turned the corner they came upon a bistro that was bursting at the seams with customers. *Raoul's* was scripted above the French doors.

Alex walked up first and nodded at the bouncer.

"Drinks only?" the gruff doorman grunted at Alex. He stood well over six foot tall but opened the door courteously and deftly.

Inside it resembled a French brasserie from the height of the Art Noveau period. Tulip-shaped lamps dotted the walls and booths filled with champagne-drinking clients lined them.

The main attraction stood tall and proud behind the bar wearing a crisp white shirt and a pout.

Even Eve pulled her shoulders back and walked upright as they approached the bar and the stunningly attractive bartender. Deep-set dark eyes, clearly sculpted jaws, a Roman nose and gelled black hair stereotyped him as the classical tall, dark and handsome stranger. Eve couldn't take her eyes off him but was anxious not to attract attention from the others.

Nicky was less candid as she neared the barman. "Wow, he is absolutely gorgeous!" she gasped. "Any chance of getting that guy on your books, Eve?"

"He wouldn't be a suitable client for Just for Coffee. We usually only take on professional people that earn above a certain threshold," Eve said, attempting to hide her interest in him.

"I think you'll find he earns a damn sight more than you do!" Conor said sharply.

As the barman put another ten-dollar tip into the overflowing tip jar Eve felt that possibly she would have to agree with Conor on this one.

A large oil painting of a nude hung over the bar and Alex caught Rachel staring at it.

"What do you think?" he asked.

"It's nice. I don't know how anyone could do it though."

"Paint with oils or pose nude?"

Rachel giggled. "The second one, silly!" she said, giving him a mocking thump.

"It's easy – you just take off all of your clothes and lie there," he said wickedly.

Rachel's gaze fixed on Alex's for an instant and they both felt the room stop. The intensity of their stare was private, for their own eyes only.

"Would you pose for me?" Alex said, not even blinking as he delved into her eyes further.

Rachel didn't know what to say. The idea was shocking but exciting. A part of her longed to do something as daring as posing nude and another found her own body so repulsive that the answer would have to be definitely no.

"Well ...?" he pried.

"I don't think I'd make a very good model," she said shyly and turned her head. There were other reasons why she wouldn't want Alex looking at her naked. Even though she had ventured up to his apartment earlier, she wondered now if she would have been able to show him her body – part of her was horribly ashamed of it. And there was always the matter of the scars and bruises which nobody ever got to see – apart from Derek of course.

"I wonder what his name is?" Nicky asked Eve with her eyes fixed firmly on the tall barman shaking a cocktail with the charisma of a movie star.

"Why don't you ask him?" Conor interrupted the two women mid-stare.

"I couldn't do that!" Nicky exclaimed, turning to face him.

"I'll ask him for you," he said and called over to the barman. "Jack Daniels, and what's your name?"

The barman glanced over at Conor and then turned to the two staring women.

"Franco!" he said – he obviously had heard Nicky's question.

Both women were embarrassed and turned their heads away. Eve reached into her pocket to distract attention from herself as she searched through her phone for missed calls.

"Cool name," Nicky said. "But we'd be more surprised if he was called something like Walter, wouldn't we?"

Eve nodded, still staring at her phone. "I've got a text message here from Stephen and I see two missed calls from him."

"What does he want?" Nicky was beginning to dread the mention of the man who seemed to be everywhere she went in New York.

"He wants to know if we can join him in the Soho Grand later for a drink."

Nicky was beginning to feel sorry for the way she had treated him earlier. He had after all been nothing but kindness itself, rescuing her from the rain and being so friendly at the spa.

"What are you going to do?" she asked Eve.

"I guess I have to go – I mean he's the reason I'm here after all. This is the bit of the job that bores me. Clients don't usually need so much pandering at this stage but I can see that he's on his own and lonely."

"Why don't you tell him to join us here?"

"And meet Van Gogh over there and Conor the Neanderthal?" Eve quipped.

Nicky's eyebrows arched. "That's not fair, Eve. They're nice guys. I know you didn't hit it off with Conor but you have managed to remain pretty civil tonight – so far anyway!"

Eve had to admit defeat. She'd realised Conor was kind of cute after she got a good look at him under the bright light of Gitanes earlier and he had definitely mellowed overnight. As for

Alex . . . "I think Van Gogh has the hots for Rachel," she remarked to Nicky.

Nicky looked over at their two heads intent in conversation. Alex had sat next to Rachel in the restaurant and they'd walked beside each other on the way to the bar. As she watched Rachel throw her head back with laughter, she realised that Eve was far more astute than she could ever be. It had taken her a long time to notice the subtle flirtation that had been going on earlier but it definitely was developing into something else after their trip on the ferry.

Conor returned from the bar with his hands full of drinks for everyone.

"Two glasses of wine, Nicky, Eve, and two beers for you, Rachel and Alex," he said, handing them out.

As he handed Eve her glass he focused on her eyes and felt thrown back to an experience that he couldn't place. "Are you sure we didn't meet in Ireland? Or maybe when you lived in New York?" he asked.

Eve shrugged. "I doubt it very much. I can't say you're familiar to me."

Conor didn't continue – he didn't want to seem foolish. But this wasn't the first time it had happened and there weren't many women with such striking colouring even in New York. He just wished he could place her.

Eve turned to Nicky, still with her phone in hand. "I have to give it to him – he's persistent," she said, flipping her phone shut. "He insisted I told him where we are and he's joining us."

Nicky took a gulp of her wine. "Do you mean Stephen?"

Since her encounter in the spa earlier she held a different opinion of Stephen. Conor was gorgeous but even she had to admit that they didn't click on a mental level. He didn't have Stephen's wicked sense of humour that was beginning to creep up and make her curious about him.

"How long do I have to keep up the false pretences?" Nicky asked.

Eve frowned. "You can't back out on me now – Just for Coffee will lose credibility if you tell Stephen that you were lying all this time."

Nicky nodded. She knew what she had to do and went over to warn the others not to blow her cover when Stephen arrived.

Stephen took a Marlboro out of the box and tapped it on the side before putting it into his mouth. The courtesy car hadn't even stopped but he was going to light it and have a couple of drags the minute it pulled up to the bar. The bouncer stood tall and ominous, wrapped in a black coat that was unseasonal for May.

"Thanks," Stephen said to the driver as he shut the door and put the lighter up to the tip of his cigarette. Through the glass windows he could see the life and atmosphere pulsating from the restaurant. Eve's tall austere figure stood out in the crowd and he wondered how he was going to negotiate his way through the crowd to get over to her.

The bouncer opened the door as he approached. He responded by placing a generous tip in his palm. He had learnt that the dollar was the most powerful language in this city and as he had never been to this restaurant before he wanted to be remembered.

Nicky's shiny brown hair came into view as Stephen neared Eve. He took great delight in approaching the girl who seemed to have a perpetual smile painted across her pretty face.

"Stephen!" Eve called as he came into view. "What can I get you?"

The room was noisier than it appeared from outside and Stephen began to wonder if he had made a mistake. Eve and Nicky were with a larger crowd of people than he had anticipated.

"Stephen, this is Rachel — an old friend from college," Eve pointed out, "and her brother Conor, and Alex from America!"

"Pleased to meet you," Stephen said and shook hands with them all even though his three new acquaintances seemed indifferent to his arrival.

"Great to see you, Stephen," Nicky said cheerfully. "With your clothes on, I mean."

Stephen smiled. She was after all the reason why he had turned up. "I think it's for the best that I wear them, don't you?"

Nicky didn't want to appear rude but his casual shirt and jeans did make him look considerably younger than the bathrobe from the Soho Grand.

"Clothes maketh the man, as the saying goes," she said, "and I have to say you do dress very well. Do you buy them yourself?"

Stephen took the glass of whiskey from Eve and nodded his head gratefully before returning his attentions to Nicky.

"I would love to say yes but I'm afraid I hire someone to shop for me — she costs a fortune and often gets my sizes wrong but I'm usually too busy to waste time looking for shirts and underpants. Louis Copeland comes around to my office and measures me up for any suits I need so that's how I manage to cover my pelt."

If Nicky had heard anyone else say that Dublin's most famous tailor called around to size him for suits she would have thought they were being pretentious, but there was something so down-to-earth about Stephen and the way he hid his wealth that made him endearing.

"I usually pop out to Marks and Spencer's for my work gear and I'm still waiting for Stella McCartney to come around and measure me up for an ensemble or two!" she said, trying not to smile.

"I'm sorry — do I sound like a prig?" Stephen said, taking a sip from his glass. "I'm so out of touch with real life — I don't know what I do with my time. Even though I'm meant to be retired I only seem to travel when it's business-related. This is the closest I have had to a holiday in four years."

Nicky knew how he felt. "Don't worry – even the working classes find it hard to get time off nowadays."

"Did you move straight from your last job to Just for Coffee?" he asked with interest. "That would have been a good time to take a break."

Nicky knew that she wouldn't be able to keep up the pretence much longer after the numerous glasses of wine in Gitanes and the two now in Raoul's. She decided to take the plunge.

"Look, Stephen, don't let on to Eve that I told you but I don't actually work for Just for Coffee."

Stephen's eyebrows rose. "You don't?"

"No, I used to go to college with Eve and we hooked up last night after a long time and she said that she couldn't drag me back to the hotel because she was meeting you. The fib and everything was my fault – please don't spill the beans because she'd be really mad."

Stephen loved the way Nicky became breathless and excited as she confessed. He looked over at Eve who was in deep conversation with the guy he had been introduced to as Conor.

"You've put yourself in a very bad position, Nicky."

She arched her wide eyes and tilted her head, wondering with a little bit of fear what he meant.

"You know, I may have to ask you to make it up to me for lying so wickedly!" He frowned, then his mouth widened as he gave her a big grin and a suggestive wink.

"What do you mean?" she asked, staring intently to hide the naughty smile slipping onto her lips.

"You have to promise to come to the Met with me tomorrow!" Alex pleaded.

"I have to see what Conor has lined up for me," Rachel said unenthusiastically.

"It's officially Mother's Day in the USA," he pleaded, "so just tell him that he has to do what you want."

"Really?" Rachel said with surprise. "It was Mother's Day in March in Ireland."

She remembered it well even though it was a couple of months back. Derek was playing golf all of the day before and made a big fuss in the local florist about the bouquet he was getting for his wife. He also bought a bottle of Moet from the children specially wrapped in a big red bow. He took her out to *Bon Apetit* in Malahide that night and later when they got home he gave her a string of bruises along her ribs. They were his favourite place because the marks he made didn't show and didn't debilitate her to the point where she needed to go to the doctor. At least it wasn't the face – she hated it when he hit her there. The heavy make-up that she had sourced to hide the numerous slaps over the years was sticky and ugly and she would invariably end up avoiding friends for the three or so days that they usually took to clear up. That's why holidays and special days were the ones that she dreaded the most as they were the ones when he was most likely to fly off the handle. It had been going on so long now that she took the beatings as a way of life. She couldn't remember what it was like to live without the fear of the next one.

"So are we going to the Met?" Alex insisted.

Rachel didn't know what to say. She didn't have control over her own mind and now that she found herself in a position where she could do as she pleased she didn't feel able to say what she wanted. She knew that she did want to feel the warmth of Alex's lips on hers again but that was all.

"If it's okay with Conor," she said eventually.

"What about you, Rachel – what do you want to do?" Alex stared at her hard. He wanted to break through and find the real Rachel that was hiding beneath the pale beautiful face looking up at him.

"Okay then, the Met, but I really think we should meet up with Conor and Nicky for lunch."

"We can go to the Boathouse," he said quickly.

"Where?" she asked. He seemed to have it all figured out.

"It's a restaurant in Central Park – just beside the Met. You'll love it – I can tell it's your type of place."

"Who did you work for before Just for Coffee?" Conor asked Eve, now that they were left with only each other to talk to and they were on more agreeable terms.

"When I came to New York I was working for an ad agency but it was the early nineties and you could say you had a degree in anything and you could get your dream job so easily."

Conor nodded as Eve spoke. "I know exactly what you mean. It was really different then – pre 9/11, I mean."

Eve's ears perked up at the very mention of those two numbers put together. A switch went off inside her and she swallowed loudly.

"Where were you?" she asked. She didn't need to reiterate the question. Anyone who lived in New York around that time spoke about the events with a sense of connection that anyone outside the city couldn't possibly understand.

"I watched from my apartment. Heard the second plane fly overhead and thought that it was coming straight for me."

Eve was midtown but could see the smoke billowing from the top of the Tower and she could picture it in her mind's eye as clearly as if it were yesterday. She always needed to ask people where they were on that day.

"What did you do?"

Conor took a deep breath. "I did the only thing I could – I photographed it. Then I ran my video for a while . . . but I've never been able to play it back."

"Did you lose anyone?" she asked.

"A couple of neighbours and friends of friends – you know . . ."

Eve nodded. She knew. She lost the man she was going to marry three short weeks after the Towers fell. He was meant to be in Paris on business that day but she had convinced him to stay in New York because she had arranged a dinner party for his birthday. He never saw that birthday. She could still remember the message he left on her voicemail. She didn't even have her phone at hand to speak to him one last time. It was the first and last time that she ever forgot to bring her phone to work.

"What about you, Eve?" Conor asked. "Did you lose anyone?"

Eve shook her head and furrowed her brow. "I think everyone lost a part of themselves that day. New York has never recovered and will never be the same again."

Conor felt a connection deepen with this woman who at first had been so curt and rude. Now he realised that she was just the same as everyone else who had lived through the changes that the new millennium had brought to New York.

"So you know why I'm not upbeat," he said, swallowing hard. "It's all gone shallow and pear-shaped, I guess."

"That's one of the reasons I left. That and the fact that I met a Brit shortly after 9/11 who dragged me back to the other side of the Atlantic."

Conor leaned his elbows against the edge of the mahogany bar, becoming more comfortable than he could have imagined earlier in Eve's company. "Don't you like London?"

Eve shrugged. "The work is good and I live in a great place

but I miss New York – it's the old New York that I miss though and that'll never be back."

"Sometimes I think of moving home but before 9/11 I'd have said that I'd be here for the rest of my life."

Eve knew what he meant. She would never have contemplated moving but after Harry's death in Tower Number One she couldn't stay. Every time she looked up at the New York skyline the Towers were missing – along with her hopes and dreams of a happy future. Harry was so full of love for life that she sometimes felt as though she couldn't breathe when she was with him. He was from Seattle and longed to move back there one day with Eve. She was happy to go anywhere in the world as long as he was there. He was only in her life for eighteen short months but those were the months that she felt truly alive. She had to admit that she married John on the rebound and was only too happy to leave New York with the prospect of getting as far away as possible from her memories and feelings of loss.

"You've gone all pensive – is there anything you want to tell me?" Conor asked gently.

Eve shook her head and took a sip from her glass of wine. "Maybe some time but not now."

There was a mellowness about the way she spoke, a softness that sounded vulnerable and Conor realised that he had jumped to the wrong conclusion about this woman with the piercing green eyes. She looked sorrowful and beautiful at once.

"Hey, why don't you guys come back to my apartment?" he said lightly. "This place is getting really crowded."

Eve looked around at Rachel and Alex deep in conversation. In the distance she could see Nicky and Stephen laughing outside the door as they smoked. This was not a scenario that she had banked on. She had to get a grip and remember that she was the director of Just for Coffee and her client was fraternising with staff – or what was supposed to be staff.

"Eh, thanks, but I have to go," she said firmly and drew back the veil that she had let slip, albeit only for a few minutes – but enough to let Conor see a vulnerable side that she had sworn since Harry's death she would not reveal to anyone. It was a side that she had not even shown to herself for years.

She walked over to Rachel and took her arm, interrupting her conversation with Alex.

"We have to go now, so will you take Nicky home before she does any more damage with our client?"

Rachel seemed surprised but agreed nonetheless. "I'll go out and get her now."

"Thanks," Eve said briskly. "I'll give you a call at some stage tomorrow – I'm not sure what I'm doing."

Then she turned without saying goodbye to Conor and met Stephen as he returned through the door from smoking his cigarette.

"Will you join me in a car?" Eve said to Stephen, quickly adding, "Nicky, I'll see you in the morning. You're going with Rachel – isn't that right?"

She was Bullish Eve again and Nicky hated it when she was like this. It reminded her of times in Dublin when they were at a party and Eve suddenly decided that it was time to go home – and as they spent so many nights in her rooms in Trinity they had to finish up whenever she said. Now fifteen years later she was still telling them all when it was time to go home.

Conor lay fully clothed on top of his bed – he hadn't turned the bedroom light on before lying down. He couldn't get the images of Eve out of his head. She was incredibly beautiful in an elegant way that not many people he knew were. It still bugged him that he couldn't remember where he had seen her before – he was increasingly convinced that it wasn't in Ireland. He had even spent some time when he returned from Raoul's searching through his albums to see if he had photographed her on some occasion and forgotten it. He jumped up and went into his file tucked away in the corner of his living-room. As he rummaged through folder after folder he still couldn't find anyone who looked like her. Lots of girls were filed under red hair but none had the same shade as Eve's. And he didn't have a green-eyed section but he couldn't remember anyone with such emerald hues in their eyes either. He took out his laptop and scanned the recent photos of models and actresses. They were stunning women but none of them looked like her.

Eventually he gave up and returned to the dark of his bedroom where he took off his jeans and slid under the duvet.

Then, as he stared up at the high white ceiling above his head, it came to him like a thunderbolt.

The woman he had rescued.

He was surprised that he hadn't remembered on Friday night, now that he recalled her smart business suit. Her dark-rimmed glasses had thrown him but he was sure that he was right. How could he have forgotten those eyes?

And she had absolutely no idea who he was. But why would she after all? She was unconscious after falling in front of the train and he had left before she came around properly. It was an amazing coincidence and he wondered how or if he would tell her that they had met before.

She was surprisingly candid during their conversation about 9/11 and he could tell that she was a woman who hid her deepest thoughts, showing them rarely. He wondered how she would react if he broached the subject. He had a suspicion she would dismiss it immediately, that she wouldn't want to be beholden to him. But, after all, he had saved her from death!

But what if he was wrong? Then he would sound and look like a fool. His memory could be playing tricks on him.

Did he really want to get to know Eve – his sister's dismissive and haughty friend? The answer was definitely yes. He had opened up to her about his 9/11 experience and she in turn had told him very little. But he knew enough to tell that her reaction was a cover-up for a deeper story that would reveal why she was the way she was. Nobody could be so cold or offhand without good reason and now he wanted to know more. Especially if she was the woman he had rescued at the subway.

He could at least find out if she was in town on that day in February. Unfortunately he couldn't remember the exact day or date.

Suddenly his mobile rang out and he looked over at his alarm clock to see what time in the small hours it was. Ten past one in the morning meant it could only be one person and he was surprised that she had been let out so soon.

He looked at the display panel on his phone as it blinked "Mandy" and sighed. He could always ignore the call but he knew that he would take it.

"Hello?"

"Conor, is that you?" the voice at the other end of the line whispered.

"Mandy," he said trying to be as matter-of-fact as he could. "How are you doing?"

"Conor, it's awful!" she sobbed. "I'm in this hospital and the staff are awful and I feel so sick!"

"I was in there earlier and they were very nice – how are you feeling?"

He didn't want to say "after trying to kill yourself" but that was what he was thinking.

"Conor, I need to get home. Will you come and get me?"

He knew that what she really wanted was someone to get her home so she could access the stash of cocaine in her flat.

"Mandy, you need to stay away from that stuff you've been taking. The few days' rest in hospital will be good for you – you know that you need to recover fully."

Mandy sniffled down the phone quietly.

"You'd better hang up – you'll be disturbing the other patients," Conor urged gently.

"I don't want to be alone – say that you'll visit me tomorrow!"

Conor didn't want to be committed to spending any time with Mandy but he would agree to anything to get her off the phone.

"Okay then but please get some rest."

"Goodnight, Conor, I love you."

Conor cringed. He really didn't want Mandy to say things like that. It only served to tie him to her with each dramatic action she took. As he placed the phone down on the locker beside his bed he thought of Eve. She was so unlike Mandy in every way.

"Wasn't that a great day!" Nicky said, taking the sleeping tablet graciously from Rachel in complete contrast to the night before.

"Hmmm!" Rachel said, trying not to sound overenthusiastic.

As days go this one was right up there with the very best of them. As she took her pyjamas from under the pillow she thought of Alex and her ride on the ferry and smiled. She had experienced the most amazing adventure in her life and she couldn't tell anyone. The strange part was that she was convinced that it wasn't over – it wasn't even the tip of the iceberg.

"Did you know it's Mother's Day tomorrow over here?"

Nicky shook her head. "No – that's amazing. We have to do something nice."

Now was Rachel's chance to make her suggestion. "Alex thinks that we should go to a restaurant in Central Park called the Boat . . . something or other. What do you think?" She tried not to sound too excited at the prospect of lunch in the middle of Central Park – of course it was the addition of Alex's company that made the arrangement so tantalising.

"That sounds good . . ." Nicky said, trying to nod, but the tablet was starting to take effect.

Rachel looked on as Nicky fell into a heavy sleep. There was nothing left to do but lie down and try and sleep herself.

She couldn't imagine feeling the way she did before travelling to New York. Even her conversation with Derek at dinner couldn't penetrate the feelings of warmth and affection that she had been receiving from Alex all day. She wondered how her children were managing. Sarah was taking over the responsibility of feeding the family in her mother's absence. Derek was always hard on her and she hoped that she was coping okay. Ben would be probably his father's pet and he wouldn't have to help in the same way as his little sister. Derek was so chauvinistic and deep down Rachel realised that she had fed his need for power with her subservient attitude for all of these years. The more she tried to keep the peace and placate him the worse he got. His tempers flared up more frequently than they used to and she worried for Sarah now that she was coming to an age where she wanted to exert her independence. All of her other friends were allowed go to the disco in the community hall but she was forbidden. Rachel wished she had the strength to stand up for her daughter and insist that she should be allowed to go but Derek would surely have retaliated with a beating and that always upset the young ones so much.

She sighed as she looked up at the high ceiling. If only there was something she could do – some way of improving things in her house of eggshells. The thought of running away passed over her as she closed her eyes and she tried to imagine living in her brother's world with all of the fabulous flavours and textures that made his life so much more interesting than her own. But no matter how hard she tried, she couldn't see a way out. Her children were still small and they needed her so badly. But she needed someone to lean on too and in her little world in Portmarnock there was absolutely no one to turn to. As Derek had told her umpteen times, nobody would believe her. She leaned over onto her side and put her hand up to her eyelid to wipe away the trickle of a teardrop that escaped, before the sleeping tablet took hold and bore her off to her only guaranteed place of peace.

SEVEN

Derek poured himself a generous glass of brandy and looked at the face of the crystal clock on his desk. Two o'clock in the afternoon. He hadn't slept all night and the tiredness was beginning to set into his bones. Rachel would be up now in New York and spending his money with that useless brother of hers – good for taking photographs and not much else. He didn't like the thought of her so far away without him. He needed her here. Friday had been a terrible day on the stock market and the last few months a rollercoaster. Saturday was spent in the golf club and finished up in front of the television in a haze of alcohol. Sunday hadn't started off in church as it usually did because he didn't feel like putting on a show without his wife at his side. If she could flit off to the other side of the world he most certainly wasn't going to do anything to accommodate the situation. Sarah was old enough to keep the household going.

He had done everything a man could do, providing so well for his family, but the interest-only mortgage on his home wasn't getting any smaller – especially since they had hiked it up to the max with the latest round of home improvements and his new Audi convertible. To think people looked to him for advice about their investments and he had made such a mess of his own finances! Rachel wasn't as high-maintenance as most of his friends' wives – she was always careful with the housekeeping money and saved by dying her own hair instead of going to the hairdresser's and other little things like that to make a difference to the housekeeping bills at the end of the month. It made him wince when he thought about how much he spent weekly in Paddy Powers the bookmakers. Playing with other people's money wasn't enough any more and he liked to do a bit of dealing on his own now but his initial bout of luck was running out and even though he had only been gambling on the horses for two years he had managed to lose more than he had earned gross in the last five. If Rachel ever found out, it would be a disaster. But she would never confront him or check up on their finances – of that he could rest assured. He hoped that she wasn't spending much in New York. If things got much worse the Revenue would be after him and Paddy Powers had already threatened to close his account. It wasn't any wonder that he found it so difficult to get a night's sleep.

"Good morning, sis!" Conor called down the phone.

Rachel sat up in the bed and looked over at Nicky who was unravelling her foetal-like limbs from an obviously pleasant slumber.

"Hi, Conor, you've woken us up," she said with a smile. "I had a great night's sleep."

"Good – are you guys going to come to the Village for breakfast?"

"Sure – have you anywhere in mind?"

"There's tons of places – will you be ready in twenty minutes?"

Rachel looked at Nicky who was having a catlike stretch and considered. "Maybe you should make that half an hour, okay?"

"There's nothing like a walk through Greenwich Village on a Sunday Morning!" Conor said as Nicky gawked and gasped at the unusual shops and grocers en route.

The sun was shining brightly and the temperature was hotter than usual for May, giving all the New Yorkers a spring in their step.

"Hey, isn't this where *Friends* live?" Nicky asked.

"There's a joke about that around here," Conor laughed. "The building that they use in the TV series doesn't exist. As you can see, there are no high-rise buildings around – compared to the rest of Manhattan."

Nicky scanned the buildings and relatively quiet roads. It was nothing like the New York that she had imagined before arriving only two short days ago. The entire experience had been nothing like she imagined. Instead of traffic jams and noise she had found a city of peace and relative harmony – she certainly felt calmer here than rushing up Merrion Square, Dublin, on her way to work in the mornings.

"Now that's a good place," Conor said, pointing across the road with his bottle of Poland spring water.

L'Aile ou la Cuisse was set on the corner of Grove Street in a typical brownstone building. The ambience from inside spilled out onto the street as the three filed under the awnings and into the bright and spacious café.

"There's a cool beer garden out back if you want to sit out?" Conor suggested.

"I love this place," Nicky said. "Maybe we can just sit at the window – what do you think?"

"Fine by me!" Rachel said.

Everything was fine as far as she was concerned – the only piece of the jigsaw missing was Alex but she was too anxious to ask Conor where he was. She didn't want Nicky making fun of her either so she tried very hard to forget Alex and focus on the menu card that the funny little waiter handed them as they took their seats.

"*Bonjour*, ow 're u today?" he said in a singing French accent.

"Good," Conor said. "Can we start with some OJ, please?"

"*Trois?*"

"Yeah, three please." Conor turned to the girls who had settled down on the comfortable wooden chairs. "If you guys don't want it I'll drink yours."

"I'll drink mine," Nicky said, running her new Maybelline Power Gloss over her dry lips. "I'm dehydrated – didn't realise how much wine I drank last night."

"That's a gorgeous colour – did you pick that up when you were shopping with Eve?" Rachel asked.

Nicky nodded. "I got some Lancôme colour focus shadow and lots of other great stuff – really cheap. Eve only buys Lancôme or Giorgio Armani!"

Conor didn't want to listen to the girls go on about their make-up and quickly changed the subject. "That guy Stephen seems very nice – but, you know, he seems kind of familiar."

Nicky laughed. "You know who he is, don't you – the property developer and business tycoon?"

Rachel and Conor looked at her blankly.

"Don't you ever watch the news, Rach? His company is doing all of the building along the quays on the south side of the Liffey."

Rachel never got to see the news. Six o'clock was dinner-time and the kids had to have eaten and be out of sight before Derek came through the doors most evenings.

"What about newspapers – please tell me that you read them?"

Rachel felt a wave of inadequacy sweep over her. She wasn't in the world of work like Nicky and she didn't usually get to talk about what was going on outside the small world of her own parochial existence.

"I read books in the evenings so I don't get a chance to look at newspapers or watch TV," she said in her defence.

"The media is pretty one-sided over here," Conor said. "If it isn't happening in America it isn't really worth reporting as far as the press is concerned – it's a joke! I sometimes read *the Irish Times* on the internet – that's good."

Nicky leaned forward, delighted to be the harbinger of inside information on Stephen.

"Anyway – about Stephen. He's very nice really. He's semi-retired after spending all of the hours God sends working and he doesn't get a chance to meet many women – from what I can tell only gold-diggers and bimbos are available in the places he socialises so his mate rang up Just for Coffee after getting fixed up himself."

Conor sat back on his seat and grinned. "I think it sounds like a great service – might try it myself."

"You've got to be rich!" Rachel said, giving her brother a playful nudge.

"That friend of yours, Eve, seems pretty hung up on money now that you mention it," said Conor. "She's always making references to how much people earn."

Rachel jumped in. "She wasn't always like that. Something has happened to her since she left college. I mean it's not fair to blame her for a habit she probably got into from working in the job she has."

Nicky thought for a moment. She didn't agree with Rachel – it was typical of her to give people the benefit of the doubt.

Eve didn't like anyone to have anything that she didn't have. "Hang on a minute," she interrupted. "Eve was always into money – much more so than either of us."

"Oh Nicky, don't be so negative about her!"

"Well, she's not so positive about you! I'd say she's jealous of you."

Rachel sat upright in her seat. "Jealous of me? Why on earth would she be jealous of *my* life?"

Nicky slapped the table gently and stared into her friend's eyes. "You've got it made, Rachel! The comfortable home, gorgeous kids and adoring husband – you can't blame her for being jealous."

Rachel shook her head vehemently. "I don't know why you're saying this – there's no way she could be jealous of me."

Nicky proceeded to ignore her friend as the French waiter returned to their table.

"Zo you know what you like?" he pouted. He gave a little shuffle with his bright blue sneakers and straightened the red baseball cap that balanced precariously on his head. His black tie was completely out of keeping with the rest of his dress as his casual shirt hung long over his jeans.

"Yeah, I'll have the pancakes with blueberries and maple syrup and a decaf cappuccino," Conor said.

"Sounds good to me," Rachel said brightly, delighted with the waiter's timing and a chance to change the subject.

Conor's phone rang out as Nicky placed her order.

"Hello!" he said, knowing that it had to be Alex. Suddenly his friend had become an early riser since Rachel had landed in the country and it was beginning to annoy him.

"Where are you, man?"

"In the Village with the girls," Conor replied. "What has you up so early?"

"I was hoping to bring Rachel to the Met this morning," Alex said cautiously.

"Well, we're hanging out here for a while," said Conor.

"I'll be there in ten — where are you?"

Conor hesitated. He didn't really want Alex for company — he was becoming a pest and he wasn't even trying to hide the fact that he wanted to be with Rachel.

"We're in that French place on the corner of Grove Street."

"I know it — just wait for me, man."

Alex hung up and Rachel waited to see what Conor had to say.

"That was Alex. He's coming over," Conor said with resignation.

Rachel couldn't wipe the smile off her face.

Eve pondered about calling the girls but then decided to have her breakfast sent to the room instead. She had acquired an appetite in the mornings on this trip that she didn't usually have. She had managed to keep the anaemia at bay since her fall on the subway three months before. The doctor assured her that if she took iron tablets, ate after waking in the mornings and never got dehydrated, she should never again black out like she did that day at the train station.

Much as she would hate to admit it to Conor, Gitanes had been a great choice for dinner and it felt good to relax in a place that was a bit different to the norm. And she had actually enjoyed seeing him again. There was something very cute about him. His Oakley sweatshirt and denim jeans were scruffy to say the least but he was so tall and had such a good figure he would probably look good in a paper bag. She berated herself for thinking this way. Arty types are bad news, she told herself. All she had to do was think about James to remind herself of that.

She really needed a steadying influence in her life if she was going to get attached again – someone solid and dependable with a decent bank balance.

Her accident on the subway had been terrifying at the time and left another scar apart from the one on her arm. Something told her at the time that it was a defining moment in her life – kind of like the attacks on the Towers. The after-effects of 9/11 were stronger than the tremor felt around the city as the Towers fell like a house of cards. Maybe she would have been better off if that stranger had never rescued her. Maybe she would now be in a state of total bliss with Harry in the next life. But she didn't really believe in the next life – much as she wanted to. This was real life and something told her that she was at a turning point or crossroads. The fact that Rachel and Nicky had turned up at the same time as she was in New York only confirmed her ideas.

She sat down on the comfortable sofa where she had spoken to Tom a couple of days before and lifted the folder of paperwork at her side. She scanned through the pages of Stephen Delaney's file, musing on what a great catch he would be for some lucky woman. Then she stopped suddenly as an idea struck her. What was she doing working so hard fixing people up with each other when she could have it all herself? Maybe Rachel did have the right idea and being a kept woman wasn't so bad. If she was looking for someone to keep her in the luxury to which she had become accustomed, Stephen Delaney certainly ticked all of the boxes. And he was ringing her constantly so he obviously enjoyed her company. It had been staring her in the face all weekend and she had done nothing about it. She turned to the page on personal wealth and reeled with excitement as she thought of the prospect of becoming Mrs Stephen Delaney.

Her decision was made. Stephen was what she needed.

She would have to be quick though – she had only one more night and day to get him to fall for her.

She picked up her phone and dialled to the penthouse suite on the other side of the building. Once she set her mind on something Eve wasn't content until she had made it happen and this was an opportunity she couldn't let slip by.

Stephen felt like the entire Chinese army had camped out on the roof of his mouth overnight. He coughed loudly before lifting the ringing phone from beside his bed.

"Hello, Stephen Delaney," he said, not checking the number on the screen of his phone.

"Hi, Stephen – I hope I haven't woken you," Eve said apologetically.

Stephen sat up in the bed and coughed again. He'd be fine after his first cigarette of the day. "No, you're fine – I was just getting up. How are you, Eve?"

Eve nervously wriggled about on the striped couch in her penthouse loft.

"Great – it's such a gorgeous day I was wondering if you would like to join me in a bit of sightseeing?"

Stephen was puzzled. The night before Eve seemed to want him to disappear – now he was being invited to spend the day with her and, he presumed, Nicky.

"Sounds great – I had no plans – was going to read the papers. Where are you thinking of going?"

A few moments before she had searched through his file carefully and she knew that he loved art – especially classical and the Impressionists.

"I was thinking of the Met actually," she said, as if it was the first place to spring to her mind.

Stephen thought for a moment. He had been there before –

twice – but they had both been whistle-stop tours. And he longed to see Nicky again.

"Sounds good – what time were you girls thinking of?"

Eve swallowed, realising he was referring to Nicky. She didn't want to be part of a threesome with Nicky – it was a pity she had turned up in New York at all.

"Elevenish?" she suggested sweetly.

"Grand," Stephen said. "Make it eleven thirty and I'll see you at the entrance – I want to pick something up on the way."

"See you then," Eve said, flipping her phone shut and tapping it off the palm of her other hand. She had only an hour and a half to make herself the most desirable woman in New York.

Alex sipped his cup of Americano with relish.

"I'm awake now!" he exclaimed and winked at Rachel. "So what have you planned for the rest of the day, guys?"

"I'd love to go to the Met like you suggested last night," Rachel said, smiling.

Conor frowned. He was in a no-win situation. The best he could do was make sure that he was with her today and not left behind like the day before. "Okay then, let's all go to the Met."

Nicky remained silent. She wasn't finished shopping – although she could probably fill both her suitcases to the brim. But for some reason all of the fuss was around Rachel and what she wanted – and she had been to New York lots of times. She really wished that her own needs might be considered.

Rachel knew her well enough to pick up on her restlessness. "Are you okay, Nicky? Do you want to see the Met?"

Nicky huffed. It was Sunday and she still hadn't even been to Times Square. "I just wanted to do a bit of sightseeing uptown!"

"Well, the Met is uptown, isn't it?" Rachel said, turning to Conor and Alex for support. "Or we could –"

"And I want to do some more shopping," Nicky interrupted.

"What is it that you want to buy, Nicky?" asked Conor.

Nicky wasn't sure what she wanted but she did know that she wanted to do lots more looking around. "I was thinking of getting an iPhone – they're much cheaper here."

"Well, you can get that up at the corner of Central Park," said Alex. "There's an Apple Store beside FAO Schwarz – it's on the way – and you can join us in the Met when you're finished." He was desperate to get an agreement between them all – he really wanted to take Rachel to the gallery and show her what art meant in his life and in doing so maybe touch a deeper part of her.

"Okay then," Nicky said, putting the last bit of fruit salad in her mouth and munching loudly. She was finally feeling brave enough to get around New York on her own. Although a bit of company would be nice. She wondered what Stephen was up to for the day. Somehow the best bits of this trip seemed to be the moments that she bumped into him!

Conor paid the Frenchman and the four hailed a cab on Grove Street. As they drove up Broadway Nicky felt isolated in the front of the car. Conor sat between his sister and his friend, protectively forcing a wedge between them. The fact that he was a head taller than either of them made the threesome look comical. The cab pulled to an abrupt stop at a large glass cube with the image of an apple on it. At the back of the structure was an entrance and escalator that led to the computer store which was hidden underground.

"Thanks, guys," Nicky said, stepping out of the car. "I'll meet you later when you're finished in the Met."

Rachel wished that Conor had fallen for Nicky but it looked as if even the initial flirtatious feelings that Nicky had for him were now fading.

"Are you sure you'll be okay on your own?" she asked.

"Fine. I feel like I know Fifth Avenue better than Grafton Street at this stage. I can always ring you if I get lost or delayed!"

Rachel smiled at her friend. She knew that shopping was her priority and there was no point dragging her somewhere that she just did not want to be. But now it looked as if she was stuck in the middle of a stand-off between her brother and his friend and she knew who she wanted to be spending the afternoon with.

Rachel waved at Nicky as the cab pulled away and they continued down the wide and open street with tall prestigious buildings on one side and a long avenue of greenery on the other. Shortly the imposing classical building of the Metropolitan Museum of Fine Art came into view and Rachel gasped as the cab came to a stop.

"Beautiful!" she exclaimed.

Conor leaned forward and paid the cab driver as they stepped out onto the sidewalk.

"It's some place!" Rachel said.

"Come on," Alex said, putting a protective arm around her shoulder.

Conor was still at the bottom of the grand steps to the entrance when his mobile phone rang out. He didn't want to answer as the others were slipping from view through the main entrance in the middle of the building.

It was a New York number but not one that he was familiar with.

"Hello?"

"Conor – you said you would come and see me today!" the voice at the other end of the line pleaded.

"Mandy – hi."

"I'm still in this awful hospital. I can't stay here – these people are nuts – I think they are trying to kill me."

"Mandy, where are your parents? I thought they were visiting you?"

"They've gone home," she whimpered. "I don't want to see them any more."

"You should have gone with them – get out of New York for a while."

"But I told them that I wanted to stay here with you. I said that you would look after me – won't you?"

Mandy was speaking in the little-girl tones that told Conor he couldn't possibly believe a word that she said.

"Look, Mandy, I didn't want to say this on the phone – you've got to mind yourself because we don't have a future."

"Conor!" she sobbed. "You've got to come and see me today!"

Conor walked along the bottom step of the long stairs that led up to the impressive entrance to the Met. He wanted to catch up with his sister – he needed to get Mandy out of his life for good.

"Mandy, I won't be calling today."

"What about tomorrow?"

"Or tomorrow. Mandy, I really have to go. Sorry!"

He turned his phone off and stared at it for a few seconds. He had to be cruel to be kind.

"Heartbreaker!" a voice whispered in his ear.

He turned swiftly to see the penetrating green eyes of his sister's friend gazing back at him.

"Eve, how are you – I was just –"

"It's okay," she interrupted. "I can just imagine the sort of girls that you date."

Conor frowned. He hated the way this woman presumed that she knew everything about him. She didn't know that he used to be Danny Clinch's assistant – the hottest rock photographer in history – or that he had helped Iggy Pop get sorted for his last album. That he had frequented the best bars and restaurants with the musical cognoscenti of New York City for the last twelve years. But it wasn't worth informing her. He wondered was it worth telling her that he had saved her life a few months ago. Because, now that he saw her again, he knew that she was the woman in the subway.

"Are you meeting someone?" he asked.

"Stephen actually," she said and then another thought hit her. "How about you?"

"I'm here with Alex and Rachel — they've just gone on ahead. Actually, I'd better follow them."

Eve's face dropped. She didn't want to meet anyone when she was hoping to woo Stephen with her knowledge of the Impressionists and European painting.

"I see — well, don't let me stop you. Give my regards to Rachel and Nicky and I'll call them later."

Conor stopped mid-step and turned to face her. "Nicky isn't with us actually — she's gone to the Apple Store."

"Oh! I'll talk later then."

It was obvious that she didn't want his company. Fair enough, thought Conor — even though a part of him was more than a little curious and wanting to spend some time getting to know the woman that he had rescued on the subway.

He hurried up the steps and thought as he climbed about a time and place where people didn't judge you for what you looked like or your material wealth. He longed for the time when New York was the centre of the universe — everything that mattered happened in New York before anywhere else — but now it was so different. People came from across the Atlantic and raped the city like it was a bargain basement. Those who were left living here wondered about a lifestyle and world in Europe and Asia that they were no longer privy to. Day-in-day-out they carried around with them a feeling of emptiness in the pit of their bellies that they couldn't explain. He had hoped last night, for the few short moments that he had connected with Eve, that he had found someone who could link the missing pieces between the two worlds. This morning, however, she seemed to have returned to the old Eve that he had met on the first night and he wondered if he had just been right about her all along.

Stephen asked the courtesy car to wait outside the Apple Store until he came out. He needed to get something for his phone and he probably wouldn't have time to do it on Monday – he would be tied up for most of the day with meetings. The escalator took him down to the basement on a futuristic trail and he wondered why on earth there wasn't a place as technologically cool as this in Dublin. He put the thought at the back of his mind as a project that he must look into when he got home.

The sales assistants were dotted around the store with apple badges and wide American smiles. He simply needed one to sort him out with a new and stronger battery than the one he already had – if it existed.

He was about to tap one of the fresh-faced assistants on the shoulder when a familiar face came into view. The same shiny brown hair as he had seen the night before attached to the face with the smile that he had come to enjoy seeing.

"Nicky!" he called.

She was wearing a sexy top with a lace print and a pair of white trousers that elongated her legs – or maybe it was the wedged espadrilles had that effect.

Nicky was startled at first but then wondered why she was, when everywhere she went Stephen seemed to be.

"Good morning, fancy meeting you here!" She was genuinely glad to see him and felt relieved to have company that wasn't concerned with Rachel and how she felt and what she wanted to do.

"I thought you were up at the Met with your 'boss'!" he said, making quote-marks with his index fingers.

Nicky's eyes widened. "Oh, you mean Eve – no, why did you think that?"

Stephen seemed surprised. "Oh, I just made that assumption," he said awkwardly, wondering why Eve hadn't corrected his error. She was just being polite, perhaps.

"The others are up there, though," said Nicky. "Rachel and Conor and Alex."

"So you *are* going up there, then?"

"I'm meant to be but to be honest I just want to see a bit of uptown – and I haven't finished shopping yet."

"What about all of the stuff you got at Century 21?"

"Oh, you mean the stuff for my son?" she said and then stopped short after realising what she had just said.

Stephen had picked up on the last word of her sentence clearly and now tilted his head and looked at her enquiringly. He was intrigued. Not only did she not work for Just for Coffee but she had lied to him about having a son as well.

"I thought those clothes were for your boyfriend," he said.

Nicky gulped. "Look, I'm sorry, Stephen, it's time to come clean – I've been telling little fibs since I met you."

Stephen looked around him and took her arm. "Come on, let's get out of here – I know just the place to bring you to see more of uptown and you can fill me in on the real Nicky."

They stood on the escalator as they ascended into the bright sunlight and came out at the corner of Central Park and the new Plaza Hotel and apartments.

Stephen waved his courtesy car to go on. He had a very different mode of transport in mind to show Nicky the best of uptown.

"Where are you taking me?" she asked.

"For a little ride that you won't forget," he said, tapping his nose enigmatically.

"What about the others?"

"Send them a text that we are stuck in the Apple Store and can't leave for at least three hours!"

"Three hours?" Nicky asked with wide eyes.

Stephen nodded and paused to text Eve while Nicky did as she was told and sent the text to Rachel.

They weren't walking for long when they came to a queue at the side of the road. A group were gathered around the horses attached to beautifully authentic carriages from a bygone age. A chestnut stallion jerked his head as his master held up a pail filled with water. He seemed oblivious to the carriage on his back even though Nicky thought it looked very heavy. It was made to seat two passengers under a canopy with a driver at the front. The horse was undoubtedly well groomed and healthy and although she had seen similar tourist rides traipse around St Stephen's Green in Dublin it had never occurred to her to have a go in one of them.

"Do you fancy a tour of Central Park in style?" Stephen asked. "It really is the most stylish way to see the nicest part of the city!"

Nicky was overcome. It was dreamlike standing next to Stephen like this under the flawless blue sky in warm May sunshine. She couldn't think of anywhere in the world that she would rather be.

"Okay," she said shyly as the driver took Stephen's money and helped her up onto the carriage.

Stephen jumped up after her and settled down cosily by her side. "Comfortable?"

Nicky nodded. What could she say? This really was a surprise and she couldn't help wonder if it was more than a string of coincidences that had brought her to this moment with Stephen.

Conor stood inside the grand entrance of the classical building that was the Metropolitan Museum of Art. It was apparent that Rachel and Alex were only too happy to run ahead by themselves. He was beginning to feel like he was in the middle of some sort of scene from a bad nineteenth-century play. He hesitated, wondering which way to go. Where was Alex most likely to take her first? He went to study the map to refresh his memory on the layout of the museum.

"Lost them?"

It was Eve again.

"Yeah. So it seems."

Just then Eve's phone rang out. She pulled it out of her handbag and read a text message, then turned to Conor with a disgruntled look and sighed. "Looks like I've been stood up!"

"Huh?"

"This is from Stephen – he's taking a sightseeing tour with Nicky and won't be finished for hours."

"What are you going to do now?"

Eve shook her head in exasperation. "I've no idea. I might go back to the hotel and do some work."

"I could do with doing some myself," Conor said. "I've a job tomorrow that I haven't prepared for properly. I guess I'll go and catch up with Rachel though."

"We could always go for a drink if you want?" Eve didn't relish the thought of spending Sunday on her own.

Conor hesitated. He felt he needed to be with Rachel – but what was the point? It was clear she and Alex had no need for his company. And he didn't really feel like traipsing around the Met on such a sunny day.

"Where were you thinking of?" he asked.

"Town?"

Conor smiled. He wasn't surprised at her choice. A part of him wanted to slag her off but it was just the sort of sophisticated joint that Eve would look good in. Besides, it was only a short ride down Fifth Avenue. He knew the maître d' – not as a frequent visitor but he had got him tickets for Sting last time he was in town and that meant that he owed him. He suspected that Eve had connections with the restaurant but decided to say nothing.

"Okay – I'll text Rachel and we can grab a cab."

Rachel jumped – embarrassed that her phone had interrupted the spiritual mood in the Impressionists wing of the museum. Her expression turned to surprise as she read the message.

"Everything okay?" Alex asked.

"Conor's bumped into Eve and he's going for a drink with her."

Alex's eyes widened in delight and anticipation. He had Rachel on his own again and he couldn't believe his luck. "Great – I mean pity but – you know what I mean."

Rachel looked up into his soft brown eyes and smiled. She did know what he meant. A tingle of excitement and anticipation ran through her as Alex put his arm gently around her waist in the same way as he had done the day before on the ferry. This time he whispered in her ear.

"There's something I want to show you – it's the reason I had to get you here."

Rachel was intrigued and let herself be led by his strong and urgent grip.

"This painting here," he said as he led her towards a corner of the room.

It was a fine collection of Impressionist paintings from Europe and America but she knew instinctively the painting that he wanted her to see.

The lady was wearing pink and her blonde curls peeped out from under her bonnet. In her gloved hand she held a china cup filled with tea.

"Is this the one?" she asked.

Alex nodded without saying a word.

Rachel turned to the picture and focused on the mid-tones and gentle hues that the painter had used to capture the mood of the subject so effectively.

"She's very pretty," she said eventually.

"And reserved – and enigmatic," Alex continued for her. "What do you think she is trying to hide?"

Rachel shrugged, surprised. "I don't think she's trying to hide anything!"

"Why do you think we get to see so little of her face?"

"That's just the way she was sitting, I guess?"

"It's never that simple. She's a woman of substance – we can see that by the way she is dressed but I think the painter only wanted to reveal a little of her sister to us."

"It was painted by a woman?"

"Yes. Mary Cassatt – it's called 'The Cup of Tea' – the sitter is her sister."

Alex talked on about the painting – its meaning and technique and how it made him feel.

Rachel listened and felt a windmill in her head. The painting was coming to life. She could feel the vibrations envelop her – the more Alex explained what they were looking at, the more she felt herself fall into the painting.

Alex was looking at her intently.

"It's funny," he said, "but the first time I met you in Once

Upon A Tart I thought of this painting and how much you reminded me of her."

Rachel jerked her shoulders back. "Of me? This reminds you of me?"

Alex smiled. "Yes – why are you surprised that I should think you are like a beautiful painting? I told you last night that I'd love to paint you!"

Rachel could feel the flush of red embarrassment creep up her neckline and she wished that she had worn something less revealing. The heat was travelling up her neck and she put her hand up to cover her reaction.

"Really, Alex, I think you've got quite a different impression of me than the one I have of myself!"

"Maybe I'm the one with the right impression, Rachel – and you're the one who's off."

He stared deeply into her eyes as he spoke, sending a shiver up her spine. She longed to feel his lips upon hers now but knew it wasn't the time or the place for that – it would be like a doctor kissing someone in his surgery. Though maybe they did all of the time! Maybe artists did it in their studios and that was why he wanted to paint her in his. She increasingly had more questions than answers in her head the longer she stayed in Alex's company.

"So where do you want to begin?" Stephen urged. "I'm looking for the truth, the whole truth and nothing but the truth!"

Nicky took a deep breath. She had been starting to relax, sitting in the horse-drawn carriage and taking in the breathtaking views around Central Park.

"Well, only if you agree not to tell Eve any of it, okay?" she said reluctantly.

Stephen crossed his heart with his index fingers. "Now go on!"

"I'm thirty-six years old and I work as a sub-editor for a magazine."

A smile developed on his face that Nicky felt sure was intended to be a compliment.

"Where?" he pried.

"Dublin."

"Continue."

"I'm a single mum and my son is fourteen – he's great but at the moment I'm an embarrassment as far as he is concerned and, to be honest, although I adore him more than anyone in the world he's a money drain. It takes most of my wages to keep up with his needs. And no, I don't have a boyfriend."

Stephen was delighted to be finally getting to meet the real Nicky and he found her fascinating. Where would he go to find someone like her in Dublin? The fact was that he wouldn't be in a position or place to meet anyone like her.

Her hair blew gently in the wind as the carriage rocked slightly over the bumps on the road when they entered the leafy park.

"I'm sorry for interrogating – I didn't mean to be like that – stop if you want."

"It's okay," Nicky said with a shake of her head. "It's good to come clean. I really like your company and it's been good to have someone to smoke with. Speaking of which, do you think the driver would mind if we had a quick puff?"

"I don't see why he would," Stephen said, reaching into his coat pocket. "We are outside after all."

He slipped open the packet of Marlboro Lights and handed Nicky a cigarette, producing a lighter with his other hand. Protectively he sheltered the flame from the gentle breeze until the tip of her cigarette had caught alight.

Nicky took a long luxurious drag from her cigarette. It really was some kind of decadence to be sitting in a horse-drawn carriage in Central Park on a Sunday afternoon smoking a cigarette.

She gave her companion a level look. "I've spilled the beans, so what's your story, Stephen?"

"I thought you were privy to all sorts of information but now that I know you aren't working for Eve I realise you aren't. I guess you're entitled to know. There isn't much to tell really. This idea that I start dating women from an agency is my friend's – as I think I told you before – but I do miss companionship. I've been separated from my wife for years and I haven't been a very good father." He dipped his head and looked sadly at his cigarette. "I've neglected the most important people in my life while I was busy building office blocks and hotels. I cut back on my workload last year and am supposed to be retired, even though I still get involved in major deals. There's more to life than work so I had to agree with my friend when he put me in touch with the agency."

The New York sunshine seemed to take years off Stephen and he was dressed more casually than the first few times she had seen him. He looked even better than the night before in Raoul's and Nicky felt attracted to him in a way that she would never have imagined after meeting him on Friday night.

"I can't believe that you couldn't find someone yourself though – I mean, you must be invited to all sorts of dinners and parties?"

"Yes, but it's always men that I seem to attract and they are usually looking for information – tip-offs or financing for business deals."

Nicky laughed. She believed him. She felt that lots of people wouldn't but she found his argument totally plausible.

"You poor thing!" she sighed and put her non-smoking hand up to gently stroke the side of his face.

Stephen leaned forward to capitalise on her gesture and steal a kiss but she jerked back.

"I'm sorry," he said, leaning back on his seat firmly.

The moment had been spoiled.

Nicky couldn't understand what was stopping her. Here was a really nice man who was available and wealthy and she couldn't respond. There was some kind of glitch in her make-up – of that she was sure. Maybe she only liked rogues and guys who would break her heart.

The horse pulled up by the side of the man-made lake in the centre of the park. It was filled with people rowing in small boats and punts – at the far end was a low building draped with red and white striped awnings.

"It's a bit like a Seuret painting!" said Stephen.

"I've heard of him – wasn't he the dotty guy?" Nicky had done the bare minimum of her art history course for the Leaving Certificate and it was nearly twenty years ago but the pointillists were a movement that she did remember.

Stephen was startled by her comment. He had jumped to all of the wrong conclusions about Nicky. She was a clever witty woman for sure but he'd never dreamt that there was a possibility that they could share a liking for other things – he longed to get to know her better and treat her the way he felt that she deserved.

EIGHT

Conor let Eve lead the way into Town. The restaurant was heaving and he was curious about how she was going to fight her way to the top of the queue. The maître d' was hassled by loud and bolshy New Yorkers fighting to get a table and Conor smiled inwardly when he saw the dismay on Eve's face. She had obviously bargained on the restaurant being quieter than this.

"If you like we can go somewhere else?" he whispered in her ear.

Eve seemed unsettled in her surroundings and pleased with his suggestion. They had little chance of getting a table and he was surprised that she had left herself open to this indignity, which was why he had assumed she had connections here.

But as they turned to retreat the maître d' rushed over, calling, "Conor! Please, Conor, come and take a table – I can always make room for you!"

Eve looked surprised and frowned when she realised that it was her companion who was being summoned.

"Hi!" Conor said. He had forgotten the name of the maître d' but, after getting tickets for a Sting concert, the maître d' would never forget Conor. "It's okay – I think the lady wants to go somewhere else."

The maître d' seemed offended – he wasn't used to people turning down the offer of a table in his restaurant. "Please, I can offer you a very nice private table in the corner!" he said, turning to Eve – although having to entice someone into his restaurant was something that he wasn't in the habit of doing.

"Do you want to stay?" Conor asked with his eyebrows raised.

Eve felt that it would be rude to walk away and, besides, she was intrigued – she hadn't banked on Conor being so *au fait* with the personnel.

"Of course I do, if we can get a table."

"Right, we'll stay."

"Thank you," said Eve to the maître d', graciously letting him take her coat.

"This way, please." He led them into the restaurant.

"I didn't know that you were connected in the trendier establishments in the city," Eve whispered in Conor's ear as they made their way to an excellent table with a view looking out on the street.

"Maybe you shouldn't judge a book by its cover," he whispered back in hers.

When they settled into their seats Eve poured a glass of water from the jug in the middle of the table and smiled.

"So tell me – how did you get so well known in Town?"

Conor grinned. "When you're in the business I'm in, you get to know all of the record producers." He pointed over at a scruffy guy leaning against the bar. "Take that guy over there, for instance – he may look homeless to you but he has one of the hottest new record labels in New York and any band that gets signed up by him is on a guaranteed ticket to fame and fortune."

Eve craned her neck. "You mean the guy in the black T-shirt with the beard and the earring?"

Conor nodded. "Exactly. So that's why I'm saying don't judge a book by the cover."

"I guess I've been in London too long and I've got used to a different etiquette."

Conor decided to let her away with it. She was showing herself to be far more vulnerable than she had been on either of the two occasions that they had met before.

"Will you stay in London?" Conor asked.

"I hated it at first but then like any city you get used to the good things and accept the bad things. I don't know how much longer I'll stay. I presume Rachel told you that I'm separated?"

Conor had to admit that he knew. He nodded uncomfortably.

"I would probably have gone to Paris or Madrid after 9/11 but the fact that I met John made it easy to follow him back to London. We were only together six months before we got engaged and as the saying goes – marry in haste, repent at leisure. And that's where I'm at, at the moment."

"Repenting?"

Eve laughed. "I don't do things like that – but I am sorry that I had to leave New York so quickly."

"Why did you *have* to leave after 9/11? I know it was grim but even though work was thin on the ground I stayed."

Eve sighed. "I lost someone very special in the Towers – Harry was his name. We were only a few weeks away from getting married. Then I met John through work – he was an advertising executive and rather than deal with my loss it was easier just to fall into a relationship. Lucille wanted me to set up in London because Just for Coffee wasn't doing great after 9/11. John was from London and happy to move back as business was bad in New York."

"I see why that didn't last. I don't know if you've been but I went for counselling afterwards and it really helped."

Eve shook her head. "I don't do that sort of thing – I can work anything I need out for myself without paying a shrink."

A waitress arrived and handed them menus.

"Thanks," Conor said, giving her a smile.

Eve lifted her handbag and started to rummage through it for her reading glasses.

"Do you wear contact lenses most of the time?"

Eve nodded as she produced the slim case from her handbag. "But now I find my close vision is getting bad when I wear them."

"Ever think of laser treatment? I got it done four years ago and it's made a huge difference to my life – especially if I have a shoot very early in the morning or late at night."

Eve slipped the spectacles onto her nose. "I like seeing things blurred sometimes – lenses never bothered me before. But I suppose I should think about it." She placed her favourite Armani handbag near the edge of the table where it teetered and then toppled onto the floor. "Oh God!" she said, as the contents spilled out under the table.

Conor quickly got down onto his hands and knees and gathered the various accoutrements that were scattered on the floor. As he looked up from his task he couldn't help notice Eve's slim ankles and sexy legs perched up on an equally sexy pair of Jimmy Choos. He had photographed enough models to recognise certain brands in fashion.

"There you go," he said as he put an expensive looking Lancôme lipstick on the tablecloth with the rest of the items that he had recovered.

"Thanks, Conor – you've saved my L'Absolu Rouge – you're very chivalrous."

Conor wondered if she had any idea just how chivalrous he could be. That he had rescued her from death on the subway? Maybe this was a good time to ask her if she had been around in February.

"Oh, my earring is missing!" she exclaimed, picking up a tiny studded diamond and pearl earring. "It was in the pocket at the side of my bag with this one but it's gone now."

"I'll pop down and have another look." Conor returned to floor level. He searched diligently but couldn't find anything on the smooth surface.

"Is it replaceable?" he asked when he sat back up on his seat.

Eve's eyes started to fill up. Harry had given the earrings to her for her birthday – of course they were irreplaceable. "They were from Harry."

Conor placed a reassuring hand on Eve's. "I think you should try getting some help, Eve – you can't just battle on through life without dealing with your feelings. You weren't on your own after 9/11 – lots of people lost loved ones. We all had to get through it."

Eve slipped her hand from Conor's grasp and wiped her eyes efficiently. "I'm fine. He got them in Tiffany's. I'll just get another one made."

But Conor could see that she wasn't fine – she was a long way from being fine.

A group of jazz musicians busked at the side of the long tree-lined lane. Stephen and Nicky's carriage had to swerve to avoid the crowd gathered around them. Dappled light fell through the leafy trees onto the pathway before them. The buzz from happy New Yorkers on a lazy Sunday seeped through the air.

"It's so beautiful here – I never in all my life imagined that New York would feel this way," Nicky declared.

"I think it's the best city in the world – apart from Dublin of course!"

Nicky wasn't one to disagree but at this moment there was absolutely nowhere else in the world that she would rather be.

"I wish my son could see this place," she said.

"He's young – he'll get here in his own time."

"I hope so – it's costing so much to send him to school – the fees are over four grand a year."

"Where does he go?"

"Belvedere College – it's on the northside."

Stephen sat up at that. "Ah, my old Alma Mater!"

"Really?"

"It's a great place – does he play sport?"

Nicky threw her eyes skyward. "Rugby is his religion. He'd rather be on the pitch than anywhere!"

"I used to play myself," he said. "When I was fitter, of course."

"You are fine," she said, giving a friendly nudge to his arm. "You're a fit-looking guy for your age."

"Thanks," Stephen said suspiciously, not sure if the reference to his age was a compliment. "Will he be playing today?"

"Oh yes – always on a Sunday," she said with a smile. "I'm usually on the sidelines screaming my lungs out but he will text me later with the score, I'm sure. He's probably playing now as we speak."

Stephen leaned forward and spoke to the driver.

"I hope you don't mind but I asked him to take us back to the Boathouse in the middle of the park – have you seen enough?"

"Absolutely," Nicky said, nodding her head. "I'd love to try the Boathouse out – Rachel was talking about it last night and said we might go there today."

"Maybe your friends will be there then?"

Nicky hoped not. Now that she had relaxed she was perfectly happy in Stephen's company and didn't want to change her vibes yet again.

When they arrived at the Boathouse, Stephen took her hand and helped her in a gentlemanly way off the carriage.

"That was lovely, Stephen," she said as he led the way into the bright and opulent surroundings of the Boathouse.

Red and white awnings shaded the tables on the waterfront from the midday sunshine. Waiters in starched white shirts and linen aprons buzzed to and fro, balancing round trays in the air as they passed. The clientele were a mix of the upper echelons of Manhattan society. Perfectly groomed wives with squeaky-clean children surrounded their wealthy lawyer-type husbands who looked like they had stepped out of an advertisement for Ralph Lauren.

"Are these people for real?" Nicky whispered in Stephen's ear. "I feel like I'd dirty them if I sat beside them!"

Stephen scanned the cover of a menu that rested on the bar where people and waiters bustled around. "I see it's Mother's Day – that's why it's extra busy!"

"Do you think we'll get a table?" Nicky asked. She couldn't imagine a nicer place to have lunch.

"There's always a table to be got!" Stephen said, tapping his nose. "Why don't you sit up here at the bar and I'll have a word with that guy over there." He gestured to the barman to come over.

Nicky realised in that instant that Stephen was the sort of man who was used to getting what he wanted in most aspects of his life but somehow he didn't have the same sort of luck in love. It gave her consolation that she wasn't the only one who seemed to be that way with affairs of the heart.

"A bottle of Bollinger for the lady, please," he said to the barman.

"God, Stephen, you can't!" cried Nicky. "That will cost a fortune!"

"It's okay," he said easily. "You deserve it – it *is* Mother's Day after all."

With a wink he sidled off to organise a table, leaving Nicky feeling like she had stepped into another world – one that she could get used to if given a chance.

"What do you want to do now?" Alex asked as his gaze went to Rachel's lips.

Rachel knew exactly what she wanted to do and where she wanted to be but she didn't have the strength or courage to admit it. She brought her eyes to look at his mouth and the lips she had kissed the day before.

"Are you hungry?" he continued.

Food was the last thing on her mind. Alex had wooed her to a point where she desperately wanted him.

"I couldn't eat a thing," she admitted truthfully.

"I could," he replied cheekily. "I'd like a Rump of Rachel on my sofa."

Rachel felt like she could melt. She could hardly breathe as Alex took hold of her hand and ushered her to the lift. Once they were alone inside Alex bent his head and ran his lips gently over hers. The lift ride was too short. Frustrated, they made their way out of the museum to where taxis lined the thoroughfare.

"Your place or mine?" Alex asked when they were settled in a cab.

They both knew what he meant.

"I guess yours," she said, flinching as he playfully fondled the palm of her left hand with his fingers. It was the gentlest of touches but enough to send her pulse racing with each stroke.

Nicky sipped on her glass of champagne and watched with amusement as Stephen returned to the bar with a spring in his step.

"There's always a cancellation if you have the right approach!" he said with a grin as he accepted a full glass from Nicky. "They will have a window seat for us in twenty minutes."

Nicky was startled – so this was how the other half lived – and did business.

"This is really nice, Stephen," she smiled. "Thanks."

"No, thank you for your company – I hate to eat alone!"

His blue eyes twinkled and she could see a glimmer of a man so brimming with intelligence and wherewithal it was no wonder that he was so successful. But why wasn't he surrounded by a throng of women? Where was the catch? As Nicky had found with any of the few men that she had dated in recent years, there was always a catch!

"You know, Nicky, I never thought when I contacted the agency that they would come through so quickly!"

Nicky took a sip from her glass. She wasn't sure if this was a compliment directed at her but it definitely seemed that way.

"I don't know what you mean," she said, prodding him playfully on the arm.

"Nicky, I have to come clean – since the first night I met you I can't stop thinking about you – and this isn't normal for me!"

"Are you trying to tell me how fussy you are?"

Stephen moved about on the bar stool before finally resting his arm on the edge of the bar and looking in her eyes.

"I don't often get to meet women that are as natural as you, Nicky. Then of course there's the matter of your eyes!"

Nicky was startled – she always felt that she had very ordinary eyes.

"The way they twinkle," he continued. "You light up a room with them."

Nicky grinned. Was he just being corny? There was something very genuine about him though and with his money any girl that knew what he was worth would latch onto him. But it said a lot about his character that he wanted more from a woman and the compliment made her blush.

"Tell me more about yourself," she said, "as we are about to have a long and leisurely lunch together!"

"I have two brothers. My mother is still alive. I have an ex-wife who hates me and two gorgeous daughters who love me, but they have their own lives and are far are too busy for their old dad."

"You must have been very young when you got married!"

"I was snatched from the cradle! Twenty-five actually. But my wife would say we were only together for a couple of months in all of our years of marriage. She hated it that I worked so hard and in hindsight now she was right. I never got to see the kids when they were small but I was driven by my career and didn't appreciate what I had."

"You were only trying to provide for your family," Nicky interrupted.

"Yes and no. I really wanted to prove to myself and everyone that knew me that I was capable – it goes back to my roots I guess …"

Nicky put her hand on his knee. "Go on – if you want to, of course!"

Stephen shook his head. "There are no big skeletons in my closet – it's a fairly common story really. I wasn't my parents' favourite – my older brother was destined for greatness and is a surgeon in James's Street. He was always the brains of the family.

My younger brother was my mother's favourite and he was allowed do whatever he wanted. My father was a Guard – which was a good job back then but they put all the family resources into sending my brother to college. My younger brother is a self-trained artist and is still supported by my mother and a poor unfortunate girl who has been living with him for years."

Nicky was entranced by his story. "Did you go to college?"

Stephen laughed and shook his head. "No way – I was advised to go out and get a job. I was lucky that I was sent to a good school – my father's brother was a Jesuit so we all managed to get into Belvedere without paying full fees. I was dyslexic and told very early on in my schooling that academia was not for me. But I was good at rugby and I got a job after my Leaving Cert and was lucky enough to get some good breaks in the property business at the right time. I suppose you could say my good fortune has been down to timing."

"What does your family think of you now?"

"My father died four years ago – he always preferred my older brother and never really acknowledged how well I have done. As for my mother, she puts no value on money or achievement and spends most of her time worrying about my younger brother. He has a bit of a drink problem – it's kind of in the family." He sipped his drink. "Have you any siblings?"

Nicky shook her head. "I'm an only child and my dad died when I was fifteen. I lived with my mum until she died a few years ago."

Stephen was anxious to know more about her son and especially his father. "So were you living with your son's father?"

Nicky shook her head. "No. To be honest, I've a disastrous history with relationships. Daniel's dad was a guy I met when I was studying in Trinity. It was a brief affair and he fled the country when I announced that I was pregnant."

"That must have been tough – bringing a child up on your own."

"I had my mum to help which meant that I was able to have a career so I was lucky that way. Daniel's brilliant but now I'm beginning to realise that he doesn't need me any more and I need something, or someone, in my life. He'll be in college in a couple of years himself and then I'll never see him!"

"I have to say you're right. I only get to see my daughters when they're looking for something." He paused for a moment, sipped his drink and smiled. "They are good girls though."

It warmed Nicky to think that he had a good relationship with his daughters. The afternoon was beginning to feel like a date and as the waiter escorted them to their table Nicky could feel admiration growing for this kind man. She was conscious of an increasing attraction between them.

To Rachel and Alex the journey downtown to Chelsea seemed to take an age although traffic was brisk and without delay. They both sighed with relief as the cab pulled up outside Alex's brownstone apartment block.

"Not long now," he whispered in her ear as he stretched forward to pay the driver.

Trembling, Rachel stood at his side while Alex opened the front door. He ran his fingers along her spine as she mounted the first flight of stairs, making her quiver even more.

Each flight of steps felt like Everest as they continued to climb, expectant of what was surely inevitable.

The front door of his apartment swung open as he pushed it in with force. They stepped inside and he slammed it with irreverence. A pile of canvases fell over and onto the floor but Alex ignored them. Peeling back her shirt from her shoulders he buried his head behind her ear before moving slowly to her cheek and finally lips.

Rachel trembled with every tantalising kiss. As he continued to unravel her clothing like the paper from a shiny Easter egg, she let out small moans of pleasure and expectancy. She didn't know how she got to the next room but suddenly she was standing next to the bed and then he was slowly and carefully lowering her on to it. As she felt his hand rub along her back she flinched. Was he looking at her skin, she wondered? Could he see any marks from the blows Derek gave her shortly before leaving for New York?

Consumed by the smell of him she let her mind drift off to a euphoria that she had never before experienced. She was in such a trance she didn't even notice him slipping off his clothing and lying down on the bed beside her. He was the gentlest of lovers and fondly kissed every crevice of her body before touching her where she longed to be caressed. Her body tingled and shook with each gentle stroke as he brought her close to climax. By then she was desperate to feel him inside. She wanted him in a way that she had never wanted anyone before in her life. His love-making was so tender she felt as if she was going to melt when they came together.

She lay in his arms for ten minutes afterwards, neither of them saying a word. Only the gentle stroking of Alex's hand along her arm made any sound. She in turn explored the soft hairs that covered his perfectly formed chest with her fingertips.

"Alex, that was amazing," she said eventually and sadly – now that the extreme pleasure was ebbing, the realisation that she had committed adultery was creeping up to spoil things on her.

"You are amazing," he replied, gently stroking her face and staring at her as if trying not to blink.

Rachel became suddenly aware of the other bodies hanging in canvases scattered around the room. They weren't all on the wall although it was difficult to see the brick in places. Some were on the floor and some were resting on chairs and drawers. Most of the paintings were figurative and they were all painted with zest and a remarkable use of colour. Rachel was no art critic but she could see something special in his work.

"I like your paintings," she said, staring at the largest canvas that hung on the wall directly in front. "Who is she?"

Alex turned to look at the canvas and smiled. "It's my sister. That was painted after we took a trip to Walden Pond one fall."

"Where's that?"

"Not too far from where I grew up – outside Boston."

"Where do you exhibit your work?"

"I've a couple of regular galleries that take my stuff – there's one on Twenty-fifth Street that takes commissions so I never starve!"

"It must be so exciting living here and painting for exhibitions," she sighed – her own life in a Dublin suburb seemed drab and uneventful in comparison. There were her children for compensation and she adored them but she wished that she had a relationship that completed her. Now she had even jeopardised that by giving in to lust with a stranger who she probably would never see again after tomorrow.

"You're a gorgeous woman, Rachel." Alex turned his head and saw the trickle of water escaping from the corner of her eye. Softly he wiped it away. "Hey, why are you so sad?"

"I'm married, Alex, and I have a family – I shouldn't be here with you – like this . . ."

"But we both wanted it. You only have one life, Rachel, and you need to experience it to the full."

"Sometimes I feel like I just exist – like I have no real purpose."

"You're a mom – I told you how lonely it was not having a mom at home when I was a kid. You're doing a great job!"

Rachel turned her head swiftly until she was almost touching his face with hers.

"Then why do I do everything so badly? How do I get it so wrong?"

Alex sat up in the bed. "Where does this come from, Rachel? Why these negative feelings? Everybody that meets you loves you."

Rachel shook her head. "I can't expect you to understand. I'm not easy to live with. I get it wrong all of the time. My husband is under terrible pressure in work and I annoy him."

"And what about the pressures you have minding the kids and keeping house?"

"I . . . I . . . you just don't understand. I'm not good at anything and I probably deserve it!"

Alex's face scrunched up. "Deserve what? Rachel, what are you trying to say?"

Hesitantly, Rachel rolled over on to her side and pointed to a large bluish-brown patch around the back of her ribs.

Alex's eyes widened as the bruises became clear.

"Jeez!" he gasped. "How did you get those?"

"A little going-away present from my husband."

Alex had drawn many models over the years. In art college sometimes drug addicts modelled for money – some even lived on the street – but he had never seen bruises like these. He leaned forward and kissed them ever so gently.

It was all that he could do.

The waiter was far too handsome to be working in his profession. Nicky was mesmerised by his penetrating blue eyes and blond hair as he filled her glass from the chilled bottle of Sancerre. He could be a member of the Swedish Royal family or a model for Hugo Boss. But this was the Boathouse after all and it appeared the Boathouse was something special. Nicky stared all around from her perfect corner table covered with a crisp white linen tablecloth. Everyone who sat or passed through seemed to be even more stunning than the last person she saw. Then her gaze fell on Stephen's smiling demeanour and she realised that she was with the best.person in the world to enjoy such an experience.

"What do you think so far?" Stephen asked, although he could tell that she was impressed.

"I don't think I've ever had such a gorgeous starter in my life," she said truthfully.

"Truffles were a good choice," he nodded in agreement.

Their table was a perfect vantage point for viewing the rowboats and gondolas that slowly floated by like man-made swans. The people inside the vessels were enjoying the New York sunshine as much as those in the restaurant watching them through the open windows.

"This is so nice, Stephen!" Nicky let out a little sigh. "It's all a bit like a dream."

He lifted his glass and clinked it off hers. "I don't think I've enjoyed a lunch like this since... do you know, I can't remember the last time I felt so relaxed! It's a pleasure not to have someone asking advice on shares or property."

"I don't have any cash to buy shares so that's not going to come up in conversation!"

Stephen waved over to the waiter and pointed at the now-empty bottle of Sancerre.

"Will we have another one?" he asked Nicky.

"I'm tiddly after the champagne we had first and we haven't had the main course yet!"

"That was ages ago!"

Nicky noticed that he had drunk most of the bottle without

her noticing and a part of her wondered just how he could consume so much so quickly. He seemed perfectly sober so obviously he could handle it.

"Tell me more about your life in Dublin," he said, leaning on his elbows and staring intensely at Nicky, making her feel like the only woman in the world.

"Well, I do a bit of Salsa dancing actually – I go to classes in the Floridita."

"Sounds good – can I come?"

Nicky laughed. Stephen didn't resemble the typical students who went to her Tuesday-night classes. However, if he put on a red shirt with shiny black shoes he could pass for a dark Latino lover.

"I can move, I'll tell you. When I was in Argentina on business I was brought to a tango show and the lead brought me up to dance with her – she said I only needed a little practice and I'd be able to join her on stage sometime!"

She didn't know if he was joking and she didn't care. They were having such a wonderful easy time together and she didn't want the meal to end.

Conor and Eve stepped out into the bright sunshine, leaving Town and their revealing lunch behind. As they paid the bill Conor had asked the maître d' to contact him if the earring was found but he hadn't held out much hope.

"Where are you off to now?" Conor asked. He was starting to enjoy the cat and mouse game with Eve where she revealed tiny bits of herself but only by accident.

Eve took her phone out of her bag to check for messages but was disappointed when her text to Stephen hadn't been answered. She really needed to hunt him down – she had little over twenty-four hours left in the city to charm him.

"I'm not really sure – I might just go back to the hotel," she said. Stephen had to go back there eventually.

Conor was disappointed as he hadn't found the right moment to approach the subject of the subway and, though he was quite sure, he still wanted confirmation of the fact she was the woman he had rescued.

As Eve looked impatiently at her watch, he decided just to ask her outright.

"Eve, were you in New York in February?" he asked. "When we had the bad spell of snow?"

Eve looked up at him and furrowed her eyebrows. "I think so – well, early February – we had our AGM. Why?"

Conor decided that it was best to plough ahead, now that he had started. He took a deep breath.

"One morning on the subway a woman fell onto the track …" He felt foolish now that he was asking her – what if she didn't have a clue what he was talking about? "And … someone jumped down and rescued her . . ."

Eve's eyes widened. "Really?" There was a pause, then she said, "I never get the subway . . . Just for Coffee always supply courtesy cars." Her hesitancy showed that she was lying.

Conor had his answer.

An empty yellow cab passed at that instant. He raised his hand as it pulled to a stop beside them.

"There's your cab, Eve."

"Do you want a lift downtown?"

Conor shook his head. "No, you're okay. I'll go hook up with Rachel – she should be finished in the Met by now."

Eve nodded as she sat in the cab. "Thanks for lunch – it was nice."

Conor closed the door of the cab and waved as it drove off.

Even though she had implicitly denied she was the woman he had picked off the train tracks, a gut instinct told him that she was.

Eve moved about uncomfortably on the black leather seat of the cab. How did Conor know about the incident in the subway? It would be the most remarkable coincidence if he was the man who had rescued her.

She could remember very little of the event – nothing of being carried off the tracks.

How could he have known that it was her – as he had implied? There might have been something about it in *The New York Times* but she had never identified herself and she hadn't left any details. Unless he was just a passerby who had witnessed the event?

Why hadn't he said anything before? Perhaps he was unsure if it was her. He had often looked at her strangely since that first night. Then she remembered her glasses. People often didn't recognise her with her glasses on.

All the way back in the cab she toyed with the idea of Conor being the one who had saved her. She really didn't want to be reminded of that incident ever again but she naturally wanted to know if Conor had been her rescuer. That would be so extraordinary. She paid the driver and walked slowly into the hotel and up to the reception desk.

She needed to clear her head of the entire matter and focus on her new mission – if she was going to get to know Stephen Delaney any better. She did have a masterstroke up her sleeve, however – she was the one who had to find him an appropriate partner and she could make sure that he never got to date a woman who was suitable and use her own charms on him in the meantime.

After all, there was no fear of her ever finding true love again

185

as long as she lived. Deep down she believed that there was only ever one man for her and there would never be anyone to come close to him – and he was buried under a pile of rubble. By now he would be in a landfill somewhere outside the city – in an anonymous grave.

"Can I help you?" the receptionist asked politely as Eve stood in a daze in front of the desk.

Eve shook her head and tried to bring her thoughts back to the present.

"Sorry!" she said, standing numb and confused. "I was wondering if you have seen Mr Delaney – is he back yet?"

"I have a message here for him and a package but there was no reply from his room ten minutes ago."

Eve walked away without replying. She wanted to go to her suite and sit in the bath and try and wash the torrent of emotions and thoughts that Conor had conjured up out of her head.

Alex walked around the apartment, so comfortable in his nakedness that it made Rachel laugh.

"Are you not worried that my brother might be looking for me?"

"I sent him a text saying that we were still in the Met!"

"You are wicked!" She hesitated and breathed deeply. "And so am I!"

Alex threw himself on the bed and put his hand out to caress the side of Rachel's pale face.

"You are not and I won't let you talk about yourself like that – not in front of me anyway!"

Rachel shook her head. "I can't believe what I have just done."

"It was unbelievable all right but we did nothing wrong. We're two consenting adults, right? Grabbing this short time that we've stolen from the universe!"

Rachel stared deeply into his brown eyes. She loved the way he spoke. He had a way about him that made everything all right. But she was thousands of miles from home and she needed to make contact with her brother and get some semblance of reality back into her life before she returned to Dublin.

"I have to ring Conor," she said, fumbling beside the bed to find her bag. "This was lovely, Alex, but I'm a wife and mother first."

Alex reached out and caught her wrist in a way that made her wince and jerk away.

She had been programmed to believe that wrist-grabbing was a prelude to something more sinister.

"Rachel — why did you jerk?" Alex was appalled to see this beautiful woman staring back at him like a frightened creature.

Rachel pulled her wrist away. "I really have to phone Conor!"

"That's not it. Rachel, I'd never hurt you — or anyone. Even the thought of doing such harm makes me physically sick!" He gently stroked her arm. "You may be a mother and wife but you're a person first. You deserve the right to feel safe in your own home and that's something you don't have as you've just shown!"

Rachel threw her eyes up to heaven and bit on her lip. She knew that he was telling the truth but she didn't feel like she was capable of being herself any more.

"I have to call Conor," she said again.

This time he let her get her phone.

But, she thought, what was she going to say to Conor? How was she going to explain her presence in Alex's flat? She hung up abruptly before he answered and turned to Alex.

"We have to get out of here — where will we say we'll meet him?"

"Tell him we're in Tarts. By the time he makes it downtown we'll be there!"

Rachel spoke briefly and abruptly to her brother.

She didn't feel the same as she had before going to Alex's apartment. She wasn't sure how she felt now but she knew that she would never be the same again.

The waiters arrived at the table in duplicate with large silver covers keeping the delights of the main course under wrap long enough to tantalise their taste buds even more. As the covers revealed the delicious dishes of pork and duck, Nicky laughed in delight.

The waiters retreated and Stephen put his hand gently on hers.

Nicky felt a sudden urge to kiss him. She wondered why she had stopped him in the carriage earlier. Her eyes widened and this time Stephen knew that he wasn't going to be pushed away. She pursed her lips and moved her head close enough to his so that he could easily reach them. As they briefly met and retreated Nicky realised that she had to have more. She wanted to kiss him again and not in this public place but privately where she could get to know him better.

"Bon appetit!" he said.

Nicky carefully spooned the delicious vegetables onto her plate from the dish in front of her and then eagerly picked up her knife and fork.

As the first tasty morsel reached her lips, her phone rang out. She was tempted to ignore it as Eve had been texting her more than once and she really didn't want to be disturbed by her or anyone. But this was a phone call, not a text, and she felt obliged to answer.

"Excuse me a moment," she said to Stephen.

As she drew the phone to her ear nothing could have prepared her for the news she was about to receive.

Conor sat at one of the two small tables outside Once Upon A Tart. If Rachel and Alex had phoned from here, they certainly weren't here any more. His suspicions had been right and Rachel and Alex were now more than likely in a post-coital embrace and he wanted to thump his best friend. How dare he take advantage of her naivety while she was here on holiday?

Two figures came into focus as they rounded the corner of the street. Conor knew that the best thing to do was to stay calm but he didn't feel like it. He wanted to go straight up and confront Alex but that would only serve to upset Rachel. He bit his tongue as they walked slowly up to him with guilt etched all over their faces.

"Hi, Conor," Rachel said first. "The Met was fantastic – what can I get you inside?"

"I've got a coffee, thanks."

The curtness of his reply told her a multitude. She gave Alex a nod and he simply said "Americano" in a way that suggested his relations with Rachel were now on a different plane.

When she had disappeared out of sight Alex took a seat next to Conor and waited for the onslaught.

"What the hell do you think you're playing at?" Conor demanded. "She's a married woman – not that that seems to matter to you!"

Alex was ready for the attack and he had his answer. "She may be married but, man, she sure isn't happy."

"Hold on a second – you've only just met her – I've known her all my life and even though Derek wouldn't be my favourite person in the world he's still my brother-in-law and you shouldn't be messing her about."

Alex looked directly at Conor – not flinching for a second. "Just how well do you think you know your sister?"

"That's none of your business – I want to know what you got up to?"

Alex raised his eyebrows enigmatically. "Well, I'd make it my business if I were you. Your sister isn't who she makes herself out to be at all – not by a long shot."

Conor's face turned red. "I won't have you talk about her like that!"

Alex lifted his hand in defence. "Listen, man, I don't want to fight with you but there's a much bigger picture going on in her life and I think it would be good if you asked her how she really is – I mean, this is huge – so huge that a little fling with me isn't even the tip of the iceberg."

Conor shook his head adamantly. "What are you trying to say?"

"I'm just saying she's in trouble, man – big trouble. And I'd rather you heard it from her than me. Listen, I'll just go. Tell her to call me as soon as you guys have talked. I'll be in my apartment – okay, man?"

Conor watched Alex walk away and was left feeling even more anxious than before. He hadn't a clue what Alex was talking about.

Rachel arrived at the table with a laden tray.

"Where's Alex?" she asked, putting the tray down.

"He's gone back to his place."

She said nothing but looked startled, even upset.

Conor stared at his sister as she took the seat opposite. "Rachel, please, can you tell me – what's going on?"

Rachel put her elbows on the table and sank her head heavily into her hands. The last thing she felt like after committing adultery was a third degree from her brother about Alex. She raised her head to confront Conor.

But then, a thought struck her. Now that Alex knew her dreadful secret, had he gone and spilled the beans to her brother so quickly? Looking at Conor's solemn and troubled face, she knew that Alex had. She should have known not to trust him.

He had seemed so sincere and kind and now ... She felt sick inside.

"What's he told you?" she whispered.

"It's what he hasn't told me that intrigues me," Conor said vehemently.

So he hadn't told him everything. Maybe she could retreat from this situation after all. "I don't need this, Conor – I came here for a break, not a life-changing makeover."

"I need to know what you told him that you wouldn't tell me – I mean, I am your brother after all!"

Rachel nodded. "That you are, but there are some things best unsaid. You have been here for years, Conor – we see each other intermittently but what do we really know of each other's lives?"

"I thought I knew you well!"

Rachel wiped her face with the palms of her hands. "Nobody knows me well, Conor. And do you want to know why? I don't even know myself any more!"

"You're not making any sense."

"I never make sense – I make sandwiches – I make beds – I do taxi service for my kids and ..."

There was something stopping her from saying it. There was always something stopping her and it was the fear of not being believed. None of her friends or neighbours in Portmarnock would believe that she was a human punch-bag for her husband. There were times when she even denied herself the luxury of believing what was happening to her.

But if she was ever going to get out of her situation she needed to be truthful and tell her family. Conor was probably the best one to start with – after all, he was far enough away to keep a secret.

"Are you going to tell me what it is?" Conor demanded.

Rachel sighed – she was left with no choice.

"Derek hits me," she blurted.

Conor furrowed his eyebrows. "What do you mean 'hits'?"

"I mean – he beats me."

Conor's scrunched-up face only confirmed her worst suspicions. If he didn't believe her – who would?

Then she thought of Alex. He hadn't doubted her for a second – but then, he had seen the evidence. Why had he told Conor? Why had he betrayed her like that? Then she realised that she didn't doubt him either. If he had betrayed her confidence it was because he cared about her and wanted to protect her. Now she wished he hadn't left. She needed him to talk to her brother again. Maybe he could get him to believe her.

NINE

The colour completely drained from Nicky's face as she put the phone down on the table.

"What is it? Who was that?" Stephen asked urgently. He could tell that something dreadful had happened but Nicky had hardly spoken through the entire phone call.

Nicky rose to her feet and looked around in total panic.

"I've got to get home," she said frantically.

Stephen stood up and gestured for her to sit back down. Whatever was wrong in Dublin she was too far away to be going anywhere quickly.

Nicky started to sob out loud and heads at the tables nearby started to turn.

"It's Daniel – he's been injured playing rugby and I have to get home."

Stephen held onto her arm gently and firmly while handing her a napkin to wipe the tears from her cheeks.

"Hold on, he's been hurt but it probably isn't serious – I

broke a couple of bones over the years playing rugby. Where is he now?"

"He's on his way to hospital. They think he may have broken his neck and they wouldn't let me speak to him."

Stephen didn't want to sound alarmist but it was the worst possible injury and he had lost a friend in school to a broken neck. The only thing he could do was calm her down until he got her on a flight home. He put his arm around her with great care in a gesture of support and empathy.

"Don't worry! You'll be home soon – leave it to me to book a flight. Rachel can pack your stuff and bring it back – is there anything you need urgently from the hotel or can we go straight to the airport?"

Nicky shook her head as the trickles of salty tears continued to flow down her cheeks.

"Your passport?"

Once her passport had been located in the zipper pocket at the side of her handbag, he assured her that she had everything she needed.

Stephen beckoned to the waiter for the bill and asked for them to order a cab.

"Come on outside and we'll have a fag while we're waiting."

"What about Rachel?"

"Give me your phone. I'll call her – you just relax and we'll go straight to JFK. The five forty is a direct flight and it will be ready for boarding in an hour."

Nicky touched his hand as they stood up.

"Thanks, Stephen. I don't know what I'd have done if I was on my own getting that call."

Stephen handled the next hour like a military operation. In the cab he phoned ahead and managed to book her a seat on the five forty flight. Then on reaching the airport he sat Nicky down and, taking her passport, ticket and credit card, approached the Aer Lingus desk to deal with the change of flight and any extra charge. A few minutes later he beckoned her over, everything arranged.

Stephen held her hand as they made their way to the boarding gate. He wished that he could join her on the flight so she wouldn't have to be alone but he really had to be at the meeting the next day – it was the reason he had travelled all the way to New York. Now he felt as though his reasons for travelling had been to find the woman he had longed to meet but was never given the opportunity to before.

He hesitated at the gate, then said, "Ring me when you get back and let me know how Daniel is."

Nicky nodded. "Thanks," she said, giving him a polite but distracted kiss on the cheek.

He watched her disappear without looking back and felt as if he was letting a real chance for happiness pass him by. He suddenly realised that she didn't have his number and, worse than that, he didn't have hers. All of his communications by phone had been to Eve. At least he could get it off her, he thought, and breathed a sigh of relief.

Rachel hung up abruptly with her mouth half open in disbelief.

"What is it?" Conor asked.

"That was Stephen – he's with Nicky and she's heading back to Dublin right now – Daniel had an accident playing rugby."

"I hope it's not serious."

Rachel shook her head. "I don't know how serious. I didn't talk to her and by the sound of it she's going home unsure herself."

"What a bummer! I'm sorry your weekend isn't turning out for your friend, sis."

"It's not exactly turning out the way I had planned!"

Conor looked at his fragile and anxious sister. She had made a huge revelation about her life and he had to believe her but he found it so difficult to imagine Derek as a wife-beater. He could be pompous and didactic underneath the subtle charm that he used with everyone but he was never a physical type of guy in any way. Why couldn't he believe her as easily as Alex obviously could?

"What do you want to do?" he asked.

"I don't know – I need to clear my head."

"I think you need a drink!" Conor said with a smile. "Why don't we go to the Spotted Pig?"

"Will you tell Alex where we're going so he can join us?"

Conor nodded grudgingly. It was his sister's last evening in New York and it was up to him to make it as pleasant as possible for her.

Nicky took her seat listlessly. The air stewardess had kindly ushered her to the seat as if she were a visually impaired person. She was in a trance since taking the phone call earlier and had her seatbelt on before she noticed that the seats were unlike the ones she was familiar with.

A mature and perfectly groomed stewardess came up to her with a crystal glass filled with champagne and a copy of *the Irish Times*. Only then did Nicky look around and notice that there were only four seats in each row and the man in the seat beside her had his footrest raised to take the weight off his feet.

"Is this first class?" she asked the woman holding the silver tray with the perfectly balanced champagne glasses.

"Yes, madam."

"Oh, I shouldn't be here ..."

"Have you got your boarding pass?" the stewardess asked

politely. It wouldn't be the first time someone had accidentally wandered into the wrong seat.

Nicky searched her pockets and produced the card. It said 3B in clear bold print.

"This is the correct seat, madam," said the stewardess, glancing at the card.

Then the thought struck Nicky that Stephen had handled the change of flight at the desk before boarding. He probably took it for granted that first class was the only way to travel but she cringed when she thought about the weight it would put on her already overly stretched credit card. Anyway this was no time to be worrying about money – she had to get home to Daniel and as quickly as possible too. The glass of champagne might help the journey pass faster. Nicky raised her hand and took both the glass and the newspaper.

"Thank you," she said, putting the paper on her knee although she knew there was no way she felt like reading it at the moment.

All she could think about was her son and what state he must be in. Although he was a big strapping lad on the cusp of manhood he was still her little boy and after all there was only the two of them. It was another of those moments when she wished she had a companion – ideally a father for Daniel. He had missed out on so much at the most important times in his life. All the special occasions and rites of passage that involved family were sadly lacking that second parent as a support and carer. She had muddled through well considering and he was turning out to be a fine lad with top grades in school. He was popular with the other guys in the class and on the couple of occasions that he had been to socials where members of the opposite sex were involved he always grunted that he'd had a good time. It was enough to assure her that he was a good mixer and could easily carry himself in all healthy aspects of life as a teenager. But now she worried. What if this injury was as sinister as it sounded? Karen had been so good to let him stay with her for the weekend and she felt sorry for her now that this had happened while he was in her care. Her son had been such a good friend to Daniel and made him feel like a member of the extended family. But Karen had made out on the phone that he might have broken a bone in his neck and then told her not to worry. But what else would she have said from so far across the Atlantic? *Your son is in a life-threatening situation and get here quickly?* She didn't think so. Karen was perfectly clear that it would be best if she got home soon and that was enough. If it was a broken wrist she probably wouldn't have told her at all.

Nicky took a look at her empty glass and hardly remembered sipping from it. Had she built up such a capacity for alcohol after two nights in New York? She hadn't even got a chance to stay a third. The lunch with Stephen had been so enjoyable but the abrupt way that it came to an end said it all about her luck in love. Maybe she should forget about men completely. If Daniel's injuries were bad she would be busy for the foreseeable future nursing him back to health. For the moment she had to believe that they could be remedied because the alternative was unthinkable.

Stephen felt a tremendous sense of loss when he returned to his large suite in the Soho Grand. The lunch in the Boathouse was going so well and he was feeling emotions that he hadn't experienced for years. The thought of Nicky on her own on the long journey home left him feeling sad and helpless. He went over to the mini-bar and poured himself a straight whiskey. It was the surest way to relax and the safest company by far. He could always rely on it and it didn't get destroyed like flesh and blood and bones. He said a quiet prayer for Nicky's son even though he wasn't religious. It was all he felt he could do.

Suddenly the phone in his suite rang out and he rushed to get it, hoping that it might be Nicky before she took off but realising quickly that the voice on the other end of the line belonged to another Irishwoman.

"Hi, Eve," he said, not trying to hide the disappointment in his tone. "Sorry about earlier – what can I do for you?"

Eve cleared her throat. "I was hoping I could do something for you, Stephen – have you plans for later or are you still with Nicky?"

Stephen took a stiff gulp from his whiskey glass. "Nicky has gone back to Dublin – I've just come from JFK a few minutes ago. Her son has been involved in a rugby accident."

Eve was shocked. As far as Stephen was concerned, Nicky worked for Just for Coffee and so a part of her was furious with Nicky for telling him so much personal information and taking off for Ireland without even informing her. What impression did that give of the company? "I'm surprised she hasn't told me about this, as her superior. I hope it's not serious."

"We don't know at this stage. But don't worry about keeping pretences up with me, Eve. I know that she doesn't work for Just for Coffee – she told me not to say anything to you but I guess in the scheme of things, with her son ill, none of that matters."

Eve was hugely embarrassed and couldn't come up with a suitable response. She just muttered "No, no, of course it doesn't." This was typical of Nicky – she always put herself first and disregarded what others needed – especially when it came to Eve. Her son had probably only sprained his wrist and now she was causing a commotion with one of the most important clients that Eve had ever had on her books. She wished she had never called Rachel and let the two girls back into her life. "I'm sure he'll be fine," she added lamely. "Um . . . what are your plans for the rest of the day and this evening?"

"I don't have any – I'll probably stay in my room for dinner."

Eve's head buzzed. She could call on him in his room – it was only across the corridor.

"I hate eating on my own," she said, "but I'll probably do the same – I need to catch up on some work before my return to London tomorrow."

Stephen swirled the remaining contents of his tumbler around and finished it off with a quick gulp. "I'll talk to you before you go, I'm sure. See you, Eve," he said abruptly and hung up in a rush to refill his glass.

Eve hadn't had time to say goodbye but that didn't bother her because she had no intention of that being the last he would hear from her that night. It was easy – she would call around to his suite, looking casual but seductive, and woo him until he no longer needed a dating agency.

Conor stood up. "I'm going for a wiz," he said.

It was a term that Rachel hadn't heard in years but one that her sibling had always used when needing to go to the toilet. It meant that she was finally on her own with Alex again and he responded by putting his hand on her arm as soon as Conor was out of sight.

"Rachel, you've gotta stay with me tonight," he urged. "It's your last night in New York!"

"Thanks for the compliment, Alex," she said in a tone that told him she couldn't.

"I'm totally crazy about you, Rachel, and you gotta let me draw you – even for a few minutes."

"And we both know what that would lead to, don't we?" she said with a small smile.

"Have you forgiven me for telling Conor that something was wrong?" Alex asked with doe-shaped eyes. "Did you tell him that your husband beats you?"

Rachel lowered her head. She didn't want to say that her brother didn't believe her but he was still relatively silent on the issue.

"You left me with no choice but I'm glad he knows, for what it's worth."

"What's he going to do about it?" Alex asked with urgency in his voice.

"I'm not sure he totally believes me!"

Alex shook his head. "You're kidding, right?"

"Conor knows Derek and he can be very charming – even though he's not exactly Conor's favourite relative, he finds it hard to believe that he would hit me."

"Did he say that?"

Rachel shook her head sadly. "He didn't have to – I could tell. Maybe when I've gone home you can approach the subject again?"

"Rachel, you can't go back to him. You're in danger."

Rachel threw her head back and laughed. "Well, if he was going to kill me he'd have done it by now."

"You gotta be kiddin' – you have to tell someone. The police?"

Rachel shook her head. "The police wouldn't want to know. And I have three children, remember, and absolutely no way of supporting them – so I must stay with Derek. And I know for a fact that Derek would take it out on me any way that he could – even if it meant doing it through the kids."

"He's a monster to make those marks on your back!"

Rachel shook her head again but this time even harder. "That's just where you're wrong. Nobody would think he's a monster. He's a pillar of society in fact. He gives generously to all the charities – even drags us all to Mass on cold Sunday mornings!"

"The church always gets that kinda creep – even over here. I'm glad I'm a pagan."

"I don't see any way out of the life that I have built for myself. I couldn't even buy a bottle of milk – I have no income of my own whatsoever!"

"You've been working in the home – doesn't that count for anything?"

Rachel shrugged. "Not that I know of and anyway I love my family – I couldn't rock the boat and Derek would make sure I suffered if I did."

Conor approached with a fresh round of drinks on a tray and a big smile. He intended to make sure that he kept close tabs on his sister for the rest of her stay.

"What do you think of this place, Rach?" he asked.

"It's good – like being in London – it's like an English pub, isn't it?" she said, glad to be changing the subject.

The less she talked about her situation the less she would have to think about dealing with it. She had no options – leaving the home with or without her kids was not going to happen and anyway Derek had told her, on the one occasion that she had stood up to him, that if she ever tried to leave he would kill her.

Conor heard a bleep go off in his pocket and cursed his phone. The familiar number that had plagued him all weekend was flashing in the screen.

"Hello, Mandy," he said with a sigh. "How are you feeling now?"

There was a brief pause and then his face became more animated.

"I'm not at my apartment. Have you been released from hospital? You need to go straight home!"

The saga of Mandy and Conor was becoming painful for anyone to watch and most of all painful for Conor.

"Look, Mandy, I'm not going back there tonight – call Tonya or one of your friends." He shook his head. "No, I'm not going to Pravda either and probably never again – look please, Mandy, just take care and get yourself home, okay?" He didn't wait for a detailed response and was quick to hang up. He turned to the others. "Let's do something fun tonight and go somewhere we won't find any models!"

"That's easy," Alex said. "What about the Comedy Cellar? I think we could all do with a laugh!"

"That's a great idea, man!" Conor said. "Just what you need on your last night, sis – a good laugh."

Rachel looked awkwardly at the two of them, unsure if she felt able to laugh at the prospect of the long flight home on her own tomorrow, going to an uncertain future. If having sex with Alex had shown her one thing, it was that there was another life out there where she could feel love like she hadn't with Derek since before they were married!

Eve lay in the bath of bubbles in her suite and soaked. She tried to get thoughts of Conor out of her head but she couldn't. She had jumped to all the wrong conclusions where he was concerned. His contacts with Town, the restaurant earlier, were a surprise – his recognition of her as the woman on the subway in February an even bigger one. There was something very attractive about him and she had definitely been prejudiced in her judgement of him. He knew New York very well and had been touched like everyone else who had lived through the tragedies of 9/11 – just like she had. And he was thoughtful and considerate when she lost her earring. But he was one of those arty bohemian types that she had always said she would never have a relationship with. In any case, he hadn't given any real indication that he was attracted to her.

She turned her thoughts to Stephen – a much more appropriate partner for someone of her age and status. He had children already so he wouldn't necessarily want to start a second family – which suited her very well indeed. There wasn't any real chemistry there but she was a good-looking woman and she could make him desire her – of that she was sure. The hardest part would be making him desirable to *her*. He was attractive in a powerful kind of way but the Pierce Brosnan look wasn't her typical preference. He could knock five years off by dressing younger and stopping the grey from slipping into his hair with a bottle of dye. But he was a wealthy and successful man and he was looking for a partner – otherwise he wouldn't have contacted Just for Coffee.

She stepped out of the bath and dried herself with the soft black towels that were complimentary with the room. This was a night for her sexy La Perla underwear. Then a simple wraparound top that would unravel easily and a skirt that would fall to the ground in an instant would do the job. She pondered her lace-top stockings and decided that they were definitely needed to complete the ensemble. She would leave Stephen no choices.

Her make-up was flawless after ten minutes of pampering and preening and she slipped her stocking-covered feet into her relatively new Christian Louboutin black high heels. She adored the signature red leather soles and admired how they looked on her feet.

Now she was finally ready! She reached into the mini-bar and took out a bottle of Bollinger. He had the same glasses in his suite as she had so there was no point in carrying them across.

She slipped her room key and mobile into her tiny Prada handbag and pulled the door closed behind her. Although she wasn't sure of the reception she would get, at least she had her armour in place. When she reached his door she gave a loud short knock and was startled by the speed at which it opened.

Stephen stood at the other side of the door with a look of total shock on his face.

"I thought you were room service!" he said distractedly. By his glazed expression and the smell of alcohol on his breath he had obviously had a lot to drink.

Eve wasn't deterred nonetheless. "I hope you don't mind me calling – I was just thinking maybe you'd want some company?"

Stephen looked down at the bottle of champagne that Eve was swinging in her left had.

"You don't have any whiskey – do you?"

Eve was close to suggesting that he'd had enough whiskey – but she had come with the intention of seducing him.

"Only champagne!" she said, moving into the suite after him.

"Would you shut the door, please!" he said, waving his lit cigarette at her. "I have to go back out to the balcony or I'll probably set some bloody alarm off or get arrested or something."

Eve followed him out onto the veranda, to the spectacular view of Manhattan that sparkled all around. The table on the deck was littered with an over-full ashtray and empty baby bottles of Irish whiskey and a few of brandy. Great – Eve thought – he's sloshed. How do you seduce a man who is intent on drinking his bar dry?

"Can I get you a drink?" he said.

It was obvious to Eve that he was totally oblivious to the

huge effort she had put into getting ready for him. Still she was undeterred.

"I'll have a little bubbly if that's okay with you?"

Stephen took the bottle of Bollinger from her and started to open it clumsily.

"Would you get some glasses from the cabinet inside, please," he said as he wrestled with the cork.

Eve made it back to him just in time as the frothy bubbles started to escape from the top of the bottle.

"Will you have some too?"

"May as well," he shrugged, taking a glass from her. "They are very slow with the whiskey."

"I was going to order something for dinner and then I thought I'd see what you were doing," she said seductively. "We could order something from room service and watch the sunset over Manhattan."

Stephen squinted from over the top of his glass of bubbly. It was odd that she should be so concerned about him now but he could do with the company. Otherwise he would be left on his own, drinking into the small hours.

"Allright – but I'm not very hungry," he said. "Why don't you order something for me?"

It wasn't exactly the start to the evening that Eve had anticipated or wanted but she would make the best of the situation. She went back into the suite and scanned the room service menu for something that she would eat herself. He was easy to order for – a steak well done with a side order of fries. She found a pasta dish that looked appetising and phoned in her order. It was not exactly the perfect set-up for an evening of seduction but she was resourceful!

Rachel felt as though she was flanked by two bodyguards. Alex and Conor were vying to see who could get closest. It wasn't how she had imagined her last night in New York. She was getting very worried about Nicky and wished she had spoken to her personally before she took off on the flight. All she got was a text telling her that she was sorry and would ring her next day to tell how Daniel was. By now she would be well across the Atlantic Ocean.

Conor and Alex slowed down as they came to a gate that led to a basement cellar.

"This is it," Conor said. "I've got tickets."

The three made their way into the dark bar – lit only by lamps that hung low over the dark wooden tables. The brick walls were covered with effigies of some of the famous American and European comedians who had played gigs in the cellar over the years. Conor led them to a small table in the corner and they sat on the hard benches. A waitress rushed over the minute she spotted them and took a tab.

"What'll you have, Rach?" Conor asked.

"A beer!" she said.

It was her last night of decadence and she would rebel one more time before she returned to Derek's world where she could only drink one glass of wine in his presence per night.

Alex nodded. "A beer for me too, man."

Now that they were all sitting and the warm-up act hadn't yet taken his position, Conor wondered if it was such a good idea after all. The beers had hardly arrived when his phone bleeped with a text message that he had to strain his eyes to read. It was from Nat Lincoln, the record producer who had fixed him up with the guitarist to shoot next day.

Can you meet me in Pravda at about eleven – I'd like you to meet Jim. Thanks Nat

Conor could see that it wasn't a question by the thanks at the end of the text. Of all the bars in Manhattan why did Nat have to choose the place where Mandy was going to be?

"I don't believe it," he said taking a swig out of his Tiger beer.

"What's wrong?" Rachel asked.

"I've just had a text from a guy who wants me to meet someone in Pravda – that's where Mandy's going."

Just then the warm-up act came out on stage – he was African American and had the crowd reeling in seconds but Conor didn't feel like smiling. If he left Rachel with Alex they would end up back at his friend's place and he wouldn't see his sister until morning. If he went to Pravda there would be a big scene with Mandy and probably tears and tantrums. If he didn't go to Pravda, Nat might be mad and then he mightn't get the gig.

Rachel let out a loud giggle and Conor could see that a night of laughter was just what she needed. So what if she had a good a time with his friend? Alex was a good guy and maybe a short affair wouldn't spell the end of her marriage – although right now he wasn't sure what sort of a marriage his sister had after her revelation earlier.

Rachel turned and saw the look of distress etched all over Conor's face. "What are you going to do?"

Conor shook his head. "I don't know!"

"Why don't we all go to Pravda? That way Alex and I can distract Mandy and you can do business with your producer friend."

That was a perfect solution.

"You don't mind, do you, Rach?"

She shook her head. "This place is all right but I wouldn't mind doing some bar-hopping – it's my last night in New York!"

Eve opened the door for the room-service waiter. She had managed to curtail the amount Stephen was drinking. A good plate of food was needed to soak up the rest of the alcohol and then she could set to work on her mission.

"That's okay – I'll bring it inside," she told the waiter and gave him a tip from her tiny handbag that she had left on the entrance table.

She rolled the trolley covered in crisp white linen out to the deck and Stephen stood up to help her as she approached.

"Thish looks good," he said, removing the silver lid from the platter.

By now night had fallen on the city and the illuminations from the hundreds of buildings dotted around the city made the most spectacular backdrop to their meal.

"Not many restaurants have a view like this," she commented.

"No. It'sh a good choice. I usually shtay uptown in the Waldorf," he said and gave a small hiccup. "Thish is a mush better locashion – for me and work." He searched under the table. "Where'sh the wine?"

"I didn't order any," Eve said, hoping that maybe he would take a break from drinking alcohol.

Instead he went into the suite and searched through the bar. A bottle of white Californian wine that he was familiar with came to hand and he reached for the corkscrew from the top drawer of the drinks cabinet.

Eve watched as he took a generously filled glass of white wine and held it up to his lips. At this rate he wouldn't be able to eat his meal without falling into it. She would have to be quick if she was going to make her move. She held out her glass, urging him to pour a large measure of the wine from the bottle before he drank it all. In an effort to encourage him to eat something she started to eat herself even though she wasn't hungry.

Instead he gulped back the wine and refilled his glass. Then, almost tripping over, he took his seat in front of Eve and tried to cut his steak. When it proved difficult he ate some fries instead. His silence spoke a multitude.

He's totally sloshed, Eve thought. What am I going to do?

Taking the bottle of wine in hand, she stood up.

"Do you mind if I put this in the fridge to cool it down a little – it's quite hot out here."

Stephen waved his approval with his fork and returned to his fries.

Eve poured it down the sink in the bathroom and returned to the table with a spring in her step.

"How is your food?" she asked, her tone as if they were sitting in a cosy intimate restaurant.

Stephen nodded and arched his eyebrows. "For room shervish itsh fine," he slurred as he sat back on his seat, leaving his steak untouched. He reached into his shirt pocket, took out a packet of Marlboro and lit up a cigarette.

It would normally irk Eve if someone did this without asking but she had other things on her mind. She hoped she had got to him before he passed the brink of intoxication. Each drag he took from the cigarette reminded her of how much she disliked smokers. However, the balance of his accumulated personal wealth more than compensated.

She had to think out her next move carefully. This was a game and she was reminded of the other night on Thompson Street as she walked with Conor and watched the Greenwich Village locals playing chess. The next move was crucial and it would make or break her chances with Stephen.

"Would you like a coffee?" she asked.

Stephen shook his head. Then like a bold child he jumped to his feet.

"Hey, they never shent up my whishkey!"

Eve had to take the opportunity any way that she could. She jumped to her feet and sauntered over until she was close enough to smell him.

"How could you need more alcohol when we are on top of the world? Look, the sky has turned to black while we ate and now the city is twinkling as if it's putting on a show just for us!"

Stephen took a long drag from his cigarette and looked out over the balcony at the Empire State Building in the distance as if it was the first time that he had noticed the stunning view of Manhattan at night.

"Ish very nice!" he said with another giveaway hiccup.

Eve took the cigarette from his hand and rested it on the ashtray in the middle of the table.

"And it's very nice to be spending it with you, Stephen," she said seductively as she moved closer until she could smell the cigarettes and alcohol on his breath. It didn't deter her. She had a mission and she was going to succeed – no matter what the cost.

Stephen looked dazed and confused at the bright green eyes that sparkled at him. As they neared he focused on Eve's full red lips. How had he not noticed them before this? She smelt of flowers and femininity and suddenly he found those soft ripe lips on top of his and he let himself respond. He hadn't been with a woman for nearly a year and that had turned out to be a disaster. On this occasion he was taken totally unawares. Why was she kissing him? His masculine urges quickly overtook any other thoughts he might have, had he not been in an inebriated state.

Eve slipped her tongue into his mouth and the alcohol tasted bitter and sweet at the same time. He was a gentle kisser and she could tell by the way he held her waist so clumsily that the rest was going to be easy. Carefully she took his large hand in hers and started to walk backwards, leading them both into the suite. This evening she would give him an experience that he would never forget.

Pravda was only a couple of blocks away from the Comedy Cellar. A lone red lamp stood out from the top of an iron railing as the only indication that a bar was hidden underneath. Rachel looked down at the dark and ominous basement. There was a sleaziness about the place and she felt it from the moment they walked through the red velvet curtains at the entrance.

Heads turned as they strolled by candlelit cocktail tables and burgundy parlour chairs.

"This place should have pick-up joint written on the front door!" Alex whispered in her ear.

Rachel nodded but with wide eyes she surveyed her surroundings carefully.

A waiter dressed in black brushed by them, holding a round tray high up in the air with six vodka shots on it. Cyrillic lettering scribed on the low arches evoked an atmosphere of pre-Cold-War decadence.

"I know it's sleazy but it's quite nice in an old-fashioned kind of way!" Rachel observed.

"Conor hates this place," Alex whispered back. "Not just because he met Mandy here."

Rachel watched as super-thin models paraded by. "Is everyone drinking vodka?"

"Leave it to me," he said with a wink and gave an order to the barman. "Where's Conor gone?"

Rachel looked around and saw him sitting in a corner, flanked by a scruffy-looking guy in his early forties and a younger equally scruffy companion.

Alex handed her a tall glass filled with a pale yellow liquid. "Try this – it's the house special."

Rachel took a sip, observed by Alex as he took a generous gulp from his identical drink.

"It's nice!" she exclaimed. "What is it?"

"It's a Nolita – best thing about this place."

"Nolita? What's in it?"

"Well, the name means North of Little Italy – called after the neighbourhood – all I know is there's plenty of vodka in it and an apricot liqueur!"

"I like it!" Rachel sipped again. "Eh, do you think we should go over to Conor or stay here?"

Alex looked over at the three men intent in conversation in the corner. "Maybe we should leave them at it – it's nice to get you all to myself again!" he said with his eyes widening.

He didn't need to elaborate any further – his desire to spend the night with her was as strong as her desire to feel the warmth of his body against hers at least one more time.

"I'd really love to stay with you tonight but I have to go back to the hotel."

"I could always come with you?"

Rachel wanted to say yes and leave straight away but too many thoughts clouded her head. She had let herself get spun up in a web of passion and desire that she could not see through. She had a life on the other side of the Atlantic that involved more people than just her. Life would go on as normal once she returned and she didn't want to fall for Alex in a deeper way than she felt she already had.

"Today was wonderful ..." she started.

"Don't say but!" he interrupted with doe-shaped eyes.

"I did something wrong earlier – we both did – and although it was very nice I can't let myself fall in love with you,

Alex. And I'm already in danger."

Normally a woman using the word love in a sentence would have Alex running a mile but when Rachel said it it sounded different. He understood what she was trying to say because he could feel emotions around her that were different to other girls he had relationships with. She was a woman who had experienced so much of life – the pains of childbirth and childrearing, the harshness of a relationship laden with fear. How she bore it all with such gentleness and realism amazed him – he wondered how she continued on. This was a person that he could really communicate with – talk about life and feelings – and he wanted to get to know her better but they only had the chance of one more night together and he didn't want to let it slip away.

"I know what you're saying, Rachel – but I'm not too happy that you're going home tomorrow. I really wish we had more time!"

He let out a sad sigh and she reciprocated by placing her hand gently on his cheek.

"Maybe it's better that we don't have more time – maybe this is all the time we are meant to have."

Alex looked deeply into her eyes and thought he saw her soul for an instant. He had to paint her – even if he could only do it from memory. She was so beautiful and fragile that he longed to touch her. He couldn't stop himself from stealing a kiss and he leaned forward until their lips met.

Rachel embraced the moment and felt the same wave of contentment sweep over her as she had felt on the Staten Island Ferry when they had shared their first kiss. This stolen moment in amongst the dark and shadows made it even more difficult to pull away.

"Let's go over to Conor," she suggested.

Reluctantly he gave a nod.

Conor stood up as they approached.

"Nat, Jim, this is my sister Rachel – and I think you've met Alex before, Nat."

The unshaven Nat stood up and held out his hand. Clad in a black T-shirt with a skull emblazoned across it and earrings in his left ear and lower lip, he wasn't exactly as Rachel had imagined.

"I see why your brother hides a looker like you away!" Nat said with a wink.

"Oh, I'm only here on a visit – I live in Dublin."

"You've got such a cute accent – must be why I like working with Irish artists – Jim is from Ireland too," he said, gesturing to the third person at the table.

Jim's long hair, tied back in a pony-tail, and bearded face threw Rachel and she didn't recognise him until he opened his mouth.

"Pleased to mee –" He stopped speaking at the exact moment of recognition for both of them.

"James?"

He stared blankly for a second, trying to remember her second name. "Rachel – Trinity College – you did English?"

"James Holden – music!"

"You guys know each other?" Nat burst in excitedly. "That's just great – I have to go over to your little country sometime – everybody seems to know everyone!"

Nat beckoned over to the waiter. "More drinks here – these guys are having a reunion!"

Conor could tell that this was not necessarily the warmest of reunions – even if Nat couldn't. "Let's sit down," he said. "So, Jim, you went to Trinity?"

"Yeah, well, I studied music but knew that really I needed to get out and find my own sound. It's kind of Celtic rock that's inspired by the Irish musicians who fused traditional with rock in the eighties – but I've put in some dance beats – I did mixing when I was a DJ in the nineties."

Rachel was unable to speak. It was incredible that after all this time she should bump into James, the father of Nicky's child. Maybe it was just as well that Nicky went home. What was she going to say to him if he asked? By the look of him he was so obsessed by his own career maybe he wouldn't ask.

"So where are you living, Rachel?" James – now Jim – finally asked.

"I'm still in Dublin – I don't know if you remember Derek Sloan from Trinity, but I married him and we live in Portmarnock – we've three kids." She bit her lip after she mentioned kids. What if he asked about his own child? She would have to tell him the truth.

"Have you written any novels – if I remember rightly you were the star of your English class?"

Rachel flinched. The thought had never occurred to her as she cleaned and washed and cared for her family for years. Writing a novel was a dream she had back then when she had confidence and she was her own person. What on earth would she have to write about that anybody would be interested in, ferrying kids from ballet to gymnastics?

"I don't get a chance – family takes over!"

"Right," he said, nodding his head in a way that told her he was absolutely disinterested in what her life was like. "What about the other girls you were friends with – Eve and eh – eh –"

Rachel was horrified that he could hardly remember Nicky's name – the woman he left pregnant in Dublin while he shirked his responsibilities.

"Nicky," she hinted.

"Yeah, Nicky. Do you still see those girls?"

Rachel was unsure what to say – what would Nicky want her

216

to do? She couldn't possibly have any feeling for him now – but he was the biological father of her child and, even if Daniel hadn't wanted to meet his father yet, the chances were that at some time in the future he would. She had to answer quickly.

"No, I haven't seen them for years!" she said.

Alex listened avidly and wondered why she should disown her friends when talking to this guy – obviously there was a bigger story surrounding these three Irish girls and he would help by changing the subject. "So where are you playing in New York?"

Jim's eyes lit up as he began to talk about himself and his music.

"I'm playing support in Radio City for the next three nights."

"That sounds great!" Alex applauded. "And then?"

"I'm going to travel around a bit. The east coast first and then I'm going out to San Fran and LA."

He spoke like had been living in America from birth. Rachel felt sick and wondered what on earth he'd been up to for all of these years.

"Do you ever go home?"

"Been back once since I left college – for my father's funeral."

"Oh, I am sorry," Rachel said automatically. "Where have you been living?"

"Spain, Greece, then I was in Brazil for a bit. I've been here five years and finally making it doing what I love."

Alex could tell that there was something untoward about this guy. He didn't feel this way about many people but it was clear that Rachel was not enjoying the reunion either.

Just then a familiar voice cried out from halfway across the bar.

"Conor! I knew you'd come!" Mandy rushed up to the

group and draped her left arm on Conor's right shoulder like a limp lily.

Conor flinched and put on a weak smile. "Mandy – do you know Nat and Jim …"

Mandy immediately threw her hand out to Nat who took it and kissed it.

"We haven't met before because if we had I'd have remembered!" Nat said, raising his eyebrows suggestively.

Mandy giggled.

Conor wasn't sure if it was the effects of alcohol or drugs that had her so relaxed but he was glad to avoid a scene at any cost.

Mandy sat down beside Nat and he beckoned to the waiter to come over and serve a round of drinks.

Rachel observed those around. Conor was uncomfortable now that Mandy had arrived on the scene. Jim seemed uninterested in anyone there but himself and Mandy and Nat were hitting it off famously. All she wanted was to be on her own with Alex for one more night but instead she felt trapped in a scene from a play that she didn't want to be in. If only she could be transported out of here and back to the safety of Alex's apartment.

Conor gave his sister a knowing glance which she reciprocated. "We can leave if you like," he murmured. "I've said all I need to say to Nat and I've met Jim. Tomorrow's gig will be straightforward so we should be finished by lunch-time and I can hook up with you then – that sound okay?"

Rachel nodded. She had planned to spend her last morning in New York shopping. She wanted to spend some time in the Pottery Barn store and get some accessories for her house. At least that had been her plan before coming to New York. Now, however, she found it difficult to even think of her home. She longed to see her children of course but leaving New York also meant not seeing Alex again and in the short time she had spent with him she had gained so much confidence and self-esteem. Maybe she needed to go to bed and take a sleeping tablet – then it would all fade away.

Conor stood up first. "We're going, guys – enjoy the rest of your night."

Mandy looked up and was about to stand up too but Nat reached out his hand.

"You can't go on me yet – I haven't even heard your voice!"

Mandy giggled and sat back down, much to Conor's relief.

"See you tomorrow morning at nine!" he said to Jim who nodded his reply.

Alex stood up and followed Rachel and Conor out to the door.

"I'll walk her home – it's okay, man!" Conor said protectively.

"Fine. I'm going to hit the sack too. See ya tomorrow, Rachel!"

Rachel gave him a small peck, that said so much, on the cheek. "Thanks for taking me to the Met today – it was lovely."

Alex nodded. "Yeah, I really enjoyed it."

Both were talking about something else but neither needed to explain.

"Come on, sis," Conor said, putting his arm around his sister. "Let's get you home."

Rachel looked over her shoulder as Alex walked away in the opposite direction – feeling as though she had let a part of herself leave with him.

Stephen was snoring.

It was two o'clock in the morning and after a short sleep Eve was now wide awake. Her eyes felt like they had been rubbed with sandpaper and she wished she had taken her lenses out. Maybe she should go for laser eye surgery after all! She got out of the bed and reached for the black bathrobe that was hanging in the closet. She tied a knot in the belt as she walked out to the veranda and the stunning spectacle of New York at night. She loved it here but she couldn't stay. Every time she returned she was reminded of Harry and all that she had lost. She wasn't the only one to lose someone in 9/11 but she found it so hard to live with the scars and time didn't seem to make it any easier. Getting out of New York was the most painless thing to do and the best. Maybe it was time to return to Ireland. By all reports it had come a long way since she had left it.

But her heart would always remain in New York. Broken and in pieces with memories of Harry and the life that could have been – should have been. She edged out to the railings and leaned over. How easy it would be to throw her leg over the side and leap into Harry's arms where she could be at peace forever. But she didn't really believe that he would be on the other side any more. All she could imagine was an abyss. Before she met Harry she'd believed in reincarnation and after-lives and the next life – but that was before he was taken away from her.

She let out a cry – it was primal, coming from the very pit of her solar plexus. What had she done with Stephen? Why was she here? He was a good man and wealthy but there was more to life than money. She had built up a nice nest egg for herself with an apartment in London that she now owned. None of it mattered. None of it would bring Harry back. Sleeping with Stephen and everyone before him only reminded her that Harry was gone – no matter how hard she tried to move forward she was stuck.

Stuck somewhere around 7.15 a.m on September 11th 2001, the last time Harry kissed her before leaving for work.

"Hey – tell me about Jim," Conor asked as they strolled through the stillness of Washington Square. "How well did you know him?"

Rachel shook her head. "I can't believe it was him after all this time – that's the guy that Nicky and Eve went with – he's the father of Nicky's son!"

Conor seemed to have trouble believing his ears. "Are you serious? The guy that you told me about – the one she stole from Eve!"

"It's pretty incredible, isn't it? Could you imagine Eve with him now?"

"I couldn't imagine either of them with him – I mean, he seems like a cool guy and all –"

"Unless he's had a personality change in the last fifteen years," Rachel interrupted, "I would call him a selfish pig and I think he probably hasn't changed at all."

Conor shrugged. "It's hard to say when you only speak to someone for a few minutes but –"

"He didn't even ask about Nicky's child!" she cried. "He never tried to make contact afterwards and he has been back to Dublin since!"

Conor wasn't used to seeing Rachel with fire in her belly and the new spunky attitude came as a shock. "Hold on there, sis – this is me! I'm just talking about first impressions – he's like a lot of the guys that I shoot."

"Yeah, well, if Nicky or Eve were there tonight I think your subject could be looking forward to a different kind of shooting tomorrow!"

Conor laughed. Meeting one of Eve's ex-boyfriends made him wonder about her taste in men. Maybe she wasn't always a hard-headed business executive and there was a softer side hidden underneath all that austere beauty.

"I can't imagine Eve with a guy like that – did he look different in college?"

"Younger of course, but he was always on the scruffy side. His hair wasn't long but he was an arty type of guy. It was different in the early nineties."

"Isn't it amazing that I should be shooting him at precisely the time when you guys are over here?"

"It's incredible. I hope Daniel hasn't broken anything serious but in a way it's just as well that Nicky has gone back. Did I tell you that she had a nightmare our first night here that some man was trying to take Daniel away – it was his father."

"No! These coincidences are pretty spooky all right – I understand now why you told him you never see the others."

Conor hadn't ever taken much notice of coincidences before but meeting Eve again after saving her from the train made him believe that there was something bigger going on for all of them.

"I didn't get a chance to tell you earlier but I had lunch with Eve and it turns out she was in town three months ago and I'm almost one hundred percent certain that she had a near miss with a train on the subway and I picked her off the train tracks."

Rachel shook her head. "Hold on – you mean you saved Eve's life? Did you tell her?"

"She denied ever using the subway – said it couldn't have been her, but I'm pretty sure."

"Maybe it was her doppelganger!"

Conor frowned. "I'm certain – even more so now that she says she was in town in February."

"Okay – but she would have said if something like that had happened."

"Why don't you believe me?"

"Why didn't you believe Derek hits me?"

Conor lowered his head. "You know, I'm sorry if I wasn't very supportive earlier – about Derek. It's just hard to hear something like that and to imagine someone you love in that position. And I don't want to read about you in *the Irish Times* as another casualty of a violent marriage."

"I don't think he'd kill me!" she said and then bit her lip. There were a couple of times when she had feared for her life.

"Maybe I could come home and talk to him?"

Rachel shook her head vehemently. "No way. Look, I promise I'll get real help when I get home."

Conor wrapped his long strong arms around his sister as they approached the steps leading up to the Washington Square Hotel. "You'd better because I'm going to keep in touch more often when you go back."

"Thanks," she said. It felt good now that someone in her family knew. Maybe she would have the strength to do something about her situation when she returned.

"See you tomorrow," he said, unwrapping his arms.

Rachel nodded. "For lunch?"

"Why don't we meet at Pottery Barn? You always finish off your shopping there."

"Good idea – I'll text or call you at noon. Thanks for a great time. I'll never be the same after this weekend."

"It's been good," Conor agreed. "Sleep tight – you'll need all your stamina for Pottery Barn!"

The night porter opened the door for her to enter the hotel.

"See you, sis," Conor said, giving her a warm kiss on the cheek.

"Night night," she said as she entered the foyer.

It was dark in the Washington Square Hotel and she felt a

little scared and lonely as she stepped into the lift on her own. The walk through the corridors was long and there was a deathly silence from the bedrooms as she passed. In the distance she could make out a silhouette crouched down outside her door. She felt fear at first and contemplated turning around and getting the night porter but as the figure stood up she realised that she had nothing to fear. That familiar spiky hair that she had come to love came into focus and before she could say anything Alex's dark intense eyes were fixed upon her.

TEN

The Aer Lingus Airbus touched down on Runway One Zero at Dublin airport and Nicky breathed a sigh of relief. She didn't have long to wait now to see her son. Travelling in first class had been an experience but she was so worried about Daniel she had only been able to catch a few minutes sleep here and there. The food looked gorgeous and was served with silverware but still she had no appetite. Now that she was on Irish soil her only concern was getting a taxi to the Mater Hospital as quickly as possible.

She hurried through emigration and, without luggage to collect, was in the back of a Toyota Avensis in minutes. Dublin was grey and dreary compared to the sunshine she had left in New York. It was all like a dream and part of her felt like it wasn't really her who had been sitting in the middle of Central Park with Stephen Delaney only a few hours earlier. She didn't have to travel for long before she saw Delaney Developments emblazoned across the side of a site where apartments were being constructed. She would probably never see him again and maybe it was just as well. Now that she was back in her world there was no place for someone like him. It was a shame but a reality.

She checked her watch for the time and phoned Karen – not sure if her friend would be still in bed.

"Hello. It's me – I'm on my way to the hospital now."

"That's good, Nicky. I'm here and we're looking forward to seeing you – especially Daniel."

Nicky panicked inside. Had Karen stayed there all night? It was good of her if she had.

"How is he doing?"

"Well, considering. We'll talk when you get here."

"Can I speak to him?"

"The nurse is with him. You'll be here soon."

Nicky felt butterflies build inside her stomach. There was something about Karen's tone that suggested things were far from okay. If only she hadn't gone to New York! Maybe Daniel would have done something different yesterday and that would have set off another chain of events and now he wouldn't be lying in a hospital bed. She had tried to give him independence when it would have been easier to wrap him up in cotton wool but she had always felt that he was disadvantaged, growing up without a father, and she had overcompensated in any way that she could.

As the taxi drove down Drumcondra Road the familiarity of Dublin made the past days feel like a dream. New York with its tall buildings and buzz was now a distant memory. The glorious time spent in Central Park and the Boathouse felt as though it had happened to someone else. She found it difficult to visualise Stephen's face. They had only spent a short time together and one kiss had passed between them – she would be silly to read much into the relationship, searching for something that wasn't there. He had handled her awful situation with great care and thoughtfulness. It must be wonderful to have someone there to lean on through the good times and the bad, she thought, as the taxi pulled in through the gates of the Mater Hospital.

She paid the driver and hurried up the hospital steps. The receptionist looked blankly up at her as she approached the desk.

"Hello, I'm Nicky Blake – my son Daniel was admitted yesterday after a rugby accident."

The receptionist checked her files on the computer. "Oh yes, Mrs Blake. He's in A and E at the end of the corridor – take a right through that door."

Nicky didn't try to correct the error of addressing her as Mrs Blake – it was one most people made. She would have made a similar assumption if their roles were reversed.

"Thank you," she said and walked quickly through the double doors.

The smell of hospital detergent wafted in the air and she felt her stomach muscles tighten as she approached the hustle and bustle of the Accident and Emergency ward. It was difficult to see Daniel at first, then she noticed a trolley in the corner with Karen and a nurse beside it. With an ache in her heart she hurried over to her son who was lying with numerous contraptions and wires coming out of his arms.

It was his stillness that frightened her the most. He stared blankly up at the ceiling and when Nicky rushed over and kissed him he jerked but didn't speak. The nurse helped her onto a chair.

"Mrs Blake – Daniel is resting – he's being monitored very closely and has only just woken up."

Karen moved over to Nicky's side. The pressures of the previous day's event showed in her face. Her eyes were sunken with dark rings underneath and her usual smart blonde bob was flat.

"Oh my god – tell me what's happened!" said Nicky.

"I'm afraid we've had a terrible scare with Daniel but we have carried out a lot of tests and it looks like he's going to be fine," the nurse answered reassuringly. "A doctor will be here in a few minutes to speak to you, Mrs Blake."

Nicky turned her gaze to her son's expressionless face. "Darling, speak to me – tell me how you feel," she pleaded.

But Daniel didn't move.

"But what happened?" Nicky asked Karen helplessly.

"I was on the sideline – it was all very vague – it happened very quickly," Karen started to explain. "Daniel was stuck in the scrum and fell out of it badly – it was a simple accident, the coach said."

Nicky looked at her son and leaned forward again to kiss him, her face creased with shock and concern.

"Your son has been very lucky, Mrs Blake," the nurse said, placing her hand supportively on Nicky's arm. "He's in shock – and it's been a long night – but thankfully there are no spinal injuries."

Nicky sighed. It was always her worst nightmare and secret fear since Daniel discovered the joys of playing rugby. She had to thank her lucky stars that she hadn't come home to worse news.

But, if he was given the all clear, then why did he look so limp and weak?

Rachel woke with the comforting feel of Alex's warm limbs wrapped around hers. She couldn't remember a time when she had felt so good before falling asleep or equally happy on waking. His breath gently tickled her left shoulder and she wanted to stay in this position forever.

Alex kissed the bare flesh on her back and gave it a tantalising lick before grabbing her gently to flip her around.

"Let me see your beautiful face," he said with the familiarity of someone who had been a lover for more than one day.

Rachel gazed up at his dark brown eyes and felt as if she were falling into them all over again. The night before had been so amazing she'd felt at times as if she couldn't breathe.

"I'm glad you're still here," she said.

"I'm not leaving your side for the rest of the day – no matter what Conor wants to do with you this afternoon!"

"My last night in New York – I can't believe it's over and I'm going home today," she said sadly, biting her lip.

Alex lifted his finger and ran it gently across her bottom lip. "Those lips are too gorgeous to bite! Promise me you won't do that any more!"

"Sorry, it's a habit!"

"And stop apologising – you're too beautiful. I want you to promise that you'll look after yourself when you get home – don't let your husband hit you or I'll be over to sort him out."

Rachel sighed. "That'll go down really well – don't touch me or my American lover will be on to you!"

Alex saw the futility of his offer too but didn't like the helpless feeling of watching the woman he was falling in love with returning to a man who not only didn't appreciate her but also abused her.

"Why don't you go see your doctor – promise me you'll do that when you get home!"

Rachel's GP, Tony Crosby, was kind and empathic but Derek attended him as well. He treated the kids brilliantly over the years but she seldom went for herself or her own ailments – although Tony always asked her how she was doing.

"I'll think about it!" she said reluctantly.

"Promise and then you'll have to do it!"

Rachel nodded. "Okay. I promise."

Alex leaned forward and gave her a delicious wet kiss. "Now there's only one more thing we need to do before we get up and enjoy your last day in New York."

Rachel didn't need to ask what that was. His warm body was tense and aching for her as much as hers was for him. It was going to be a great start to the day.

Stephen opened his eyes slowly as the heavy feelings that alcohol leaves behind took hold of his head. He glanced at his watch and almost didn't notice his own nakedness until he felt bare flesh against his leg. He shuddered with surprise on seeing Eve lying in the bed beside him and the memories of the night before came hazily back to him.

At the same moment Eve turned her head and with some reservation gave Stephen a smile.

"Good morning!" she said, her voice as smooth as silk.

"G-g-good morning, I-I-I . . ."

"It's eight – I guess we've both slept late," she said evenly. "I have an appointment with Lucille at nine so I'll dash across to my suite."

Stephen nodded and turned his eyes away as the naked Eve stepped out of the bed.

Inside he felt a surge of panic. He hadn't orchestrated this strange predicament. He certainly hadn't tried to seduce Eve at any stage during the weekend. How did they end up in bed together? His drinking was taking him out of control. He had already ended up in a couple of bad situations relating to work – missing meetings and losing documents while working on his laptop under the influence of alcohol. Now he was waking up with a woman that he had no recollection of seducing – what was going on? Eve was stunningly attractive but she wasn't his type.

"Will I call you later?" Eve said as she slipped into her

Christian Louboutins. "Wall Street at lunchtime is such a buzz!"

Stephen didn't turn around. He hid under the covers, still struck by the thoughts running through his head. "Eh, I don't know if my meeting will run on – I'll talk to you in the afternoon."

"I'm getting a BA flight back to London at five so I guess we could hook up in Dublin if we can't get it together today."

"Sure," he said reluctantly. "That's probably the best thing to do."

Eve knelt on the side of the bed and leaned forward to give Stephen a goodbye kiss.

He reciprocated clumsily and watched as she walked briskly out of the bedroom. Why had Eve come to his bed so readily the night before? Maybe she was interested in him after the time they had spent talking on the first night. Or maybe she was interested in him because she was aware of his cumulative wealth? He hated himself for jumping to this conclusion, but felt that it was the latter.

When he was certain that she was gone he jumped out of the bed and pulled on his dressing-gown. He didn't take risks with unprotected sex but couldn't remember using a condom. What if she got pregnant? He felt sick and sad and longed for a drink but the meeting with his New York counterparts was important. He wondered how Nicky was doing – she would be in Dublin now with her son. How could he have spent such a good lunch with Nicky and then ended up in bed with her friend later on the same evening? It was uncharacteristic behaviour even after drinking copious amounts of alcohol. But in any case Nicky probably wasn't that interested in him. Downbeat and angry with himself, he strolled into the lounge and opened the door of the bar. A bottle of port rested on the shelf and he pulled out the cork.

Rachel and Alex walked hand in hand through the foyer of the

Washington Square Hotel and out under a clear blue sky filled with New York sunshine.

"It's going to be a good day!" Alex said, smiling widely.

Rachel nodded. Deep inside she was feeling guilt and concern for Nicky. She was still in New York while Nicky was whisked back to a terrible situation at home.

"Do you mind if I call Nicky? I'm concerned about Daniel."

"Sure – call her."

Rachel dialled her friend's number and the dial tone went immediately to her mailbox. She didn't know whether to trouble her by leaving a message or if it would be better just to try again later. By now she would definitely be in the hospital receiving the prognosis. She thought of her own children and hoped they were coping well in her absence. Sarah was such a capable girl she felt certain that at least they would all be fed. In less than twenty-four hours she would be home with them and back to her daily routines of caring for them, so she would make the most of the little time she had left in New York.

Rachel looked longingly at Alex – she wanted to hold tight to every moment they spent together today and remember it forever. Once she arrived in Dublin it would be hard to recall the feelings of warmth and love that she shared with him, as she went about her daily tasks as wife and mother.

"I was going to do a bit of shopping for my house – and told Conor I'd meet him in Pottery Barn later."

"We could snoop around the Village, then I'll take you to some great shops in the Meatpacking District."

Rachel nodded. "I'm happy wandering wherever you take me!"

He gave her hand a gentle squeeze. "We'll always have today, Rachel," he said softly. "No one can take this time away from us."

"I know," she nodded.

"I'm feeling grateful to the universe for any time with you," he continued. "Imagine how bad it would be for both of us if we had gone through our lives and never met. I feel like I've been waiting to meet you for all of my life and, even though I can't be with you every day, I feel as if we'll always keep this secret feeling for each other."

Rachel stared at him with wide eyes – transfixed by his words. He had described exactly the way she was feeling about him inside. Both of them were given this short time together for some strange cosmic reason. And although they couldn't have a future together, this special time was enough to transform how they both felt as individuals forever. They would not be able to share their lives physically together in the future but they would always have their memories and the knowledge that there was someone on the other side of the Atlantic Ocean that they really loved.

Alex leaned forward and kissed Rachel spontaneously on the lips. She smelt of roses and home and peace and he knew that as soon as she was on the aeroplane later that she would be taking a part of his soul with her.

"Come on," Rachel said with a nudge, when she felt they were getting too morose. "Show me something different about New York!"

"We are coming up to West Fourth Street courts – do you fancy shooting some hoops?"

Rachel gasped. "I haven't held a basketball since I was in school."

In the distance three guys were playing a game on an almost empty court behind high mesh walls, showing great skill and speed.

"You gotta be good to play with these guys!"

Rachel gave Alex a playful thump on his upper arm. "No

way – I'm not going to make a show of myself. Those guys are brilliant."

Alex opened the mesh door that led into the court and waved at the towering figure with the ball in his hands.

"Mind if we play?" he asked casually and, Rachel felt, a little cautiously as well.

The tallest guy, who must have stood over six feet six and was dressed in a hoody and bandana, laughed dismissively.

"You gonna play one on one with your lady friend?"

Alex shrugged. "I thought we might play with you guys!" He didn't want Rachel to see how edgy he was feeling inside but he betrayed himself by the way he was swaying from foot to foot uneasily. He hoped that having such a pretty companion would make the guys more welcoming.

"Hey, we don't wanna get beat by some pretty lady – it's all yours, man!" the player said as he bounced the ball over in Alex's direction.

"Thanks, man," Alex responded and started to dribble over to Rachel who by now was in position to do battle with him.

She dislodged the ball from Alex's hand and started to dribble it up to the net.

"Hey, cheeky!" he called and tickled her waist.

It didn't deter her and she continued bouncing until she was clear of him. Then she aimed and took her shot. The ball teetered on the edge of the ring for a few seconds and toppled into the hoop and out through the net.

The three guys who were now watching started to applaud and Rachel felt red rise in her cheeks.

"Hey – you never told me you were good at sport," Alex said with a smile. "Wanna try again?"

Rachel laughed. "I think I'll quit while I'm ahead."

"Thanks, guys," Alex said, bouncing the ball back to its

owner. "She's too good for me!"

The three players laughed at the interlude and Alex was relieved that he had hit on the courts when some ordinary guys were playing and not members of the heavier gangs who also frequented the courts.

"That was fun," Rachel said – still giggling as Alex took her hand on leaving the court.

"Do you play any sport in Ireland?" he asked.

Rachel's eyes widened and she laughed loudly. "I never get a chance to. My days are packed out – when the kids are in school in the mornings I'm playing catch-up with myself!" She shook her head and continued. "I'd love to do something because I liked games in school and I even played cricket in college – but not any more."

"It's good to do something for yourself."

The mention of college reminded her of James Holden. Suddenly she wanted to tell him. "You know, meeting that guy last night from college was an amazing coincidence. You won't believe it but he's the father of Nicky's son."

"What?" Alex stood stock still in astonishment. "Are you kiddin' me?"

"No. I'm dead serious." She looked him directly in the eye. "And he's never seen his own child."

"I'd hate that," Alex said sternly. "I can understand how some guys just shirk their responsibilities but I'd hate to have a child and not know them."

"Well, Jim was always self-centred." She brooded as they walked on. "Funny though, for all his self-centredness, he said something about me last night that made me think – I used to really love literature and he reminded me that I wanted to write a novel when I was in college."

"And can you write?"

Rachel shrugged. "I suppose so. At least I could. I haven't tried in years though. Now I don't have anything to write about!"

Alex gave her hand a tug and let go swiftly. With his hands on his hips he took two steps backwards, looking almost comical.

"Hey – are you a mother of three children whose every need you look after each and every day?"

She nodded, puzzled.

"And for how long now?"

Rachel shrugged. "Thirteen years!"

"And have you been married to a man who doesn't appreciate or treat you properly?"

"Yes. But what do you mean?" she asked defensively.

"That sounds like you have a lot to talk about and I don't even know what else you do that you haven't told me about!"

Rachel laughed. "You've heard it all."

"Well, I knew you were fit but I didn't realise that you were good at sports too!"

Rachel laughed and started to run a little as Alex got set to pounce on her playfully. He threw his arms around her waist and started to tickle her.

"Oh no, you don't," she said, pulling away and starting to run in earnest.

Alex chased her jokingly until he caught her again and this time he took a stronger grip and moved his head close enough to give her a warm delicious kiss.

"You won't escape from me now!"

Rachel stood still and wide-eyed. "Maybe I don't want to escape!" She took a hold of his hands and removed them from her waist gently – then swung around and started to pick up speed again, calling, "And maybe I do!"

They ran like adolescents up Sixth Avenue and into the

Meatpacking District, racing past beautiful boutiques and shops until Rachel felt a stitch in her side from laughing so much.

"Hey, you can forget about Pottery Barn – this place is much cooler!" he said when they eventually slowed down in front of a store with large windows displaying all kinds of things for the home.

Rachel knew he was probably right. The district was now considered one of the trendiest in New York, a far cry from its origins as home to slaughterhouses, packing plants and prostitution.

"Myx-pilpyuks!" she stuttered as she looked at the name over the front door.

"Mxyplyzyk – but you say it like 'Mix-ee-pliz-ik' – he was a character in the Superman comics – you know, the Marvel ones?"

Rachel was enthralled. "I just love the way you know things like that, Alex."

"Well, I am a doctor after all!" he said with a wicked wink. "Come on!"

They rummaged through the shelves of brightly coloured homeware and furniture.

"I think I'll buy this," she said, holding up a plastic duck watering can. "Holly would love it!"

"How old is she?"

"Six."

"Maybe she would like this better," he said, holding up a pink fluffy handbag.

"I think you know my kids better than me!" Rachel smiled as she took the bag over to the cash register.

"What did you get your other kids?"

Rachel had to think. "I got a load of clothes for Ben in Old Navy and he'll probably refuse to wear half of them. Sarah wants perfume that I'll get at the airport – and money!"

"I can't imagine what it's like to have kids!"

"It's just great," Rachel said with a smile. "They give me a reason for living – for going on."

Alex took her hand firmly once she had purchased the bag. "Come on, I want to show you somewhere," he said secretively.

Rachel trotted along behind him as he took off out of the store. "Where are you taking me?"

"I'm going to show you somewhere only a real New Yorker would go – we don't tell the tourists about it."

"Sounds good," Rachel laughed as they raced up Greenwich Avenue.

On 12th Street she watched, with a mixture of astonishment, horror and fear for his safety, as he shimmied up a drainpipe.

"Come down! Where do you think you're going?"

"I'll be back in a minute," he said as he disappeared over the corrugated iron at the top of the wall.

Suddenly a rope ladder fell down, almost hitting Rachel where she stood. Alex popped his head over the wall and beckoned.

"Come on up!" he called.

Rachel looked around her but none of the local residents in the Meatpacking District blinked an eyelid as she started shakily to ascend the ladder.

"That's it – take it easy – it's perfectly safe," Alex urged encouragingly.

Nothing could have prepared Rachel for the sea of green when she reached the top of the wall. It was like an oasis in the middle of all the vast manmade structures. She stepped down onto overgrown railway tracks where daisies and wildflowers now grew abundantly. Alex put his arm around her waist and guided her over the steel girders to the shade of a deciduous tree.

"What is this place?" Rachel asked with awe.

"It's the High Line – a section of the railroad used by the

meatpackers to ship meat all over America. It's been out of action for years. Parts of it runs through buildings – one stretch goes through a music studio! It's been overgrown and disused for as long as I've been in the city."

"It's like a little park!"

"It's better than that – it's a mile and a half long and up on 30th street you get a great view of the river. There's a group of artists and residents who have set up a Renewal of the High Line campaign to turn it into an elevated park – and it's going to happen soon. Apart from Central Park it's the only stretch of green in Manhattan."

They lay down under the shade of the tree and looked up at the cloudless blue sky above their heads.

"Here's something – when you're back in Ireland on a sunny day you can lie down in your back garden and have the same view as we have now."

"What a great idea!" she said with a smile. No doubt there would be plenty of times when she would desperately want to be back in New York with Alex when her life returned to normal in Dublin.

"But you're here now," Alex said, sitting up and leaning tentatively over Rachel's taut body.

Her eyes widened as she moistened her lips in anticipation of his kiss. Although they were in the middle of the city and out of doors Rachel felt as though they were hidden in a private world of their own.

Alex melted into Rachel's embrace as he fell deeper in love than he wanted to – with a woman who was married and whose life was in a country so far away.

Conor arrived at Radio City with minutes to spare. Charlene, his regular make-up artist, was already ensconced at a table in the corner of the stage surrounded by boxes of paraphernalia.

"Hey, Conor!" she said, lifting her head – covered with a new spiky blue hairstyle.

Conor smiled inwardly. He never knew what she was going to look like from one shoot to the next. "Hey, Charlene – love the look!"

"It's only gonna stay 'til Tuesday – I'm bored with blue!"

Conor smiled and looked around for his assistant. No sign. He was new and not as reliable as his last one who had been with him since he set up on his own.

"Any sign of our gig?"

"There's a guy with a pony-tail and guitar backstage. Nat rang and said he wasn't going to make it – something about meeting a hot new chick last night in Pravda!"

Conor put two and two together and smiled to himself. With a little bit of luck the hot new chick was Mandy. He suspected that the stash of narcotics Nat had hidden in his Porsche would have appealed greatly to Mandy – not to mention his fat wallet. If it got Mandy off his own back for good that was a good thing.

"What way do you want to do this?" Charlene asked.

"My sister's in town and I want to get it done as quickly as possible. This guy is solo and we need to just get some promo shots that Nat can send out ahead of his gigs – from what Nat told me last night he has his album cover shot – and they want me to do some more when he plays live here on Wednesday."

"Cool!" Charlene said, returning to her mixtures and potions.

Conor set down his equipment beside Charlene and went searching for Jim. He had found the door with the star on front easily enough, he thought. This guy had a high opinion of himself.

Jim spun around on his chair as Conor entered. He was wearing army pants with a sleeveless T-shirt and dog-tags on top.

"How ya doing, man?"

"Hey!" Conor couldn't figure this guy out. He was laid-back and Conor didn't feel he was anything like the malicious guy his sister had described. But there was also something odd about him that he couldn't put his finger on. "Are you looking forward to your gig on Wednesday night?"

"Can't wait, man — it's been a long time coming."

"It was crazy that you knew my sister — it never stops amazing me when coincidences happen in this town. A city of so many million yet you always meet the people you are meant to."

Jim nodded. "It's easy to forget home when you've been travelling as long as I have. College was cool but Ireland didn't have much to offer me back in those days."

Conor didn't want to get into a discussion with him about his parental obligations — it was his job to take a few shots and go — but, if the tables were turned, he would most certainly like to know how the child he had back in Ireland was growing up.

"Ireland's come a long way," Conor said with a smile. "I was home three years ago and it's become really hip."

Jim shook his head. "I'm not going back there."

Conor's decision was made for him. There was no way that he would interfere with fate.

"Do you want to get started? I want to meet my sister for lunch."

Jim jumped to his feet and took his guitar by the neck. "I'm ready."

Charlene set about working her magic as Conor's assistant at last arrived.

The scene was set as Jim perched himself up onto a high stool and started to strum.

"Do you mind if I play while you shoot?"

"Go ahead!" said Conor.

Jim relaxed and his eyes started to close as he opened his mouth to sing.

The first words of the song echoed round the stage and filled the hall. It wasn't familiar but the name he used was unmistakable. Conor felt an eerie flash of revelation as Jim hit the first high note and sang about a boy he'd never met – his son. He didn't have to wait long before he heard the name again – it was the same name that Rachel had mentioned the night before.

It was a song about someone called Daniel.

Nicky waited with bated breath as the doctor came to speak to her.

"Mrs Blake?" he asked, looking from Nicky to Karen and finally at the nurse.

God, Nicky thought, he's only a kid himself.

"I'm sorry that we took so long to see you. We were waiting for confirmation of the X-ray results and I am pleased to say that he is out of danger – there are no fractures."

Even though the nurse had reassured her earlier and the doctor looked about twelve, she felt a great sense of relief.

"Is there any injury?" Nicky asked, still wondering why, if her son was supposedly all right, he looked so awful.

"He has a soft-tissue injury of the neck."

"But Daniel is complaining of pins and needles in his arms and a headache," Nicky said with concern.

"He pulled nerves in his neck. Give him a day or two and he'll be right as rain," the doctor said confidently. "I would think he's had a terrible shock more than anything else."

Nicky looked at the tired and gaunt eyes of the young medic who had clearly been working right through the night. Traces of acne were sprinkled under his early morning beard.

"Will he be able to come home?" she asked.

"Absolutely. He can go straight home with you now. Give him

Paracetamol every four hours and a day's rest in bed and he'll probably be ready for school tomorrow! I have to go, excuse me!"

Nicky looked at Karen for reassurance but she was so tired she seemed just glad to hear the words "go home".

Daniel lay quietly on the trolley as the nurse removed the collar that had been supporting his neck.

"How are you hoping to travel – have you a car or taxi?" the nurse asked.

"I'll give you both a lift," Karen said.

"No, you've done more than enough – I don't know how I can thank you for looking after him so well. We can get a taxi!"

"I won't hear of it. Come on, I'm sure you're exhausted. I can go straight home to bed after. Bob will have the kids off to school by now."

How lovely to have someone there as a sidekick and support, Nicky thought. She had never known the luxury of a partner in times of crisis. A flash of Stephen's kind and caring face came back to her and she cherished the feeling of support that she had felt at JFK airport when he had helped her reschedule her flight.

Daniel moved slowly and carefully off the trolley as Karen supported him by the left arm and Nicky took hold of his right elbow.

"Take your time, love," Karen said reassuringly. The fact that Daniel wasn't speaking much since the accident had her feeling concerned. "Is there anything you want to get on the way, Nicky?"

"No, thanks," Nicky said, exhausted. "I just want to get him home."

Alex held on tightly to Rachel's hand as they walked down Sixth Avenue – also known as the Avenue of the Americas. Neither speaking, not sure where they were going. Making love on the High Line had left them both dazed and exhilarated at once.

"Oh, I nearly forgot!" she said. "I'm meant to be meeting Conor at Pottery Barn!"

"Send him a text – tell him we'll be in Café Habana – it's close to Pottery Barn. He'll join us there. I know he likes the place."

Rachel did as he suggested but she secretly didn't want her brother to come. She loved him but she was enjoying having Alex to herself. With him, her eyes had been opened to a whole new world that existed alongside hers but didn't touch it in any shape or form. Their stolen moments on the High Line were precious and she would treasure them for as long as she lived. Plus, he had shown her some strange and quirky stores that she would never have got to see normally – his taste in shopping was as good as his taste in everything else that he did!

When she had finished sending the text message she stopped and stared at Alex. He responded by gently placing his lips on top of hers.

"Are you going to be okay when you get home?"

"Please, Alex, let's leave it – I don't want to think about it. We have only a few hours left and then I'll be on the plane."

"Do you think Conor would mind if I came to the airport with you?"

Rachel nodded as they started to walk again. "I think he just might. I've spent more of this weekend with you than him. With his crisis with Mandy and shooting Jim Holden I think he's had a hard enough time but, you know, I'm a great believer that things happen for a reason and if he hadn't been so busy we wouldn't have got to spend so much time on our own."

Alex nodded. "That's true – I feel sorry for the guy – he got the short straw!"

He released his grip on her hand and put his arm protectively around her shoulders as they walked. Rachel was becoming used to these feelings of warmth and security and each time she received a loving gesture from Alex it gave her just that little bit more strength to go home and face Derek and do what she knew must be done. She wasn't doing her husband any favours either by succumbing to his moods and angry outbursts. She had the power to do something about her situation and she had to do it – not only for her own sake but also for her children's.

Rachel's phone bleeped to acknowledge a text had been received.

Will be there soon – whats Eves number? C

Rachel arched her eyebrows in surprise. Why would her brother want Eve's number?

ELEVEN

Eve packed her bag despondently in her penthouse. She didn't usually feel this way after sleeping with someone – no matter what the motive. But Stephen wasn't just anyone – he was a client and what she did was utterly unprofessional. If Lucille found out she would be furious and if the roles were reversed she would feel the same.

She had slept with enough men in her life to realise when someone wasn't interested in developing a relationship. Stephen was a gentleman and was obviously feeling awkward after spending the night with her, so he had tried to camouflage his feelings as best he could. But Eve knew that he wasn't interested in anything more and now she would have the task of finding him a date. However, she could be fortunate and he might terminate using Just for Coffee if he was too embarrassed. At least she hoped that was what he would do. As long as he said nothing to Lucille.

She wasn't looking forward to returning to her lonely

apartment in London and she didn't want to go back to Ireland. But to stay in New York would be equally difficult – at the moment she felt that it would be the wrong thing to do even though it was what she really wanted.

She jumped for her phone as it bleeped. The number was American but unfamiliar.

The text message was strange, asking her to ring Conor, and for a moment, seeing his name out of context, she had to think who he could be. But why did he want her to contact him? Did he want to meet up with her? She wasn't sure that she wanted to see him again. Especially if he had notions that he was some sort of knight in shining armour. She didn't want to be reminded of that embarrassing episode on the subway.

She hit the reply button on her phone and listened as it rang.

"Hi, Eve?" the voice at the other end of the line said.

"Yes, Conor – how are you?"

"I left a text message on your phone a few minutes ago. I've got good news – they found your earring and they have it in Town at the front desk waiting for you!"

"That's great! Thanks, Conor!"

She had three hours to be in JFK – she could call in and get it on the way.

"I'm glad they found it for you. Are you going home soon?"

"I've a couple of hours left – have to drop into the office – it's near Town."

"That's good. All the best in London. I gotta go – I'm meeting Rachel for lunch."

"Tell her I'll give her a call her when I get back to London – things got a bit tight with time to meet up!"

"Sure – safe journey home."

"Thanks," Eve said, hanging up. 'Safe journey home' sounded strange – she felt more at home in New York than anywhere in the world. It felt wrong to call London home. Why was she leaving this city – the city that she loved so much – to go to a place that was never really home? She knew the answer. She was running away from the city she loved because she couldn't deal with what had happened to her after 9/11. Conor was right – she wasn't alone. At least while she was in New York she was around people who were also touched by the attacks – who had experienced loss the same way as she had. But it was easier to run away than to deal with it. It was easier to sleep with one man after another and tell herself that it didn't matter than to grieve for the one man that she had truly loved in her life.

She walked over to the sleek and stylish dressing-table in the corner of the suite. As she sat in front of the mirror and stared at her reflection she didn't recognise the woman that stared back. She didn't know who she was any more. Sleeping with Stephen, marrying John, all the affairs on the side meant absolutely nothing to her. Conor was the only man who had spoken any truth to her in years. She used to communicate truthfully with Harry but only superficially in all of her relationships since then. The thought of London and the loneliness waiting for her in her apartment made her stomach churn. Conor was right – she needed to speak to someone but her behaviour had left her with few friends or acquaintances that she could talk to. Her eyes filled up as they had a tendency to do when she was feeling sorry for herself. The fact that she had let her guard down in front of Conor the day before had left her feeling foolish and cross with herself. There was something about that guy that was brutally honest.

Maybe he *had* saved her from the train in the subway back in February. Was it possible that he could now save her from herself?

The rays of sun from the day outside filtered in to highlight the thin lines that were starting to find their way onto her usually flawless skin. The GA designer foundation worked a treat for concealing the signs of age but she knew what it was covering beneath.

For someone in her prime she still hadn't found herself. She needed to settle somewhere and make a home – stop running from here to there and this relationship to that. She needed to go back to basics. Maybe she needed to go home to Dublin or even Galway – back to her roots. She stood up and went over to her suitcase to shut it.

Always one for making impetuous decisions, she was about to make another.

"Here he is now!" Rachel exclaimed as Conor squeezed through the queue of patrons waiting patiently at the door.

"You did well to get a table!" he said, looking to Alex first and then to Rachel.

"Got the last one before the lunch-time rush," Alex said with a smile – suddenly aware that he and Conor's sister had the flush of post-coital pleasure written all over their faces.

Conor took a seat in the small space at their corner table.

"I'm glad you're getting to see this place before you go, Rach," he said. "The food's amazing."

A waitress rushed over and placed a beer on the table in front of Conor. It was part of the service given to regulars and Conor and Alex were often spotted in the Café Habana.

"What did you want Eve's number for?" Rachel asked suspiciously.

"She lost an earring in Town when we were having lunch yesterday," Conor said, taking a sip on his Brooklyn Lager. "The maître d' rang me earlier to say that he had found it."

Rachel raised her eyebrows suggestively and turned to Alex. "Do we believe him?"

Conor frowned. "She's not my type!" he said dismissively. "So what are you guys having?"

"I've ordered my usual *Cuban sandwich*," Alex said with a smile, "and Rachel is having the mango and jicama salad."

Conor looked at his friend's beaming face and noticed a glint that he didn't usually see in his eyes when he was with a woman.

"How did your work go this morning?" Rachel asked, also with a beaming smile.

"Pretty standard job," said Conor. "He's a dull enough character – no great romantic or musician either! But he's done something weird – he's written this song about a kid called Daniel."

Rachel nearly choked on her beer. "Are you serious?"

"Yeah – mad, isn't it?"

"What was the song about?" she asked, astounded.

"It was something about the son he never got to see and the day he walked away and wishing he could walk back to him – something like that."

"I don't believe it! What did he say about it?"

"Nothing."

Rachel's eyes widened. "Did you not ask him about it?"

Conor shrugged. "No, I didn't."

"You are hopeless – you should have said something!"

"Like what?" Conor asked with eyebrows arched.

"Like … I don't know … ask him if the song was about someone he knew! Ask him if he has ever tried to contact Nicky? Something! Anything!"

"Rach, it wasn't my place – my remit was to take a few pictures. I have his number if you want to talk to him."

"God, no!"

"There you go – and I don't even know the guy! I'll send Nicky the number if she wants it."

Rachel thought for a few seconds – now was certainly not the time with Nicky's son in hospital. But then maybe James deserved to be told that his son was ill? It was so confusing she didn't know what to do. "Maybe I'll wait until I get home before I tell her anything – and see how Daniel is doing."

"That's probably the best idea. I've booked a cab for you to get to the airport – we'd need to head about four to give you plenty of time."

"Oh," Rachel said meekly. "So you're coming with me then?"

"Of course – have to look after my girl," Conor said with a wink.

Rachel wished that Alex was taking her to the airport instead of Conor. She couldn't stand the thought of saying goodbye. She looked over at him and he threw her a look that told her he was feeling exactly the same way.

Eve entered the lobby of Just for Coffee and smiled at Arthur as he rushed to take care of her bag.

"Let me take that for you, Miz Pawtah!"

"Thanks, Arthur," she said appreciatively. "You're always in such good form – can you let me in on your secret?"

Arthur turned his head and beamed his white teeth. "That's cos I live in the best city in the world, Miz!"

Eve nodded. She had to agree with him.

Lucille's secretary was fussing over paperwork as Eve entered the foyer.

"Miss Porter, Miss Baron is expecting you!" she said with a half smile.

Eve opened the door and was met with a great reception from her boss.

"Come in! I've just had the most amazing phone call from Stephen Delaney – most unusual!"

Eve felt the colour drain from her face. Had he rung to complain that she had come to his room and seduced him the night before? Or something worse – even though she couldn't think what that could be – maybe something about Nicky and the company's lack of professionalism?

Eve had to keep cool. She wore her untouched expression as she took a seat in front of Lucille.

Lucille continued. "Absolutely coincidently, Stephen met someone special in New York this weekend and he doesn't need our services any more."

Eve was dumbstruck. She didn't know how to interpret this information. Had Stephen fallen in love with her after one clumsy night of lovemaking? She didn't really think so.

"He said that the company was very nice and professional and he felt that, as he had broken the contract, he wanted to pay us in full for our services and he threw in an extra five grand bonus for your helpfulness," Lucille beamed. "So well done, you!"

Eve felt like a call girl. Was Stephen trying to pay her for sex or pay her to get rid of her?

Lucille's beam faded a little. "You don't seem very pleased?"

"It's just that it seems like it was a bit of a waste for me coming over here at all!"

Lucille smiled her cheesy grin that she usually only wore for clients. "You can't spend too much time in New York – did you have a nice weekend?"

Eve didn't know how she would describe it – eventful and thought-provoking, maybe – but nice wasn't a word she would use. "It was good but I have a flight to catch now and I need to pick up something I left in Town."

"Oh, did you go there? I just love that place." Lucille continued beaming. "Needless to say, Stephen asked if we could destroy his personal and financial details etc."

"Of course," Eve said professionally. "Actually, Lucille, I've been thinking while I've been here that I miss New York and if there was an opening in this office I might consider coming back."

Lucille's expression changed dramatically. "Gosh, we couldn't move you, honey – you're our woman in Europe ..." She paused for a moment in thought. "In fact I was thinking of opening an office in Paris – how is your French?"

"Adequate," Eve replied unenthusiastically. "Would our service go down well in France?"

"Absolutely – we've been getting calls from there. I never thought that you would be interested. What do you think?"

Eve didn't know what she thought. She was confused. Before coming up in the lift she'd wanted to stay in New York – she couldn't have cared less if she never saw Europe again. Only the day before, she had told Conor that she considered moving to Paris after 9/11. It was strange that now she was getting an opportunity to do just that.

"I don't think I want that sort of upheaval, Lucille – I don't feel like taking on a whole new project. I was hoping that I could find a way to come back to New York. I realised this weekend how much I miss it."

Lucille seemed perturbed. This was the last thing she'd expected from Eve. "Honey, it's not like you're just an employee that could hop from office to office – you're a director and there isn't a need for two of us here in New York."

Eve knew what Lucille was getting at. Before she left New York she was high on the corporate ladder but not a director. It would mean a step down to return to New York.

But moving to Paris would mean making huge changes in her life and huge commitment would be involved in setting up the business. There was no easy solution. She had to make changes but was even more confused than she had been earlier.

"You aren't normally so quiet, Eve – what do you want to do?"

Eve had no idea what she was going to say. She had no idea what she wanted to do. At least she had choices but they all involved enormous change.

"Can I think about the Paris option?"

"Sure, honey," Lucille said, cool and crisply. "Just don't take too long – I need to appoint someone for Paris by the end of the month."

"It all sounds very quick – you hadn't decided to open an office in Paris at the AGM in February."

Lucille shook her head in disbelief. "We spent a good part of the meeting discussing expansion but you were a little distracted that day, if you don't mind me saying so – I was really concerned about you after you left the meeting – it was like you were dazed or something."

Eve remembered why she was so vague that day but she didn't reveal it to Lucille – she felt foolish enough about the whole subway incident.

"I think I remember, now that you mention it," she lied. "Look, I have a flight to catch. I will be in touch by the end of the week."

"Don't take too long," Lucille said with a wry smile. "Well done anyway with the Stephen Delaney affair."

Eve didn't want to hear that man's name mentioned ever again. He was another reminder of the foolish impetuous things that she was prone to doing, despite her austere controlled exterior.

"Talk soon, Lucille," she said as she stood up and they air-kissed.

Eve didn't look back as she left the office. She took the lift down to the foyer where Arthur waited, bright and breezy as always.

"There you go! Miz Pawtah, you want me to get you a cab?"

"That would be great – thanks, Arthur."

They both stepped out into the May sunshine as Arthur caught the attention of the first available taxi. She thanked him with gratitude that she didn't usually show those in the service industry – but Arthur was different. He would be here the next time she called to see Lucille and right now she had no idea under what circumstances that might be.

Arthur opened the door of the yellow taxi in front of her and then she was on her way.

Eve wished she still had her apartment in the stylish upper-east side. She often thought of it – she had been so happy there. It was Harry's apartment but his mother was quick enough to take the lease on it after Harry died and chuck her out of it. Eve had quit her apartment shortly after meeting Harry. They lived together so happily in his that there was no need to keep two places and they agreed that his apartment was the better located to the stylish lifestyle they were going to be living as a couple when they got married. John had come along at the right time and offered her a home and a whole new life and it was just what she needed. But looking back now, it wasn't what she needed at all. She wished that she had dealt with her grief like Conor and sought out counselling. Staying in New York with those who were going through the same trauma as she was would have been a better thing to do. But there was no point thinking about that now.

"Please, could you stop off in Town restaurant," she said to the driver. "I'll only be a minute."

The maître d' sprang to attention when he recognised Eve. It made her wonder just how Conor came to be so well connected in the place.

"Miss, I am so glad that we found your earring," he said,

fumbling with papers and envelopes on the front desk.

"Thank you so much," Eve said as he handed her the tiny object in a small white envelope.

She opened the flap and took out the stud. The thought of losing it made her shiver.

"Do drop in next time you are in Town!" he said. "It's a pun but we only say it to our important customers."

"That would be lovely!" Eve said with a smile. It had been a lovely lunch and she had enjoyed Conor's company so much. The awkward unsatisfactory evening she had spent with Stephen only highlighted that even more. There was definitely something of the knight in shining armour about Conor Moore.

In a frenzied panic Rachel tossed the clothes that Nicky had purchased out of their paper bags and piled them on top of each other into the large suitcase that Nicky had bought in Century 21. There were still plenty of garments left to be piled into Nicky's old suitcase. Thankfully her own suitcase held all of her own purchases and everything was packed in ten short minutes. She took a final check under the bed and a last look in her empty paper shopping bags before calling out to Conor at the other side of the door.

"I'm ready!"

Conor and Alex took a case each and dragged them down the corridor until they reached the lift. It was a tight squeeze to get everyone to fit but they were only a couple of floors from the ground.

When they reached the entrance steps of the Washington Square Hotel Alex shuffled anxiously, knowing that it was his time to go.

"I guess it's time to say goodbye," he said reluctantly.

Rachel's eyebrows arched. She really didn't want him to go. How could she tell him that she wanted him to go with her to the airport? This was something she should have organised earlier but now it was too late.

"Have a good journey," Alex said sadly and leaned forward to place a gentle kiss on her cheek.

She put her hand up to touch the spot where his lips had been. She would love nothing more than to slip into a long warm embrace.

But Alex was aware of protocol and nodded at Conor. "I'm off – probably see you later, man."

Rachel gave a little wave and swallowed hard to fight back the tears that were welling in her eyes.

"Take care and remember you promised!" Alex said, shaking a stern finger at Rachel.

She had to think for a moment – what had she promised? Then she remembered – she was going to go to her doctor as soon as she got home.

As he disappeared down the street Rachel felt as though she could cry.

A long white custom car drove up and stopped at the sidewalk and Rachel knew that this was for her. She sat quietly in the back of the car while Conor talked on about how great it was that she had come and how awful it would be when she was gone. As they drove through Brooklyn and Jamaica, Rachel stared out of the window in case Conor saw the tears in her eyes because he would know who she was crying for. As the taxi drove up the ramp of departures at JFK Rachel knew that her dream was now well and truly over and it was back to life as normal on the Old Portmarnock Road.

"Thanks for coming over," Conor said as he wrapped his arms around his sister for one last time.

"It was wonderful – I'll never forget this weekend as long as I live."

Conor knew that he wasn't the reason why she would never forget it or why it was so wonderful but he didn't begrudge his sister the experience. He just hoped that she would be okay and settle back to normal life when she returned.

"If Derek hits you again, will you ring me at once?"

Rachel smiled. What could she say? – "I can guarantee that he will strike me again but what good will it do telling you? It would take 24 hours to get home and rescue me!" – It was easier just to nod.

"Tell Mum I'll be back for a visit before the year is out – who knows, I might be home for good some day!"

"That would be great," Rachel smiled but felt sure that it would never happen.

"And remember, if he lays a finger on you, ring me immediately."

"I will!"

But Rachel knew already that she wouldn't.

Another brotherly and sisterly loving embrace and a short while later, Rachel sat nervously on her own in Terminal Two waiting for departure of the large green Aer Lingus airbus back to Dublin.

Just then an alarm went off at a nearby boarding gate, sending security into a frenzy. Police with loaded holsters ran past and she wished that she wasn't on her own. It was so different to her light-hearted departure from Dublin four days before. She worried about Nicky and how she must be coping. As for her own situation, Sarah had been vague when she rang earlier and she hoped that she had coped with her father and younger siblings while she was away.

The alarm suddenly stopped and the police returned to their positions. She hoped that she would get some sleep on the flight but the cramped conditions in economy would make it difficult and she would probably have to sit beside a stranger instead of Nicky. She reached into her handbag and took out her last sleeping tablet. With that at least she had some chance of sleeping. She swallowed the tiny pill back quickly as the air stewardess in green came up to the desk at the boarding gate and started to take boarding cards.

Rachel stood up and made her way to the desk with heavy steps. She could still see Alex's brown eyes in her memory and hoped that she would be able to hold that image forever. She'd never forget the way he made her feel for those three nights in New York. A part of her felt like she would never be the same again.

When she embarked on the aeroplane she took her seat towards the back and half-heartedly opened the plastic on her complimentary pillow. A teenager wearing an iPod turned up too loudly to be polite sat down on the seat next to her.

She felt like crying but had to put on a brave face as the chief steward came down to her row and leaned across the teenager to convey a message.

"Mrs Sloan – there has been a mistake with your seat number – we apologise profoundly. I had hoped that I would spot you coming in. Check-in sometimes can make mistakes when a passenger upgrades on a different day to travelling. Follow me."

Rachel wasn't sure what the mistake was but felt glad that she at least was rescued from sitting beside a noisy iPod for seven hours.

She followed the steward up to the front of the aeroplane where he ushered her into her new surroundings in Seat 2A.

"A Mr Delaney changed your ticket yesterday and the stewardess didn't upgrade it on the system properly. I hope you will be comfortable now."

Rachel didn't know what to say. She had never been in first

class before. Derek always travelled first class for business but he had never treated his wife to the expensive seats on the few occasions that they had travelled for pleasure. Suddenly she remembered her sleeping pill and panicked. This was her first and possibly only time that she would get to travel first class and now that she had a big comfortable chair with a footrest and reclining back she wouldn't be awake long enough to enjoy it! Of course she could always run to the restroom and try to vomit it up! That would be disgusting – besides, the effects of the tablet were beginning to take effect and it might already be too late.

The chief steward returned with a silver tray in his hand holding champagne in crystal glasses.

"Would you like some champagne, madam?"

"Yes, please," Rachel said – feeling like a child that was being treated to anything she wanted in a sweet shop. "Thank you so much."

Her eyelids felt heavy as she took the first gulp.

"Let me put your legrest up for you," the kind steward said, manoeuvring her seat and putting a wool blanket over her legs.

Rachel wasn't used to this pampering and fuss. She put her glass down on the table and took the menu from the steward.

Finally she was on her own in the midst of this luxury. She smiled to herself. She didn't know how or why Stephen had upgraded her ticket but it was wonderful to have this experience. After enjoying four wonderful days in New York where she had avoided pain and fear, she was ready to take a new hold of her life. It was time that she stood up for herself and her family. She opened her menu card and pictured Alex's smiling face. Slumber fell on her like a veil and unbeknownst to herself she was asleep before take-off.

Alex turned the key to his apartment and pushed open the door. The smell of oil paint sometimes filtered through his nose when he had been away from his studio for a while. It felt right to live and work in the same space – his work was his life and vice versa. All that was thrown on its head this weekend as Rachel had shown him what it was like to get really close to someone. He didn't turn the light on immediately as the city lights were sparkling through the window. He felt more peaceful in the darkness and sat on the big brown armchair where he usually read a book. The room seemed different, or maybe it was he himself that had changed. If he had a drink he would probably finish the bottle and fall asleep. If he tried to read he would probably be too distracted by thoughts of Rachel to concentrate.

He contemplated going out but felt that would only delay the inevitable grieving he had to do since saying goodbye to Rachel. Then he realised that the choice had been made since the first time he laid eyes on her. There was a reason why she had come into his life and he had to do something about it. While her face was still so easy to visualise and the smell of her was still strong on his hands and skin he had to immortalise his vision of her.

He jumped up and hit the lights – every light in the room. He could mope and miss her but that wouldn't be doing their relationship any service. Instead he would paint an image that he would have forever and encapsulate the part of her soul that remained with him in New York.

With speed and alacrity he took a canvas five feet square and hooked it up to an easel. He searched through the pile of half-opened tubes and squirted yellow ochre onto his mixing palette first. He followed with ultramarine, titanium white and cobalt blue. Crimson next and Naples yellow – it was as if he was possessed by a strange force controlling his every move. He took his brush in hand as if it were a weapon and dipped it in a sepia tint that he used to sketch. The simple lines that would turn this two-dimensional board into Rachel fell swiftly and easily onto the canvas. Her face shone out at him through the canvas as he added each brushstroke. He didn't know where this power was coming from but he was no longer the painter – he was simply a channel that the universe was using to paint this picture. As he added the spot of titanium white to the centre of her pupil he felt like crying. Inside he could feel her pain and understand how she suffered each day in her life. It was only now that he knew why they had met. He was taking away her pain and putting it into the picture. She could leave it with him in New York and he would mind it for her so she could feel only joy in the future. They hadn't met for just any reason. She would give him the ability to move from being a painter of merit to an artist of giftedness and he would give her the freedom to live her life without fear.

He worked through the night, not stopping for a break. He was working with his soul and normal bodily functions were on standby and would remain so until the canvas was finished. As he placed the final stroke of crimson on the canvas he let out a deep breath and a ray of light from the new dawn shone in through the window. He stood back from the canvas as if he would be blinded by staying any closer.

Then he realised that he had completed his best work.

TWELVE

Rachel woke up to the smell of freshly baked bagels. She looked around – disoriented for a moment. What had she missed? She looked at the tiny screen in front of her and switched it on. It showed the aircraft's location over Athlone in the centre of Ireland. She looked out the window to her right and saw a blanket of green beneath her.

Letting out a loud sigh, she considered that maybe it was for the best that she had slept all night. It might give her the strength to face the next few days with some energy.

"Would you like a bagel and some fruit, madam?" the air hostess asked in a sprightly fashion. "I'm afraid we don't have time to serve you with a Full Irish!"

"No, thank you, I'm fine," Rachel replied with a smile.

But she wasn't fine. She felt sick at the thought of going home. She longed to see her children but she trembled inside as she pictured Derek. What if he took it out on her for going away? He had made it clear before she went that he wasn't keen on the idea but in a fit of good humour agreed when Nicky told them about the Aer Lingus seat sale. He had made her pay already with the marks on her back for making the decision to go but now she dreaded what the repercussions would be.

The captain gave his final address to the passengers as the aircraft started its descent into Dublin airport. In the distance Rachel could see the outline of the coast at Portmarnock and shivers ran up her spine. Already the feelings of inadequacy and insecurity were surfacing and she was only a few hours apart from Alex and the confidence-building that she had relished and cherished for the last three nights. Now she would return to her world of watching, waiting and reacting to Derek's every move. She no longer felt beautiful or worthy. She slid back into her usual habit of thought: after all, she was lucky to have a home and support for herself and her children and if she wanted to keep things that way she had better put up with whatever Derek was going to lash at her.

For a change her luggage was first through baggage reclaim and out through to the carousel. She struggled for a moment with the weight of the case, pulled the handle and it fell to the ground. Nicky's two bags came trundling out five cases later. It was a good time of the morning to arrive and she would have no trouble picking up a taxi for the short fifteen-minute ride to the Old Portmarnock Road.

A kindly old driver was waiting in a Skoda outside arrivals and she felt guilty watching him grapple with the weight of her cases as he put them into his boot. Nicky's new case was so heavy that Rachel was glad she didn't have to pay extra for it – as she'd had to do at the airport check-in in New York.

"Where to, love?" he asked.

"Old Portmarnock Road please – just by the new driving range."

"No problem, dear. Did you come from the States?"

"Yes, could you tell by the weight of my case?"

The old man smiled — his reflection visible in the rear-view mirror. "You girls just love shopping over there — were you in New York or Boston?"

"New York, just for three nights."

"Can't see the attraction myself. You can get anything you want here now — but I suppose with the cheap dollar you get more value."

Rachel didn't feel up to small talk even though the man was only trying to be kind. She wanted to be alone with her memories and relish the image of Alex that was still so clear in her head before it faded like she knew it was going to — and sooner rather than later.

"It's just here," Rachel said as the taxi drove past a large and comfortable detached house built in the American style. It was such a statement of Derek's rise to prominence as a respectable member of Celtic Tiger society. But that Tiger was no longer purring and, even before she left, the markets had another bad day's trading and Derek was in foul humour yet again. In the bull market he couldn't lose but now the bear was roaring and she knew that each day he had been to work for the past year had been hard and fraught with uncertainty.

"Nice house, love," the driver said, smiling as he leaned back in his seat.

Rachel didn't comment. "How much do I owe you?"

"Fifteen euros," he said, getting out of the car and hauling the bags from the boot.

Rachel watched as the car drove off down the gravel driveway. She looked over at her Renault Scenic. It sat small and square beside Derek's Audi. It was strange that Derek's car should be there at all. She looked at her watch — why wasn't he in work at a quarter to nine in the morning? He was usually gone by seven thirty most mornings. The children were getting lifts to school from her friend Veronica so they would all be gone by now.

She rooted through her purse and put the front door key into the lock. There wasn't a sound from the house. As she turned the key she heard nothing but the birds singing softly in the large cherry blossom at the side of the driveway. She pulled her case into the hall and rolled it along the wooden floorboards and into her newly decorated open-plan kitchen.

"Hello?" she called but only silence rang through the house. Maybe Derek got the Dart to work? On the odd occasion when he was involved in after-work entertainment he would leave his car at home. That would be the icing on the cake – it would be so nice not to have to see him too soon.

It was good to be home in some ways and she could look forward to collecting Holly in a few short hours' time. She hoped that the little girl would be pleased with the pink handbag that Alex had picked out for her. Without thinking she flicked the switch on the kettle and took a mug down from the cabinet above her head. The deep sleep had been relaxing and she felt better able to face whatever her return had in store. She popped a pyramid teabag into her mug and tidied up the breakfast bowls that were filled with half-eaten cereals. Back to cooking and cleaning and caring – it couldn't be further away from her experiences in New York. But this was her reality.

As she reached into the fridge and pulled the milk carton out, the sound of a footstep made her jump, spilling most of the contents onto the cream tiles.

She turned quickly to see Derek's hollow grey eyes staring at her with a penetrating and frightening gaze.

"I've been waiting for you – I wanted to make sure that you got home safely."

Rachel looked down at the wet floor and back up at her husband. "Y-y-y-es, t-t-thanks."

Derek pursed his lips. "Only home a few minutes and already you're wreaking havoc," he said with a solemn shake of his head.

"I'm sorry!" she declared. That didn't take long, she thought to herself. Only two sentences home and she was apologising already. Why couldn't she say that was his fault for creeping up on her like that? What stopped her? Where was her voice? Did she leave it back in Manhattan?

"Really, Rachel – I wonder how you managed these last few days. We, on the other hand, got on very well without you." With that, he sniggered.

She had expected him at least to miss his regular punching-bag – a frisson of horror ran through her at the thought he might have been hitting out at someone else while she was away . . .

Words failed her and even though she opened her lips nothing came out. What could she say? Whatever she did say would be the wrong thing. Eventually she came up with something that she hoped would be safe.

"Would you like a cup of tea?"

"And make a total mess of the floor with the hot water, hmm?"

Rachel trembled as his expression changed and he smiled broadly.

"Come on, Rachel – I didn't stay at home to see what you got me in New York – I've got something for you!" His piercing eyes looked her up and down.

Oh God, she thought – not now!

Derek reached out his hand and smiled widely. "Come now. Upstairs?"

It was a rhetorical question. There was no point in saying

anything. When he smiled that wide smile he always wanted sex. If she was lucky it would all be over quickly.

Conor took the steps up to Nat's office deep in the Meatpacking District. It was an ultra-cool set-up and a testament to Nat's success. In the crook of his arm he held his laptop with an array of shots that he had taken the previous day. Conor had made the shots cool. It was his gift and that was just the way it was.

Nat's secretary was a looker, like most of the women that walked around the offices of the music label. Nat had a keen eye for pretty women and they in turn flocked to him – more for his influence in the city and the size of his wallet than anything else.

"Morning, Conor."

"Hi, Donna. Is Nat in his office?"

"Go right in, he's expecting you!"

Conor passed down a corridor filled with black and white images of rock bands – many of which he had taken himself. Platinum records decorated the wall around Nat's door as Conor gave it a loud knock.

"Come in!" a voice called.

Conor turned the handle and stepped inside.

Nat looked as dishevelled and wrecked as usual but it was only nine thirty in the morning – very early for him to start a day's work.

"Conor, my man!" he said, getting up off his red leather swivel-chair. "Am I glad to see you! How did you get on with Jim?"

"Hey, Nat! Good. How's it going with you?" Conor unzipped his laptop case as he approached Nat's desk.

"Good, man – the best – there's a hot new babe just driving me crazy – you were there when I met her in Pravda. Her name's Mandy!"

Conor nodded. "Good call – she's a looker all right!" There was no point in saying anything to Nat about his history with Mandy – he was relieved that she must have said nothing either. "I won't delay you," he said, starting up a slide show. "Do you want to check these out now?"

Nat observed photograph after photograph but, Conor felt, didn't show a lot of interest in them.

"You know, man – things have changed a bit," said Nat, sweeping back his long fringe from his forehead, "but I haven't had a chance to sort it yet. A new group has come on the scene that's going to need a lot of my time, and promoting Jim isn't really as important as it was last week."

"Really?" Conor said with eyebrows raised. Jim obviously had no idea of this.

"I haven't signed along the dotted line with Jim yet and I'm beginning to think that maybe he's getting a bit old for the market that he's trying to break into. You don't do festivals old unless you're Bob Dylan."

Conor knew what Nat was getting at.

"I'll pay you in full, of course, for your work yesterday and I'll be looking for you to photograph these guys, Destiny Sparks. When can you take a look at them?"

"Anytime. Where do you want me to shoot them?"

"I'll leave that up to you but I swear these kids are the hottest thing on the scene at the moment – there hasn't been anything this different since the New York Dolls!"

Conor liked a challenge and working with a raw new talent. He had felt that Jim Holden was particularly lucky to be getting a break with Nat and his label. But it looked now like it wouldn't be happening for him after all.

THIRTEEN

Eve stood at the door of her fine apartment beside the Thames. It was so lonely. She never spoke to her neighbours who lived on either side, or anyone in the block for that matter. Young single professionals who worked all day and partied all night surrounded her and she didn't feel like she fitted in.

She turned the front-door key in the lock and went into her hall, picking up a pile of envelopes on the way. It was more convenient to go straight to work from the airport but now she realised that she hadn't even a bottle of milk in the fridge and the thought of going out again didn't appeal. She dumped her suitcase in the hall and slammed the door behind her. She could run a bath – that would be the best thing to do. She strolled into the bathroom and turned on the taps.

The bright evenings of May allowed enough light in through the long windows. She went into her small but sufficient kitchen and flicked the switch on the kettle. A box of green tea rested on the work surface and she decided to have a cup – at least she wouldn't need milk. Opening the freezer door she took out a frozen meal for one from M&S and popped it into the microwave. It was the silence that she hated the most. It was eerie and sad and she wished she didn't live alone.

Suddenly her mobile phone rang. She didn't want to answer but at least the voice on the other end would be company even if it was only for a few minutes.

"Hello," she said.

"Eve, hi, it's Nicky."

"Nicky, how are you?" She had to think for a moment – there was a reason why she didn't get to say goodbye – what was it? Oh, yes . . . "How is your son?"

"He's doing great. Thankfully he didn't break any bones and his spine is fine which is what we were all worried about. He's a bit shook up after his ordeal in hospital but it could have been much worse."

"I'm glad to hear it." Eve walked over to the kettle and put a green tea bag in a porcelain mug.

"Actually I was wondering if you could help me. I'm looking for Stephen Delaney's number to thank him. He brought me to the airport . . ."

"I've finished with his file – actually I left it in New York. He doesn't require our services any more. I have to tell you I think he's got a bit of a drink problem – he was sloshed on the Sunday that you left and we ended up sleeping together. He was very odd the next morning too."

Nicky felt as if she had been dealt a blow to her stomach. How could he have slept with Eve when he was kissing her over lunch in the Boathouse earlier? Maybe he was a womaniser and laughing at them all behind his back. But deep down she didn't think that – he had seemed so genuine.

"Nicky? Are you still there?"

"Yeah, sorry. That's fine then. I won't trouble him."

"You didn't do Just for Coffee any favours with your little confession but at least he paid up in full before terminating his contract with us."

"I'm sorry. That's good that he paid the company." Nicky didn't want to talk – she felt sick inside.

"Have you spoken to Rachel?"

"Yes, I got your number off her. She's at home now."

"Tell her I'll give her a call!"

"Sure I'll tell her."

"I've left the bath running – have to go – bye, Nicky!"

"Bye!"

Eve hung up. Of course she still had Stephen's number in her phone but she didn't want to give it to Nicky. That would make it too easy for her. She had noticed the disappointment in her voice after she said that she had slept with Stephen. She had nothing to feel guilty about – after all, hadn't Nicky slept with her boyfriend and had his baby?

Nicky stared at her mobile phone and put it down on the table. How could Stephen have slept with Eve after what they had been through only a few hours before?

Daniel shuffled into the kitchen and opened the fridge door.

"Is there anything to eat?"

"You didn't touch your dinner," Nicky snapped. If she hadn't left New York so quickly the day before maybe she would have spent the night with Stephen and not Eve. If she hadn't rushed home so quickly from New York – if Daniel hadn't been playing rugby – if, if, if only!

"I felt sick earlier," Daniel said grumpily.

"Go and lie down and I'll bring you a sandwich," Nicky said a little more caringly. She was lucky that her son was well and she berated herself for being so selfish after such a near miss.

She went over to the fridge and took out the sliced ham. While spreading butter on the sliced white bread she considered what she would do the next day. Her boss wasn't too happy that she had taken another day off work. She would have to go in tomorrow. Maybe Daniel would feel better in the morning and be able for school. It was one of those times when lone parenting was extra difficult.

Imagining that anything could develop between herself and Stephen had been only foolishness on her part. He was a rich and successful businessman – why on earth would he want to have a relationship with her? A holiday fling for a weekend maybe, but she was stupid to think that it would have turned into anything else.

Nicky cut the sandwich in two first and then in four. She placed it on a plate and poured a mug of milk. It was only herself and Daniel that she had to think about and she had to put him first. She lifted the plate and mug and brought them into the living-room where Daniel was lying outstretched on the sofa.

"There you go, love," she said, putting them down on a table beside him, then leaning forward to give him a gentle kiss on the forehead.

Daniel grunted his thanks and started to munch ravenously on the sandwich.

Nicky returned to the kitchen and went straight for her phone. She had to talk to someone about her feelings so she dialled Rachel's number.

"Hello?"

"Hi, Rach, it's me."

Rachel had spoken to Nicky a little earlier to arrange collection of her suitcases and was surprised to hear from her again so soon.

"Everything okay?" she asked.

"Yeah, Daniel is fine – I just rang Eve and you'll never believe it but she spent Sunday night in New York with Stephen!"

"Really? Where did they go?"

"You don't get it!" Nicky's voice rose. "She spent the night with him!"

The penny dropped but Rachel didn't understand why Nicky sounded so upset. When they had spoken earlier Nicky had only made reference to the upgrade that Stephen had made on their flights. When Rachel had teased her about him she had dismissed the notion that there could be any romance between them.

"I guess they're two adults – why shouldn't they?"

"You still don't get it, Rach – well, I didn't tell you – while I had lunch with him we kissed – I thought he liked me."

"Why didn't you tell me?" Rachel gasped. "And do you like him?"

Nicky realised, and not for the first time, that she did and it was more than just 'like'. He was someone that made her laugh and the only man that she felt truly relaxed with. He even smoked, which was becoming a rarity.

"I suppose I do like him. But I think I was wrong."

"Well, he wouldn't have upgraded your ticket if he didn't like you at least."

"He upgraded your ticket too – maybe he's just generous."

Rachel had thought it overly generous and even the richest of men wouldn't make such a gesture unless they had a reason. It was her suspicion after seeing them in Raoul's restaurant on Saturday night that Stephen liked Nicky – but maybe he was just a player after all. Poor Nicky – she really did pick them. Now was not a good time to tell Nicky that she had met James Holden. Knowing Nicky, she would worry herself sick and come up with all sorts of unfounded complications. She would tell her tomorrow.

Just then Nicky heard some odd noises from the living-room. "Rach, I have to go! I think Daniel is being sick!"

"Okay but ring me back – to tell me how he is!"

Nicky ran into the living-room to see Daniel lying on the floor, holding his head as vomit spewed out of his mouth.

"Daniel, are you okay?" Her heart pounding she knelt by his side and held him until he stopped vomiting and fell back exhausted. Pulling a cushion from the sofa, she placed it under his head. "I'll go get a tea towel, love."

She rummaged around the kitchen, frantically grabbing a bucket and cloths.

Daniel hadn't been himself all day. For such a usually loving boy he had been bad-mannered and aggressive.

"Here, let me clean that away." She gently wiped his mouth and then began to tidy up around him. "What's hurting, love?"

"I've got pins and needles in my arms."

Something was seriously wrong. Her mother's intuition told her that.

"I'll get you a drink of water and then I'm ringing the medical helpline to see what to do."

Nicky went into the kitchen and groped around looking for the number. Whatever was happening was related to the incident on the rugby pitch, of that she felt sure.

Stephen fumbled with the key as he opened the front door of his beautiful apartment on Aylesbury Road. He had pottered about in head office for as long as he could but left feeling surplus to requirements. The new acquisition in New York would be a definite winner but that didn't give him the buzz that it used to. There was a time when any large purchase left him excited but now little moved him. He was only involved in the signing of papers nowadays – his company had so many directors there was really little or no need for him to be around at all. It made him consider again something that he thought about a lot – going back to work on a more permanent basis. He needed to feel the sense of responsibility again that he had handed over to find a new life – this new life that hadn't been all that he hoped it would. All he was left with was empty hours filled with bouts of drinking that he never indulged in when he was working hard. Those bouts had led to mistakes – not least the one he made in New York.

He hated himself for sleeping with Eve and letting Nicky slip out of his life so quickly. The one woman to create any impact on him emotionally for years and he left her at a departure gate without even taking her number. If only he could remember where she worked – he couldn't and wouldn't ring Eve to get it.

Throwing his briefcase on the table in his study he went over to pour himself a Tyrconnell whiskey at the drinks cabinet – it was his favourite single malt. He hit the switch on the remote and strains of Chopin filled the room. He was definitely in the mood for Chopin.

He sat on a large black leather reclining chair and ran his fingers around the rim of the crystal glass. Taking a sip, he closed his eyes and tried to picture Nicky's face. It made him feel like a cigarette so he lit up a Marlboro and reached across to grab an ashtray from a nearby table. Just then his mobile rang and he jumped up to answer it – maybe, just maybe, it was Nicky – surely Eve would give her his number if she asked? He winced as he remembered the awkward encounter with the tall auburn-haired woman the previous morning.

The name on the screen of his mobile flashed *Frank* and he considered whether to take it or not. When it stopped he felt the decision had been made for him. But a few seconds later the phone rang again. This time he answered.

"Hiya, Frank!"

"I knew you'd answer if I kept ringing – I missed you today – where are you?"

"At home."

"Alone?"

What a stupid question, Stephen thought. "Sure – I'm going to hit the sack."

"I'm down the road from you in the Four Seasons and Jessica has a few very attractive single friends with her – come on over!"

Stephen sighed. "I'm really tired."

"Don't go all funny on me – you have to get in the swing of meeting women – those Just for Coffee girls will be fixing you up for dates soon."

Stephen took a sip from his glass. "I won't be doing any dating – I terminated any dealings with them – it was a crazy idea."

"Ah, Stephen!" Frank groaned. "You desperately need help – get into a taxi and get down here now – okay?"

What had he got to lose? He gulped back the remaining contents of his glass and grabbed his jacket. But he wasn't giving up on Nicky – he didn't have her number and he would have to be resourceful to find it – but find it he would.

Rachel closed the door of Holly's bedroom – she was sleeping soundly. She checked the next room and Ben was also asleep. The bedside light in Sarah's room told her that her daughter was still awake. Quietly she entered. Sarah jerked as she saw her mother and slid something under her pillow.

"Are you reading, love?"

"No – I was just writing in my diary."

"Was everything okay while I was away?" Rachel asked, sitting down on the bed. "You've been very quiet since I got home."

"Yeah, it was fine," Sarah replied, placing the pen on the bedside locker. "The others did nothing around the house but I knew they wouldn't."

"What about your father? Was he nice to you?"

"Whisper, Mum! He's only downstairs and might hear us!"

Rachel looked at the fear etched across her daughter's beautiful young face and shivered. Was Sarah turning into another of his victims? Maybe she had been selfish going to New York – she should have guessed that Derek would take his angst out on someone while she was away.

"Sarah, did your father give you a hard time while I was away?"

"He was in a terrible mood – all of the time."

"Did he shout at you – or . . .?"

"He didn't hit me."

Thank God, Rachel thought. She would never forgive herself if he laid a finger on their daughter.

"Mum – when are you going to do something about him?"

Rachel moved uneasily around the bed. She had wondered when she would be having this conversation with her daughter. "He's been in good form since I got home this morning."

Sarah arched her eyebrows. "How long will that last?"

Rachel knew that she was right. There was no way that it would. "What do you think I should do?"

"Go and talk to one of the crisis helplines. I've heard about them in school. They came out and gave us a talk one day."

Rachel would never do that. But she knew that she had to do something.

"I'll see – give me a couple of days."

"I bet he'll have hit you by then!" Sarah said adamantly.

Rachel hated to admit it but she knew that her daughter was right.

Stephen passed the impressive collection of Irish art as he made his way through the corridors of the Four Seasons Hotel. The Brian Bourke was one of his favourites and he reminded himself to check out White's auctioneers during the week – they could definitely acquire a nice piece of Bourke's for him.

Eventually he came to the grand doors of the Ice Bar which was heaving with glamorous models and well-heeled men. Stephen stood conspicuously at the doors for a moment while he tried to locate Frank and the harem of women that he had described. It didn't take him long to spy his tall friend with silver-grey hair in the corner. His stunning wife Jessica was holding a glass of champagne and standing by his side, talking to three other women. Stephen considered getting a quick whiskey before he joined the group but it was too late as Frank's long arm waved in the air and he beckoned to Stephen to join him.

Through the bodies and bar stools Stephen strolled over to his friend. He wished desperately that the smoking ban had never been introduced.

"Glad you could make it, old man!" Frank said, patting Stephen on the back.

"Hi, Stephen," Jessica said with her perfectly smooth Dublin 4 accent. "I'd like you to meet Emma, Caroline and Gina."

"Hello, girls," Stephen said and nodded at them in turn. "Can I get you another bottle of Bollinger?"

"That would be lovely," Emma said with a wide smile.

She must be the outgoing one, Stephen thought to himself. Caroline had flaming red hair and a frown and Stephen wondered why she was there at all. The third girl, Gina, was pretty – she had brown hair and lovely eyes – not too unlike Nicky if he were to compare them. She gave a warm and natural smile and although she was dressed in a sharp black business suit it was obvious that she was softer than the other two.

Jessica picked up on the attraction immediately. "You know, Gina and I were associates together when we started off," she explained to Stephen. "She's a partner now at Coyle & Brennan and I wouldn't be surprised if she's a senior by the autumn!"

Stephen raised the glass of whiskey that Frank had just handed him. "Congratulations – that takes some doing!"

"I just work too hard. If I had a good social life I'd probably be an associate still!"

Stephen liked her modesty. There were plenty of pushy women trying to sing their own praises when they first met him – modesty was one of the things that attracted him about Nicky. The similarity between the two women was really amazing.

"I'm just slipping out for a cigarette!" Gina said, reaching for her handbag.

"There's some company for you, Stephen," Frank said, giving his friend a nudge. "The rest of us don't smoke."

Gina led the way as Stephen followed with his box of Marlboro in hand. When they reached the tall ashtrays at the entrance pillars to the hotel Stephen offered Gina a cigarette.

"Thanks," she said, taking one from the box.

Stephen leant forward to light it and watched as she took a long deep drag from her cigarette.

She really was remarkably like Nicky.

"Where are you from, Gina?"

"The northside originally – I get a hard time in work about that!"

"Me too. Griffith Avenue."

"I'm from the Malahide Road – so we were practically neighbours!"

"Where do you live now?"

"I've an apartment in the IFSC but I need to get out of the city," Gina said, releasing a long cloud of white smoke from her lips. "I'm never at home and if I was somewhere like Sandymount or Clontarf maybe I'd be more inclined to walk on a nice summer evening – like tonight!"

"I know what you mean. I'm on Aylesbury Road and I wouldn't mind moving out to Dalkey or Howth but I know I'd never walk no matter where I lived!"

They both laughed at the same time, each understanding where the other was coming from.

"How come I never met you before, Gina?" Stephen was entranced by her simple classic beauty and tilted his head to get a better view of her profile.

"As I said, I don't get out much. I was living with a partner in the firm and he was as much a workaholic as I am. We weren't having much fun and grew apart – we were like strangers after living together for three years."

"Same thing happened with my ex-wife!"

"I wish I could just let it go – not take my work home with me."

Stephen nodded in agreement. "I officially retired last year, thinking that it would make me stop but I'm still involved in deals here and there and I realise that I need something – I'm not into cars or golf or any other leisure activities."

"I tried sailing and skiing – hated them both!" Gina said with a roll of her eyes.

Stephen laughed. "I have a 40-foot Beneteau tied up in the National Yacht Club in Dun Laoghaire – I've been out in it twice!"

"How long have you had it?"

Stephen laughed and took another drag from his cigarette. "Ten years!"

"What are we like!" Gina said, shaking her head. "Sometimes I wish I could just leave work early and go to the pictures or do something totally normal."

"I haven't been to the pictures for years either," Stephen nodded.

"Actually," Gina suggested with eyes widened, "do you fancy going one night during the week?"

Stephen thought for a minute. "On a date?" He wasn't sure how he felt about a date with a woman he'd only met a few minutes before. It had been a long time since he'd had a date and now suddenly in a few short days three attractive women had come his way – they were like the Number 42 bus!

"Yeah, why not call it a date!" Gina shrugged. "Thursday night? I'm not in court Friday and I could leave reasonably early on Thursday."

Stephen wasn't sure but at least she wasn't a man-eater like Eve and she seemed more down to earth than most of the women Frank's wife introduced him to. Finally he decided to take a leap of faith – why not? He wasn't doing anyone any harm. It was only a movie!

"Thursday it is – you'll have to give me your number." He took his mobile phone out of his pocket.

He wasn't going to make the same mistake twice.

It was one o'clock in the morning and Nicky couldn't sleep. The phone call to the medical helpline hadn't alleviated her concern so she rang the hospital and they weren't much better. Daniel was asleep now but he had vomited again before going to bed. He didn't seem to want liquids even though it was obvious that he was getting more and more dehydrated each time that he vomited.

How could everyone be so flippant when he could have broken his neck so easily? The injury didn't seem to be hurting but he was having bad headaches. She would make it her business to take him back to the hospital the next day. She knew that something was wrong and it was up to her and nobody else to come to his aid, just like it had been on every other occasion in his life.

She heard her stomach rumble and realised that it was still on New York time. She had forgotten to eat any dinner with her concern over Daniel. She slid out of the bed and shuffled into her slippers. Pulling on her dressing-gown she dragged her feet along until she was out on the landing of her modest three-bedroom home.

Daniel's breathing was heavy and coarse. If only she had support. Her boss would be mad if she took the next day off but she felt left with no choice – Daniel needed further medical attention and she had to get it for him soon. Nobody seemed to be able to help. She thought of Stephen and felt even more lonely than usual.

"Rachel, it's wonderful to see you," Tony said, giving her hand a warm shake. "Looking lovely as usual!"

He gave her a peck on the cheek and she smelt the pristine aroma of his aftershave and soap. His suit was smart with pinstripes and he wore a lilac silk tie over a white shirt.

"Thanks, Tony," she said with a weak smile. The kind GP was always cheerful and caring with her and his surgery was a place where she felt safe.

"Sit down there and tell me how all the family are!" His lilting West of Ireland *blas* meant that young and old alike loved listening to his voice.

"Grand, thanks." Rachel didn't think she could go through with it. She had promised Alex that she would but now she was here she wondered if Dr Tony Crosby would believe her.

"And how are you yourself – hope you're not doing too much – I know what you mums are like, rushing around caring for everyone."

Rachel swallowed hard. How would she phrase it? Would she show him the fresh marks that he'd made on her arm and legs? Rachel felt the tears well up in her eyes and a lump swell in her throat.

"I'm in a bit of trouble," she managed to say.

Tony sensed the seriousness of the situation instantly and put a supportive hand on top of Rachel's. "Take your time, love – there's no rush."

Rachel thought of the big queue outside in the waiting-room – this was the reason Tony was so popular – he always had plenty of time for everyone.

"I'm scared. I don't know how to say it."

"Take all the time in the world," Tony urged gently.

"Derek gets angry sometimes and hits me!" She felt as if she was vomiting out the words.

Tony didn't looked shocked or like he didn't believe her – quite the opposite.

"Rachel, where does he hit you?"

Rachel retracted her hand and shrugged. "Different places – mostly arms, ribs, back and sometimes legs."

"Ever in the face or head?"

Rachel shook her head at first and then considered it best to tell all. "A couple of times across the face – just black eyes."

"How many times has this happened?"

"It's been going on for years – since Sarah was born!" It was getting easier to tell now that she had started.

"What about the kids – does he touch them?"

Rachel shook her head. "I've never seen him and they would tell me – I think – I hope."

"But it will be affecting them – have they seen him hit you?"

Rachel nodded. She felt ashamed and wasn't sure why. It felt like she was the one who had instigated this whole pattern from the beginning.

"Do you want me to take a look at where he hit you?"

Rachel wasn't sure. Alex had seen the bruises. Maybe Tony didn't believe her and he needed to see them.

"Do you have to see them?"

"No, pet, not at all – it's completely up to you. When did he hit you last?"

"Last night – I was in New York with my friend for the weekend – I came home on Tuesday and he hit me the next night."

Tony took a sharp intake of breath. It was something that was cropping up more and more in so-called respectable society. Husbands coming home and taking their angst out on their wives – he hated it and wished they all had the bravery to tell him like Rachel had.

"I have a number here that you have to ring, Rachel. There is very little I can do but these people will help you and you need to get some good counselling. We need to get you strong. This isn't going to be easy but it can't go on. You would be wise to go to the police as well just in case.

"In case what?"

Tony didn't want to scare her but sometimes a wife-beater could go too far and the consequences could be fatal. "Well, it would just be better for everyone's sake." He scribbled some names and numbers down on his notepad. "Take a good course of vitamins. Have the guards' number handy at all times. And I want you to speak to this woman tonight – she's a terrific counsellor and she'll see you quickly if you tell her that I sent you. Now, do you hear me – you have to do this!"

Rachel nodded. She knew she had to do it – she had promised Alex and Conor. Sarah had been right about Derek and it was too painful to hear her daughter speak as she did about her own father.

"Thanks, Tony," she said, taking the page from him.

"Ring me anytime – here's my mobile number," he said, scribbling it down on the notepad. "You'll always get me on it."

He gave her a gentle hug before opening the surgery door. It meant a lot to her that he had believed her. Maybe others could see through the other side of Derek too.

She paid the receptionist on the way out and made her way to the car. The thought of returning home was traumatic.

She could hardly remember Alex's face – it had faded much quicker than she had ever imagined. With the phone numbers Tony had given her still clutched in her hand, she got into her car and started the engine. Only one more hour until it was time to pick up Holly from school – she wondered how her youngest had been affected by the trauma in her family. Such a bright and happy child normally, she hoped that she would remain so and not become affected by it like Sarah obviously was. Sarah had become angry and not just with her father but with all men in general.

The drive from Raheny to Portmarnock was quick today and she was soon home. As she got out of her car she remembered the diary that Sarah had hidden from her two nights before. Dare she invade her daughter's privacy and see what had happened while she was away? Tony did seem concerned about the children and he was right to be – she was worried sick about them herself.

When she was only a few steps in the hallway she couldn't resist the compulsion to sneak up to Sarah's room while her daughter was in school. Slowly she opened the door handle and looked around the tidy small bedroom. Sarah was practical by nature and Rachel had thought it odd that she should choose to move from a bigger room to this until the young girl explained that she would find it easier to keep it tidy. How organised and applied her daughter was – so unlike her.

She sat down on the bed and cautiously put her hand under the pillow until she felt the hard cover of Sarah's diary – it was pink with the Playboy Bunny embossed on the corner. A part of her winced at what she was about to do – she had always promised herself that she wouldn't invade her daughter's privacy but she needed to get inside Sarah's head and see if she really was safe in her own home.

Inside the front page was a warning: *If anyone opens this diary you will go to hell!* Rachel stopped before turning to the next page – such a threat left her disturbed.

She turned the page and her eyes widened in surprise. It was laid out completely differently to the way that she had imagined it would be – instead of script in paragraphs, the whole text was in bullet-point format with lots of figures and numbers.

May 13th
6 stone 10 pounds. Shouldn't have eaten that chocolate bar *
two apples
40 sit-ups
must try harder
* *
May 14th
2 packets of cheese and onion
bag of chips *
had to eat dinner – tonight Mum home
*
bag of jelly beans

And so it went on and on, accounting food and dotted with more and more astrisks which seemed to Rachel to have some ominous meaning. She pored over page after page of the diary. It wasn't what she had expected to find. Sarah had a lovely figure and although she was thin, she was definitely not skinny. Rachel had thought it perfectly natural that the puppy fat should start to fall off once she started secondary school last year. This obsession with what she was eating clearly spelt something more awful than a desire to lose a few pounds. It was either anorexia or bulimia.

And what did those sinister asterisks stand for? What was so secret that it could be written only as a symbol? And why were they sometimes attached to items of food while at other times they stood on their own? As she flicked through the diary a flash of intuition told her what they were: the asterisks meant that Sarah was vomiting.

Rachel was horrified. Had she been so preoccupied with herself and keeping Derek appeased that she had ignored her beautiful daughter who was obviously screaming for help? This was the very sign she needed to act immediately. She felt inside the pocket of her jacket and pulled out the numbers that Tony had given her. She knew what she had to do.

Alex hadn't fully recovered from the experience of painting Rachel's image. He sat and stared at it – half expecting her to come out of the canvas but, as he did that, he realised that he would probably never see her in the flesh ever again. The thought hit him like a blow to the gut and he had to look away from the painting. There was a collective exhibition in one of the galleries that he used and he toyed with the idea of submitting it. But first he had to ask himself if he wanted to show it to others – or maybe he could just keep her locked up in his studio forever – keep her all to himself.

Suddenly his phone rang and he smiled when he saw Conor's number in the screen. They hadn't spoken since Rachel had gone back to Dublin – at least it meant that his friend wanted to talk to him still.

"Hey, man!" Alex answered. "What's up?"

"Hiya, Alex – do you fancy meeting in Tarts? I'm on my way there now."

"Sure – I don't feel up to doing anything today. See you in ten!"

Alex relished the chance to meet Rachel's brother. Maybe he would have some news of her. He grabbed his keys and shut the door behind him. New York was heating up and it looked like summer was starting early. Alex liked to get out of town at the height of summer and had considered going to Maine a few weeks before. Maybe he needed a change of scenery – his work was definitely taking a shift in a different direction. Getting away from New York might help him to find some new inspiration in the same way as meeting Rachel had.

He caught a cab to Once Upon A Tart where Conor was already sitting at one of the small round tables out the front. Two mugs rested on the table and Alex was pleased that his friend had already got him his favourite Americano. It meant that things could and would return to normal between them.

"So – what's happening?" Alex said, sitting down and taking the cup of coffee up in his hands.

"Things are good – Nat has signed a band that he thinks are really hot – like the New York Dolls!"

"Interesting! This town needs some inspiring acts – especially since CBGB's closed. What's happening with that guy we met in Pravda the other night?"

"I did the shoot but it turns out Nat's not signing him after all. Did you know that he was the guy Nicky and Eve went out with in college?"

"Hmm?" Alex didn't seem to register what Conor was talking about.

"The row in Kelly and Ping – when Eve said that she didn't want everyone knowing her business! Years ago Nicky had taken her boyfriend off her and that's why they fell out."

"I'm sorry, man, I'm a bit distracted – I think I remember something about it. You see, I've painted a picture that I'd like you to see."

Conor raised his eyebrows in interest. "Really – what of?"

Alex swallowed, unsure how Conor would feel about his subject matter. "It's of Rachel."

"Did she pose for you?" Conor asked as he frowned.

"No, man – I did it from memory."

"That can't have been easy!"

"Normally I'd say it's impossible but something took me over, man – the other night – just after she'd left. I wasn't in the mood for sleep or going out and I started to paint – I couldn't stop – worked through the night."

"That's not like you, Alex!" Conor knew Alex to be one of the most pragmatic and clinical artists of the set that he had become acquainted with on the New York art scene.

"Do you want to see it?" Alex persisted.

"Sure," Conor said. "Next time I'm in your place."

"You don't understand, Conor." Alex was becoming more animated as he spoke. "I don't know what to do with this – she's just beautiful!"

Was he still talking about the painting? Conor cleared his throat. It was time that Alex was brought back down to earth.

"Listen, man, I know you liked my sister but she's got a whole life in Dublin and she doesn't need you messing it up. I mean, you got to promise me you won't try and contact her!"

Alex's expression froze. He didn't feel that he could do that but he knew that he didn't want to upset her either. "I'll never do anything to hurt her or cause her any pain!"

"And you won't contact her?"

"Not unless she contacts me first!"

Conor took a sip from his coffee, feeling as satisfied as he could be with the answer Alex had given him.

With quivering hands Rachel carefully pressed the digits on the piece of paper in front of her into the phone. She could barely focus on the woman's name. Darina – that was it. When the ring tone was answered by a voicemail she almost hung up – but that would have been too easy.

"Hello, my name is Rachel Sloan and Tony Crosby gave me your number – I was wondering if I could make an appointment – my number is . . ."

"Hello?" came a voice on the other end of the line.

"Oh, hello – is that Darina?"

"Yes, I was working on something and didn't get to the phone before the voicemail clicked in," the friendly and warm voice informed her. "Tony is a very good friend and I like to look after his patients well. What can I do for you?"

"I was wondering if you could fit me in for an appointment?"

"I work Monday, Wednesday and Thursday evenings – or would you be able to make a morning?"

"Actually, that would suit me better," Rachel said, her spirits lifting on hearing the helpful tone of Darina's voice.

"I do Wednesday and Friday mornings."

"Either would do, I'm keen to see you as soon as I can."

"I've just had a cancellation for this Friday if that suited?"

"That would be perfect, thanks. What time?"

"Eleven okay for you?"

Rachel hadn't expected the arrangement to be made so quickly or smoothly. "Eh, yes."

"Do you know where I am?" Darina continued to be brief and businesslike.

"Yes, Tony gave me your address. That's great – I'll see you on Friday. Bye."

"See you then."

Rachel hung up, with a great sense of relief.

She had a lot to think about before she met Darina. What was she going to say? What was Darina going to ask her? She would go on to the internet to find out everything that she could about eating disorders – after she rang to see how Daniel was doing.

There was also the matter of James Holden . . . it really was time that she told Nicky about him.

"Hello?" Nicky answered the phone in a breathless and hesitant voice.

"Hi, Nicky – how's Daniel?"

"Oh hi, Rach!" Nicky sighed. "I'm in bits – Daniel has gone off to school and I'm not happy about it. He's all over the place since that bashing he got on Sunday. I wish he didn't play rugby."

"At least he's well enough to go to school!"

"That's just the thing – I didn't want him to go but he insisted – he's been so stroppy since I brought him home from hospital."

"Sounds like Ben – he's been stroppy since I brought him home from the maternity hospital!"

Nicky laughed. Rachel did have her moments and she was glad to hear her say something funny to relieve the tension.

"So how are your lot?"

Rachel swallowed hard. She didn't want to upset Nicky with

her problems – she had enough of her own. "Just getting back to normal – you know?"

"I envy you with your steady life, Rach."

If only you knew, Rachel thought. Should she tell her about James? Nicky sounded so flustered it seemed this was not a good time to do it.

But as the days went by she wondered if there ever would be a good time to tell her friend that she had met the father of her son.

"Hello," Conor said into his cellphone.

"Hi, Conor, it's Jim here – from the photo shoot on Monday."

"Oh, hi," said Conor cautiously. "How are you doing?"

"Not great, man. I've just had a call from Nat."

Conor could hear the disappointment in his voice and cleared his throat. He didn't want to let on that he had already heard that Jim had been dropped. "Oh? Bad news?"

"Yeah, Nat's not closing the deal – I'm really pissed off!"

"That's terrible, man," Conor said sympathetically.

"Yeah, I'm going to go on the road anyway but I wanted to use the photos if that was okay? Nat said I could."

"Sure – do you want me to email them to you?"

"I don't suppose I could see them first and then maybe save them on a CD? My computer isn't great."

"Call around to my studio – it's in Chelsea."

"Nat told me where it was."

"I'm here now and should be for another couple of hours so call on up."

"Thanks, Conor."

"No probs." Conor felt genuinely sorry for the guy. This wasn't the first time that Nat had built an artist's hopes up and then left them hanging out to dry.

FOURTEEN

Gina looked at her watch. It was ten minutes before she was due to meet Stephen at the Irish Film Centre and there was no way she was going to be finished with her work. It wasn't exactly the start she wanted to give to a possible new relationship but she didn't want to leave any stone unturned for her client. This case was turning out to be more complex than she had first thought. Should she ring Stephen and ask him to meet her later or cancel altogether?

This was how she dealt with everyone in her life and it had left her with few close friends. Eventually, when you put work before those around you, they get tired and don't call any more. This wasn't the way she wanted to start things off with Stephen but she felt as if she had no choice.

She dialled his number on her mobile and stuck it between her chin and her shoulder. She often continued working while having conversations on the phone.

Stephen answered so quickly it startled her.

"Hello?"

"Hi, oh Stephen – I'm really sorry but I'm after losing track of the time and I still have at least another hour's work to do before I can leave."

"You sound like I used to!" he said with a laugh.

"I'm sorry – can we make it for another night next week?"

Stephen was sitting in a Mercedes – the taxi company that he used was always available to pick him up from anywhere and at any time he wanted in Dublin city.

"No!" he said curtly.

Gina was startled by such a response and not sure how to take it. "I'm sorry if I ruined your plans but I have to look after this client …"

"I'm going to the Clarence – I'll be waiting for you in the bar – see you in one hour exactly – I'll be timing you!"

Gina mellowed when she heard the humour in his voice and let out a loud sigh. "I see – so you're not the kind of guy to take no for an answer?"

He had already let one girl that he liked slip through his fingers. He wasn't about to do that again.

"Exactly – I'll be waiting!" he exclaimed and turned off his phone.

It suited him not to sit through a movie – he'd feel more comfortable meeting Gina with a drink in his hand. He would have to be careful not to overdo it before she arrived. He had already got into one regrettable situation this week with his drinking habits and would have to be careful that it didn't happen again.

He wondered how Nicky was managing and how her son was getting on. It was amazing how she'd had such an impact on his life in such a short time. It was a shame that she left without giving him her number. Suddenly it struck him that he could find her through her work! There couldn't be that many Irish women's magazines. But what was her surname? He tried to imagine the ticket in JFK airport but the events had all happened so quickly he couldn't remember clearly what it was. He thought it started with P – or was it B? Without hesitation he rang his personal assistant. She was an efficient girl and would find her number easily – he hoped.

The chauffeur was used to driving Stephen around and, even though he hadn't been informed, realised that he was not going to the Film Centre. Still, it would be polite to check first.

"The Clarence, is it, sir?"

"Yes, please," Stephen replied before his assistant's voicemail clicked on.

Jim rang on the buzzer of the studio door. The buildings around Chelsea were really cool.

"Is that you, Jim?" Conor asked through the intercom.

"Yeah, it's me."

"Come on up – I'm on the second floor."

Jim pushed the door open and walked into the lofty hallway. He ascended the narrow staircase to the second floor. Conor was waiting at the door to his studio.

"Come on in."

Jim followed Conor into the work space – covered with filing systems and photographic equipment.

"You've got a great place."

"It's in a good spot," Conor said, guiding him over to a large desk and a widescreen computer. "Tell me which ones you want and I'll save them into a folder. We're better off making a couple of CDs while we're at it."

"Whatever you say, man!"

Conor felt genuinely sorry for this guy whose dreams had

been shattered since the last time they had met. And he was increasingly curious about him. He wondered just how much Jim knew about the son he had growing up on the other side of the Atlantic.

"Did you write that song you were singing the other day? The first one you sang."

"'Daniel'?"

"That's the one!"

"I use that as my warm-up – Daniel's the name of my son."

Conor was dumbfounded. This guy didn't add up. How come he had written a song about his son and yet didn't try and get in touch with him or his mother in all the fifteen years they had been apart? Should he tell him about Nicky – and Eve? Would he want to know if the shoe were on the other foot? That was easy to answer – definitely he'd want to know. But would Nicky want to see him again?

"Wow – that's really cool!"

Jim shrugged. "I wrote it a couple of years ago – after my father died I finally admitted to myself that I had a son, but it was too late to do anything about it. Meeting your sister the other night really brought me back – I had a relationship with her friend when we were kids in college."

"It's probably a bit late telling you this now but her friend Nicky was over here with her last weekend."

Jim flinched. "Nicky?"

"Yeah . . . she told us that she had a fourteen-year-old son."

Jim was visibly shaken by the revelation. "I haven't seen her in fifteen years." He shook his head in disbelief. "She was here! Man, I don't know how I'd handle it if I had to face her."

"She's really nice."

"I bet she hates me!" Jim looked down at the palms of his hands.

"I wouldn't say that. It can't have been easy raising a kid on her own though – she's doing a really good job." He had to stop himself from elaborating. He didn't know if he should tell him about the accident – after all, he didn't know the correct prognosis.

Jim looked up. "Do you have her number?"

"I could get it for you."

Jim looked down at his palms again. "I really wanted to get in touch a few years back – I didn't know that she called him Daniel until I ran into someone who knew her in Spain just before I left for the States. I've been really curious to see him and get in touch but I feel so guilty when I think of the way I left her on her own. I never loved her, you see – it was just a fling."

Conor understood and nodded his head in solidarity.

"You see, I was crazy about her friend Eve. She really broke my heart."

Conor empathised completely. He had come to understand how the austere yet stunningly beautiful Eve could have such a hold on a guy.

"So what are you going to do now?" he asked.

"I don't know what's best – I'd love to see my own flesh and blood but I don't want him to hate me – like he has every right to."

"He won't hate you."

"I bet his mother hates me, despite what you say – and if she's told our son the truth about me I'm sure he hates me too."

"Why don't you try? What harm could it do?"

"That's just it – I don't want to cause any more pain than I already have."

Conor felt for the guy – he wasn't as bad as he had seemed at the beginning. Maybe the letdown from Nat had mellowed him in some way.

Conor took out his phone and texted Rachel.

"I'll give you Nicky's number now and then you can decide later what you want to do with it. This is probably a good time to get in touch with your son – before he's a grown adult and then mightn't want to ever know you."

Jim nodded in grateful agreement. "Thanks, man. But, you know, I wonder if I'll ever have the guts to make the move to call her."

"At least now you'll have the choice."

Eve had to hand it to Lucille as the phone rang for the fourth time today – she certainly was persistent.

Would she take the job? Moving to Paris sounded glamorous but it wasn't where she wanted to be. Matchmaking people who didn't have the time to put into a relationship didn't seem like a good enough reason any more to continue what she was doing. Sleeping with people like Stephen and her old affair with Tom seemed futile and left her feeling dirty. But to stay in Chiswick didn't feel right either.

She needed someone to talk to but her acquaintances in the UK were just that – none were real friends. She had blown it now with Nicky too and if she had confided in Rachel about what she had done with Stephen she wouldn't be surprised if Rachel didn't want anything to do with her either. It was suddenly sad to feel so lonely at what was supposed to be the prime of her life. What was it all for? Maybe Conor was right and she needed to sort her head out. To deal with her demons!

As if on cue her phone rang again. This time it was a familiar number but one that she hadn't seen flash on her screen for months.

"Eve?" the Surrey accent at the other end of the line asked. "Is that you?"

"Yes, John," she said with a smile. "How are you?"

"Good, good – and you?"

"Fine – to what do I owe the pleasure?" There was no animosity between them but there was certainly no regret.

"Just wondering if we could meet up for a beer?"

"Darling, you know I don't meet for beer but a G&T will do – where are you?"

"I'm down at the Red Lion – I was meeting Bart for a quick one after work and as I'm in the neighbourhood I thought I'd give you a call to see if you were on your tod."

"Actually I am and that would be surprisingly nice!"

At least she could be civil – John hadn't done anything bad during their relationship – he'd just been there at the right time – or wrong time!

"Great – see you then, girl!"

Eve gave a little laugh. It was his use of words like "girl", that had grated on her so irritatingly when she was married to him, that made her smile now. He certainly wasn't the worst man she had been in a relationship with. It was a shame that their sex life hadn't been as active as it should have been for a couple in their thirties. But John was patient and understanding with her for that horrible time after Harry died and that was a virtue that she admired to this day.

She rummaged around the make-up bag that sat permanently on the ledge of the window in her en suite bathroom. Her Flash Bronzer came in handy at times like this as she put some of the gel on her finger tips and spread it over her arms and legs. Her suit wasn't appropriate attire for the Red Lion at any time of the day or evening so she quickly changed into cropped jeans and a T-shirt. It was nice to be able to slip on open-toe sandals of a May evening. The short walk to the Red Lion meant that she would be there before her mules pinched her feet.

She grabbed her handbag and keys. Leaving the apartment behind, she walked through the leafy street. It was a surprise to hear from John – she hadn't given him much thought since he moved out of their apartment. It went to show how separate their lives had become for the months and years before they eventually split up. A part of her felt sad, now that she had heard his voice this evening. She wondered why he was asking to see her.

Stephen ordered another Tyrconnell whiskey and small jug of water from the pretty Chinese waitress. The wood panelling of the stylish octagon bar reminded him vaguely of New York. He knew that the Clarence was a popular choice for solicitor types. He had arranged to meet many at different times in his career at this venue. It was nice to feel anonymous as he sipped the remains of his glass.

He hardly recognised Gina as she entered the bar with her briefcase swinging at her side.

He waved over and she caught his eye instantly. She looked even lovelier than he had remembered from the Ice Bar.

She quickened her pace as she approached him and in her smile he saw the reason why he had made a date with her so impetuously.

"Hi there!" he said, standing up to give her a peck on the cheek.

"Sorry I'm a bit late –"

"Perfect timing – I'm just going to pop out for a cigarette – join me?"

"Love to!" she said as they walked out to the smoking area. "I've only smoked three cigarettes all day."

"I thought this was a quiet day for you?" Stephen said as he held open his packet of Marlboro and she took one gratefully.

Gina shook her head. "Tomorrow is generally my quietest day of the week but there isn't any day that I'm not run off my feet!" She took a light from him and breathed in the smoke deeply.

"If you're only smoking three a day you're not a real smoker then, are you?"

"I think I could give them up if I had to but I look forward to them – they're my treat – as long as I don't smoke too many."

"I wish I could give them up completely," Stephen sighed. "They have become downright debilitating!"

"I think some people use them to pull the opposite sex!"

Stephen nodded. "Well, it got us together, didn't it?" And in a way it got him and Nicky together, he thought.

Gina laughed. "I think Jessica got us together – how unsubtle can she be – arranging for her three single girlfriends to be available when she just happens to be meeting her husband's single friend!"

"Actually, to be fair to Jessica, I was only a last-minute invitee."

"Jessica doesn't leave anything to chance – I bet that whole scene was orchestrated!"

Stephen shrugged. "Maybe – but if she did plan it I'm glad!"

Gina put the cigarette up to her lips and whispered under her breath. "Me too!"

Eve almost didn't recognise John. He sat hidden in a corner away from the bar. It was very unlike him – usually he went automatically to the high stools and counter. His thin sandy hair had grown and he was wearing a scruffy T-shirt, not a designer shirt as she had expected.

He looked up as she approached and got to his feet. He leaned forward to embrace her and Eve reciprocated.

"Looking gorgeous as always, Eve!"

"Thanks, John. And you are as charming as always!"

"I'm really glad you were free – I tried the apartment a couple of times over the weekend and you weren't there."

Eve sat back and crossed her legs on the Victorian padded chair to get more comfortable.

"Actually I was in New York for the weekend."

"Lucky you – I can't remember the last time I was there."

"Summer 2002 – we went back for a weekend – remember?"

John nodded his head awkwardly. "Right – that was when we got engaged, wasn't it?"

Eve nodded silently.

"You know I still love you, Eve!" he said smiling.

Eve hadn't expected John to come out with this – it was the very last thing she expected him to say.

"You'll always be like a really good flatmate," he said, now grinning, "or sister!"

Eve berated herself for entertaining the thought that John could have any amorous feelings towards her. She hadn't treated him well – hadn't she been having affairs for most of the time they were married? John was a good man and he deserved better.

"So why were you looking to speak to me this weekend?" Now that it was clear that he wanted something Eve felt it was time to get to the point.

John picked up his pint glass and took a quick sip. "I was wondering if we could speed the divorce up a bit – if it suited you of course!"

Eve didn't mind his request in the slightest but she was curious about the sudden hurry. When John left shortly after Christmas he'd said that he didn't care how long the divorce took and there was no need to hurry the process up by declaring one partner had been unfaithful or any of the usual causes needed to apply for a speedy decree nisi.

"Why the hurry now?" she asked, knowing in her heart that there could only be one answer.

John took another sip from his glass and put it back down heavily onto the table.

"I've met someone and we want to get married."

Eve smiled. John was so impulsive – hadn't they married hastily too? "I don't mind if you want to move ahead with the divorce application," she said, "but you can't be with this girl all that long. I hope you don't think I'm interfering but I do care about you and maybe you could do with more time – I mean, we jumped into marriage too quickly!"

John started to fidget with the beer mat before lifting the glass to drain the last sup of beer. "This isn't easy, Eve. I don't know how to explain."

Eve saw a flush of red creep up his cheeks and she almost felt sorry for him. He was always a sensitive guy but this behaviour was uncharacteristic.

"Who is she?" she pushed. There had to be some reason why he was so anxious.

"Look, I'm getting another beer – do you want one?"

"I've hardly touched the G&T you got me," she said, finally taking a sip from the Hi-ball glass.

"I've got to get another beer."

Eve watched as he fumbled about for loose change in his pocket. From behind he looked like a guy in his twenties and the new scruffy look made him look cuter than he had been when they were together as a couple.

John returned and put his pint down as he took his seat.

"Do you remember when we met first and you used to talk about Harry?"

Eve nodded. Where was this going?

"You spoke about him like he was your other half – your soul mate."

Eve lifted her glass to conceal her face. She didn't like to be reminded of those grim days. John had been so caring and understanding. He really didn't deserve the affairs and lack of commitment that she gave their marriage.

"Look, if you've met a nice girl then I'm really happy for you – there's no need to explain."

John rubbed the back of his neck. "That's just it, girl – I do need to explain – because the person I want to marry is a bloke!"

Eve could have dropped her glass if she hadn't put it down to rest on the table seconds before. Unable to reply, she just gasped. A deep frown developed on her forehead.

"So you see why I needed to tell you this in person!"

Eve wondered how little she knew him at all. John was always so heterosexual but now that she came to think of it he was never ever jealous or suspicious and he was sensitive in a feminine way, unlike most men that she had relationships with in the past – including Harry.

"I know this must come as a bit of a shock ..."

Eve shook her head. "Look, it's fine – I mean as long as you're happy!"

John's face lit up. "Eve, I've never been happier in my life. I've always known that I was gay and I did everything to refute it. I'm really sorry for marrying you and not being totally honest."

"Did you have any gay relationships while we were married?"

John shook his head. "I've denied this part of myself for my whole life. I've never tried to do anything about my real feelings until I met Keith."

Eve wasn't sure whether she wanted to hear about it or be

spared the details. She thought that she was a good judge of personality and human nature. But this revelation did go a long way to explain why John was so sensitive and caring. He was so compassionate and patient with her after Harry died. This also explained why their sexual relationship had never been right. Eve had blamed herself for the numerous affairs that she was having but now felt somewhat vindicated.

"John, I'm really happy for you. Everyone deserves to meet that special person."

"You know I can understand now why it was so hard for you to lose Harry. I'm so sorry, Eve."

Eve nodded. This was the best conversation she had ever had with John – the first time that she could open up and be herself because he was being truthful with her.

"Thanks for letting me know."

"Hey, I want you to come to the wedding. You're a special woman, Eve, and when I couldn't make my marriage with you work there isn't another woman in the world that it would have worked with!"

Eve knew there was a compliment in there somewhere and smiled as she took a sip from her glass. "I have to say I was a bit shocked when you told me first but I think it's great. I hope Keith realises how lucky he is too."

John's gaze turned starry as he talked about Keith. "Keith wasn't like me – he'd been active sexually when he was still in school. He's lived with four blokes but now he's found his Mr Right and he doesn't want to let me go!"

"Keith's dead right. When you find that person who is totally honest with you and you can trust, you've got to grab the chance and make the most of it."

Eve gazed at John's beaming face. She envied him. How wonderful to be with someone who was honest – someone who you could be straight up with too. She thought of Conor in New York and smiled. He was the only man who said it like it is!

"Good morning, Mr Delaney."

Stephen held his head as he realised who was on the other end of the line.

"Hi, Doris, how are you?"

"Fine thanks, Mr Delaney – I have the number of two sub-editors with the name Nicky in the city."

Stephen looked over at the body splayed out on the other side of his bed – he'd done it again. This type of behaviour was completely uncharacteristic – especially twice in the one week. When was he going to learn to curtail his drinking?

"Sorry, Doris, could you email me that information and I'll call you back!"

Stephen put his iPhone down on the bedside locker and turned his attentions to the woman who was lying at his side.

"You realise I'm late for work!" Gina said, sitting up in the bed hastily.

"You put enough hours in last night – you don't want the company to own you!"

"It's because I own a part of the company that I have to work the hours I do!"

"I forgot – sorry!" Stephen said with a smile as she ran her fingers over the few curly hairs on his broad chest.

"I hope you don't think I normally do this!" she exclaimed. "It was that lethal cocktail that you ordered for me that did it!"

"Did I have one as well?"

Gina frowned. "We had three each!"

Stephen nodded. He recalled the trip to his apartment in the courtesy car with the kissing and fumbling that led to his bedroom but he couldn't remember how many drinks he'd had the previous evening.

"You know, you can certainly handle your drink, Stephen – and heaven knows how many you'd had before I got there!"

Stephen didn't try to count. He had given up counting. At least he must still have had his wits about him as Gina approved of his company enough to come back to his apartment.

"I'm sorry if I stepped out of line last night," he said.

"Don't worry," Gina giggled. "You were the perfect gent – when we got back here you took all of your clothes off and said 'have a good sleep'. You were out cold in minutes."

Stephen felt a flush of colour rise in his cheeks – he wasn't sure which was more embarrassing – if he had slept with her or the fact that he hadn't! "I hope you don't think it was because I didn't want to!"

Gina slid out from under the bedcovers, revealing a camisole top and matching lace underwear. She grabbed her clothes from the floor and held them up high enough to cover her torso. "I really have to go to work. Do you mind if I use your bathroom?"

"Work away!" he said, gesturing to the door.

When she was out of sight he picked up his iPhone and read the message Doris had sent. Nicky Thornton and Nicky Blake – that was her name – he remembered now – she was definitely Nicky Blake.

Now that he had her number he had to ask himself if he had the nerve to do anything about it. The other question was: did he want to do anything, now that this other wonderfully attractive woman had entered his life?

He had to give the matter some thought.

Nicky dumped her Clio in a reserved staff parking spot – she didn't care if she got clamped or got one of those annoying stickers plastered across her windscreen. Daniel hadn't improved overnight and Nicky was frantic as she watched him stumble out of the car.

"Are you okay?"

"I'm fine – stop fussing, would you!" he snapped.

Nicky walked alongside her son as he wavered up the steps to the entrance of the Mater hospital. The receptionist looked blankly at her as she approached the desk.

"Excuse me, my son was admitted on Sunday with a suspected broken vertebra and sent home on Monday but he hasn't been right since. I was wondering if you could get someone to take a look at him."

The receptionist blinked her long eyelashes, heavy with mascara. "You'll have to take him to A&E down the corridor," she said and lowered her head into the open file on her desk.

"Thank you," Nicky said in a tone that was far from appreciative.

Daniel was oblivious to the conversation. After one day in school he was worse than ever. Nicky had tried desperately to take his temperature but he was an awkward patient, not wanting his mother to come near him. And when he had vomited in his sleep Nicky was beside herself with concern.

The triage nurse ushered Nicky and Daniel into a line.

"We're very busy today," she said with her left hand resting on her hip. "If any of you can see your GP instead I would recommend it – you're all in for a long wait."

Is this what I've been paying my medical insurance for all these years? Nicky asked herself. She stood up and approached the uniformed woman.

"I was here on Sunday with my son and he was allowed to leave but he has been very ill all week."

"Maybe you should have brought him to your GP?" the

nurse said with a smirk and walked briskly away.

Nicky was incensed. There was no way she was leaving without a conclusive diagnosis of what was wrong with her son.

"We'll wait here," she said to Daniel, loud enough to be in earshot of the triage nurse.

A young man was rushed into the theatre on a stretcher and Nicky winced as she witnessed the fuss and upset around him. She overheard a doctor say that he had definitely broken C2 and his spinal cord was severed. Nicky felt a thankful knot in her stomach develop as case after urgent case was admitted and seen to before Daniel. At least her son was walking.

She looked at the clock on the wall which seemed to be travelling at a snail's pace.

"Would you like me to get you a sandwich from the canteen?" she asked. "It's almost lunch-time."

Daniel looked vacantly at her, then his head fell forward and he started to vomit on the linoleum flooring.

The triage nurse rushed over, calling out for a porter.

"You really should have brought him to your GP," she said dismissively to Nicky. "It's obvious that he has some sort of tummy bug."

While the porter mopped up the mess in as dignified a manner as he could, the triage nurse finally saw to Daniel.

"Come this way!" she instructed and pointed to a spot behind a curtain. "I'm just going to take your details."

"He can't talk," Nicky explained. "I'll tell you everything you need to know."

The nurse tossed her eyes heavenward and took Daniel's details. "So he's had no other symptoms apart from vomiting and a slight temperature?"

"He's a bit confused."

"Like most lads his age!" the nurse replied dismissively.

"Now, young man, give me your arm and we'll take your blood pressure and then you can go home!"

Daniel lifted his arm and the nurse wrapped the canvas around it and read the dial as the digits on the blood pressure machine rose. Nicky looked on angrily – rudeness like this display by the triage nurse only confirmed the decline she saw in Irish society since the emergence of the Celtic Tiger. Why couldn't a country as well situated economically and socially as Ireland have an adequate health system?

The nurse's brow furrowed as the digits continued to go up on the machine and Nicky could tell that there was something wrong.

"What is it?"

"It's 180 over 120," she replied abruptly. "I have to get a doctor!"

The nurse jumped to her feet and hurried outside, grabbing a woman in a white coat who was passing by. A lot of muttering went on between the two women before the second woman – a doctor presumably – rushed over to Daniel and spoke very kindly and gently.

"Daniel, is it?"

He nodded.

"We need to do a couple of tests. There's nothing for you to worry about – we'll have you seen to in no time!"

The triage nurse sat by his side and held his hand firmly. "I'll stay with him until we get him to CAT scan."

Nicky looked from one woman to the other – what was going on? Why this fuss all of a sudden? Her stomach felt as though it had been given a swift blow. The prognosis couldn't be good.

Pierre danced to his feet as he spotted Alex coming through the gallery door laden with a cumbersome canvas.

"Quick, help him!" he called to his assistant.

She duly obliged and they laid the canvas against a large pillar in the middle of the exhibition area.

"Quick, quick! Take that wrapping off!" he shouted at the poor girl who was already in the process of removing the paper.

Pierre took two steps back once the image was revealed. He rested his head on his right hand and stared silently at the painting.

Alex couldn't tell by his expression if he was concentrating or frowning. Either way he didn't care. He didn't really want to share the image of Rachel with anyone else but Conor had insisted that he showed his patron as it marked a turning point in his style.

Finally Pierre spoke. "Remarkable. It's really remarkable!"

Alex had only heard Pierre use this word when a fine example of Hopper's came into the gallery by chance a couple of years before.

"Would you consider selling it?"

Alex shook his head adamantly. "I told you that I would show it to you but it's not for sale."

"Have you others?"

"Just one!" Alex had stayed up for much of the previous night and painted another image of his muse. It was not as dramatic or luminous as the painting in front of them now but it was still a worthy piece in his new style.

"Can you do others?"

Alex scratched his head. "I'm not sure when or if I will be painting any more in the series."

"This is preposterous, Alex!" Pierre started to shake his wrist as was his habit when he didn't get his own way. "I need an exhibition of these. Where is this woman – you must get her to model for you again! She has unleashed a new passion in your work."

"It's not that simple," Alex said. He didn't like saying no to Pierre – he was one of the most important art dealers in New York. Showing your work consistently in his gallery was the best seal of approval an artist could hope for.

"I want more – when can you give me ten pieces of this calibre?"

Alex couldn't answer. He didn't know when he would get the inspiration.

"Well?" Pierre asked impatiently. "Will you give me an exhibition?"

Alex didn't know whose voice he was using but the words flowed out. "I will have your paintings in three months!"

Pierre's face changed expression instantly. "Excellent – I am very happy – make sure the canvases are all as big as this one – no, make them bigger – okay?"

Alex had really been thrown a gauntlet and he had to produce the work because an artist didn't upset Pierre and stay working in New York!

Nicky was close to tears. The doctor had tried to be sympathetic and understanding but her bedside manner couldn't appease the distraught mother. Daniel was under sedation and she was left in bewilderment in the corridor while he had a CAT scan.

She had forgotten the most important rule of the hospital and left her phone turned on. When work rang she wanted to scream on recognising the number.

"You'll have to take that outside," the Sister said brusquely to Nicky, making her even more agitated.

Nevertheless she took the few short steps out to the courtyard and dialled the office to see what they wanted. The youngest member of the secretarial staff was there to answer the phone.

"Good morning, Nicky – someone rang for you this morning – and she asked for your number and I gave it without thinking and then I thought she could be some sort of psycho or something but it was too late. She hung up once I gave it."

Under normal circumstances Nicky would have been mad with the young girl but, in the light of this new information regarding her son's health, she felt it frivolous to be annoyed.

"That's all right," she said quietly – relieved that it wasn't something serious. "Bye."

She flipped her phone shut and sat back down on the plastic chair outside of the CAT scan theatre. Finally the doctor that she had spoken to earlier reappeared with concern etched all over her face.

"Mrs Blake!"

Nicky hated it when someone started off so formally – it usually meant bad news. She nodded and swallowed hard.

"I'm afraid Daniel has a subdural haematoma," she said in a hushed tone.

"I'm sorry – that is?" Nicky conjured up all sorts of terrible thoughts.

"It's a bleed just outside the brain – we're lucky that we found it. We don't know but can only presume that it was a result of his accident playing rugby – did he say that he was struck on the head?"

Nicky shook her head. "He never said – he's just been vomiting and dazed all week."

"He will have to be operated on and the sooner the better."

Nicky gulped. "On his brain?"

"Yes – we will drain the blood off and he should be fine but there are only a handful of neurosurgeons who can do this kind of work and the delay will be getting one that is available – we will do everything that we can."

This didn't sound good enough. She was angry with the system and angry with the world. What would happen if they didn't operate quickly?

"Get someone – I don't care what it costs – I'll sell my house if I have to."

The doctor shook his head. "It's not a question of money, Mrs Blake."

"Well, what the bloody hell is it a question of?" Nicky screamed. "And stop calling me Mrs Blake!"

Rachel got out of her Renault and looked up at the smart early-twentieth-century semi-detached house where Darina had her practice. She felt butterflies flit inside her stomach. Now that she was here, she wondered how she would be able to tell a complete stranger about her problems. Since making the appointment she had unravelled a completely new problem that was even more difficult to cope with. In a way the beatings had become a part of her life but her daughter's eating disorder was something she never had to deal with before and she felt swamped.

Slowly and steadily she made her way up the path until she came to the front door. There was no bell but an old-fashioned knocker hung in the centre of the door. Darina answered quickly and Rachel knew the instant she saw her smiling moon-shaped face that she was a kind woman.

"Hello – Rachel?"

"Yes, Darina," Rachel replied holding out her right hand. "Pleased to meet you."

"Come on in," Darina said, giving her hand a warm shake. "I'm the first door on the right."

The counselling room was cosy and simply decorated. Two odd armchairs sat opposite each other, a small table with tissues and a bowl of stones between them. The unused fireplace was filled with dried flowers and ceiling-high bookshelves covered the walls either side of the fire-breast.

"Do sit down," Darina said kindly as she picked up a notepad and pen.

"Would you tell me a bit about yourself – your file will be kept completely confidential so don't worry!"

Rachel crossed her legs uncomfortably. She didn't want to give too many details about herself – what would Derek do if he ever found out where she had been?

"I live in Portmarnock with my husband and three children."

"Do you work outside the home?"

Rachel shook her head.

"And how old are your children?"

"Sarah is twelve, Ben is eleven and Holly is six."

"So tell me, Rachel, why have you come to me today?"

Rachel looked down at the sweaty palms of her hands. She didn't know where to begin. She could defer telling Darina about Derek if she told her about Sarah.

"I was looking in my daughter's diary because I was worried about her – you see, I was away for a few days last week."

Darina said nothing.

"I didn't know if she had coped while I was away and I know I shouldn't have looked in the diary but ..." Rachel hesitated and looked appealingly at Darina, who still didn't respond. "Sometimes I think she is more grown up than her years – she speaks a lot of sense. Then I find out she has been keeping an account of everything she eats and putting coded messages beside the lists."

Darina still said nothing.

"She's always been a really good kid and she looked after her father and the kids while I was away." Rachel stared up at the corner of the room while she spoke. She didn't feel comfortable any more – talking to someone who wasn't even responding and obviously wasn't going to tell her what to do. She needed answers and quickly! She stood up suddenly. "I think I might have made a mistake coming here today. I need to take my daughter to get help." She started to search through her handbag for her purse. "I'm sorry for wasting your time – maybe you could make an appointment for her or give me the name of someone that could deal with eating disorders."

Darina had seen women like this hundreds of times before. The nervousness, the lack of confidence, were a cover for something more sinister that was happening to them.

"Rachel, why don't we start again?" Darina said gently, pointing to the chair. "I'm not in any hurry and I think you probably have a few things that you would like to talk about. I'm really more interested in you than your daughter and we can sort something out for her at the end of the session – my real interest is your concerns and why Tony recommended that you came to me. Do you want to start again by telling me about you?"

Rachel sat shakily back down onto the chair with her handbag resting on her lap. How different she was now to the woman who had confided in Alex the week before! It was so easy to tell him the truth. It was so easy to be herself and true to her own feelings. Now she was in flux and she didn't know how she was going to tell this strange woman what her life was like.

"I'm afraid for my family," she started with a loud sigh, "and I am afraid for myself."

"Right – do you want to elaborate on why you are afraid?"

"It's more who I am afraid of really." Now that she had started to tell it was getting easier. "You see, my children have seen their father hit me."

"How often does he hit you?" Darina asked quietly.

"There's no big pattern really. It's more a case of whenever he's in a bad mood – which is a lot of the time, I guess."

Darina could see how hard this was for the pretty blonde woman sitting in front of her and she wondered once again how any man could lay a violent finger on such a beautiful face and body.

"There are usually two types of men that hit their wives, Rachel," she started to explain. "The pit bull and the cobra. Their reasoning is the same – it's all about control. You have to be strong to counteract it and that's the hard bit. The fact that you have come to me today is the first step and believe me it's a huge step."

Rachel felt very proud of herself all of a sudden and the feelings of strength that she had experienced in New York with Alex began to trickle back.

"So which describes your husband best – the pit bull who attacks relentlessly and wears you down or the cobra who lashes out occasionally and when you least expect it?"

Rachel considered that question carefully. She couldn't say that she knew exactly when or how he was next going to hit her and he used this as a device to control her and keep her in constant fear.

"I'm not sure – I guess he's more of a cobra." Rachel was still not quite sure of the analogy. "I can't say exactly how it starts but it's usually over something that I have done wrong."

Darina looked at the beautiful and frail woman in front of her. She was thinner than most women her age and although her skin was flawless she had an expression that told a multitude. This woman was showing an act of great courage by coming to see her and she owed it to her to help her out of the abyss that she had fallen into.

"Rachel, will you do something for me today?"

318

Rachel nodded. She would do anything to get out of her situation and help herself and her children and ultimately Derek.

"The next time he goes to hit you, say 'Stop – I will not allow you to hit me'. If he doesn't listen, then take yourself to the police. It might not be any harm to tell them of your situation in advance, to warn them so that they have it on the record."

The police! Surely that was going too far? "But there's no need really. I mean, he would never harm me badly."

Darina stared hard at Rachel and shook her head very slowly. "I had a client recently in a similar situation to yours who said the very same words to me. I don't want to frighten you but I do think you need to be aware that this condition of Derek's is very serious and he needs help or he could go too far."

Rachel felt like she was running out of breaths. She didn't want to believe that Derek would kill her but she did live out most of her days in fear of his temper and the next time that he was going to lash out. And there were those few times he had gone a bit further . . . She needed to do something before the whole situation got out of hand. Already her daughter was at risk with an eating disorder.

"I know what you're saying but I don't really think he would – I mean he's holding down a very good job in the IFSC and we've got a lifestyle to maintain ..."

"Do you really want to keep this lifestyle?"

Rachel gulped. She couldn't go on the way she was and she knew it.

"Have you got any family or good friends that will help you at this time?" Darina asked.

"My mother is in Dublin but I don't see that much of her – she has her own life, I have a brother living on the southside and my youngest brother is in the States – I was with him last week and I told him about the beatings."

"That's good – it's just a pity that he's so far away. Do you talk with him much?"

Rachel shook her head. "We've spoken a couple of times since I got back and he texted me looking for my friend's number but that's it."

"Well, it's good to have someone at hand if you need them."

If only she had someone else – and one particular person sprang to mind. It was easy to talk to Alex but he was thousands of miles across the Atlantic Ocean and she would possibly never see him again. Maybe she should tell Nicky – she was a good and trustworthy friend but she had enough troubles of her own right now.

FIFTEEN

Stephen had procrastinated over whether or not to dial Nicky's number all day. There would never be a good time to ring so the best thing to do was just dial the digits and let fate take charge. He wanted to know how her son was and a part of him wondered if he was making a mistake engaging in a relationship with Gina after he had such strong feelings for Nicky. He waited for the ring tone and tried to picture her face – it wasn't difficult. Nothing could have prepared him for the noises coming from the other end of the line once she answered.

"Hello?" Nicky's voice was sharp and distracted.

Stephen considered hanging up, but that would be foolish as she would be able to read his number on her caller ID – and he wouldn't be able to ring back without looking foolish.

"Hi, Nicky – this is Stephen!"

"Hi, Stephen!" she said in surprise. "L-l-look, I'm in an ambulance – just leaving the Mater."

"What's wrong?" he asked, concerned.

"It's my son – he has a bleed on the brain and they've only just discovered it." She was close to tears as she spoke. "They're taking us to Beaumont Hospital where they hope to operate as soon as they can find a neurosurgeon."

Stephen looked at his watch – it was almost five o'clock. "That's awful, Nicky – I was trying to get your number and my secretary only found you this morning. I was hoping your son would be okay by now."

"I'm so scared, Stephen. He's lying here beside me and I feel so helpless – I don't even know when they will be able to operate – they can't get a neurosurgeon!"

Stephen pictured Nicky sitting in the ambulance with her son and wished that he could do more. This was not how he had expected to find her and he felt that his timing couldn't have been worse. Then suddenly he thought of George – his old friend from Belvedere. Surely he could take care of the lad? He had the best reputation for neurosurgery in the top medical circles. There was something he could do after all.

"Look, Nicky, hold tight – I'm going to give my pal a call – he's a neurosurgeon. I'll ring you back in a few minutes."

Nicky wiped away the tears streaming down her cheeks. "Oh Stephen, that would be wonderful – I'm so worried." Her voice trembled from tears and the bumps on the road penetrating through the ambulance.

"Of course you are – talk in a few minutes."

When he hung up Nicky felt a shiver down her spine. Why was this happening to her now? Here was Stephen ringing and she wasn't even able to speak properly – she was a disaster when it came to the opposite sex but she had to remember that he was just being kind. He had, after all, slept with Eve only hours after kissing her. If Stephen could do anything to help her son – that was all that mattered now.

Eve's entire value system had changed overnight. One drink with John and a conversation that should have taken place years ago and she suddenly saw the world as a very different place. She couldn't continue on in the job that she had been doing. She didn't believe in it any more. Love couldn't be found through the pages of a catalogue nor could it be calculated from a database like a supermarket list. Love was delicate and ethereal and it was up to each individual to find their own way in the world. If Lucille wouldn't give her a job in Just for Coffee, New York, then she would just find another job that suited her better.

Eve didn't relish the prospect of telling Lucille that she was leaving – Lucille was banking on her taking over the entire European operation and expanding it. What she needed to do now was find a place to live where she felt comfortable and at home. That was a big enough task to take on at present.

She looked at her watch – it was time for lunch. It was also a week since she had returned from New York and she felt like a whole lifetime had passed in between. Suddenly her mobile rang and she looked to see who it was. Then she wondered what sort of mood the caller would be in – considering they hadn't spoken since New York.

"Hi, Rachel."

"Eve, hi! I was meaning to call you last week but I don't know where the time went since we got home!"

"It has flown," Eve agreed. "Did you enjoy the rest of your stay?"

"Yes, absolutely. Have you spoken to Nicky?"

"Just briefly – she was looking for Stephen's number. How is her son?"

"A good deal better – he had to have an operation – bleeding on the brain."

Eve gasped. "Poor lad – I thought he was okay after she got back!"

"It was one of those things – a freak blow to the head and it didn't show until he had a CAT scan on Friday – they were concerned about his neck naturally and didn't suspect anything like this."

"I hope he'll be okay."

Rachel sighed. "Yes, well, it looks like he will be now. Stephen came to the rescue and got his neurosurgeon friend to perform the lifesaving operation."

"Stephen?" Eve asked curiously. Obviously those two were meant to be together. A green envy crept over her as she listened to Rachel. "So is everything going to be okay now?"

"Yes – there's no reason why he won't make a full recovery. Poor Nicky though – it can't be easy for her on her own, having to deal with something like that."

"I agree – I wish there was something I could have done." Eve felt guilty for not giving Nicky Stephen's phone number. Karma had a way of coming back to get you if you didn't do the right thing! "How is life in suburban Dublin?"

"I've been busy myself," Rachel said brightly. If only Eve knew how life really was in suburban Dublin, she would certainly get an eye opener. "Um, the reason I'm phoning now, I never got around to mentioning to you or Nicky that I bumped into James Holden in New York!"

Eve gasped again but this time even louder. "I don't believe you!"

"I know. I hardly recognised him despite the fact that he looks almost exactly the same."

"What's he doing in New York?"

"He's playing music. Would you believe, Conor was photographing him for some record producer."

"Did he say much?"

Rachel laughed inwardly – what Eve really meant was did he ask about her. "He didn't give much away – he was acting so cool. I could hardly keep a straight face – it was totally surreal."

Eve smiled to herself. "Imagine him surfacing after all of these years – was Nicky there?"

"No, she had gone back home thankfully – I think she'd have had a heart attack on seeing him."

"What's he like now? Is he still scruffy?"

Rachel laughed. "I think that would describe him well but he would prefer to see himself as really cool."

"It was a good few days, wasn't it?"

"Yes, it was." Rachel wondered how much Eve would be willing to reveal. She decided to push it. "Eh, did something happen with you and Stephen?"

Eve frowned. "Who let the cat out of the bag?"

"I was talking to Nicky…"

"Look, it was just a mistake – no big deal – two adults in New York for the weekend – you know how it is?"

"Sure do."

Rachel knew how it was exactly. It was only a pity that her little affair was as far away as it could be now. Everything was back to normal – almost. She had made the huge stride of seeing her doctor and a counsellor in the one week. Derek, however, had behaved as he normally did and life was just as unbearable as ever. It would be lovely to be able to tell Eve her feelings and her own problems with Sarah but Eve had no children or any understanding of how hard her old college friend's life was.

"I just wanted to let you know that I met James," she said, "because I have to tell Nicky now and I'm not looking forward to it."

Eve nodded into the phone. "I'm amazed that he cropped up after all of this time. I wonder how Nicky will take it! What a coincidence that Conor was photographing him!" And that might not be the only coincidence, she thought. "How is Conor?"

"Good – I only called briefly to let him know that I got home in one piece. Stephen upgraded our seats – wasn't that nice of him?"

"Very!" Eve said haughtily, not sure why she was put out with the revelation – after all, she always travelled first class. Maybe it was the fact that she had slept with him and he hadn't called – that was not a thing that she was used to – it was usually her prerogative to decide whether or not to speak to a man after sleeping with him. Maybe she was losing her touch?

"So have you any plans to visit Dublin?" Rachel asked. "It would be nice to catch up again on home turf."

Eve pursed her lips and thought. Visiting Dublin was the least of her problems. She didn't know what she wanted to do with her life – inside she realised that she was at some type of crossroads but had no idea which way to turn.

"I've no plans to come to Dublin. Just for Coffee is well set up there and to be honest I'm considering a career change."

"Really? To do what?" Rachel was startled by the revelation.

"I know it sounds crazy but I'm not really sure – I don't know what I want to do with the rest of my life – all I know is that I have to get out of London – it just doesn't do it for me any more – to be honest, I miss New York!"

"I can understand that!" Rachel sighed. She missed it herself – she missed the dreamy unreality of the city. And she missed

Alex. "It was good to see you, Eve, and we should try to keep in touch now!"

"Yeah – that would be good. I'm not really sure where I'm going to be but I will call you if I change city or address."

"Take care, Eve."

Rachel hung up. Eve wasn't someone she could confide in but it was worth the call.

Nicky gently stroked her son's limp arm. He was resting well after the operation and George Osbourne, the neurosurgeon, was the most charming man that Nicky had ever met. His bedside manner was old-fashioned and comforting. It had helped when Daniel was released from theatre. The Sister told her that if George had not stepped in and operated so quickly her son's chances of survival would have diminished as each day passed.

Nicky wished she could say thank you to Stephen but the two times that she called him she was put straight through to his voicemail and she didn't feel leaving a message was appropriate thanks. She wanted to tell him personally how grateful she was. She would try again later.

Daniel moved his head to the side and smiled a watery smile that melted his mother's heart.

"How are you feeling, love?"

"Good!" Daniel said, nodding his head and then wincing when he realised that it hurt so much.

"Try not to move," Nicky said comfortingly. "You're going to be running about in a week!"

Daniels's heavily bandaged head was covered with all sorts of wires and tubes but he was on the mend and that was all that mattered to Nicky.

The vibrations from the phone in her pocket told her that she had a call. She had no doubt that it would be work. They were less than sympathetic to her situation and Nicky felt let down and angry about the way they had treated her.

"Back in a minute, love," she whispered to her son and went out to the corridor to take the call in private. "Hello?"

"Nicky – I hope your son is getting on okay?"

"Yes, Trudy!" Nicky was losing patience with her boss who had little or no compassion for anyone with children.

"Good – that's very good. Because we need you to finish the edits by tomorrow night – if I email them to you now, will you be able to get them back to me?"

Nicky sighed. The audacity of the woman! If she didn't need the job so badly she would tell her where to stuff her magazine. "I'm afraid I'm really tied up here with Daniel – I don't like leaving him – can one of the other sub-editors finish it?"

Trudy cleared her throat. "Well, I didn't want to suggest that because you've always been very particular in the past about your sections of the magazine but I can get one of the others to take care of yours – in fact, I was thinking a bit of reshuffling might do everyone a little good."

So this was what it was all about! Nicky wondered when she was going to get pushed sideways. It was obvious that Trudy was enamoured with the new girl who was training in sub-editing and it was only a matter of time before she made a position for her – but never would she have expected that the position in jeopardy would be her own.

"So what do you want me to do?"

Trudy cleared her throat again with a nervous cough. "I was thinking maybe you could do more research and interviews – you know some hands-on pieces like you used to do so well!"

Don't try and pacify me, Nicky thought angrily. *I know when I'm being shoved aside.*

"Do whatever you have to do, Trudy," Nicky said sharply.

"You've got a magazine to run and I've got a sick son to tend to. We can only do so much."

Trudy gave an annoying little giggle. "I'm so glad you see it that way, Nicky. Take all the time you need and we'll discuss your new remit when you're back in the office – okay?"

"Okay!" Nicky grunted. She was demoted to general run-around and no matter what way Trudy tried to butter it up, the fact was that she had been slapped in the face and it wasn't much gratitude for the years of hard work and dedication that she had given the magazine. It made her want to chuck her job in entirely but that simply wasn't an option. There would be medical expenses to pay for Daniel even with her medical insurance.

She needed cheering up and she longed to hear Stephen's voice – she wanted to feel desirable again like the way he had made her feel during their wonderful lunch in the Boathouse in Central Park. She dialled his number and waited – when the voicemail answered she turned off her phone. She didn't want to speak to anyone else for the rest of the day. She would tend to Daniel's needs because he was the most important person in her world and always would be.

The sultry tones of Miles Davis filled the high ceilings of Stephen's apartment. 'Kind of Blue' was his favourite album of all time. It was a test to see just how perfect Gina was as a mate and companion. So far she had passed with flying colours and they had only been on three dates. Making dinner for her was a big one – he didn't cook often and was generally happiest of all with a good steak, Shanahan's on the Green being his preferred venue for dining in the city. If she liked this Thai green curry he was making, choice of wine and Miles, then he had probably found his perfect mate. She was certainly his match socially.

Frank was pestering him with phone calls twice a day to see how they were getting on.

He found it difficult to forget about Nicky but having two women on his mind was hard to deal with. He knew that he had to choose one and his head told him that Gina was the sensible choice. She didn't have any children either which made her practically baggage-free.

He topped up the large John Rocha crystal glass with his favourite St Emillion vintage and took a sip. He had to be careful tonight – he had been drinking more in the last year than in the previous twenty and he had been doing things that were uncharacteristic – especially where the opposite sex was concerned.

Suddenly the doorbell rang and Stephen grabbed a tea-towel to wipe the traces of green sauce off his fingers. He glanced in the hallway mirror as he passed by and felt good in his casual Hugo Boss shirt and jeans. When he opened the door he couldn't see Gina's face at first – it was concealed by a huge bunch of tulips. She let them slip, revealing a big grin.

"Hi, Stephen," she said, handing them over along with the bottle of Moet that nestled in the crook of her arm.

"Gina!" Stephen was startled – no one had ever bought him flowers before. "I don't know what to say!"

"How about opening the Moet? I bought it chilled!"

Stephen hadn't realised how forthright Gina was but he figured that to hold such a powerful position in a man's world she had to be a ball-breaker!

"Come in!"

Gina stopped when she was midway through the hall. "Is that 'Kind of Blue'?"

"Yes," Stephen said with a smile. It was only a small question but one that told him a multitude. Had he finally found the companion of his dreams? "Yes, let's open this!" And he held the bottle of Moet in the air like a trophy.

Eve crumpled up the sheet of paper in front of her and started again. Before any important meeting or discussion she wrote down everything that needed to be said and put it in order so that she didn't miss anything. She had to be totally clear before giving Lucille her notice because she would use every trick in the book to convince her to stay.

Two hours later Eve still had not written anything. The best thing to do was to pour a glass of wine. The cabinet where she kept her good bottles was right beside a bookcase. Protruding out past the ledge was a large and out-of-date Atlas. She had enjoyed flicking through it when she was in college and used to tick off all the places that she wanted to see. She would be thirty-six soon and hadn't managed to visit half of her list of countries. Some of the countries had changed name and shape since she was in college. So much had happened in the lives of others – like Nicky and Rachel – they had children. She pulled out a bottle of Chateauneuf du Pape that needed to be drunk before it aged past its best. It was a shame that she had no one to share it with. She thought of John and felt very pleased for him. It was only right that everyone got to meet their soul mate – even if it was only for a short while.

By the third glass of wine Eve felt much more able to confront Lucille – it was four o'clock in the afternoon New York time. Lucille would probably ring before it turned five – but she would do her the favour of saving her the call. She felt sure now that she knew what she had to do.

She pressed speed dial. Lucille's chirpy voice answered almost immediately.

"Hi, Lucille – it's Eve."

"Eve, honey, I hope you have good news for me."

Eve took a sip from her glass of wine. "Lucille, I've been doing a lot of thinking this week and I'm sorry but I'm going to hand in my notice."

Lucille gasped.

"I haven't made this decision lightly but I think it's time I made some changes in my life and moving to Paris isn't one of them."

"Don't be hasty, Eve. Won't you stay on in London?"

"I really want to get out of England. I've decided to sell my shares and take a year out – maybe do some travelling. There's a lot of the world that I haven't got around to seeing and if I don't do it now I never will."

"Well, well, well – this is a turn-up for the books. I don't know what to say!"

"I'll call in to see you on the way – I might start my great voyage off in New York."

"Yes, well, that would be good." Lucille sighed. "Would you not consider a sabbatical – six months may be all you need?"

"Just for Coffee doesn't need me any more, Lucille – it was always your baby and together we got it up to be the great service that it is but it's time for me to move on."

"I hear you, honey, and I wish you all the best. Come and see me soon – we will have to do some paperwork!"

"I will – it shouldn't take me long to tidy things up here – I might keep the apartment as an investment or sell it and buy somewhere in New York – I'm not sure yet."

"Sounds like an exciting adventure!"

"I think it's what I need right now. Thanks for understanding, Lucille."

"Talk soon, honey, take care!"

Eve hung up and felt a huge weight lift off her shoulders. There was no denying that it was time to move on. She would have enough income from the sale of her shares to live a comfortable but more frugal existence for the next couple of years. The future was uncertain but seemed much more real. It had been an amazing day – she was now jobless and soon without a country to call her home. It was strange that people from her past were cropping up again and she was getting closure in different aspects of her life. Even the vagabond James Holden was located and put to rest. Meeting her old college friends had helped her to find a part of herself that she had hidden away since leaving Dublin, and meeting John had helped her find peace with Harry at last. Then there was Conor – what had he shown her? He was the only odd piece in the recent puzzle. He had spoken to her with truth and honesty and she had him to thank for saving her life – maybe with the few words that he had spoken in Town restaurant he had saved it again. She raised the glass to her lips and took another sip. She was alone in the world and that was all right.

Rachel had done everything that she was told. Now she was standing in Malahide Garda station and felt the police were looking at her a little strangely. The sergeant called on one of his female colleagues to take her aside where she could talk privately.

Garda Marion Walsh was small but stocky. She led Rachel into a pleasant room, carpeted with floor tiles and painted a mint green.

"Take a seat, Mrs Sloan, and make yourself comfortable." Her country accent was quiet but strong. "Now why exactly are you here today?"

Rachel felt nervous when she considered the information she was about to impart. First she had spoken to Tony, then Darina and now the guards – she wondered who else she would have to tell.

"I suppose you could say I have been attacked."

"In your marital relationship?"

How could she tell just by looking at me? Rachel thought and gave her bottom lip a nervous bite. "My husband is violent towards me."

"Do you want to make a statement?"

Rachel wasn't sure if that was what she wanted at all but now that she was here she might as well talk – so she nodded.

Garda Walsh gave her a gentle knowing smile. "How long has your husband been hitting you, Mrs Sloan?"

Rachel cast her eyes heavenward and tried to count silently. "I guess ten years or more."

"I see," Garda Walsh sighed, jotting notes down on a large sheet of paper. "And you never went to the guards before?"

Rachel shook her head. She felt like a schoolchild being chastised by the principal for playing truant. "I hit the panic button a couple of times in the hall."

"Did the guards come?"

"Yes," Rachel nodded.

"And then what happened?"

"Derek would tell them that the kids were messing and that it was an accident."

Rachel bit her lip again. She had told the guards that story herself on more than one occasion.

"How many children do you have?"

This was all too painful. "I have three children – he doesn't hit them," she added. "But it's affecting them – I think my daughter has an eating disorder – I can't let this continue – the youngest will be next."

"Mrs Sloan, you know that you could go into the Family Law Courts today and get an interim barring order."

"What's that?"

"It's an order from the court that will force your husband to leave the family home until you continue with prosecution."

Prosecution – court – barring order – the words were too awful. How could she have let her life come to this? How could she survive without Derek supporting her? How could she continue with him hitting her?

"I don't know if I can –"

"Have you got someone who would go with you?"

Rachel thought of Nicky – she was the only friend that she could bear to tell. The women she knew in Portmarnock would shy away from her – or so she presumed. Most probably wouldn't believe her – their husbands wouldn't want her any way near them.

"If I get this order, what do I do then?"

"Come straight to us and give us a copy. We will give the order to your husband and assist him in getting his things and leaving the home peacefully."

After thirty minutes Rachel couldn't take any more. She thanked the guard and bundled out of the station with her coat held over her head like a convict. She got into her Renault feeling sick inside. What if Derek had seen her – there was no earthly reason why – but if he did, what would she say to explain? All of the people she had called into her life to help her said the same things – it wasn't easy to be strong and stand up to a bully. She was so scared that when he turned on her she froze and felt it was better to suffer the consequences than to make him even madder.

She needed help and although she felt bad she knew that Nicky was the only person she could turn to. She rang her number and waited.

"Hi, Rach – how are you?"

"I'm not the best, Nicky – how's Daniel?"

"He's doing well – what's up?"

"Is there any chance we can meet – I need to talk?"

Nicky recognised the anguish in her friend's voice instantly – it wasn't like Rachel to be alarmist.

"I went back to work today – I'll be visiting Daniel after – what about lunch – could you get in to town to see me?"

Venturing into Dublin city was something Rachel seldom did – most of her shopping needs were fulfilled in Swords. She could ring Veronica and get her to take Holly for a playdate – that would give her two and a half hours before she would have to pick up Ben from basketball.

"Okay – I can be in to you for one. Where?"

"Insomnia café – the one around the corner from my office?"

"Great – see you then."

Rachel was shaking – she had put enough cogs in place. She was making the moves to change her life completely. She shivered when she tried to imagine how Derek would take it. Was she ready to give up her lifestyle? The choice wasn't hers to make. Something had to be done before her children were left with permanent scars. Sarah wouldn't talk to her honestly either and, even though she had been monitoring her food carefully, she found it impossible to find out what she ate during the day. The counsellor in Sarah's school had been very nice and supportive but there was little she or any of the teachers could do to ensure that she didn't vomit up her lunch.

The decision to do something had been taken out of her hands. She knew that she was left with no other choice.

Nicky was already there, sipping a latte grande and looking out through the large glass window. It was so unlike Rachel to ring urgently like that. She wondered what the matter could be. This would be as good a time as any to try Stephen again.

She dialled his number and waited – this time he answered.
"Hello? Nicky?"

"Hi, Stephen – I tried to get you a couple of times but was sent to your voicemail and I wanted to thank you personally for getting your friend to operate so quickly."

Stephen sounded pleased to hear her voice. "How's your son?"

"Great, thanks to you – I don't know what you did but it was only a matter of hours before George was at the hospital and operating."

"He owed me a couple of favours – it was good timing – I'm glad I could help."

"You've been so good – with New York and now this –"

"Honestly, Nicky – I'm just glad I could help," he said, his voice becoming quieter.

"I'd like to repay you – how about dinner?"

After an awkward silence Stephen eventually spoke. "There really is no need, Nicky – it was no trouble."

Nicky had hoped for an enthusiastic response – after all, why had he gone to so much trouble helping her if he didn't like her?

"I'd really like to see you again," she said. "I mean, we were having such a good time in the Boathouse – weren't we?"

"It was good," he chuckled lowly.

Nicky wondered if there was someone else around – why else would he be talking so quietly? "Look, I won't keep you but I really am so grateful," she said reservedly. "For everything!"

"Thanks for calling, Nicky – I've got to go. It was no trouble."

Then he was gone. Nicky stared at the mobile phone. How odd. She liked to think that she had learned something about character since making such a bad choice for her son's father but she obviously had got the wrong end of the stick with this guy.

There was little she could do now apart from wait for Rachel to arrive.

"Who was that?" Gina asked.

"Just a girl I helped out – she needed a surgeon in a hurry and I got my pal George to help!"

Gina put her hands on her hips. "And are you in the habit of having strange women calling up to thank you?"

Stephen smiled as she walked over to him.

"Is this what happens when you date a solicitor – the Spanish Inquisition every time you take a call?"

Gina shrugged. "I like to be kept in the picture, that's all!"

"Does this mean you care?" he asked wickedly.

Gina moved closer to Stephen who rested with his back against the island in the middle of his kitchen.

"I wouldn't be missing meetings with clients and slipping off during my lunch break to meet you in your apartment if I didn't!"

Stephen put his hands carefully on Gina's hips. "Well, that's always good to know!"

Gina lunged forward and placed her lips on his, taking him unawares.

"Now!" she demanded. "Take me to bed now!"

With an image of Nicky still in his mind's eye he followed her upstairs. He had to choose which he wanted to be with because he wasn't being fair to either of them. Gina had laid her cards on the table from the beginning and it had been much easier to fall into a relationship with her – but there was something about Nicky that he didn't want to let go of. A part of him felt as if the decision was being made at that very moment.

When Rachel arrived, Nicky was looking even more frazzled than she did.

"I'd trouble finding a parking spot – sorry!" said Rachel.

"That's okay," Nicky said, giving her friend a kiss on the cheek. "It's been crazy since we got back – I still have to get those suitcases off you!"

"I'll drop them over some evening when Daniel gets back – sorry, I didn't even think to bring them today!"

"What are we like – a few nights in New York and we are both snivelling messes. What's up?"

Rachel sat down and picked up the menu card. "I just had to talk to someone but I didn't want to hassle you with all Daniel has been through."

"Thank God he's on the mend – but what's up with you?"

The waitress interrupted as Rachel was about to launch into her confession.

"A cappuccino please and a glass of water – that's all," said Rachel.

"So what's happened?" Nicky asked urgently when the waitress had gone.

"Nicky, there are a couple of things I need to say. First of all, I'm going to try and get a barring order against Derek."

"A what?" Nicky nearly spit out her latte as she took a sip.

"I've never told you because I suppose I just wasn't ready to deal with it – but Derek hits me – he's been doing it for ages."

Nicky's eyes widened. "Derek – your husband, Derek?"

Rachel nodded. "I know it sounds crazy but things have been bad for years. Then, when I got back from New York I found Sarah's diary and she has an eating disorder – it's time I did something about the situation before my kids get as messed up as me!"

"Jesus, Rachel, I don't know what to say!" She really was gob-smacked. "Never in a million years would I have put Derek down as a wife-beater – I mean he's such a straight-up kind of guy."

"Didn't you ever think it funny the way he controls my every move?"

"I thought you didn't want to go out much – I envied you with your security and family."

Rachel shook her head vehemently. "Don't envy me – I live in fear every minute of the day. I never know when he's going to hit me next."

"Your coffee!" said the waitress, startling them both. "And the water."

Nicky watched the waitress flounce off and then leaned forward towards Rachel. "But I never saw any marks!" she whispered.

"He seldom hits my face – and if he does I camouflage it well. He's got the knack of hitting without leaving scars but he also knows how to make them really hurt!"

Nicky put her hand out and rested it on top of Rachel's comfortingly. "I had no idea – oh Rach – why didn't you tell me?"

"I never felt safe enough – until I was away from my home in New York. I told Alex first and then Conor. Since then I've spoken to my GP and the police – I can't stop talking now!"

"I wish you'd told me!"

Rachel shook her head. "I wasn't ready. I had to be pushed to the brink. Now I have to deal with Sarah and I'm so worried about her – I need to get me and the kids to a safe place – so that we can all heal."

"Well, if there's anything I can do ..."

"Actually, you could if you can get off work – I need to go into the family law courts and I don't feel I can do it alone."

"Of course I'll come with you."

Rachel gave a half smile. "Thanks, Nicky. I rang Eve by the way but there's no point in telling her – we aren't really close any more."

Nicky smiled. "I think it was interesting meeting her again. We've all gone in very different directions, haven't we?"

Rachel nodded. "And we didn't exactly take on the world like we thought we would either!"

"At least we have our kids," Nicky added.

There was a pause.

"Actually, Nicky, I've been meaning to tell you – it was mad really – when you went back on the last night in New York, Conor took me to this bar and we met someone you know."

"Who?"

Rachel gulped before divulging. "James Holden!"

Nicky's mouth dropped. "Oh my god, I don't believe it ..."

"I'm sorry for not telling you sooner but with Daniel sick and all the stuff going on at home there wasn't a good time."

"Never would be too soon to see that bastard!"

"Well, he's changed very little – except he's scruffier and has this unbearable American twang."

"Did he ask about ...?"

Rachel shook her head. "I'm sorry. He didn't ask about Daniel – but when Conor met him the next day at the photo shoot he revealed to him that he had a son."

Nicky was aghast. She started to tremble and had to put her coffee cup to rest.

"What made him come out with it to Conor?"

"Well, he did it indirectly – he started to sing a song about his son – Daniel."

Nicky gasped. "A song! But – what does he know about him – how does he know his name?"

"I'm not sure of the details but I can get Conor to talk to you if you like?"

Nicky shook her head. "I don't want James Holden coming anywhere near me or Daniel – ever!"

341

"Nicky, I realise that you feel that way now but you must consider that Daniel may want to know more in the future."

Nicky looked down at her coffee cup, feeling numb.

"I know this is all a bit of a shock," Rachel said with a sigh. "Who'd have thought that a few days away could lead to this?"

Nicky was still speechless. She hid behind her latte, closing her eyes every now and then.

"Are you okay?" Rachel asked sympathetically.

"I'll be fine," she replied, putting her cup firmly down on the table. "It's just the shock of knowing where he is. I'm relieved really that he's not in Dublin. Did he say that he would be staying in the States?"

"That seems to be very much his intention – touring."

"God – I hope he doesn't become famous – Daniel's been strumming away on his guitar and his music teacher says that he has great potential."

"Daniel is nothing like his father so don't worry. He's a great kid!"

"Yeah, he is," Nicky nodded. "But I'm not the best at picking men – I rang Stephen to thank him for getting his friend to help Daniel and he seemed completely preoccupied!"

"He's probably a very busy man!" Rachel tried to reassure her.

"He's meant to be retired but he was certainly distracted when I rang!"

"It could be a number of things causing that – don't worry! I bet you'll hear from him again!"

Nicky shook her head. "Something has changed – I don't know what but he sounded very different."

Rachel didn't know what to say. It was a terrible side-effect of holiday romance and she was suffering from it herself – even though she had more serious problems on her plate since returning home.

"But, anyway, back to more important things," said Nicky. "When do you want to go to the family law court?"

"In the morning?" Rachel asked hopefully.

"I can be out doing some research – they've changed my remit in work and in a way it's a blessing – it will give me more flexibility to move around during the day."

"Good – that's really good!"

"Right. Meet you there at what time?"

"Nine thirty?"

"See you then."

Rachel left the café shaking inside. She was really going to do something about her life.

Dinner would be very different this evening – it might be the last meal that she would share with Derek. The thought terrified her as much as the thought of continuing to be his punch-bag.

She drove steadily all the way back to Portmarnock and pulled up in front of her local deli. She didn't feel like cooking and they made a really nice lasagne that she could put in a dish and pass off as her own. She had very little money but her credit card that she was allowed use only in emergencies would do. After all, he would be so mad after he got the barring order, what would twenty euros on the card be in comparison? Before it would have been a good thumping but now she felt a sense of relief that the thumping might finally stop. She breezed into the bright and friendly shop, picking up strawberries and salad, and putting them in her basket as she browsed.

As she finally made her way to the check-out, she passed the newspaper rack and the headline in *the Irish Times* caught her eye. "Husband acquitted for murdering his wife". The words sent a shiver up her spine. She picked up the paper and, after she had put her groceries on the conveyor belt, she quickly scanned the article. The jury had found this man not guilty. But what if he *had* murdered his wife? The evidence was purely circumstantial but if he was innocent why did his own children break down crying in the dock. This was becoming a common story in modern Ireland. Husbands who killed their wives were cropping up in the headlines more and more and this acquittal would send out the wrong signals to men who wanted to get rid of their wives permanently. Did Derek want to get rid of her? She liked to think that he wouldn't go too far but there were those couple of times that he had hit her on the head. Once he had left her with internal injuries and she had been traumatised for weeks. She had almost eradicated those ordeals from her memory and hadn't even admitted them to Alex or Darina – she found it difficult to admit them to herself. Would he want to get rid of her if she got a barring order against him? Probably!

"Is that everything?" the girl at the counter asked.

"Yes, thanks," Rachel replied, putting the newspaper back – the last thing she needed was to be putting ideas in Derek's head. She passed her credit card over to the girl and took the paper bag filled with groceries.

"No, hold it – I have some cash in my purse – don't use that card."

She didn't feel so sure that a barring order was the answer any more.

She quickly counted her cash – luckily it was enough.

Nicky was driving home from work. It was good to be out on the road again – she could make her new appointment a positive move within the magazine or go under completely and the latter did not sound attractive. Rush-hour traffic wasn't as bad as usual today and she felt like her world was moving into a better phase. Daniel was going to be fine and that was the most important thing. At least she didn't have to suffer the horrific situation that

Rachel was in – she would never have believed it but the trip to New York had bonded them in a close way that they hadn't experienced since their college days.

She looked out at the steady stream of cars moving swiftly in the opposite direction and sang along to the radio.

When her mobile phone rang she didn't think too hard about who it could be.

"Nicky? Nicky?"

She almost crashed into the car in front as it came to an abrupt standstill. She pulled in off the road.

"Hello?" he said.

Though the accent had changed, the voice was unmistakeable. Especially the way he had said her name.

"Yes, this is Nicky," she replied shakily.

"Nicky, it's Jim – James Holden."

"Yes." She didn't know what to say – she was dumbstruck.

"I got your number from a friend of yours – Conor Moore."

"Right, okay!"

"Nicky, I won't blame you if you want to hang up – I genuinely have been meaning to make this call for years."

Then why didn't you, she thought angrily.

"I don't want to cause you any trouble," he continued.

Then why are you calling now?

"I'm ringing about Daniel and I was wondering if there is anything I could do to help?"

"Well, he's out of nappies now," she snapped, then berated herself for revealing too much emotion.

"I know – I'm sorry."

"It's okay – there's no need to apologise."

"Too late for that, I guess?"

"About fourteen years too late."

"I don't blame you for hating me, Nicky."

"I don't hate you, James – to hate someone implies emotion and I really don't have any feelings towards you."

This was turning out harder than he had anticipated. He didn't know what he expected but this was not going his way.

"Nicky, I'd love to do something for your boy and if you think we could talk again or maybe I could speak to him sometime then that would be great but, equally, if you don't want me around, that's fine too."

Nicky was trembling inside – the cheek – the utter audacity of the creep!

"I'm driving home in traffic and this isn't a good time to be talking, James. I think it's best to leave things just the way they are."

"Sure – whatever you say, Nicky. If you want my number Conor Moore has it."

Nicky wanted the conversation to end as quickly as possible.

"Okay – thanks for calling – bye!"

Nicky turned off the engine of her car. She put her head on the steering wheel and sobbed as loudly as she had all those years ago when she discovered that she was pregnant.

SIXTEEN

Three months later

September

"I want you to do a special on high-flying women in the city who are getting married soon!" Trudy said with a big grin etched on her face.

Nicky looked up from her desk and grinned cheesily at her boss. "Why do you want *me* to do it?"

"I think you would give the piece the right amount of detachment – so many of the other girls are engaged or newlyweds and they may go over the top with it!" Trudy shook the two-carat rock that protruded on her left hand.

Nicky wanted to hit her. "Sure – no problem."

"Great. I knew you'd be fine – here's a list of the women that I want you to interview. They are all expecting your call to fix up an appointment."

Trudy left the sheet of A4 paper on Nicky's desk and breezed off.

Nicky glanced over the list of names – three unbearable women who had it all – it was so bitchy of Trudy to give her the feature. But it didn't matter. Daniel was thriving. Rachel was alive!

The names of the prospective bridegrooms were listed at the bottom of the page. Nicky felt a jolt shoot up her arm as she read them – it couldn't be! Maybe it was a different Stephen Delaney!

She grabbed her packet of Marlboro and lighter and headed for the front door of the building with her mobile shoved into the pocket of her jeans. She could feel herself hyperventilate. What was going on? He hadn't been in touch since she called to thank him for helping Daniel but she had been longing to believe that there was a good reason for that – a reason better than finding someone else. Maybe he had this Gina person at home all along and he was only messing with the Just for Coffee agency? She lit the tip of her cigarette and inhaled deeply. Why had she such lousy luck with men when other women seemed to have it all?

She hadn't contacted James again and hadn't mentioned the call to Daniel – why should she go through so much herself and inflict it on her son too? Another part of her feared that Daniel would want to get to know James and follow him out to America and she definitely didn't want to create a scenario like that. As each day passed she convinced herself that she was doing the right thing by her son and herself.

Stephen wasn't as easy to forget. She could still see him, tall and striking, with those dark eyes and his hair peppered with grey making him all the more sophisticated. She wondered how she was going to have the strength to do the piece on his fiancée – deep down she knew that she would simply have to.

Eve stood in Departures at Heathrow airport, clutching her boarding pass. Her whole life had been packed into three suitcases and her apartment in Chiswick was ready to be taken over by an upwardly mobile young woman who was working nearby. The income would help supplement her way around the world.

She had a small but smart apartment waiting for her in the East Village and she relished the thought of spending some time confronting her ghosts. It was a totally different part of New York to the Upper East Side and she could get a whole new perspective on the city. The last three weeks in Portugal had been inspiring and relaxing but they also made her realise that she needed to be in a city. She needed to be kept busy – her route around the world was changing with the days. Rome was lovely in June but she was lonely seeing the beautiful sights on her own – she wished that she had someone to share it all with. She met a waiter in the Piazza Navona who had helped spice up a few nights but that was towards the end of her stay and it was never going to go anywhere. All roads lead to New York and not Rome as far as Eve was concerned.

The flight across the Atlantic seemed quicker than usual – maybe it was because this time she had a sense of homecoming about the journey.

Before she knew it she was sitting comfortably in the back of a yellow taxi and staring out through the window. She wasn't thinking in words – only pictures. This trip felt different to any other.

A well of tears filled her eyes as she came to Brooklyn Bridge and the space that filled the sky where the Twin Towers had once stood. Why was she only crying now? She had been to New York on several occasions since Harry had died. Why was this journey different? Maybe because she knew that she wouldn't be returning to Europe any time soon or maybe because she wasn't a top executive in a thriving company. Whatever the reason she didn't care – it felt good to be home.

"Alex, this is outstanding work. I'm getting goosebumps all

over!" Pierre said, scratching his bald head. "I didn't think you could do it – this is wonderful!"

Alex was exhausted. It had been a long hot summer in New York and it wasn't over yet. He had seen little of it, cooped up in his studio most of the time with the odd burst of energy taking him to the High Line and the place he felt closest to Rachel. He often lay on the grass and looked up at the sky – comforted by the notion that it had shrouded Europe only a few hours before and maybe Rachel had looked up at the same spot that he was looking at now.

Those were the things that mattered. He didn't have time for drinking or going to parties – he'd only been to two exhibitions since he started working on the Rachel series and it was the right thing to do because he didn't need distraction. On the very odd day he travelled up to the Met and looked at the painting of the lady with the teacup and he'd mentally whisk back to where he had stood with Rachel and that helped him to go on.

Conor said he was obsessive but that wasn't doing his creative process any harm – even he could see that Alex was creating something special. Conor was working in a different medium – he couldn't understand what it meant to start with a blank canvas and see images jump out at him from underneath. Michelangelo described the process of sculpting his captive slaves as releasing them from the marble. Wasn't he doing the same thing – allowing Rachel to fly out from beneath the canvas – allowing her to be free? Something had happened the other night – something inexplicable – just before he finished the tenth and final painting in the series. Rachel had moved on in some way and he couldn't understand how or why but he felt that something had happened.

He hoped that she was okay . . .

"Alex – are you with me?" Pierre demanded.

"I was daydreaming – what do you think we should do with them?"

Pierre started to pace up and down, glancing from canvas to canvas as he passed.

"I think we must show them in the fall – October, maybe November – are you willing to sell them all?"

"Except that one," Alex said, pointing to the original portrait that he had shown Pierre three months earlier.

"That is fine – I think you could go to Europe with these. It is as fine a collection as I have seen in years. You have crossed the Rubicon, Alex – the world is now ready for you!"

It was very high praise indeed from one of the most cantankerous but also most powerful art dealers in the city.

Even though he knew that these compliments would kick-start his career into a totally new dimension, they didn't touch him the way he thought they would. Instead he felt a dreadful sense of loss at the prospect of his Rachel paintings leaving him. He hadn't received a call or text from her in the last three months but at least while he had this project to complete her image was scattered around his studio and home. To release these canvases would mean that he would be left on his own and he didn't relish the thought. He would be so lonely – he hadn't even had time for his friends since she left. Conor was down to one coffee a week instead of the usual daily afternoon meetings like they used to have before he met Rachel. He had worked so hard and it had obviously paid off in his paintings but every other aspect of his life had suffered in the process.

"I said, are you ready for Europe?"

"Sure," Alex said with a shrug – he wasn't going to disagree with Pierre – he wasn't a fool!

"Good! Because I have somewhere really special in mind for these. First I will take four and show them in New York and that will get the critics excited. We will put them up for sale to the highest bidder with a ridiculous reserve!" His voice was becoming more animated as the excitement rang through.

"Sounds good," Alex said with a nod of his head.

"Then we can show the rest in one of my favourite galleries in Dublin – the IMMA – they want me to put together an exhibition of contemporary American art for the spring and I think that your work will be the *pièce de résistance*! The media will be so hyped!"

Alex flinched on hearing the word Dublin. Could this be? Were his paintings of Rachel going home?

Nicky set off for Aylesbury Road at eleven forty-five. Lunch in the lavish setting of Gina's fiancé's house was the order of the day and Nicky would happily have swapped her feature for a week in Mountjoy Prison – but that option wasn't on offer.

Luckily she had been able to confirm from his bride-to-be that Stephen was away on a trip abroad and so wouldn't be there for the interview.

"What a shame!" Nicky had said, thanking her lucky stars.

She hoped that Gina wasn't too good-looking or nice – it would only make it more difficult to cope with the fact that Gina was marrying the only man that she had fallen for in years. The leafy sidewalks led the way to a manor-type development of stylish apartments and Nicky knew instinctively that she had reached her destination.

There were several parking spaces available and Nicky took the first and nearest one. With a sharp intake of breath, a notepad and her best and only designer Louis Vuitton handbag, she was ready to take on the might of Stephen Delaney's fiancée.

The intercom at the doorway was hidden discreetly behind climbing clematis and she searched for Apartment 4. Delaney was imprinted on the second button and she pressed until she heard a buzzing from the intercom.

"Hello?"

It wasn't the excruciating high-pitched Dublin 4 tones she expected to hear from the future Mrs Delaney but a very ordinary down-to-earth accent that sounded like her own.

"Hello – I'm meeting Gina Hall – Nicky Blake from *D Scene* magazine."

"Come on up, Nicky – I'm on the second floor."

Once inside the building the trappings of wealth were everywhere. Original paintings hung on the plush wallpaper that lined the stairway. It would have been easier to get the lift but Nicky didn't want to miss a thing – she wanted to see every inch of the apartment and its surroundings. She wanted to see just what she was missing.

The solid oak door sprang open as she made it to the top of the stairs and standing in the doorway was the woman who had won the heart of Stephen Delaney. Nicky smiled her professional smile and held out her hand politely.

"Very pleased to meet you, Gina," she said brightly.

"Welcome to our apartment."

The cheeky mare, Nicky thought – had she already put her name on the deeds?

No expense was spared on decoration – this was easily the most beautiful interior Nicky had ever been in. It was an eclectic mix of period furniture with modern styling and made the smart interior of Rachel's house pale into insignificance.

"It's a very elegant apartment," said Nicky.

"I had nothing to do with it," Gina said, tossing her shiny brown hair and batting her long eyelashes. "This was Stephen's but we are planning to buy a house a bit further out – Killiney or Dalkey."

Lovely, Nicky said to herself. Gina was a plain girl but with a large enough budget to groom herself into the very attractive league. Nicky wished that she had passed on this assignment – she hadn't thought it would be this hard.

"Take a seat," Gina said, pointing to a Queen Anne chair.

Nicky sat down and prepared to take notes.

"So where do you want to start?"

"I suppose where you two met would be as good a place as any," Nicky began. Pen in hand like a weapon, she wrote as Gina spoke.

"I was with friends in the Ice Bar and Stephen had only returned from a trip to New York that morning ..."

Nicky's ears pricked up with interest at the mention of New York – so he had met Gina right after their special time together – this really rubbed salt into the wound.

"His friend Frank married my colleague Jessica Marshall and She is always trying to match-make her friends!" Gina continued.

Nicky's shorthand was shaky but she didn't mind. She guessed that she would remember every syllable of their conversation without a notepad.

Gina rattled on, every word a barb to Nicky who had to struggle to hold it together. "Where do you plan to have the Big Day?" she said eventually, cutting into Gina's romantic reminiscences.

"We are going to make it small – only close friends and family – about two hundred guests!"

Please don't make me puke! Nicky thought.

"Stephen wanted to go away – Italy – but in the end I convinced him to choose an Irish Castle. It will be much more convenient for organising and I don't want the wedding planner to take over the entire arrangements of our day!"

"Of course – it's terrible the way they can just take over!" Nicky said, sympathetically enough to sound convincing.

"For the honeymoon I fancied a cruise in the Caribbean but Stephen said we were too young for that and he always wanted to go to St Petersburg so that has to be ironed out yet!" Gina gave a little giggle. "Would you like a cup of tea – I just realised we've been nattering on and I never offered you anything!"

"I'm fine, thanks," Nicky said quickly. "I don't want to take up your time – I think I've got lots here for the piece."

"It's no trouble – I have to say I'm quite enjoying talking about it all!"

Well, I'm not enjoying listening, Nicky thought silently.

The front door slammed and Nicky jumped.

"It'll only be Stephen – relax," said Gina. "He must have got an earlier flight. Great! Now you can interview him too!"

Nicky's heart had started to hammer. "No, no need, I'm sure what I have is fine!" Stephen dragged his briefcase into the living-room casually behind him.

"Hello!" he said, not realising at first who the person sitting before him was.

"Hi, Stephen," Nicky said shyly.

Stephen's face spoke a multitude. "Hi, N-n-nicky, I n-n-never realised that it was your m-m-magazine coming today!"

"Do you know each other?" Gina asked with a startled expression on her face.

Stephen turned to his fiancée. "Yes, we met in New York – it's a long story."

I could spill the beans about Just for Coffee, Nicky thought, but that wouldn't be very nice – after all, Stephen had only ever been kind and helpful.

"How is your son?" he asked Nicky.

"Good, thanks – he's made a complete recovery and been given the all clear," Nicky said with a nod of her head. "He'll be back playing rugby in no time!"

"That's good."

Nicky became painfully aware of the awkwardness in the room and made the first move to alleviate the tension.

"I think we've covered everything really well. Our photographer got great shots the other day and we'll send you a copy of the ones that we will use."

"Have you got my email?" Gina asked.

"Yes, and here's my business card with my email address." Nicky handed the card over to Gina.

Then she moved over towards the door and the other two followed hesitantly. She was very aware that her every move was being studied by Stephen. She also realised that his fiancée was studying her even closer. If the ground could have opened up and swallowed her she would have been the happiest woman in Dublin.

"Goodbye," she said stiffly but politely while Stephen Delaney and his fiancée waved her down the stairs and back to her job in *D Scene* magazine.

Derek opened the top button of the collar of his shirt and loosened his tie – inside he was seething. There was no other way to consolidate his finances other than to declare bankruptcy. It made him mad to think that his career, which had flown so high with the Celtic Tiger, had come to this. He had been on a downward spiral for the last year and a half and now he was about to reach the bottom. He didn't relish the prospect of handing over the keys of his house to the building society – where would he take his family?

Rachel had been out of line and it had taken a good deal of willpower and a few heavier thumps than usual to get her back into her place. It was a big mistake allowing her to take that trip to New York but things were back to normal now – she had really lost the run of her place in the family. The kids were bearable – apart from Sarah who was getting so like Rachel that he'd had to spell it out to her clearly on two occasions recently that she would simply have to toe the line or else she would have to get the same treatment as her mother. So far the threats had worked. He didn't need this type of hassle on top of all the crap he had to deal with in the office. His gambling had brought him a couple of healthy wins with Paddy Power in June but those gains were swallowed up again by the horses in July. Work would be on to him sooner rather than later – especially as he hadn't been making repayments on the renovation loans and the mortgage top-up. The houses he had purchased in Dunboyne were now in negative equity and the apartment in Swords had dropped so much in value it was hardly worth selling – he couldn't remember the last time he made a repayment on it. He was a man in so much debt that his once-healthy wages would no longer be sufficient to cover the interest that he owed.

That was why it was important that Rachel stuck by his side – they needed a front. It was a pity he hadn't put a large life assurance policy on Rachel . . . but she was worth more to him alive – who else would be able to look after the kids?

He strummed his fingers on the steering wheel of his Audi to the beat of the rhythm coming from the drive-time radio show. He had to think and quickly about what he was going to do. Maybe he could convince the bank that he was going out on business on his own – they might give him a large enough investment to cover the debts he carried. But not even the banks were interested in stocks at the moment – their own were in such a sorry state – a stockbrokerage would be the least favoured business proposition he could come up with. He had little choice but he would have to do something soon because it would only be a matter of time before his boss found out the state of his finances and then inevitably Rachel would find out too.

As he approached the Malahide Road roundabout he swerved quickly, nearly hitting a motorcyclist.

"Learn the rules of the road, punk!" he roared through the open window of his car door.

Life was full of rules and he hadn't always played by them but he had done well for a while – that was why it was so unfair that he might now lose everything that he had worked so hard to gain.

Rachel sobbed into her cup of coffee at the kitchen table. Derek had been concealing the truth for years and she knew it but it wasn't until she opened the envelope a few hours earlier that she had any idea of the depth of his lies. It was no wonder that he kept the family finance paperwork well hidden in a locked cabinet in his study. He had been squandering money on a level that she couldn't even contemplate while he had made her manage on a frugal allowance from week to week. She felt her stomach churn but nothing was coming up. She couldn't even invite Nicky over to the house any more without causing a scene.

She felt as though she had let her friend down. Nicky had sat with her in the small waiting-room of the family law court for six hours back in May and when her turn came to speak to the judge she had bottled out. Why had she bottled out? Because she didn't have anywhere to go or any way of supporting herself and, no matter what Nicky said, she couldn't convince her that she would find a job in the modern-day workplace.

This morning some strange force had caused her to open the letter from the building society. After all, weren't both their names on it? So she was entitled to see what was inside. Nothing could have prepared her for the shock of seeing the figure outstanding on the bottom line of the page. By now she had thought that they would be almost mortgage free with only a couple of years and nominal payments left – they had bought their house before the property boom of the late 1990s so the amount outstanding simply didn't make sense. Where was all the money going? Did she have the nerve to ask him or would she try and stick the letter back together so he wouldn't know that she had seen it?

Holly was at a friend's and Ben was going for a sleepover so that left just Sarah in the house. She was upstairs as usual – Rachel couldn't reach out to her any more – she had let her daughter down. Apart from Nicky, she had nobody to talk to. The sessions with Darina had started out well but after four consultations she wasn't dealing with Derek or Sarah any better so what was the point? Now this.

She trembled at the prospect of telling Derek that she had seen it. She clung to the mug in her hands and took a sip. Her mind spun and she had no idea what she was going to do.

The front door banged open. Rachel looked up at the clock on the wall. Five past four – what was he doing home so early? Hastily she grabbed the document from the building society and clumsily tried to shove it back into the envelope that it had come in. But it was too late…

"What have you got there?" Derek demanded, slamming his briefcase down onto the kitchen table.

Rachel's mouth opened but nothing came out.

Derek glared at her like a man possessed. "I said, what have you got there?"

Rachel handed the wrinkled envelope over and Derek tore its contents out. His eyes scanned the page and he crumpled it up into a ball.

"This is none of your business!"

"My name is on the envelope too!" she chirped nervously.

"You don't earn anything – you don't bring any money into this house so how would you be able to pay it back?"

"It looks like you haven't been paying it back either." Her voice quivered.

"Bitch – you cheeky fucking bitch – after all that I have given you!" he roared as he grabbed the pony-tail of blonde hair at the back of her head. "How many times have I told you to mind your own fucking business!"

With a swing he flung her across the kitchen until she hit the back door with a thud and slid down onto the marble floor. Before she could get up he was ready with a punch to her right cheek – quickly followed by a swing to her left.

She looked up at the red that seemed to flash in the corner of his eyes. He was possessed and she was scared. For a few seconds they froze in suspended animation. It was only as she tried to get up that he walloped her again but this time in the stomach, leaving her wheezing and winded.

"*Stop!*" roared a voice from the other side of the kitchen.

Derek turned and glared at his daughter.

"*Get out!*" he howled. "*Get the fuck out!*"

"You can't keep doing this to her – you're a pig!"

Derek was incensed. "I won't be spoken to like that by anyone!" he bellowed. With a swing of his nearest arm he hit his daughter across the head and sent her flying out into the hall with the force.

Rachel looked at her beautiful daughter who had crumpled like a leaf with the blow. She only realised then how skinny her little body had become.

"Leave her alone!" she cried, rushing to Sarah's side.

Derek intercepted and grabbed Rachel by the neck with

both of his hands and forced her up against the wall.

"I've had enough crap – you've no fucking idea how hard life is for me – you swan about without a worry in the world while I'm left doing everything to support this family!"

Rachel was gagging for air. Never before had he tried to throttle her and she felt sure that he was going to kill her.

Sarah slid along the wooden flooring in the hall – she had to get to the front door.

"Where are you going?" Derek roared at Sarah.

This was her chance. Sarah jumped to her feet and made it to the panic button beside the front door. She pressed the red switch and the house alarm rang out.

Derek let go of Rachel's neck and she gasped as she fell to the floor.

"You're in big trouble now!" he bellowed as he launched a swing at his daughter's head. Her nose burst open and blood spat out with the first blow, sending her to the floor yet again.

"Get into the kitchen – you've done it now – little bitch!" he snarled.

Sarah slid meekly along the floor – desperately hoping her mother would be all right.

Rachel was on her knees but breathing freely when her daughter reached her. Tears streamed down their cheeks as they looked into each other's eyes.

Derek fumbled with the numbers at the alarm box. This was their chance to escape.

Rachel pointed to the back door and Sarah made a run for it. She had the key turned before Derek made it back into the kitchen and Rachel threw herself in front of him to give Sarah enough time to get the door open.

"Get back in here!" he roared to Sarah – but she was gone.

Rachel stood bravely in front of him with terror in her eyes.

"Leave her alone – please, I beg you!"

Derek lifted his arm and smacked it across her face, sending her flying across the floor once more. Then he stomped ominously over to where she had fallen. He grabbed her wrist, then stood on her arm and snapped it like the twig on a branch.

Garda Marion Walsh was on duty when the alarm sounded in the Sloan's house on the Old Portmarnock Road. She wondered when it would happen because she knew it was only a matter of time before it would.

"Gerry – that's the house that woman lives in – the one I interviewed a couple of months ago – she hit the button before when her husband was beating her," she told her colleague.

"Do you want me to check it out?" Gerry was munching a ham and cheese bap and not in the mood for rushing to the scene of a crime.

"Would you please – I'll get someone to take over here – I'll go with you!"

Gerry threw his sandwich onto the table and grabbed the keys. "Come on!" he said with his slow Donegal drawl – slipping his sunglasses onto his nose.

"Can we step on it?" Marion asked impatiently once they were finally in the car.

"It's probably kids messing – that's what it usually is!"

Marion gave him one of her earnest looks. "I just have a feeling – humour me!"

Gerry put his foot heavily down on the accelerator and the Ford Mondeo took off. They were a couple of hundred yards from the house when a young girl with blood streaming down her face flagged them down.

"Pull in!" Marion yelled, grabbing some cloths from the glove compartment.

The young girl was trembling and sobbing as Marion helped her onto the back seat of the squad car.

A call came over the radio from the station. "The owner of that house rang in to say everything's okay – that was a false alarm!"

"That's grand," Gerry reported back. "We've a minor here we've picked up on the road – she's been beaten. Roger Juliet Charlie!"

"Now slowly – tell me what happened – who did this to you?" Marion asked.

"My dad – he's going to kill my mum!" Sarah spluttered as the blood seeped down her face and onto Marion's uniform.

"Do you live near here?"

"Yes – down the road."

"What's your name?"

"Sarah – Sarah Sloan!"

"Quickly – we have to get to that house." Marion urged Gerry, slamming the back door and jumping into the passenger seat.

Gerry picked up speed.

Sarah called out, "There – that's my house!"

The squad car swerved to a stop in the gravel driveway and Gerry sprang out. The front door was open and he ran into the hall where a woman was sitting at the end of the stairs shivering and shaking. Her face was battered black and blue and she held her arm protectively.

"Are you on your own?" he asked.

Rachel nodded.

"I'll get an ambulance – we have your daughter in the car."

Rachel's gaunt eyes stared up at the tall figure of the guard. "Is she okay?"

"She's going to be fine – and so are you!" he said comfortingly as he sat beside her on the bottom step. "Where is your husband?"

"He drove off a few seconds ago – I think I've broken my arm!"

"It's all right – everything's going to be okay."

"I know," Rachel sobbed as she burst into uncontrollable tears.

"Pull that piece you did on Gina Hall," Trudy said curtly, slapping a page on her desk. "Thankfully we haven't gone to press!"

"What's this?" Nicky asked, picking up the sheet of paper.

"It's a memo – they've parted already – would have made a good story if they had actually gone through with the wedding! *C'est la vie!*"

Under normal circumstances Nicky would have thought Trudy a callous bitch but this piece of news brought nothing but a smile to her face.

"And while you're at it can you find me a celebrity bride – a soap star – anyone!"

Nicky nodded. "Don't worry – I'll find someone."

When she had left the desk Nicky grabbed her cigarettes. This was definitely a cause for celebration. She dialled Rachel's number before she was out of the building and cursed when she heard only a voicemail at the other end of the line.

Damn – I need to talk to someone who will understand, she thought. Taking long and leisurely drags from her cigarette she panned through her list of friends in her mobile phone but there was nobody she could talk to. She was so curious to find out what had happened. She felt sorry for Gina – then stopped and considered maybe it was her and not Stephen who had called the wedding off. Instinctively she felt that it had to be him. She took a final drag from her Marlboro and as she stamped it out made a resolution. If she could get Stephen back into her life she would do something huge – something momentous – she might even consider giving up smoking! It was a wager with herself that she was willing to gamble – she would do absolutely anything to get another chance with Stephen. No man had touched her in this way – ever.

As she sat back on the chair at her desk she tossed her cigarettes into the basket beside her. It was time to Google the engaged celebrities in Dublin city and this time the task wasn't nearly so ominous – she didn't care who was getting married because Stephen wasn't!

This was such great news. She had to tell someone – she dialled Rachel's number and waited.

"Hello, Nicky?"

"Hi, Rach – you'll never guess whose engagement is off!"

Rachel was sitting in the back of an ambulance with her bloodstained daughter at her side – she wasn't in form for guessing anything.

"Nicky, I'm on my way to hospital – Derek lashed out big time – he broke Sarah's nose and my arm!"

"Oh my God! Is there anything I can do?"

"No thanks – the younger ones are with friends and Derek has driven off to God knows where!"

"What hospital are they taking you to?"

"Beaumont."

"I'll call in on my way home from work," Nicky said. "I'm leaving now!"

"Only if it's no trouble."

"Stop it, Rachel – I'll see you soon." Nicky hung up and gave her desk a quick tidy. If she could get her hands on that bastard Derek she would kill him. Maybe she had been blessed to be on her own all of these years?

She rang to check that Daniel was all right and set off

through the city traffic. She berated herself for not doing more in May – they both knew that one day it would come to this – thankfully he hadn't done more damage.

The lease on the apartment was for three months with an option on three more if she wanted to stay longer. It was the nicest time to be in New York – Eve always loved the onset of the fall. While sitting in her new favourite coffee shop in SoHo and browsing through the *New York Times* she decided that she could be productive – all of this free time was getting boring and she could do with a job – one that would be a new challenge yet not too taxing! Definitely something that didn't involve dating or relationships.

She took a sip from her cup of coffee as something tickled the back of her neck under her long auburn hair. She put her hand up to scratch the spot then turned around, sensing someone behind her.

"It's you!" she gasped at the tall dark figure dressed in a Che Guevara T-shirt and faded jeans.

"What are you doing back in town?" Conor asked, eyeing the more youthful-looking Eve wearing a lime-green Abercrombie top and sexy white shorts.

"I couldn't keep away!" she said with a smile and lifted her Dior sunglasses off her nose to hold her hair back. "Call it an epiphany I had last time I was over!"

"Really?" Conor pulled back the free chair at the table and sat down. "Mind if I join you? This is my favourite coffee shop."

"I've been here a week and haven't missed a day – those tarts are amazing – Rachel mentioned this place when she was over – speaking of which, how is she?"

Conor shrugged. "She calls every couple of weeks but seems to be just mulling along – I guess she's busy with her family."

Eve nodded. "It's the fact that I don't have one that leads me back here – I have to say you opened my eyes to a few things last time we met."

Conor's eyebrows arched. "Really?"

"Yeah – I've decided to confront my demons – put them to rest – plus I'm now jobless and deciding whether to do something about it!"

"How long are you staying?"

"My original plan is three months, then I'm going to do some travelling on the west coast and then go to Australia – maybe finish up in Asia."

"A world tour?"

"Something like that!" she nodded, taking a sip from her cup of coffee. "My apartment in London is on lease for a year. I don't think I'll be going back there though – I'm hoping to find my new home on my travels!"

"Sounds great. I've been here so long I don't know if I'd ever leave – but a world tour sounds very appealing!"

"I decided it was now or never and when I got back to London my ex announced that he was getting married again – to a guy!"

Conor made a funny face and Eve smiled. "I do pick them! So I'm going off to find myself – I'm thirty-six and if I don't do it now I never will."

"I think that's a really brave move – sounds cool."

"Thanks," Eve said with a smile.

Conor looked at the beautiful woman in front of him who now appeared so much younger and more relaxed. She was so different to the one that he lifted from the tracks and wasn't shrouded by the veil of reserve that hung over her during their lunch in Town. Then he noticed the diamond studs that were covered by the cascade of her hair.

"You got your earring back!" he grinned.

Eve put her hand up to her earlobe. "Yes, thanks to you! There's something else – I've decided to take your advice and see a counsellor. I need to talk through what happened on 9/11."

"Well, you can have my counsellor's name if you like – she's cool and she specialises in trauma."

"I might take you up on that, thanks. Why don't you order a coffee – I'm not going anywhere!"

"Sure," he said, standing up and displaying his fine tall physique. "Back in a minute!"

Eve watched him walk into the shop and smiled. It was more than coincidence bringing them together – it was fate! Maybe it was time to just let herself go and be real with a man – and who better than her very own knight in shining armour? In a way she hated and despised that woman she used to be and wanted to make a fresh start with a man who was always honest with her. She wasn't looking for a relationship – she had a terrible track record. But maybe they could be friends.

"I can't thank you enough, Nicky," Rachel said as she sat down at the kitchen table.

"I'm glad to be of help – that Garda Walsh is really lovely!"

"It's great to get the barring order. Are you sure you don't mind sleeping here tonight?"

"Not at all – Daniel is thrilled to be staying with Matthew again – let's hope he doesn't get into any trouble this time!"

"Where's Holly?" Rachel panicked.

"In her friend's," Nicky said calmly. "Now stop fussing and we'll sort everything out tomorrow."

Nicky realised that things were much worse than she had ever imagined for her friend. Derek had left his family penniless and it was only a matter of time before the house would be repossessed but now was not the time to reveal all of this to

Rachel. For now she needed plenty of rest and support.

"What will happen when you go to work tomorrow?" Rachel asked with fear across her eyes.

"Derek is in custody – he can't get out because of giving you and Sarah such a horrific beating.

"I can't believe that it has come to this – how am I going to manage?"

Nicky wondered how her friend would. At least she had been working since they left college and supporting herself and her son – Rachel wasn't even aware of the huge gambling debts that Derek had mounted up over the last five years. Garda Walsh had told her that he was about to be fired from his job for embezzling cash. How could she have let her husband get away with so much for so long? It wasn't for her to judge – for now all she could do was offer her friend support.

SEVENTEEN

November

Alex was at a loss to know what to paint next. The exhibition in Pierre's gallery was a roaring success with all four canvases selling within minutes. Before he met Rachel he would have been happy to get three to four thousand dollars for a painting. In a mere twenty-four hours the value of his work had risen ten-fold. He smiled to himself as he wondered how Rachel would feel to know how much she had inspired and moved him.

The remaining paintings of his muse were being packed up into containers and he wouldn't see them again for three months. He decided in the end not to let his first painting go on tour – it was too precious. If anything happened to it he would feel like he had lost a part of himself. It hung now in a special place on the wall opposite his bed – so that hers was the first image that he saw every morning and the last one he saw at night.

It was better to go out and get some air – maybe meet Conor – he was always in Once Upon A Tart around this time of the day. He grabbed a jacket and headed out into the cool late-autumn air. Winter would be here soon and New York would be full of all the flavours and textures of Christmas. He loved the build-up and excitement that went with the anticipation of this time of year. The decorations uptown were worth going to see – it was the only time of year that he liked it up there. He shoved his hands deep into his jacket pockets and made his way to Once Upon A Tarts' café.

Sugar-coated snowmen and Santa Clauses filled the shelves on display and the condensation from within lined the edges of the window. Hidden away in the far corner of the café he spotted Conor sitting at a table with a red-haired woman.

"Here he is," Conor said. "He'll be too famous to sit with us in future, Eve!"

"Well done!" said Eve. "Last night was great!"

"High praise indeed, Eve," Alex smirked.

She rolled her eyes and gave him a friendly thump as he turned to go and get a coffee.

"Get me an Americano while you're up there!" she said mockingly. She didn't want him to think that she had turned too nice overnight.

Conor realised that he had better seize his chance before Alex came back. He had an idea that he was so excited about he couldn't hide it from her any more.

"Eve, I was onto Nat – you know, my record producer friend."

"Hmm?"

"Well, he has a slot that would be perfect for you – I know you've been searching for a job for a while now and I think this one would give you such a buzz."

Eve pondered for a few seconds. "I really would like a job – I've decided to extend the lease on my apartment until the summer. I'll have to get more realistic about what I can expect to get paid too."

"Well, Nat pays well and that's why I thought this would suit you."

"Go on!"

"He needs an event manager."

Eve's eyebrows arched. "Interesting."

"And Nat is really into having good-looking women around him."

"God – he sounds like a lech."

"Don't worry – you'd be well able for him."

"I don't doubt that," she said with a knowing smile.

"Anyway I told him about you and he wants to meet you tomorrow."

"Thanks, Conor – you know you've been really good to me – fixing me up with your counsellor and helping me settle back into New York – I have to admit there's a whole side to life here that I missed out on last time," she smiled. "I thought I knew it all!"

"You were a bit of a pain!" Conor nodded. He threw her a look that said he didn't feel that way about her any more.

Eve stared at his sexy blue eyes as a strong urge to kiss him took over. So far they had managed to keep the relationship purely platonic.

Conor read her expression perfectly. He wasn't willing to give her the chance to get there first.

Alex looked on miserably as Conor and Eve snogged in the corner. With a shrug he put the two coffee cups back on the counter.

"Send them over – I've just remembered I have to do something," he said to the girl behind the counter.

He pulled up the collar of his jacket and went back out into the cool New York air. Today should be one of the happiest days in his life. He had been catapulted to the heights of a big name in his profession and yet all he felt was envy for Conor. The flirtations and meetings between Conor and Eve had been heading this way for weeks. He always knew that it was only a matter of time before they clicked.

He, on the other hand, had found love at first sight with Rachel and he felt cheated by the universe that he'd only had three nights with her. He longed to know how she was and it was unfair of her brother to keep news of her a secret for so long. He should never have made that promise to Conor that he would keep away.

But Alex was true to his word and would never break it.

"This is the lounge," Rachel said as she showed Nicky the small but neat open-plan room where her children sat looking at *The Simpsons.* "Come upstairs – the bedrooms are much bigger than you would think."

Nicky followed her up the stairs to the master bedroom with a comfortable pink duvet covering the bed. "Sarah and Holly don't seem to mind sharing at all! I thought they'd hate leaving their house but Sarah said last night that it was wonderful to be able to go to bed at night without being afraid." Rachel's eyes looked dolefully at her friend. "I feel so guilty bringing them here but it was only a matter of time before the house was repossessed and it's easier to get used to our new surroundings sooner rather than later."

"I think it's a lovely house," Nicky said genuinely. "And in Malahide too which has lots of great amenities for the kids – they're still near enough to their friends in Portmarnock."

Rachel nodded. It was a lot smaller and not her own but it was a place where they could all be safe.

"How is your arm?"

"Much better thanks – I was thinking, now that the plaster is off I might learn to type – maybe even write a book," she said with a laugh. "When I met James Holden in New York he said that I always said I had a book in me – I may not have had when I was in college but I feel as if I certainly do now!"

Nicky tried not to flinch at the mention of James Holden's name. She hadn't fully recovered from his phone call and that was months ago now. But the idea of Rachel finding something for herself to do sounded good. Her friend needed all the help and support she could get after all that she had been through.

"That would be therapeutic as well," Nicky said encouragingly.

"I think so. You know when times were really bad this summer – before the big bust-up – I used to go out into the garden and lie down on the grass and think about Alex."

"You two really hit it off, didn't you?"

Rachel nodded. "He showed me that there was a better life out there for me and I will find it."

"Don't you ever feel like contacting him?"

"Every day!" Rachel sighed. "But he never contacted me. I ask about him when I talk to Conor but he always just says that he's working really hard and not going out much. He's probably got a new girlfriend and is totally in love!" Rachel felt her eyes well up with tears – she often felt desolate when she thought about Alex. "He did give me the strength to get to the point I'm at now though and that's huge."

Nicky turned and put her arms around her friend. "You're going to be okay – you know?"

Rachel sank her head into Nicky's shoulder. "Thanks – I think I will be now," she said, comforted by her friend's embrace. "Let's go downstairs and I'll make a cuppa and then you can tell me everything you have found out about Stephen!"

Nicky let go as a grin appeared across her face, reaching from ear to ear. "I feel like a stalker – I've been following his moves but so far I've come up with very little on the love front – I don't know if he broke off the engagement but I do know that he has returned to working full time!"

Rachel's eyebrows arched "Do you still think he has a drink problem?"

Nicky shrugged. "My spies aren't that well connected. But when he has been seen out in his favourite eatery, Shanahan's, he hasn't overdone it on the booze and he never leaves with a lady!"

Rachel grinned – Nicky was obsessed but in a good way.

"Hey – remember I told you that Eve has moved back to New York?"

Nicky nodded.

"Well," Rachel continued. "She's become really friendly with Conor."

"I don't believe you – is there anything happening between those two?"

"I don't think so but who'd have ever thought that they would become friends! He's even hoping to get her a job working with that record producer I told you about!"

"That's mad. It's strange that she hasn't rung us much and yet she's now friends with Conor!"

Rachel nodded her head fervently. "I think it's crazy too. I might give her a call actually – see if she'll give any more away about their friendship – he only tells me the bare minimum of what he wants me to know."

"Oh, do – for the laugh!" Nicky said, wickedness creeping into her voice.

The two fell into uncontrollable laughter and nearly didn't notice Sarah come in through the back door.

"Hi, honey," Rachel said as her daughter threw her

schoolbag into the corner of the kitchen and came over to join them at the table. "Did you have a good day?"

"Yeah," the young girl beamed. "We went to this mad gallery with lots of weird pictures and then we were allowed to go to Mc Donalds and get the Dart home on our own."

"Sounds lovely! So you won't need any dinner?" Rachel asked, beaming with pride at the life and colour that had come back into her daughter's face.

"I'm stuffed – I'd a milkshake and a Big Mac meal but I'll probably have some of that brown bread later if there's any left."

"There's plenty there," Rachel assured her.

"Right, I'll get my homework done!" And grabbing a banana and her schoolbag she headed up the stairs.

When she was out of earshot Nicky noticed the grin of pleasure across her friend's face.

"She's eating well again then?"

"Absolutely – and she seems to be really enjoying it."

"That must be a great relief."

"You've no idea," Rachel said with a loud sigh. "We've all been through so much."

"But that's over now. You can feel safe – Derek is going to be put away for a very long time – the banks will be seeing to that too!"

Eve felt her heart-rate rise as Conor took her hand and they stood up from the table. He threw a glance that asked simply 'your place or mine?'

"Let's go to mine!" she said.

He didn't reply – but then he didn't have to. They were finally on the same wavelength. The invisible layer of sexual tension that had been building between them for the last eight weeks was swollen to bursting point. They stormed along East

Houston Street hand in hand – neither able to speak.

When they reached First Avenue the realisation that they only had two more blocks to go left Eve in a state. Her lips were swollen and fingers trembling as she put the key into the door of her apartment.

Conor gave it a push.

Her legs were turning to jelly and she hoped that they would carry her through the front door and into the apartment before giving in. She just made it! They nearly collapsed on crossing the threshold. Her breathing was laboured and heavy with anticipation.

Conor grabbed her in his strong and muscular arms and she let herself go as he placed his lips on hers and the two searched frantically for each other's tongues.

Eve opened her emerald eyes for a moment and they fused with Conor's as if a mysterious and magnetic force was connecting them.

"You know," she whispered breathlessly. "You did save me on the subway – in February."

"I know," he said, nuzzling his face into her cleavage. "I've always known – but now I know why!"

Rachel cleaned up the last of the dishes that were scattered around the kitchen. Her kids were messy but she didn't care. They were happy and safe and that was all that mattered.

Ben had left his muddy boots at the back door with scattered leaves in a pile around them. Sarah's school coat was in a heap beside the fridge and Rachel picked it up – giving it a good shake down. A leaflet fell out of the pocket and she picked it up off the floor. She put Sarah's coat on a hook beside the door – how different her new home was from the house that she had shared with Derek but how much better it was to be here!

She went to put the leaflet in the bin but then hesitated – it might be important for Sarah's schooling.

She flipped it open and scanned the folded panels. It was a programme of exhibitions coming to the Irish Museum of Modern Art in the New Year. Her eyes fixed on the heading '*Contemporary American Artists*'. There were five in total.

Then her breath caught in her throat as one name leapt out – Alex Thoreau. Beside his name was a portrait in vibrant and vivid colours – it was of a woman and entitled simply *Rachel*.

The woman in the painting was blonde with blue eyes but it was a very small reproduction and the image could be of anyone. But she knew instantly who the woman was.

She gasped. If Alex had been painting a portrait of her that meant he'd still been thinking of her.

From so far across the Atlantic he was reaching out to her.

She began to weep as she held tightly on to the piece of paper in her trembling hand. A wave of emotion swept over her as she realised that she had been as important in Alex's life as he had been in hers. Her heart was thumping so loudly that she could hear it pounding in her ears. She longed to pick up the phone and tell him that she knew. Maybe she should?

But why had he never tried to contact her?

No, she may have inspired his art but that didn't mean he was still in love with her so many months later. For him, it might always have been just a brief affair – a holiday romance – just Three Nights in New York.

EPILOGUE

February in Dublin

Rachel stood under the large seventeenth-century arch as the taxi drove off behind her. Even though she had lived in Dublin for all of her life she had never visited the Museum of Modern Art or even passed through the doors of the Royal Hospital Kilmainham which housed it. She brushed the creases out of her cream-coloured overcoat and opened the buttons to show the pink dress that she was wearing underneath. She had been searching for something to wear to the opening of Alex's exhibition for months and was ecstatic when she came across a perfect little Karen Millen number in the post-Christmas sales. The shade had to be perfect – it had to be the same colour as the dress that the lady wore in the painting in the Met – the one she had seen with Alex so many months ago. So much had changed in her life since then . . .

The cobblestones made it difficult to walk in her high-heeled shoes but she negotiated them carefully, ensuring that she looked her very best when she walked into the main foyer. A porter stood at the large glass entrance door and she smiled at him as he held it open for her. Her stomach tensed and butterflies danced inside as she scanned the room to find a familiar face.

"Rachel!" a voice called out from behind – she turned swiftly in response.

A radiant woman wearing a figure-hugging scarlet cocktail dress stood before her. Her brown hair was shiny and flicked out in a glamorous new bob.

"Nicky, hi!" Rachel said, leaning forward to kiss her friend on the cheek.

"The dress is perfect," Nicky whispered in her friend's ear. "I knew it would be."

"Thanks for bailing me out – I could never have afforded it, even at the sale price!"

"I'm only getting used to my new credit card – my boyfriend insists I use it as much as possible," Nicky whispered wickedly.

A few steps behind Nicky stood Stephen, looking better than Rachel had ever seen him.

"Hi, Stephen! I didn't think you guys would be so early!"

"Hi, Rachel," Stephen said, planting a platonic kiss on her cheek. "You look great. Sorry we can't stay long – I'm meeting some people in Shanahan's at eight so I'll be taking Nicky off with me."

Rachel turned to her friend anxiously. "No! You can't leave me!"

"You won't want us around when the opening is over," Nicky smiled. "Alex is going to want you all to himself."

Rachel winced. "How do you know? He hasn't seen me since last May! I mean, he might take one look at me and feel totally different!"

Nicky looked disbelievingly at her friend. "You and I both know how he's going to feel when he sees you!"

Rachel wished that she had her friend's confidence. She herself was tortured by fears and doubts.

"Have you seen Conor?" she asked, to change the subject.

"He's over there with Eve," said Nicky, pointing.

Standing by the linen-covered table and sipping on wine, Eve and Conor were very much entranced with each other's company. Rachel wished that her house was bigger and that she could have had her brother to stay but maybe he was better off with Eve in the Clarence Hotel. It made the trip more of a vacation for them both.

"I'm going to have a quick look around – Stephen is interested in buying one of the Rachel series for head office," Nicky said, giving him a friendly dig. "Aren't you?"

"I do whatever I'm told," Stephen said with a smile as she led him away by the hand.

The inclement conditions at JFK airport had delayed Alex's arrival to Dublin by two days – Rachel had hoped to get to see him before the exhibition opened but it wasn't to be. All she had tonight was the dream that he would have feelings for her when he saw her. But it had been so long since they'd been together! Secretly she was scared that he had painted her out of his system or regarded their affair as nothing more than a brief holiday fling. Or found himself a new love.

A buzz echoed around the high ceilings as Conor spotted his sister from the corner of his eye. He grabbed Eve's elbow and led her over to where Rachel stood.

"Sis, wow!" he exclaimed. "Take that coat off and let me see the dress!"

Rachel did as she was told.

"Nice dress, Rachel! What a beautiful colour!" Eve said, leaning forward and giving her friend a kiss. "We're having a terrific vacation – it's a pity Alex was delayed. Dublin is so cool

– it's changed so much."

Rachel nodded. She was now so anxious to see Alex that her legs were turning to jelly. "Is he here?"

Conor looked around. "He was being photographed by *the Irish Times* a few minutes ago – they might be interviewing him. He's very much a man in demand at the moment – you've no idea how hard he's been working this past winter."

Rachel smiled. She hadn't but she wished that she had.

"Why don't I get you a glass of wine and then you can have a look around?" Conor suggested.

Rachel nodded. She longed to see the paintings though it felt strange to be going to see images of herself.

"They're in the second room on the right," Eve informed her.

Rachel took the glass from Conor and set off on her own to find them. She didn't allow herself to rush. Each step on the parquet wooden floors she took carefully and slowly until she came to the room.

The walls were awash with strong colours and textures. The artist had ensured that the woman in the pictures reached out to touch the soul of the viewer. They were the most powerful images Rachel had ever seen and the fact that they were of her made her feel as if she was looking into a huge mirror from another dimension.

Suddenly a sensation of contact against her neck made her flinch and she jumped, turning promptly.

His eyes were upon her and so close she couldn't focus on anything else in the room. The familiar scent of his skin brought back sweet and precious memories. She was dumbstruck as a surge of bliss swept over her.

"Do you like them?" he asked.

He looked different – his hair was shorter and not so white –

more a natural blond. Instead of his usual scruffy gear he was wearing a sharp grey suit and a crisp white shirt. His familiar silver sleepers were still hanging on his earlobes. Quite overcome by seeing him in the flesh, she opened her mouth but nothing came out.

"It's probably an unfair question – but I was hoping you would like them," he said with a shrug.

"Oh Alex, they're amazing – I love them!" she said, her lips parting for a smile, her face filled with the excitement of seeing him again.

"How have you been?" he asked cautiously.

Rachel tilted her head and went to bite her lip but stopped. "It's been hard but good – did Conor tell you about my husband?"

"He tells me very little but he did mention that you're no longer with him."

Rachel nodded. "Things got out of hand. He's doing time for embezzlement and for – what he did to me." Now was not the moment to delve into details.

Sensing her discomfort, he took her gently by the arm and led her over to the corner of the room. There his eyes gazed intently into hers as he spoke.

"I'm sorry that I never contacted you, Rachel – it wasn't because I didn't want to."

Rachel wasn't sure if he was just being kind. "It's okay – I mean we only shared a weekend together – I was on the other side of the Atlantic with three kids in tow!" She laughed nervously. "Very different to your exciting life in New York!"

Alex smiled. "I've been living like a hermit since I met you, Rachel – you've filled my thoughts every day since you left."

Rachel smiled back uncertainly, unsure how to take this. Was he being his flippant funny self or was he serious? He could just be trying to be nice, now that he was on her territory . . . or maybe he fancied another affair like they had the previous May? She didn't know how to respond.

"How long are you staying?" she asked instead.

"I'm only meant to be here three nights but I'm sure I could change my flight if I had to!"

Rachel's head buzzed at the prospect of spending some time with Alex again but she answered despondently, "I'd love to show you around Dublin, Alex, but I'm tied up with the kids and school runs – and Dublin can be bleak in February. It would be very different to the time we spent together in New York."

Alex put his hand up to her face and gently stroked the side of her cheek. Her whole body responded, quivering with pleasure.

"I realise that, Rachel," he said. "I'd like to spend time with your kids."

And at those words Rachel's head filled with dreams of a wonderful future with the man she had fallen in love with and thought about every day since they'd met.

"I'm sure they'd like that too," she said breathlessly. "But we would have to take it easy."

"We can take all the time in the world," Alex said, smiling. "You are my muse, Rachel. I've been waiting my whole life to meet you and now that I've found you again I'm not letting go."

His eyes were full of so much hope and expectation that Rachel felt as if she was being swaddled in a huge cocoon of love.

Then he leaned forward and placed his lips gently on hers and she was transported back to New York – to the Staten Island ferry – to the High Line – to Alex's flat in Chelsea. But she wasn't in New York – she was at home in Dublin and she had three wonderful nights to make a new future.

The End

If you enjoyed *Three Nights in New York*,
don't miss out on *Two Days in Biarritz*,
also published by Poolbeg.

Here is a sneak preview of Chapter one . . .

Two Days
in Biarritz

MICHELLE
JACKSON

Two Days in Biarritz

MICHELLE JACKSON

POOLBEG

ONE

Friday 10th March, 9.25p.m.

"Sometimes it's better not to tell."

"What do you mean?" Kate was curious. Maybe she didn't know her friend as well as she thought she did.

"Look, some things are best kept in the past." Annabel's tongue was loose after the alcohol, still she beckoned to the waitress to bring another two glasses of the liqueur. She sat back in her chair. "Okay, maybe I did go back to Nico's room last night and have sex while you were with Brett!"

"Yeah, right!" Kate scoffed. "I think I know you well enough by now, my very married friend! And, besides, in the unlikely event that you did, you'd have told me. We spent the whole day together and even after meeting him in Bayonne this afternoon you never said a word to me! So I know you didn't!"

"Well, I was with him and I'm riddled with guilt, so don't ask me any more about it!"

Kate stared at Annabel. She did, in fact, look guilty. It couldn't be true! Could it? "You're kidding me, right?"

"No."

The waitress placed two more liqueurs on the table before them.

"Thanks," said Annabel and tossed most of hers back at once.

"I don't believe it!" said Kate.

"What don't you believe?" Annabel frowned.

"That you slept with Nico, of course!"

"Why?"

"Why?" Kate echoed, exasperated. "Because you just don't do that kind of thing!"

"Wha's this called again?" Annabel said, raising the glass of ruby-coloured liqueur to her lips in slow motion.

"Floc!"

"Well, Kate, I think I'm flocked!" Annabel drained the glass and licked her lips. She ran a hand through her dishevelled long blonde curls and beckoned to the waitress again.

Kate took a sip of her floc. "Come on! Tell me the truth! Did you really sleep with Nico?"

"Why d'you find it sho hard to believe?" Annabel was beginning to slur a little.

"Because: you're married, you don't play around, you're the sensible one −"

"Hold ish right there!" Annabel held up a hand. "I'm the shenshible one?" Realising she was slurring, she paused, and then made a big effort to speak distinctly. "Oh, yes, of course. You're the artistic one, the exotic one − I'm the dull one, the boring one −"

"I'm not saying anything like that!"

"Yesh, you are! I've always been the little mouse and you've been the − the −" she took in Kate's long-limbed frame, jet-black hair and tanned skin, "the panther! Or sho you think!"

The waitress deposited another two flocs on the table.

"Well, Annabel," said Kate, "the fact is, in all the years I've known you, even before you married Colin, you have never allowed yourself to be swept away by passion –"

"Thatsh what you think!" Annabel drunkenly pointed a finger in Kate's face.

Kate pulled back and drained her old glass, before picking up the fresh one. "What do you mean by that?" she said, becoming irritated now at this nonsense.

"All I am saying is, maybe I have known passion, a great passion. Mush mush more zan anyone!"

"Oh? Is Colin on Viagra now or what?" Kate's tongue always sharpened the more she drank.

This cut much too close to the bone and Annabel felt quite hurt. "I had my great moment!" she said, flushing. "Before I ever met Colin!"

"Oh yes – a moment so great you never even thought to mention it to me!" said Kate scornfully. "Some great moment!"

"It was!"

"Okay, okay," Kate pretended to yawn, "when and where – and what? First kiss, age twelve, school bicycle shed? You already told me that one."

Something snapped in Annabel. She was tired of Kate's presumptions about her sexual needs and desires, and the experience with Nico the night before had awakened a new confidence in her. "On the boat – with Damien – sho zere!"

"You dark horse!" Kate said, shaking her head. "You never told me about a Damien – who or when was he?"

"On the boat! You were there! Damien, it's always been Damien. I've always loved him. Zat's why it was so easy to marry Colin!"

"I don't know any Damien from our past," Kate declared, now more than a little upset and agitated that Annabel had kept a secret from her for all these years.

"Damien – you don't know Damien? You know him very well, Kate. You lived with him long enough!"

For a long frozen moment Kate stared at Annabel. Then her mouth dropped. She felt as if she had received a sharp blow to her solar plexus. "My dad! You were . . . no, you couldn't have been . . . you were in love with my dad?" Kate couldn't believe she was uttering the words.

"I sure was, and he loved me too. On the ferry, in the storm, all those years ago."

Kate felt as if she was going to pass out. Was Annabel only talking rubbish with the copious glasses of wine and floc inside her or was she telling the truth?

"What happened on the ferry?"

"I made love to your father, Kate!"

"Tell me you're joking, Annabel! You couldn't have!" Kate's head was shaking frantically as if she could shake the image away.

"I sure did and I'll never forget it." Annabel was relieved to be telling Kate the truth at last. "I need more drink – where's zat waitress gone?"

Kate sat there expressionless – unable to respond. If what Annabel was saying was true, she had been deceiving her for most of their friendship.

"I feel mush better after telling you at last, Kate – it'sh been hard keeping it from you all this time." Annabel gave a little hiccup. "I'm glad I told you now."

Kate wasn't able to drink any more. She put the napkin up to her mouth and pushed her chair back slowly.

"I'll be back in a minute," she said, finding it difficult to catch her breath.

She quickly walked to the toilets. Her stomach was churning inside and her heart was racing. There was no way – Annabel and her father! She couldn't hold the raclette back. She felt her dinner rise back up her throat and she spewed its contents into the bowl. Her head was dripping with sweat and she felt as if she were being choked by a pair of imaginary hands.

Standing in front of the mirror, unable to wash her hands they were shaking so much, she stared at her reflection and the tears sprang to her eyes. How could Annabel do such a thing? To her mother as well, who had been so good to her! And how could she have kept that secret all those years, despite all the memories they shared together? They'd never had a true friendship. Annabel had made a fool of her. She could never trust her again.

Walking on trembling legs, she made it back to the table but had to steady herself before taking her seat.

Annabel gave a lopsided smile, oblivious to the effect her revelation was having on Kate. She looked a lot drunker than when Kate had left her only a few minutes before.

Kate leant across the table, gripped Annabel's hand hard and stared straight into her bleary eyes.

Annabel blinked, startled.

"Annabel," said Kate slowly, deliberately, "I'm really upset. I need to know if what you're telling me is true."

"Ish true."

Kate took a trembling breath. "You had sex with my father on that ferry crossing – in the storm – all those years ago?"

"Yesh."

"You've been in love with him ever since?"

"Yesh, I have. Thash why I married Colin."

Kate let go of her hand. "But you never told me."

Annabel's eyes widened. "How could I tell you something like thash?"

It was true, thought Kate. This horrible thing was really true.

"I need to go to the loo now. You took ages," Annabel

grinned. She wobbled slightly as she stood up and went off in the direction of the rest rooms.

Kate was feeling numb. She thought quickly and knew she had to get away. Digging down deeply into her bag, she took out sixty euros. She threw the notes down on the table, anxious to be gone before Annabel returned from the toilet.

She didn't want to have anything to do with Annabel Hamilton again for as long as they both lived.

Nico was anxious to be on time for his arrangement with the Irishwomen.

"You're jumping around like a hare, Nico – relax and finish your beer," Brett said with a shake of his head.

"I told Kate and Annabel we'd meet them in Desperados," Nico said reluctantly.

"I wish you hadn't included me in your arrangements. One night with them was enough." Brett took a sip of his beer. "Anyway, we're a threesome this evening." He nodded towards their drinking companion, one of the other surfers.

"Hey, I don't want to get the blame for Nico missing out on his fun!" the scrawny Londoner laughed.

"He already had his fun with this bird last night," Brett grinned. "That's the bit I can't understand."

Nico felt awkward. Usually one night would be enough – they were used to picking up women all over Europe as they went from beach to beach – but Annabel was intriguing.

He took another drink from his glass and scanned his watch. Nine forty-five – they weren't the type of women to sit around waiting.

"Will you have another beer, mate?" the Londoner asked Nico.

"Not right now," he replied sullenly, making sure not to

make eye contact with Brett. "I'm going out to get some fresh air." He stood up.

"Tell the truth. Are you going to Desperados?" Brett asked.

"I'm going to tell them that we can't make it. It's only around the corner – I'll be back in a minute."

Brett shook his head scornfully and returned to his beer.

Kate tossed the clothes into her hold-all with great urgency. She didn't want Annabel to catch her packing. It wouldn't take her long to realise that Kate had left the restaurant and returned to the hotel, and by then Kate needed to be well out of Biarritz.

The receptionist was startled to see her packed and ready to go, paying her bill at such an hour.

"Un taxi, s'il vous plaît," Kate asked, and the receptionist obliged.

Kate's plan was simple – she would spend the night in one of the many hotels in Bayonne. The Ibis would certainly have plenty of rooms available this time of year. The drunken Annabel was not her responsibility and anyway she couldn't look her in the eyes after their conversation.

Suffering as she was at being betrayed by her best friend, Kate's thoughts now swung to her father. Her insides twisted at the thought of him. How could he have done it? How could he have done it to her mother? The night of the storm. No wonder her father hadn't passed any comment when she was missing from her cabin all that night – Annabel was curled up under the covers in his! The thought repelled her so much she felt dizzy and had to sit down in the small foyer. She wanted to be at home in her small house under the gaze of the Pyrénées.

The waitress came over with the receipt on a saucer as Annabel returned from the ladies'.

"Where's Kate?"

"Your friend, madame? She has left."

"Left?"

"Oui, madame."

Why did she do that? Annabel sat down heavily and felt around under her seat until her hand fell on her bag. Where did she go? This was odd. Annabel was anxious to continue her discussion about Damien. Her mind was a dizzy haze of twinkling lights, delicious tastes, and aromas from the kitchen. She reached into her bag and put some money on the table.

"Your friend paid, madame," the waitress said.

Annabel stood up on unsteady legs and felt around for her coat that had fallen off the back of her chair. This was most strange.

"Would you like a coffee?" the waitress asked, noticing her condition.

"No, thank you. I really have to go," Annabel said, and slowly made her way to the door. She had flashes of her conversation with Kate. She had taken it very well, considering. There were no outbursts or condemnations – but where could she have gone? She carefully stepped out on to the street, anxious not to fall, but felt the ground swaying up to greet her. She couldn't remember the way back to the hotel but the steady roar of the ocean called her to take a left.

"Annabel!" a voice called but she didn't register it.

She hobbled down the road, the cobblestones feeling like pebbles in her shoes. A strong arm grabbed her from behind and she turned to see deep brown eyes stare back at her.

"Nico!" she exclaimed and flung her arms around his neck. Her legs went from under her for a second and he held her up with his arms gripped around her waist.

"It's lucky I found you, Annabel," he whispered. "You should not be on your own with so much to drink."

"'Ave you seen Kate?" Annabel was disoriented and her memory had turned to mush.

"I was on my way to Desperados," Nico said, surprised to find her in such a state. Where was her friend? "I will take you back to the hotel."

The receptionist had seen some sights that night already but was shocked when Annabel was assisted up to the desk only a short while after her friend disappeared into the night in the taxi.

"What is your room number, Annabel?" Nico asked.

"Can't remember," Annabel said, her head slumping under its own weight.

"Vingt-sept," the receptionist replied, handing the key over to Nico, judging that Annabel was in no fit state to make it to the second floor on her own.

Annabel was getting heavier with every step. Nico negotiated the bedroom door like a fire-fighter and plonked her down on the bed where she collapsed in a heap. She moaned and flipped over to the other side of the double bed.

Nico put the key down on the dressing-table and left the drunken woman in her slumber. The night before had been passionate and exciting – but maybe he had been wrong about her after all.

A few hours later the sun beamed through the window and burned onto Annabel's closed eyelids. She ruffled around the bed, unsure of her surroundings. She raised her head with some difficulty. The room was empty. She floundered around, looking for her watch. 8.02 a.m.

Where's Kate? What happened last night? How did I get back?

It was all incredibly vague – she had only snatches of memories to cling to.

But she remembered telling about Damien. Why did she do that?

She went to the bathroom in search of Kate but all of her belongings were gone. She looked for Kate's bag but that too was gone. There was a sinking feeling in her stomach. It was a nightmare. She looked around for her handbag and was grateful to find her mobile phone still sitting in the pocket. She dialled Kate's number but it rang out for a few seconds before stopping suddenly. This was serious. She really needed to find out where Kate had gone. And she only had a couple more hours until her flight back to Dublin.

She wished she could turn the clock back. Just forty-eight hours back and everything would be as it was before, as it should be.